International acclaim for *Insurrection*

"Young's fans will not be disappointed.... Brings to the... most enigmatic characters." —*Daily Mail* (London)

"If you love Scottish history, you won't want to miss this fresh take on Robert the Bruce.... [A] vivid, action-packed thriller." —Ken McGoogan, author of *How the Scots Invented Canada*

"Action-packed.... A fighting start to a new trilogy." —*The Sun* (UK)

"[A] thrilling, thoroughly engrossing historical novel by a first-class writer at the very top of her game." —Angus Donald, author of The Outlaw Chronicles

"Immaculately researched and carefully written, evoking a very particular— and largely unexplored—time and place." —*Daily Telegraph*

"The fast and furious start to a majestic new trilogy." —*Woman & Home*

International acclaim for the **Brethren Trilogy**

"Combining rich historical detail, clever plotting and engaging characters, Young has crafted a historical thriller that will have readers turning pages and envisioning the sequel." —*Publishers Weekly*

"One of the best historical debuts in recent memory. Exciting and enthralling." —John Connolly, author of *Every Dead Thing*

"A sweeping historical adventure with strong characters and serious verve." —*The Baltimore Sun*

"Exhilarating.... Evokes the atmosphere of the times brilliantly." —*Birmingham Post*

Also by Robyn Young

Insurrection

The Brethren Trilogy

Brethren
Crusade
Requiem

ROBYN YOUNG

REBELLION

HarperCollins*Publishers*Ltd

Published by HarperCollins Publishers Ltd

First published under the title *Renegade* in Great Britain in 2012 by Hodder & Stoughton
An Hachette UK company

First published in Canada by HarperCollins Publishers Ltd in this original trade paperback edition: 2013

First Canadian edition

HarperCollins Publishers Ltd
2 Bloor Street East, 20th Floor
Toronto, Ontario, Canada
M4W 1A8

www.harpercollins.ca

Library and Archives Canada Cataloguing in Publication
Young, Robyn, 1975–
Rebellion / Robyn Young.

ISBN 978-1-44340-808-0

1. Robert I, King of Scots, 1274–1329—Fiction. I. Title.
PR6125.O943R42 2013   823'.92   C2012-906099-2

Part title illustration designed by Lee Wilson
Maps drawn by Sandra Oakins
Typeset in Perpetua by Hewer Text UK Ltd

Printed and bound in the United States
RRD 9 8 7 6 5 4 3 2 1

ACKNOWLEDGEMENTS

As usual I have a host of people to applaud, so please bear with me. First, thanks go to Donal O'Sher and Ann McCarthy in Waterville, County Kerry, for the unforgettable boat trip to Church Island and the wealth of local knowledge they were willing to share. Many thanks also to the helpful steward at St Patrick's Church of Ireland Cathedral, Armagh, and the Reverend Ted Flemming for information on the building's history. A general round of appreciation goes to all the knowledgeable curators and guides I spoke to at historic sites across Ireland and Scotland, with special thanks to the usher at Westminster Abbey, who let me into the shrine of Edward the Confessor.

I am, once again, indebted to historian Marc Morris for reading the manuscript so thoroughly and bringing his considerable knowledge to bear upon it. His red pen is very much appreciated. Indeed, I should thank all the historians whose books I have pored over, dog-eared, scrawled on and gleaned so much from while working on this trilogy. Any mistakes that remain are my own.

My sincere gratitude goes to my editor Nick Sayers for all his support, with a huge thank you to the rest of the fantastic team at Hodder & Stoughton, especially Laura Macdougall, Emma Knight, Lucy Hale, James Spackman, Auriol Bishop, Catherine Worsley, Ben Gutcher, Alexandra Percy, Laurence Festal, Abigail Mitchell, Laura del Vescovo and Jamie Hodder-Williams, as well as to my copy-editor, Morag Lyall, proofreader, Barbara Westmore, and Jack Dennison for looking after me on the road. Many thanks to everyone in the art and production teams, marketing, sales and publicity, and foreign rights – too many good people to mention here, but their hard work is very much appreciated.

Many thanks as ever to my agent, Rupert Heath, all at the Marsh Agency, Dan Conaway at Writers House, and to my editors and publishing teams overseas; I continue to be enormously grateful for all your support.

A nod to my fellow committee members on the Historical Writers' Association, Stella Duffy, Michael Jecks, Ben Kane, Robert Low, Anthony Riches and Manda Scott; it's been a pleasure to have 'colleagues' to share the experience of this mad career with over the past year. With special thanks to Manda and Michael for the pertinent details on corpses. It's very handy knowing people who you can ask, What would happen if I shaved a dead body? – and they don't immediately call the police.

Last, my heartfelt thanks go to all my friends and family, most especially Lee, without whom this journey wouldn't mean much at all.

CONTENTS

ENGLAND, SCOTLAND & WALES 1299AD

ORKNEY

SCOTLAND

BUCHAN

BADENOCH   MAR   • Aberdeen

ATHOLL ANGUS
MENTIETH   • Dundee
LENNOX   Perth •   • St.Andrews
Stirling   • Kinghorn
Falkirk   DUNBAR
Glasgow • Edinburgh • Berwick
Irvine Peebles   • Roxburgh
• Ayr Lanark
ISLAY   The Forest   NORTHUMBERLAND
ARRAN   Turnberry • Lochmaben
CARRICK ANNANDALE   • Newcastle
GALLOWAY
                • Carlisle   • Durham

THE NORTH SEA

ENGLAND

• Lancaster
YORKSHIRE
• York

ANGLESEY
LINCOLN
• Conwy
Caernarfon Snowdon
Nefyn GWYNEDD
POWYS   • Leicester   NORFOLK

WALES   WARWICK
HEREFORD   Cambridge •
PEMBROKE   ESSEX
GWENT GLOUCESTER • Oxford
London •
Canterbury •
Salisbury • Lewes •   Dover •
Portsmouth •

CORNWALL   ENGLISH CHANNEL

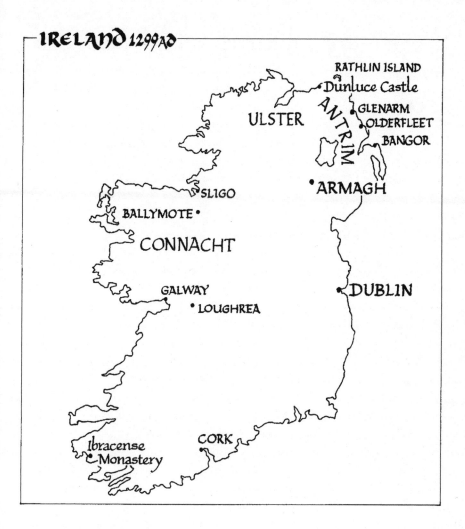

IRELAND 1299 AD

RATHLIN ISLAND
Dunluce Castle
ULSTER
ANTRIM
GLENARM
OLDERFLEET
BANGOR
ARMAGH
SLIGO
BALLYMOTE
CONNACHT
GALWAY
LOUGHREA
DUBLIN
CORK
Ibracense
Monastery

Brutus! there lies beyond the Gallic bounds
An island which the western sea surrounds,
By giants once possess'd; now few remain
To bar thy entrance, or obstruct thy reign.
To reach that happy shore thy sails employ;
There fate decrees to raise a second Troy,
And found an empire in thy royal line,
Which time shall ne'er destroy, nor bounds confine.

The History of the Kings of Britain, *Geoffrey of Monmouth*

PROLOGUE

1135 AD

. . . the reliques of the other saints should be found, which had been hidden on account of the invasion of pagans; and then at last would they recover their lost kingdom.

The History of the Kings of Britain, *Geoffrey of Monmouth*

Armagh, Ireland

1135 AD

*O*n the brow of Ard Macha, whose ancient slopes bore the name of a goddess of war, a band of men were waiting. They stood close together outside the cathedral's doors, eyes searching the mist that shrouded the hilltop. A golden light was starting to suffuse the haze, the memorials of the saints in the cemetery just visible, but, beyond, the city of Armagh remained veiled in white.

A crow cast from one of the yew trees that guarded the approach to the cathedral, the beat of wings disturbing the hush. The eyes of the company darted in the direction of the bird to see a figure emerging from the mist. It was a man dressed in a hooded black robe that ill-fitted his gaunt frame. As he walked towards them, their hands tightened around their weapons. Some of the younger men shifted uneasily. One at their centre, as broad as an ox with a hard, craggy face, pushed through their ranks to the front. Niall mac Edan stared past the approaching figure, scanning the amber gloom. After a moment something large appeared, trundling in the man's wake. It was a cart, drawn by a mule. Two men in black habits were leading the beast. Niall's eyes narrowed in expectation, but there was no other movement. As ordered, Malachy had come alone.

The men with the cart halted on the edge of the cemetery, leaving Malachy to continue up the slope, the hems of his black habit flapping around bare feet. His head was shaven in a severe tonsure, his bald crown burned livid by the July sun. His face was pinched, the skin stretched over the bones of his cheeks and sinking into the hollows of his eyes. Niall sensed the tension in his men; saw some of them edge back. Last month, when Malachy came to this hillside, attempting to enter the cathedral, he brought an army with him and blood had been spilled. But Niall knew it wasn't the memory of violence that unnerved his men. They would be calmer facing spears and axes than this solitary, whip-thin man whose feet were callused from years walking the land, preaching the word of God. They had all heard the stories.

It was said that Malachy once cursed a man who defamed him, causing the unfortunate's tongue to swell and turn putrid, worms gushing from it. After seven days *vomiting out the maggots that filled his mouth the wretch had died. A woman who harangued Malachy during a sermon was known to have fallen to the ground after the oration, convulsing so hard she swallowed her tongue. He was said to be able to cure pestilence and create it, cause rivers to rise and burst their banks, and it was believed that the vengeance of the Lord would fall upon any who stood against him.*

Despite this, Niall mac Edan held his ground, not bothering to draw his sword. He had denied Malachy entry to Armagh and its cathedral for ten months now and he was still standing. His eyes moved to the cart, which, even at this distance, he could see was piled with chests. The sight of it strengthened his confidence. Only a man, as fallible as any born of Adam's line, would need to resort to a bribe to get what he wanted. He gestured his men to move aside as Malachy, Archbishop of Armagh, approached.

Malachy watched the men before him part. Beyond, the doors of the cathedral were open into shadow. Ard Macha, encircled by mist, was as familiar as a friend. Born in this city almost forty years ago, he had grown to manhood with her green slopes in his view – upon which the blessed St Patrick had founded his church. The stone cathedral had changed in the years since he was a boy. It was only a decade since its ruined roof, struck by lightning in a time no one living could recall, had been replaced by Archbishop Cellach. The shingle still looked new. Malachy was pleased to see that although his friend and mentor had died his labours lived on. The thought of Cellach made him turn his attention to Niall mac Edan, at the head of the waiting company.

For almost two centuries, men of Niall's clan had held sway over the cathedral, claiming to control the diocese by hereditary right, along with its wealth and the tributes of horses and cows from the people of the province. Few of these men who had stood as bishops had taken holy orders, or been consecrated in Rome. Most were married laymen, whose hands were more accustomed to weapons than scripture; men of avarice, lust and violence, whose control of Ireland's Holy See was anathema in the eyes of the Church.

This evil had been uprooted by Cellach. A son of the clan, but a true man of God and a staunch reformer, he had elected Malachy to be his successor, but after Cellach's death, Niall and other members of the family had defied this decree and kept Malachy out of the city. And so he had come to defend his right; first with an army, which resulted in bloodshed, now alone, with ten chests of coin. The payment was large, but the prize invaluable.

Malachy halted before Niall, wondering how such a brute could have sprung from the same womb as a devout man like Cellach. Cain and Abel, came the thought. 'It is inside?'

'As soon as I've seen my fee you can have it.' Niall's Gaelic was abrasive.

'It is with my brethren.'

Niall motioned sharply to two of his men. 'Go. Look.'

Moving warily past the archbishop, they headed down to the cart.

Malachy stood waiting while Niall's men inspected the chests. It was not so many moons ago that the people of Ireland bartered with animals and goods. The plundering Norsemen had changed all that, bringing the tainted silver with them. How often these days it seemed a man's worth was measured in such things, rather than in the fortune of his faith.

Once they were done, the two men hastened back up the slope. Both were grinning.

'It's all there,' said one to Niall. 'Ten chests.'

Niall's eyes flicked back to Malachy. He gestured to the cathedral with a mocking sweep of his hand. 'Enter then, your grace,' he said, his voice biting down hard on the title as if it were a piece of gristle in his mouth.

The fires of hell cleanse your soul, Malachy thought as he moved past Niall and walked between the rows of armed men towards the doors of the cathedral. None of them lowered their weapons, but Malachy paid the barbed points and keen blades no heed. He paused at the entrance, his bare feet suddenly reluctant to take him from the dewy grass on to the flagstones beyond. He had not wanted this. Any of it. Now, more than ever, he missed the wild solitude of his beloved monastery, Ibracense. But Cellach had entrusted him with this position. It had been his mentor's dying wish that he become Archbishop of Armagh. Moreover, the pope had commanded that he take control of his see and oust the men who continued to defy the laws of the Church.

Malachy stepped over the threshold and entered the shadows of the interior. The place had a smell of sweat and men about it. He didn't look back as footsteps and triumphant voices faded behind him, Niall and his band swarming over their prize. Ahead, at the end of the nave, was the high altar. On the altar, where the flames of candles flickered, was a long object wrapped in white cloth.

Malachy dropped to his knees in front of it, resisting an overwhelming urge to seize the object; to hold in his hands what had once been held by Lord Jesus Christ. When the proper prayers had been said, he rose and carefully unwrapped the cloth. From out of the folds he drew a staff; a crosier, covered in an exquisite sheath of gold, encrusted with gems. All the candlelight and hazy morning sun filtering through the windows seemed caught in its precious length so that it blazed like a flame in his hands.

The staff had belonged to St Patrick who brought the word of God to Ireland seven hundred years ago. It was said that the saint had been given it by a hermit who received it from Jesus, although some heathens proclaimed Patrick stole it from the Druids. It was the holiest relic in Ireland. People would swear their most solemn oaths upon it; oaths that if broken would cause great plagues to sweep the land. It was the *staff of the King of Kings, a symbol of righteousness and supreme authority.*

It did not matter that Malachy had been chosen as Cellach's successor, or that he had been consecrated in Rome. Until he was in possession of this relic his appointment would not be accepted by the people of Ireland. This was why he had agreed to Niall mac Edan's demand for payment; for whosoever had control of the Staff of Jesus could claim to be not only rightful Archbishop of Armagh, but successor to St Patrick and spiritual ruler of all Ireland.

PART 1

1299–1301 AD

He was in suspense for some time, whether he had better continue the war or not, but at last he determined to return to his ships while the greater part of his followers was yet safe, and hitherto victorious, and to go in quest of the island which the goddess had told him of.

The History of the Kings of Britain, *Geoffrey of Monmouth*

1

The frail glow from a single candle danced over the walls of the crypt, throwing monstrous shadows up the sides of the octagonal pillars and across the ribs of the vaulted ceiling. The light's bearer slowed his footsteps, cupping a hand around the flame as it threatened to flutter out. Around him the voices of the others were breaths in the darkness.

'*Hurry.*'

'*There, Brother Murtough. The chest.*'

'*I see it. Bring the light, Donnell.*'

As Donnell moved closer to the whispers, his flame illuminated a collection of chests and boxes stacked on the floor. There were many such items stored in rows down the length of the sixty-foot crypt: baskets of cloth, sacks of grain and barrels of salted meat. The cathedral and the city it dominated had suffered much violence over the centuries, from destructive raids by neighbouring Irish chieftains and pillaging Norsemen, to the determined, tide-like expansion of the English. Thirty years ago, when Archbishop O'Scanlon ordered a great edifice built in place of the original scarred structure, the underground chamber had formed the base of his new choir, granting the cathedral and the people of Armagh a safe for their treasures.

Donnell halted beside his four companions, the candlelight staining their faces. The chests here were decoratively carved and painted with biblical imagery. It was clear they belonged to the cathedral and no doubt contained its collected wealth: chalices and plates, vestments, jewels and coin. The chest Murtough and the others had spotted was larger than the rest. Inlaid with inscriptions in Latin, barely legible under a layer of dust, it was the only one that could store what they had come for.

Murtough negotiated his way to it. The shadows highlighted the scar that furrowed the left side of his face, cleaving right through his upper lip, in sharp relief to the pale, unblemished skin that surrounded it. He reached out to lift the lid. When the chest failed to open, his brow knotted.

On the stillness came an eerie moaning, drifting towards them as if flowing down a tunnel, rising and falling in pitch.

One of the men crossed himself. 'Lord, spare us!' His exclamation resonated in the vaulted space.

Murtough's scar creased with his scowl. '*Matins, brother. The canons are singing the matins!*'

The younger man let out a breath, but the fear didn't leave his gaze.

Murtough rose and scanned the gloom until his eyes fell upon a pair of large silver candlesticks. He crossed to them and hefted one in his hands, testing its weight.

'They will hear,' said one of his companions, catching Murtough's arm as he moved back, the candlestick brandished in his grip. The man's eyes flicked to the ceiling, where the distant chanting continued.

'*There,*' murmured Donnell, the flame guttering in the rush of air from his lips. He pointed at a basket covered with cloth.

Seeing what he meant, Murtough went to it. Dust swarmed as he wrapped the cloth around the candlestick's base. Returning to the chest, he rammed it at the lock. The muffled thud echoed like a drum. The chest shuddered, but although the wood was dented by the impact the lock didn't break. Steeling himself, Murtough tried again, ears attuned for any change in the chanting descending from the cathedral choir. After three blows, the lock buckled. Murtough lifted the lid, sending shards of wood scattering. He stared inside at a neat collection of breviaries and Bibles.

As the others saw what it contained they began speaking in rapid whispers.

'*We cannot search every chest here.*'

'*We have lingered too long already.*'

'I will not leave without it,' replied Murtough grimly. 'We were told beyond doubt that they are coming for it. I will not let it fall into their hands.'

'But if we are caught . . .?'

Donnell moved down the chamber, his eyes on something that shimmered up ahead. He had glimpsed it earlier, but had thought it the reflection of his candlelight on one of the many barrels or coffers. Now he was accustomed to the gloom he realised that the glow in his cupped hand was too feeble to penetrate that far. Whatever it was, it was standing in its own source of light.

Drawing closer he saw a stone plinth, like an altar, the top of which was covered with brocaded cloth. He could smell the smoky perfume of incense. The chanting of the canons was louder here, the psalms of the dawn office rippling down to him. Upon the plinth lay a slender, gem-encrusted crosier.

'*Praise be.*'

Looking up, Donnell saw an aperture cut into the roof of the crypt, tunnelled through the rock right up to the floor of the choir. Beyond the bars of an iron grate he made out the pillars of the choir aisle stretching to the far ceiling, bathed in candlelight. The Staff of Jesus lay hidden at the cathedral's heart, displayed only to the canons who worshipped above.

According to their abbey's records, one hundred and sixty-four years had passed since St Malachy had wrested the staff from Niall mac Edan. In all the time since it had rested on this hallowed hill, the cathedral, the city and Ireland itself changing around it. If sentient the staff would have perceived the distant convulsions of war as the English had come, first as adventurers, then under the command of their kings. It would have smelled the fires of destruction and heard the marching footsteps of the conquerors as they took the east coast from Wexford to Dublin and Antrim; felt the hammer blows as the earth was quarried for stone to construct new towns and castles that were heaved up to dominate the country they now controlled. Would Malachy, their blessed founder, even recognise what had become of the land outside these walls? Donnell turned, his eyes shining in the candle-light, as his brothers emerged from the darkness he had left behind.

Murtough moved past him, slowing as he approached the plinth, his gaze going from the staff to the iron grate above. Cautious, but eager, he stepped forward and took hold of the crosier. One of the others opened a cloth bag for him to lower the relic into. With the staff secured and Donnell lighting the way, the men hastened through the crypt, leaving the psalms of the cathedral's canons to fade behind them.

By a door in the east wall, a figure was waiting. His pale face came into view with the approaching candlelight. 'Do you have it?'

Murtough nodded, his eyes on the prone form of the doorkeeper his companion was crouched beside. There was a smear of blood on the man's forehead. His sword was still in the scabbard at his side. He had not been expecting the attack. Why would he, from men in the garb of a holy order? 'Has he stirred?'

'No, brother. I fear we wounded him gravely.'

'We will pray for him and suffer penance for the sins we have committed tonight.' Murtough's voice was gruff. 'When the staff is safe.' He nodded to Donnell, who pinched out the candle flame as the door was opened into the crisp dark of a spring dawn.

Leaving the body in the crypt, the six men stole across the grass, threading silently between the wooden crosses and memorials of the saints, their black habits making them one with the great shadow cast by St Patrick's cathedral.

Antrim, Ireland, 1300 AD

The horse plunged through the forest, snorting steam and kicking up clods of earth. All around the trees surged, scattering rainwater through the canopy. Snatches of white sky flickered between webs of brown and brittle leaves. November's fury had flayed the branches and the valley floor was covered in a rustling shroud.

Robert leaned into the furious pace, the wooden pommel jarring his stomach as he compelled the animal on through the trees. Fleet, a dappled grey courser, was so responsive to the bit that the merest tug of the reins would compel him up and over fallen boughs or across the narrow cuts of streams. The horse was smaller, but far swifter than Hunter, the destrier he had left back in Scotland in the care of his friend and ally, James Stewart.

The hood of Robert's green cloak had slipped back miles ago and rain drenched his cheeks. His ears were full of the rushing wind and his own fierce breaths. Exertion raised a metal taste in his mouth. A small branch whipped his face, but he barely felt it, all his attention on the backs of the twelve running-hounds as they veered up a steep bank, barking furiously. Robert pricked his spurs into Fleet's sides, urging him to follow.

Cresting the rise, he put his horn to his lips and blew several rapid bursts, indicating the change of direction to the others, whom he'd left some distance behind. Through a break in the trees he glimpsed a bald sweep of headland rearing over the mouth of the wooded valley. Beyond, the sea filled the horizon, slate grey beneath a sky ragged with clouds. Across the expanse of water, visible as a faint, broken line, was the coast of Scotland. Robert felt his chest tighten at the sight of his homeland. Then, he was goading Fleet on.

Ahead, through the tangle of oak and rowan, he got his first glimpse of the quarry – a flash of light-coloured rump with a darker stripe down the tail. Determination shifted to anticipation as the blind pursuit delivered the prospect of reward. The hounds had picked up the trail of a good-sized fallow buck. It switched this way and that, trying to elude the dogs, but they were fixed on its scent now, blood-lust impelling them through their exhaustion. The deer was following the natural line of the valley, through which a river ran down to the sea. Robert blew the horn again. Answering calls echoed from different parts of the forest, some behind, some ahead. Without warning the buck turned and reared, hooves striking the air. It wasn't as big as the great red harts they had hunted until the season ended, but its antlers would still maim, even kill any hound that got too close.

Robert pulled on the reins, bringing Fleet to a wheeling halt as he shouted commands to the circling dogs. Uathach, his faithful bitch, was at the front of the pack. Despite having recently given birth to a litter of six she was fearless in her ferocity, her sinewy body hunched forward as she snarled at the buck, which lowered its head and tossed its antlers this way and that, raking the soil. Robert glanced over his shoulder, hearing the mad ringing of horns as the rest of the hunting party converged on his position. He caught sight of his brothers, Edward and Thomas, at the front of the company. The buck veered away through the undergrowth, but it was too late. The huntsmen, lying in wait further along the valley, had let slip the mastiffs.

Robert spurred the courser on, pursuing the deer in its final, desperate flight as from the left hurtled two massive dogs, the spikes on their collars flashing like metal teeth. The buck raced on despite the danger. Robert admired its tenacity, even as the mastiffs emerged from the trees and threw themselves upon it, one leaping up and under to tear at its throat, the other raking its hind. The buck's bellow became a roar of pain as it crashed into the mud, limbs thrashing. Bringing Fleet to a stop, Robert swung down from the saddle, shouting for the huntsmen. They came sprinting through the bushes, sticks at the ready to whip away the mastiffs who had pinned the buck, their jaws embedded in its flesh. The animal snorted deeply and shuddered. As Robert went forward through the line of hounds he slid the silver-ringed horn back into its silk baldric — both gifts from his foster-father. The buck's legs were twitching. Robert nodded to the huntsmen, who beat the ground menacingly with their sticks, until the dogs released their hold, licking bloody slaver from their jaws.

As Robert crouched by the deer he saw himself reflected in its eyes: wet hair falling in dark hanks around a strong-boned face, green cloak hanging heavy from broad shoulders, sodden with rain. The buck snorted again, blood trickling from its nostrils and pumping from the mortal wound in its neck. Robert eased off his glove and placed a hand on one of the antlers. He ran his palm along the curves of velvet bone and remembered his grandfather telling him that some believed an animal caught in the hunt would imbue its captor with its properties. Words, long forgotten, sang in his mind.

> From the hart power and nobility; from the buck swiftness and grace.
> From the wolf cunning and agility; from the hare the thrill of the race.

Drawing his broadsword, balanced by its ball-shaped pommel, he rose and placed the tip of the forty-two-inch blade over the buck's fluttering heart. He pushed down hard.

The rest of the hunting party gathered, squires taking the reins of horses as the noblemen dismounted, calling their congratulations to him. Seeing Nes had arrived and was taking care of Fleet, Robert pulled a rag from the pouch at his belt and wiped the blood from his sword. The wood filled with the sound of frenzied barking as the running-hounds were allowed to take it in turns to tear at the buck's neck — an incentive for the next hunt — before they were coupled by the varlets. Uathach was among them, panting steam into the frigid air. As the huntsmen surrounded the buck to prepare it for the unmaking, Robert's foster-father came over.

Lord Donough's eyes crinkled at the corners as he clamped a hand on Robert's shoulder. 'Well run, my son.' He looked at the buck, nodding appreciatively. 'He'll make a fine feast for our table.'

Robert smiled, pleased by the old man's admiration. As he stuffed the soiled cloth through his belt, Cormac, one of his foster-brothers, handed him a jewelled wine skin. Two years younger than Robert, at twenty-four, he was a mirror of Donough, without the crow's feet or the white in his red hair, which he wore in the cúlán, the front thick and hanging in his eyes, the back shorn short.

Cormac grinned as Robert drank deep. 'I thought you might leap off Fleet and sink your own teeth into the beast's rump the haste you were in to catch it.'

Donough's voice cut across him. 'Mind your tongue, son. You speak to your elder and better.'

'Elder anyway,' Cormac murmured, as his father moved to oversee the huntsmen's preparations.

'Old enough at least to grow a man's beard.' Robert snatched out before his foster-brother could move and tugged hard at the whiskers Cormac was cultivating, causing him to pull away, protesting. Robert chuckled as the younger man sauntered off, rubbing his chin. Cormac reminded him so much of Edward. As Robert looked over at his brother, who was talking to Christopher Seton, his smile faded.

Fostered to Donough as children, as was the Gaelic custom, Robert and Edward had spent a year with the Irish lord and his sons, learning to ride and to fight, in training for knighthood. But while Cormac had retained his carefree insouciance, Edward's spirit had been dampened in the time since. Robert had found the return to the Antrim estates after fifteen years had only served to accentuate the changes the war had wrought in his brother, and in him.

'For the unmaking, sir.'

Robert turned as one of the huntsmen offered him a leather pouch in which were inserted five knives, each with a different blade, one for cutting through bone and sinew, another for flaying the hide, others for more delicate butchery. He gestured to his foster-father. 'I'll pass the honour to the master.'

Donough laughed contentedly and pushed up the sleeves of his shirt. Choosing a knife, he crouched with a wince and went to work on the buck, which had been turned on its back, antlers pushed into the mud to hold it steady. The hounds had quietened. Knowing their reward would be coming soon they watched the blood flow as the lord made the first cut.

As the men gathered to witness the unmaking, Robert's gaze drifted over them. Edward was lounging against a tree, arms folded. Christopher Seton was following Donough's brisk movements intently. Close by, Niall, at nineteen the youngest of Robert's four brothers, rested an elbow on Thomas's shoulders, the two so unlike one another it was impossible to guess they shared the same blood. While Niall had been blessed with the dark good looks and merry temperament of their mother, Thomas took after their father: bull-shouldered and beetle-browed. The varlets and the local men who had joined in the hunt stood apart from the nobles, watching their lord work. All their faces were flushed with exhilaration, every one of them satisfied by a hunt that had concluded with a clean kill and no injury to horse or hound. Every one, that was, but him.

The pursuit might have ended, but none of Robert's impatience had diminished. It remained in his belly, hot and unsated. That broken coastline he had glimpsed during the chase filled his mind. Scotland taunted him with its proximity. It was a year since he resigned as guardian of the kingdom and seven months since he had come to Antrim. Seven months absent from the war that ravaged his country. Seven months away from his home and his daughter, chasing a ghost.

Robert glanced round at a snap of twigs to see Alexander Seton move up beside him. His muscular form was swathed in a hunting cloak and rainwater trickled steadily down his hard face. He appraised Robert with a knowing look, as if he'd read his thoughts.

'Another good hunt.'

Robert nodded curtly, wary of the tone in his companion's voice, which augured contention. He wasn't wrong.

'But I'll say again, however good the sport, I'd rather my sword was bloodied for a greater purpose. How long do you plan to stay here?'

Robert didn't respond, but the lord from East Lothian who had been in his company for over three years, fighting at his side, wasn't to be dismissed so easily.

'We should go home where we're needed, Robert. This was a fool's errand.'

Anger flared in Robert, the words pricking him with a truth he didn't want to hear. 'Not until I've exhausted every possibility. We haven't heard from the monks at Bangor yet. It's little over a week since Donough sent word to the abbey. I want to give them more time.'

'More time?' Alexander kept his voice low beneath the conversations going on around them. 'The monks didn't respond to the first message we sent three months ago and even if they do know where the staff is, why would they tell us? It's clear from what we know – the theft in the night, the murder of the doorkeeper – that whoever took it from the cathedral intended for it to vanish without trace. The Earl of Ulster hasn't found it despite the fact his knights have been scouring the length and breadth of Ireland. By God, if a man such as Richard de Burgh, with all his power and resources, cannot find this relic, how can we?'

Robert stared at the carcass of the buck as Donough pulled the hide back from its stomach, ripping skin from muscles. His pride fought against the sense in Alexander's words. He had to believe he had been right to come here, no matter the doubt that had wormed its way in. 'You can return to Scotland. I won't stop you. But I'm staying.'

'I have nothing to return to. I gave up everything to join you and your cause. We both did.' Alexander stared across the gathering at his cousin. 'Longshanks would have Christopher and me clapped in irons the moment either of us set foot in our lands.'

Robert looked over at Christopher Seton. The Yorkshireman, whom he'd knighted two years earlier, was talking animatedly to Edward and Niall. 'Your lands may yet be won. We took back a great deal of territory before we left and James Stewart and the others will have continued the fight in our absence.'

'Territory will mean nothing if King Edward returns in strength. His last campaign almost annihilated us. We lost ten thousand men on the field at Falkirk. With William Wallace in France and you here, who will stand against the English? Tell me, are you content to leave the fate of our kingdom in the hands of a man like John Comyn?'

Robert's jaw tightened. The months absent from Scotland had not dulled his hostility towards his enemy. If anything, time had heightened it, his mind darkened by the knowledge that the longer he stayed away the more Comyn would consolidate his own position.

Two years ago, almost to the day, after William Wallace resigned as guardian of Scotland, Robert and John Comyn, the same age and heirs to the fortunes of their families, had been elected in his place. Together they had governed the king-less, war-torn realm, presiding over the fractured community of earls, lords, knights and peasants who sought an end to Edward Longshanks' English dominion. It had not been an easy alliance. There was enmity enough between the two men, but worse still was the bitterness between their families. Poisoned by an act of betrayal decades earlier that bad blood had seeped through the years since, flowing from father to son.

In invoking Comyn, Alexander Seton played a clever move. But he missed the fundamental point. When Robert left, his place as guardian had been taken by William Lamberton, but even the appointment of the formidable Bishop of St Andrews wouldn't have stopped Comyn bolstering his support among the men of the realm. In order to restore his own authority in Scotland, Robert knew he had to return with something that could prove his greater worth, something that could win them their freedom. John Comyn was just another reason he could not return without the prize he sought: St Malachy's staff.

'You told us our country needed a new king,' Alexander continued gruffly, mistaking Robert's silence for indifference. 'One who would defend our liberties, where John Balliol failed. You told us you would be that king.'

Now, Robert turned to him. The memory of the words he had spoken in the courtyard of Turnberry Castle three years ago – the year he broke his oath of fealty to King Edward to fight alongside William Wallace – was still vivid. He had addressed his men back then with fire in his heart, promising to defend their freedom and pledging to be their king. Not only did his veins flow with the royal blood of the house of Canmore, but his grandfather had been named heir presumptive by Alexander II. Before his death, the old man had passed that claim to him and Robert had sworn to uphold it, no matter the pretenders who sat upon the throne in defiance of the Bruce family's right.

His voice strengthened. 'And I will be.'

2

The hunting party made their way across the fields in the deepening gloom. The huntsman carried the buck's severed head, trailing a bright line of blood that had summoned the crows which circled in their wake. After the hounds had been given their reward the rest of the carcass had been dismembered, the best bits of venison going to Lord Donough for his table, the rest to the men who had participated in the chase. Even the local lads who jogged alongside the mounted nobles had leaf-wrapped parcels of meat and bone to take home to their families. Donough always saw that everyone was fed.

They joined the track that took them on the homeward stretch to Donough's hall, past the remains of a ring-fort where sheep grazed in the ruins that were stippled with moss and yellow rosettes of butterwort. Robert stared at the crumbling stones, struck by memory. He saw himself, lean and long-limbed, straddling the highest point of the tumbled-down walls, fists raised in triumph as his foster-brothers clambered up behind him, panting from the race. His own voice echoed down the years.

'*I am the king! I am the king!*'

He turned from the ruins as the track dipped with the slope of the land and the hall came into view. Cormac dug in his spurs and galloped ahead, his red hair wild in the wind. Niall and Thomas rode after him, racing one another. The hall dominated a grassy mound that rose over the banks of a shallow river. It was ringed by a defensive ditch and palisade, the stakes of which were unstained by weather or time. Eighteen months ago, most of the buildings had been destroyed by fire, leaving only the stone shell of the hall. It had taken months of labour, but with Donough's determination, the devotion of his tenants and coins from Robert's coffers, the place looked almost as it had when Robert lived here as a boy.

Following in the wake of the three young men, the rest of the company funnelled through the gate in the palisade. The guards nodded a greeting to

Donough and Robert, who urged their mounts up the well-worn incline to the yard in the centre of the stables and barns, which still smelled of sawn timber. Thomas and Niall had dismounted with Cormac and were issuing orders to the grooms who came out to meet the party. Robert's younger brothers had remained in fosterage when the war broke out between Scotland and England four years ago and were now more at home here than in the Bruce family's strongholds in Carrick and Annandale.

As Robert swung down from the saddle and handed the reins to Nes, he saw Donough's steward.

'My lord.' The steward raised his voice over the excited barking of the hounds. 'I trust you fared well?'

'A fine fallow, Gilbert,' said Donough, dismounting. 'We have meat for hanging.'

'I will see to it. For now, my lord, you have company.'

Donough frowned. 'Who?'

'Two monks from Bangor Abbey. They arrived shortly after noon.' Gilbert's gaze lingered on his lord's mud-caked boots and cloak. 'Shall I bid them wait while you change?'

Robert stepped forward. 'No, Gilbert. We'll see them now.'

When the steward glanced at Donough, the lord nodded. 'See there is food enough for all the company tonight. My men will dine with me.'

'Yes, my lord.'

Leaving the steward to direct the huntsmen and the varlets to usher the hounds to the kennels, Robert and his foster-father headed for the hall. As he crossed the yard, Robert caught the eye of Alexander Seton. Feeling vindicated, and satisfied with it, he stepped into the smoky shadows, his anticipation rising.

Inside the hall, by the chamber's hearth, were the two monks in black habits. They turned as Robert and Donough entered, the flames in the grate gusting with the rush of cold air. One was younger than the other and had a plain, earnest face and worried, darting eyes. The older of the two was more distinctive with a grotesque scar that carved its way down his cheek and through his lip. He stood erect, feet planted apart, meeting Robert's appraising gaze with a bellicose stare that would have looked more at home on a warrior than a man of the cloth.

Donough didn't seem at all affected by the hostility in that look, going straight to the scarred monk and clasping his hand in both of his. 'Brother Murtough, it has been too long. You received my messages? I feared the worst when you failed to answer.'

'We would have come sooner. But the danger was too great.'

The scarred monk's Gaelic was rough and guttural, different enough in cadence from the way his own family spoke it that Robert strained to understand him.

'Ulster's spies have been watching us.' Murtough's eyes roved around the hall, taking in the new beams that criss-crossed the roof. 'I am glad, Lord Donough, to see you were able to repair the damage his men caused here.'

Donough's smile vanished at the name of the man whose knights had been responsible for the destruction of his home. 'I wasn't going to let the dogs think they had won.' He turned to Robert. 'And I had a great deal of help from my foster-son, Sir Robert, Earl of Carrick and lord of these estates.'

The scarred monk's attention shifted to Robert. 'Your name and pedigree precede you, Sir Robert. Your grandfather was a great man, God rest his soul. My brethren and I honour him still.'

Robert frowned in surprise. As far as he knew, his grandfather had never visited Ireland. The Bruce family's lands in Antrim, from Glenarm to Olderfleet, had not been part of the old man's legacy. Like the earldom of Carrick, they were part of the inheritance of Robert's mother, acquired by his father on their marriage and granted to him eight years ago. Having taken his father's place, Robert had found it strange, returning to Antrim as lord, to have his foster-father kneel before him to pay homage. 'I didn't know you knew my grandfather.'

'Not personally,' the younger monk clarified. 'But we benefited from his generosity. He sent money to our abbey for years to pay for candles to burn at the shrine of our blessed founder, St Malachy.'

Donough nodded when Robert looked at him. 'Your grandfather had the donations sent to me through your mother.' He gestured to the long table that dominated the hall, where a jug of wine and goblets had been placed. 'Let us sit.'

As they moved to the trestle and benches, Robert thought of the abbey at Clairvaux in France and other holy sites where his grandfather had paid for candles to be lit in honour of the saint. How many wicks still smouldered in chapels and abbeys, kept alight by the old man's will, all in an effort to atone for the sins of their ancestor?

When travelling through Scotland, so the story went, Malachy, Archbishop of Armagh, once stayed at the Bruce family's castle in Annan. Hearing of a robber who was sentenced to hang, he requested the man be spared, a plea the Lord of Annandale granted. When, the following day, Malachy saw the man hanging from a gallows, he brought his wrath down upon the lord and his line. The curse he laid upon them was said to have caused the river to rise and wash away their stronghold, forcing the Bruce family to build a new castle at Lochmaben.

Robert's father had always mocked the legend, citing a winter storm as the cause of the damage to the castle, but his grandfather had blamed it not only for past misfortunes, but for all the events following the tragic death of King Alexander III that led to the crowning of Edward's puppet king, John Balliol, and the loss of the Bruce family's claim to the throne.

'Last year, my brothers sought me out to tell me of the destruction of Donough's hall at the Earl of Ulster's hands,' explained Robert, as he sat. 'They said Ulster's men were looking for a relic King Edward desired – a relic known by some as the Staff of Jesus and by others as the Staff of Malachy.' He studied Murtough while he spoke, but the monk's scarred features revealed nothing. 'I resigned from the guardianship of Scotland in the hope that I might find this staff and prevent the king from seizing it. Lord Donough sent messages to your abbey in the belief that your order may know of its whereabouts.'

When the two men remained silent, Donough sighed roughly. 'Come, Murtough, you may have kept your distance these past months, but word travels even if you do not.' He poured a goblet of wine and passed it to the monk. 'We know Ulster's men searched your abbey after the staff disappeared from Armagh. Why else would they do this if they did not suspect you of having taken it?'

'And why would he destroy your home, Donough?' countered Murtough. 'Are you believed to have stolen it?'

'Our support of your order is well known. We became suspects by association.' Donough scowled. 'And doubtless it presented the excuse Ulster has been looking for to remove us from Glenarm for good. Under the lordship of the Bruce family we have been protected all these years, while our countrymen were driven into the west by English invaders. I was one of only a handful of men who retained his lands. Of course Ulster wants me gone. But I say God help him and all his kind when our countrymen rise to take back what is theirs. Trouble grows in the south for de Burgh and his kin from what I hear. There are rumours of rebellion. Of war.' He thumped his fist on the table. 'A day of reckoning is coming. Mark my words.'

'Richard de Burgh was an ally of your family for years, Sir Robert,' remarked the younger monk. 'We know too of your allegiance to King Edward. How can we be sure where your loyalties lie in this matter?'

'Those allegiances are three years dead. They ended the day I joined the insurrection led by William Wallace.' Robert leaned forward, holding the monk with his gaze. 'Both our countries have suffered under the English king's dominion. If you know where the staff is, I can help you keep it from him.' As the young man glanced at Murtough, Robert caught a flicker of hope in his face. He seized on it. 'In Monmouth's *History of the Kings of Britain* it is written that Brutus of Troy, who founded these islands, had certain relics in his possession. On his death, his sons carved up the land between them into what would become England, Ireland, Wales and Scotland, each taking one of the four relics to symbolise his new authority.'

'I am aware of Geoffrey of Monmouth's works,' Murtough cut in.

Robert continued, undeterred by the monk's tone. 'According to a vision of the prophet Merlin, whose words Monmouth claimed to be translating, this division began Britain's descent into chaos. Merlin foretold that these relics would need to be gathered again under one ruler to prevent the land's final ruin. Both Utherpendragon and his son, King Arthur, came close to succeeding, but never fully achieved this. When Edward conquered Wales he discovered a lost prophecy that named the four treasures. For England, Curtana, the Sword of Mercy. For Wales, the Crown of Arthur, believed to be the diadem worn by Brutus himself. For Scotland . . .'

Here, Robert faltered, his thoughts filling with the bitter image of a block of stone in the belly of a wagon, careening down a dusty track. He was riding furiously in its wake, shield held high. Around him rode other men, blades in their hands and victory in their faces. All bore the same shield as him: blood red with a dragon rearing, fire-wreathed, in the centre. Shamefully, he had played his own part that day, in taking that most precious of relics to Edward.

'For Scotland,' he finished, 'the Stone of Destiny, upon which all our kings have been crowned.'

'We have heard of King Edward's conquests,' said the younger monk gravely. 'We know he has taken these treasures for his shrine at Westminster. Only the staff of our founder evades him.'

'Then you know how much he wants this last relic. How he will stop at nothing to get it.'

'And what about you, Earl Robert?' said Murtough, his eyes glittery in the candlelight. As he took a draught of wine, some of the liquid dribbled through the cleft in his lip. 'Do you believe in Merlin's prophecy?'

'It does not matter what I believe. What matters is that the king's subjects and many of his men believe. They fight for it, bleed and die for it. They are the sword that enabled him to conquer Wales. Now Scotland. The belief that they are saving Britain from ruin adds fire to their conviction. Edward conquers not just with might, but with the power of prophecy. He will make himself a new Brutus, a new Arthur. And all Britain will bend before him.'

'If you had the staff, what would you do with it?'

Robert steeled himself to the challenge in the older monk's stare, feeling Murtough could see right through to the desire in his heart – a desire that had little to do with protecting the relic and everything to do with atonement for his sin in the theft of another. If King Edward offered him the Stone of Destiny in return for the staff tomorrow he would gladly accept. He levelled the monk with his gaze, giving away nothing of his thoughts. 'I would prevent him from taking it. My ancestor offended St Malachy and our family has suffered ever since. For my grandfather and my line, this is my chance to right that wrong.'

For a long moment, Robert didn't think Murtough was going to respond, then the monk set down his goblet.

'After Ulster's men ransacked our abbey and found nothing we thought that would be the end of it, but then we discovered his knights were keeping watch on us, following our brothers when they left the abbey grounds, questioning anyone who visited – labourers, laundresses. A little over two months ago one of our acolytes disappeared. It emerged that he had been seen meeting with Ulster's knights. Some time later, we discovered documents were missing from our vault.' Murtough paused. 'We fear Ulster may now know of Ibracense.'

Robert frowned. 'Ibracense?'

The younger monk glanced at Murtough, who nodded. 'When Malachy was elected Abbot of Bangor he rebuilt the abbey, but soon after it was attacked by a local chieftain and Malachy and his brethren were forced to flee south. On an island in a great lake, our blessed founder built a monastery where he and his brothers remained, isolated from the barbarities of the world, for three years. Malachy called it Ibracense. He was forced to leave this sanctuary when he took up his position as Archbishop of Armagh, wresting the Staff of Jesus from Niall mac Edan. He never returned. It is only recalled in the records of our abbey, which he rebuilt once more before he passed away. The documents that were stolen from our vault speak of Ibracense – not its location, which is known to only a handful of our brethren – but the description is enough to offer a guide. Soon after our acolyte disappeared, Ulster's men vanished from Bangor. We believe they are looking for the island. If they find it, they will find the staff.'

Murtough looked at Donough, his expression now weary, defeated. 'It is why we answered your summons. We do not have the ability to keep moving it, or soldiers to guard it. The relic's concealment was all we could rely on.'

Robert spoke. 'I can take it to Scotland and secure it until both our countries are free of Edward's control. When it is safe to do so, I will return it to you.'

After a silence, Murtough nodded. 'We will take your proposition to the abbot.'

Loughrea, Ireland, 1301 AD

Richard de Burgh, Earl of Ulster and Lord of Connacht, took the roll of parchment the clerk handed to him. The royal seal hung heavily from it, the red beeswax, imprinted with King Edward's coat of arms, cracking around the edges. The earl's face, webbed with scars, was grim as he scanned the inked rows of letters and numerals. Around him the chamber bustled with servants, packing clothes into chests and removing tapestries from the lime-washed walls, emptying the chamber of its movable wealth.

'As you can see, Sir Richard,' said the chancellor carefully, 'the revenues requested from Westminster have almost doubled this past year. The exchequer has been forced to raise taxes in order to meet King Edward's demands without further impoverishing our administration at Dublin. We are stretched to the limit as it is.'

Ulster looked up from the roll at the chancellor's solemn face, thinking the man was shrewd to blame the office for the rise, rather than himself as the exchequer's chief clerk, or indeed the king.

The chancellor laced his thin fingers. 'You must know how much King Edward relies upon you, Sir Richard. You have the power to change his fortunes here. He needs the revenue only a man of your stature can provide in order to succeed in his fight against the Scots. Victory is close. His enemies suffered grave losses at Falkirk and a new campaign has been planned for the coming months, but the king's treasury was drained by the war against his cousin in Gascony and the rebellion he was forced to crush in Wales. He has been compelled to raise taxes throughout his crown lands. We, every one of us, must suffer that burden if our king is to succeed in bringing Britain under his dominion.'

'It was Ireland's grain that fed his troops in Gascony and Wales,' responded

Ulster, his deep voice grinding over the chancellor's mollifying tones. 'My tenants and I suffered this burden long before today.'

'And for that you have his gratitude. King Edward will reward your sacrifice when the war in Scotland is won. There are rich lands there, ripe for the picking.'

Ulster rose, his gold-embroidered mantle of fine Flemish cloth shifting around his large frame as he walked to the windows, through which the steel-bright February sun was streaming. Beyond the panes of leaded glass Lough Rea was spread out before him, its blue expanse ruffled by wind. His family had built this castle, their chief stronghold in Connacht, and the walled town that surrounded it sixty years ago, but their supremacy in the land extended back further still to the Norman lords who sailed to Ireland under King John, continuing the conquest begun by his father, Henry II.

Those men had carved out a broad swathe of territory from Cork to Antrim, taming the landscape under the plough, altering the face of it with castles, mills and towns. Here, in the fertile east, they settled for generations, the native Irish driven into the harsh, mountainous west. During those years, the de Burgh family had grown in prominence and power until, under Richard, they had reached their zenith. But things were changing. The Irish were pushing back. Already, there was war on the borders, native kings banding together to force out the English along the frontiers. The conquerors' control was deteriorating as the economy weakened under King Edward's increasing demands.

How galling, Ulster thought, now to be looking down from the heights of the illustrious position he had attained and seeing only the slope of decline. He turned to the chancellor. 'The building of my new castle at Ballymote has put a strain on my resources and with the exodus of so many of our countrymen, unable to protect themselves from Irish brigands, I am left to shoulder the duties of many. Whole settlements have been abandoned by those choosing to return to England. The more men leave, the more soldiers the rest of us have to find for the breach. If King Edward takes much more, we will no longer be able to hold back the tide of felons and marauders who wait on our borders, testing them always for signs of weakness.'

Ulster paused, his attention snared by a tall, well-built man in a sky-blue cloak, who had moved into the chamber past two servants carrying out a chest. 'But I will do whatever I can for my lord. You have my word on that.' Ulster strode from the window. 'Show the Lord Chancellor and his men to lodgings,' he ordered one of his servants, before confronting the man in the doorway, who looked as though he had ridden through several nights. The captain's cloak was stained with horse sweat, his hair unkempt, eyes shadowed.

'Sir Esgar? What brings you?'

Esgar inclined his head, his cloak parting to reveal the glimmer of mail. 'I bear tidings, my lord, from the north.'

'Walk with me.' Ulster headed from the chamber, leaving the chancellor and clerks to gather up their rolls.

The captain fell into step beside the earl as he led the way along the passage. All around, people hurried about their duties, making ready to move the earl's considerable household to his new castle, eighty miles north. 'I believe I may have a new trail to follow in our hunt for the staff.'

Ulster felt his anticipation stirred, but didn't allow it to consume him. There had been leads before, without success. He had several companies in the south searching for islands that fitted the description in the abbey's records, but so far they had found nothing. He made his way down the stairs, a servant who had been heading up backing hastily down before him. 'What trail?'

'My men and I kept watch on the abbey, but at a distance as you instructed. Our strategy worked and we began to notice the monks coming and going more freely. Shortly after the Christ Mass we observed the abbot's trusted man, Murtough, and two brethren leaving the abbey, equipped for a journey.' Esgar moved back into step with the earl as they descended to the ground floor. 'At a settlement they joined fifteen men and headed south. When I discovered who was leading this company, I left my men trailing them and rode straight here.'

'Who was it?'

'Robert Bruce, the Earl of Carrick.'

'Bruce?' Ulster's voice sharpened with surprise. He halted, facing the captain.

'We already knew Bruce was in Antrim from reports by our men. Travelling with him were two of his brothers, who reside with Lord Donough at Glenarm, and one of the lord's sons. The rest I did not know.'

'You believe they are going after the staff?'

'From what our informant in the abbey told us we know Murtough was involved in the relic's disappearance. The monks would have no doubt discovered their missing documents by now and would assume we are closer to finding Ibracense. I think they will try to move it.'

Ulster's anticipation now took him over. Robert Bruce – King Edward's enemy – and the Staff of Malachy in one fell swoop? How much would such a prize be worth to the king? Much more, he guessed, than those additional taxes. 'Will you be able to track them?'

'My men will leave messages at our garrisons en route. It shouldn't be hard.'

'Let them take the relic before you make a move, understand? Seize the staff, capture Bruce and bring him to me at Ballymote.' Ulster levelled the captain with a challenging stare. 'I will be waiting, Esgar.'

'Yes, my lord.'

As Esgar headed to the stables, Ulster strode out into the castle court-yard, enlivened by the prospect. Servants were piling chests into the backs of wagons, while knights and squires checked gear and weapons. It was a small army that would accompany him and his family through what had become known as the land of war. The men's surcoats were decorated with the blazons of their respective commanders, but all bore a red band of cloth around their upper arms, decorated with the black lion from Ulster's coat of arms. In these troubled times it was becoming more necessary to be able to identify friend from foe quickly.

As Ulster spoke with his men, checking preparations for the journey, he saw a young woman moving through the crowd. In her white gown she was a pearl, glimmering among the grey shells of armour. He smiled as she approached, his hard face softening. 'Are you ready to leave?' he asked, kiss-ing the top of her head, which was covered by a stiff white coif. Her sisters wore their black locks piled in braids, decorated with silver and jewels, but Elizabeth, at sixteen the youngest of his daughters, had worn hers covered since the age of ten.

'I have been praying for our safe passage to Ballymote, Father.'

As she turned up her face to his, her pale skin reddened by the wind, Ulster saw the worry in her eyes. 'I am certain the Lord will have heard your prayers.' When she didn't respond, he moved her gently to face the crowded courtyard. 'Look at the men He has provided me with.' Beneath his hands he felt the tension in her slim shoulders. She was always so anxious. When she was a child Elizabeth had been as carefree and wild as a sprite, but the accident had changed that.

On a June day six years before, Elizabeth had been playing on the banks of Lough Rea when she had slipped and fallen in. Her governess had not been watching her. The lough was deep and the child couldn't swim. By chance two squires had been passing and leapt in and saved her. At first, Ulster blessed his good fortune, then, after the shock of almost losing his daughter wore off, he thanked God in prayers more heartfelt than ever before. By that evening everyone in the castle, himself included, was calling it a miracle.

But when God had saved her He seemed to have claimed her for Himself, so that now Elizabeth was wed to Him, her prayers and piety demanding all her time, leaving little room for merriment, or indeed a suitor. It was why she remained the only unmarried one of all his children. Still, Ulster refused to send her to a convent, despite her pleas. Elizabeth's youth and beauty made her one of his greatest assets and the earl was determined that while God might have her soul, a husband would have her heart.

3

The siege engines towered out of the mist – monstrous forms dedicated to destruction. Each had been christened by the Englishmen who manned them. The Vanquisher. The Hammer. The Boar. Each was primed, ready for the day's ruin.

With a roared order from the engineers the winches were released, the beams arcing up to slingshot their loads at the sandstone walls and towers of the castle. The great stones struck with ear-splitting cracks, dust and mortar exploding on impact and a gaping hole appearing in one of the twin towers of the gatehouse. As rubble splashed into the moat, the shouts of the engineers echoed and, immediately, men began to heave on the ropes, drawing down the arm of each machine and hoisting up the massive weighted basket that hung at its opposite end. When the arm was down, a large stone ball, hewn for the purpose, was rolled into the leather sling. It was David and Goliath. Only now it was the monster who had the stone in his fist and sixty Scottish soldiers cowered within the walls, like a David with no hope whatsoever.

Beyond the industry of the siege lines, crowded among the castle's earth-work defences and outbuildings, which had fallen to the English yesterday, was a seething encampment of three thousand men. Smoke curled from fires, adding a grey pall to the morning mists. The smell of boiled meat from the cooking pots blended with the reek of horse dung and the stink from the dug-out latrines. The place blazed with colour, from the knights' surcoats and mantles to the pennons on their lance shafts and the banners that were hoisted above the great retinues of England's earls.

At the heart of the camp, King Edward watched as the siege engines were primed again. At over six feet he was an erect tower of a man, standing head and shoulder above most of those around him. His crimson surcoat was emblazoned with three golden lions, beneath which a mail hauberk and coat-of-plates broadened his muscular frame. His beard, the same swan-feather white as his hair, was clipped brutally close to his jaw and did little to soften his grim countenance. The only trace of frailty to be found in that face was the droop in one of his eyelids, a defect inherited from his father, which had become more prominent since he had turned sixty. With the gold crown upon his head and the scarred broadsword strapped to his side he was the embodiment of majesty and might, inviting comparison with legendary warriors of old – Brutus, Roland, Charlemagne. Arthur.

As the engines let loose another barrage, Edward followed the missiles with his eyes. It was only the second day of the siege and already the walls were pitted with damage. It would, however, take much more to bring the structure to ruin. Caerlaverock Castle, shaped like a shield with towers at each point of its triangle, stood isolated in the waters of its surrounding moat, drawbridge raised. Built only thirty years earlier, it was said to be one of the most redoubtable fortresses in Scotland. Stretching behind it were the salt marshes and mud-flats of the Solway Firth, beyond which lay England. With the fall of the Bruce family's stronghold at Lochmaben, Caerlaverock had become the new gateway to the west of Scotland. It was the first obstacle he faced on this campaign.

'My lord king.'

Humphrey de Bohun moved up beside him. He was clad in a blue surcoat, banded with a broad white stripe and decorated with six gold lions. His brown hair was covered by a coif of mail that framed his broad face and he carried his great helm under his arm. 'Work is progressing well on the belfry, my lord. The engineers believe it will be ready before the week is out. Once it's lowered into the moat the fighting top should come high enough up the walls to allow our men to scale them. Unless, of course, it falls to us before that.'

As Humphrey's attention shifted to the castle, the king noted the hunger in his gaze. The young man had succeeded his father as Constable of England and Earl of Hereford and Essex three years earlier, and along with those distinguished titles he seemed to have inherited the same intensity of expression, as if some thought or passion was constantly burning behind his green eyes. Edward had seen a similar fire of late in the other men of his Round Table, bound to him – as King Arthur's knights had been – by oaths stronger than fealty or homage. The war had become something personal to all of them. Some, like Humphrey, had lost family to a Scottish blade. Others were fighting for the promise of reward, or glory. But all were here for retribution against the man whose betrayal had cut like a poisoned dagger through their ranks – a man they had once called brother.

Robert Bruce.

That name was a splinter under Edward's skin. The last reports revealed that Bruce had resigned his position as guardian of Scotland and disappeared, leaving a maddening and disturbing silence. The king's best hope lay in the belief that if anyone could find Bruce it was Adam, but he had heard no word from the Gascon in months. 'The divisions,' he asked Humphrey, 'they are prepared?'

'If we storm the castle with the belfry and our men are able to lower the drawbridge, your son will command the main assault. As you instructed.'

The king seized on the trace of doubt in the younger man's voice. 'You do not think him ready?'

Humphrey paused before answering. 'I think it is a challenging assault for a first command, my lord.'

The king surveyed the crowd of men around the royal pavilion, his keen eyes picking out his son. Edward, only weeks away from his seventeenth birthday, was a mirror of himself in adolescence; the same blond hair and long, angular features. In the past year the boy's body had lengthened and begun to thicken, suggesting he would also inherit his stature. He was standing with his companions, all sons of lords or earls, apart from Piers Gaveston, who owed his position to the king's own indulgence. The son of a loyal Gascon knight, Piers had seemed an ideal companion for the young Edward. The two had since grown inseparable, but while his son seemed content to spend his days fishing and lazing outdoors it was Piers who had developed an impressive martial reputation in that time. Handsome, charismatic, arrogant, his prowess on the tournament field was already being commented on in court, while the heir to the throne languished contentedly in his shadow. That, the king was determined, would change on this campaign, which was why he had given the command of half the English army to his son.

'A victory here will be a worthy beginning to his career. I fought my first campaign at his age. It is past time he was tested. This war and his forthcoming marriage will see to it.' The king turned, fixing Humphrey with his full attention. 'On the subject of which, I am aware you have been spending time with my daughter.'

A faint wash of colour bloomed on the earl's cheeks.

Edward laughed, the sound brief and brittle. 'Do not fear, Humphrey. I am glad. Since the death of Count John, I have been pondering the question of a new suitor for my daughter. When this campaign is won, we will discuss the matter.'

'My lord, I would be honoured . . .'

Edward, however, wasn't listening. His gaze had been caught by a company of mounted men making their way through the camp, led by four royal knights. He recognised, with swift-rising hostility, the corpulent man at the head, astride a stocky black horse. It was Robert Winchelsea, Archbishop of Canterbury. With the archbishop was a retinue of black-clad clerics and two foreign-looking men in sumptuous scarlet robes and jewelled hats. Appraising their distinctive appearance, at once pious and wealthy, Edward felt certain he knew where they had come from. They had the look of men from the papal curia in Rome. The king's hostility shifted to unease.

4

Lough Luioch, Ireland, 1301 AD

Robert sat at the prow, watching the island draw near. Mountains were mirrored in the depths of the lough. Beyond their scarred heights, the sky was stained with a bloody tinge. The air was crisp, but not as cold as it had been when the company set out from Antrim, the February winds dying the further south they travelled. In the still dawn the only sound was the splash of oars. The boat, taken from the beach, was old and smelled of fish. Behind Robert, eyes gleaming in the half-light, were Edward and Niall, along with Murtough and two of his brethren. Christopher and Cormac were at the oars. Robert had left his brother Thomas and Alexander Seton with the squires on the northern shore, guarding their horses and gear. He wasn't taking any chances.

On their journey south, hampered by harsh terrain and winter weather, they had encountered bands of lawless men roaming the countryside for plunder. Most had been cautious of their well-armed company, but on two occasions they had been accosted and were only saved from a skirmish by Cormac – whose cúlán marked him as an Irishman – and by the presence of the monks in their habits. At settlements along the way they had heard rumours of pillage and murder, as the Irish grew increasingly confident in attacking areas settled long ago by English colonists.

'I see no one.'

Robert looked round at the rough voice to see Murtough peering into the gloom. The closer they had come to their destination the more subdued the monk had grown. Robert knew he was wary of what they might find when they reached the island; fearful the staff might already have been taken. But they had seen no sign of Ulster's men on the road and he couldn't imagine how anyone could find this place, even with guidance from the abbey's records. The remote wilderness, hidden by its mountain barrier, seemed as though it stood at the end of the earth. Added to the solitude was the issue of identification, for Ireland's landscape was crowded with ruins: hill forts and standing stones, cairns and barrow mounds. The crumbling remains on the island ahead were just one of countless monuments to the once living and long dead.

As they reached land, the boat grazing the shallows, Edward and Niall leapt over the sides to haul in the vessel. Robert jumped down, his mail coat shifting around him as he splashed through pools between the rocks. 'Keep watch,' he ordered Christopher and Cormac.

'We've not seen a soul in days,' Cormac responded. When Robert fixed him with a stare, the young Irishman exhaled. 'Whatever you say, brother.' He and Christopher shared a look as they stowed the oars.

Robert ignored them, unable to dispel his rising apprehension. The path to the throne he had set out upon three years ago had followed a frustratingly twisting course and these past months in Ireland he had felt further from that purpose than ever. Often he had doubted his decision to pursue the relic, fearing it would lead him nowhere. Now was the moment when his choice would be proven right or wrong.

Murtough led the way through a fringe of reeds towards the largest of the island's ruins, a church formed of the same ghost-grey stones that littered the shoreline. Birds startled from the undergrowth as the men moved towards the building, which was encircled by a low, tumbled-down wall, tufted with grass. Beyond were remains of other buildings, most of them timber, which had all but rotted away over the long years since the place was inhabited. Bushes and weeds had worked their way into the remnants, nature reclaiming its territory. On the western end of the island, Robert caught sight of a domed structure that looked like a giant stone beehive.

'St Finan's cell,' came Murtough's voice in the hush. He had stopped at the church wall and was following Robert's gaze. 'He lived here centuries before Malachy built the monastery. This island may be small, but it has a long and hallowed history.'

Robert imagined Malachy and his brethren living here; the wild solitude of their existence. It was a good place for men who wanted to escape the world.

Edward moved up beside him, leaving Niall and the other two monks to bring up the rear. 'If it is here, brother, what next?'

Murtough had moved ahead through a gap in the wall, picking his way through the undergrowth towards several slabs of stone that protruded from the grass. He was out of earshot, but Robert kept his reply low. 'We take it to Scotland, as planned.'

'And then?' Edward prompted.

Before Robert could reply, Murtough's voice cut across them. 'Here.'

Heading to him, the men gathered around a lichen-stained grave slab, lying horizontally on top of four stone lintels embedded in the soil. It was decorated with an ornately carved cross, the spirals of knot-work entwined with beasts and birds. Murtough's brethren bent to help him as he crouched and placed his hands on the slab's sides. Niall added his strength to theirs and, between them, the four men pushed it from the top of the grave. Stone ground on stone. In the dark hollow that appeared beneath, lined with the lintel slabs, Robert saw a grinning skull, laced with hair. The flesh had long been ravaged, the clothing reduced to threads. As his eyes drifted down the skeleton's length, he realised there was something lying alongside the corpse, wrapped in cloth.

Relief was plain in Murtough's scarred face. 'Praise God,' he muttered, sitting back on his heels.

Robert reached in and grasped it, feeling a solid shape within the folds of material. The cloth had once been white, but after almost two years in the grave it was green with mould. A fat earthworm twisted from the folds. The monks were sombre as they watched him take the staff, but made no move to stop him. This was his burden now. Carefully, he laid it on the grave slab and pulled back the soiled covering. In the bloody dawn, the gold and gems that encrusted the staff's sheath glittered. Robert felt a hot rush of triumph. The final relic named in the *Last Prophecy* – the one King Edward needed to fulfil his vision of a kingdom united beneath him – was in his hands.

As Robert stared at the golden crosier, Murtough's question back in Donough's hall came to him.

And what about you, Earl Robert? Do you believe in Merlin's prophecy?

He had spent two years in Edward's company, one of the Knights of the Dragon, whose purpose was to aid the king in retrieving the relics. While many of those who had once been his friends accepted the truth of Merlin's prophecy and were determined to prevent the ruin of Britain foreseen in it, he himself had not been able to believe. No matter the rewards, the glory and camaraderie he had found in the king's service, he had never been able to dismiss the fact that if the four treasures were gathered under one man, who would rule all of Britain, it would render the Bruce claim to the throne of Scotland meaningless. In furthering Edward's ambition, he denied his own and failed in his promise to his grandfather that he would uphold their family's right. In the end, this truth had twisted inside him, turning him from Edward's cause.

Oath-breaker, they had called him. *Traitor*.

But despite his unwillingness to believe, Robert could not deny the passage in the *Last Prophecy* that had rightly predicted King Alexander's death.

> *When the last King of Albany dies without issue*
> *The kingdom will be thrown into disarray.*
> *And the sons of Brutus will mourn that day*
> *The one of the great name.*

Alexander had plunged from the cliffs on a storm-tossed night on the road to Kinghorn. They found him next morning, his neck broken and his horse dead beside him. His granddaughter and heir, an infant in the court of the King of Norway, sailed to Scotland to take her place as queen, but perished on the voyage from eating rotten food. After that the crown had gone, on Edward's choosing, to John Balliol; not a king as it turned out, but a dog on the English king's leash. Balliol's attempt at rebellion had been a failure, the English storming across the border and crushing the uprising in a matter of months. Edward, triumphant in his conquest of Scotland, had broken the great seal of the kingdom and sent Balliol, cowed and humiliated, to the Tower of London. Disaster followed disaster.

Now, with the power to prevent Edward from fulfilling his ambition in his hands, Robert wondered. Did he doom Britain by this action? Would those days of ruin prophesied by Merlin now come upon them all?

Seeing his brothers and the monks looking at him, Robert bound the staff tightly in its mildewed cloth. He had his own destiny to fulfil. Scotland must be free of subjugation to the English crown, no matter the cost. Where John Balliol had failed, he would triumph. Balliol, now in papal custody in France, might still be the rightful king in the eyes of many Scots, but to the Bruce family he had only ever been a puppet. Robert's ancestor, the great Malcolm Canmore, had overthrown his rival, Macbeth, and had taken the throne. Now, God willing, he would do the same. Pride and blood demanded it.

'It was there?' called Cormac, as the company made their way back. When Robert raised the staff in answer, his foster-brother grinned. 'I would give my horse and sword to see Ulster's face when his men tell him it was gone. Serve the bastard right for burning my father's hall.'

Robert climbed into the boat with the others, Christopher and Cormac pushing them off before leaping in behind. As they slipped out into the water, a shadow passed over them. Robert looked into the lightening sky to see the white fan feathers of a sea eagle, its wings, eight feet across, mirrored in the lough as it swooped low, heading for the north shore. In the distance, a cloud of birds rose from the trees on the banks. Robert watched the eagle's retreating form, thinking the predator must have disturbed them. Then, faint and far off, he heard the baying of a hound.

5

A s Edward approached his pavilion, the guards opened the flaps. The king swept inside, his mailed boots crushing the carpet of meadowsweet, its perfume a relief from the reek of smoke and dung that clogged the camp. Anthony Bek followed. Clad in a polished mail coat with a broadsword at his hip, the burly Bishop of Durham could easily have been taken for a knight, if not for his tonsure and the ecclesiastical robes he wore over the armour. Robert Winchelsea entered behind them, squeezing his frame through the narrow opening. After the Archbishop of Canterbury came four clerics and the two foreigners in scarlet robes and jewelled hats. When the company had dismounted to greet him, Edward's suspicions had been confirmed. The two men were official papal messengers, sent by Pope Boniface.

'Wine and food for my guests,' Edward ordered the servants waiting in the interior. Two disappeared through curtains at the back of the pavilion, while the others hastened to rearrange furniture for the visitors. 'Sit,' Edward told them, ignoring the high-backed cushioned chair one of his pages moved out for him. He waited as the two papal messengers and the archbishop sat, leaving the clerics to hover behind. Bek wedged himself into a corner, his eyes on Winchelsea.

Winchelsea frowned at the stool that was offered to him when the king remained standing. He looked for a moment as if he wouldn't accept it, but under Edward's unyielding gaze he did so. 'And how is the young queen, my lord? I hear she gave birth to a boy.' Winchelsea's smile didn't reach his eyes. 'Time passes fast. I can scarcely believe it was little over two years ago that I married you both at Canterbury.'

'Lady Marguerite and my son are in good humour at York,' Edward replied. 'But I somehow doubt you made the long journey to the front line

of my war for the purpose of enquiring about my wife's health. Let us
dispense with the pleasantries, your grace. They do not suit us. Why have
you come?'

The smile slipped easily from Winchelsea's face, his broad shoulders
hunching as he leaned forward, fixed on the king. 'My esteemed colleagues
here arrived in England two months ago. When they discovered you had
left on campaign they came to me at Canterbury. I volunteered to escort
them to your presence. I judged the message they bore important enough
not to wait for your return.'

'How charitable of you, your grace.'

The archbishop ignored the king's ominous tone. As the servants entered,
bearing jugs of wine and platters of bread, cured meat and pungent yellow
cheese, Winchelsea nodded to one of the scarlet-robed messengers. The
man stood and drew a scroll from the leather bag he carried. Bek came
forward to take it, disregarding the goblet of wine a page tried to pass to
him.

Edward noted the large papal seal attached to the parchment as the
Bishop of Durham opened the scroll. The hush inside was filled by the
muted din of the camp outside, over which the sound of splintering stone
echoed as the siege engines continued to batter Caerlaverock's walls.
Winchelsea accepted the proffered wine, grasping the silver goblet in his
fist. He was the only man who did, the servants backing away to the sides
of the tent, bearing the untouched platters of food.

Finally, Bek finished reading and looked up at the king. 'The pope, my
lord, demands that you cease all hostilities against Scotland, which his holiness describes as a daughter of the Holy See.'

With these words, Edward understood why Winchelsea had come all
the way to his siege lines to deliver a simple message. The man had been
vocal about the war since his election to the archbishopric in 1295, on the
eve of the first invasion of Scotland. That invasion had been an unqualified
success. Within months, John Balliol, the man Edward had set upon the
throne after King Alexander's death and who had rebelled, was deposed
and imprisoned in the Tower, the kingdom under Edward's command. But
it had been a victory short-lived, for a year later William Wallace had risen
to lead the Scots in insurrection. His treasury drained by wars in Wales
and Gascony, Edward had been forced to ask the Church for funds to
finance his struggle against the rebels. It was Winchelsea who stood against
him, refusing to submit to his demands. In retaliation Edward outlawed
the clergy and sent his knights to seize their goods and property, but

Winchelsea remained firm in the face of the harsh measures. A test of faith, he had called it.

Since that time, Edward and the archbishop had slipped into an uneasy truce, but it was clear, by the way he had seized upon this opportunity, that Winchelsea had not abandoned his stance.

'Why now?' Edward's voice was low, anger etched in his face. 'Why does Rome intervene after five years?'

The papal messenger who had given the order to Bek answered. 'My lord king, while in Paris, Sir William Wallace gained much support from the King of France, who recommended him to his holiness. He has since visited the papal curia and been welcomed by—'

'*Sir* William?' Edward spat the title across the explanation, his grey eyes blazing. 'I do not care whose blade or arse that brigand kissed to acquire that honour, he is as noble as a butcher's hound! He is a felon. An outlaw. Why, in Christ's name, is he being welcomed at the papal court?' The king wheeled away, thinking furiously, as the papal messenger turned uncertainly to Winchelsea. So, Philippe was interfering again, was he? He had thought the trouble with his cousin was on the way to being finished. The war over Gascony had ended, he had married Philippe's sister and his son was due to marry the king's daughter. After years of conflict, England and France had agreed a truce and Edward was hopeful that his rich French duchy would soon be back in his possession. Now, this.

'Wallace has garnered much sympathy for his cause at the papal curia,' said Winchelsea, rising to draw the king's attention. 'I strongly advise you to heed the order, my lord. The truce with France, mediated by his holiness, is still in its infant stages. Your son is yet to marry Lady Isabella and the treaty that will restore the Duchy of Gascony to you and your heirs has not been formally ratified.' Winchelsea played the statesman skilfully, his tone firm, but reasoned. 'Enter into negotiations with the Scots, my lord. Obey the papal order and end the war. Do not make an enemy of Pope Boniface. He is not a forgiving man.'

Edward didn't look at the archbishop, but the man's words, full of carefully nuanced threats, burned in him. After two years in England, during which time he never once lost sight of his aim, he had led his men north to finish what he started. John Balliol might be languishing in papal custody in France – his release from the Tower part of the deal Edward had brokered with the pope over Gascony – Wallace might be abroad and Robert Bruce missing. But that hadn't stopped the Scots continuing the insurrection begun by those three men. Edward would not stop until the entire kingdom was under his control. Neither would he rest, nay *sleep*, until Wallace was swinging from a gibbet and Bruce — well, he had other plans for that renegade.

'We should discuss this in private, my lord,' intervened Bek. 'We can speak again on the morrow,' he added to Winchelsea.

Before Edward could respond, the tent flaps opened and Humphrey de Bohun appeared, his broad face flushed with triumph. 'My lord, Caerlaverock's garrison has surrendered. The castle is ours.'

The king stared at the young commander, realising that he could no longer hear the crashing of stones. 'Bishop Bek, draft a response that these men will take back to Rome with them tomorrow. In it you will defend my policies in Scotland and you will explain to his holiness that I have a right to subdue a people who owe me their allegiance and yet rise in rebellion against me. I set John Balliol upon the throne and he paid me homage as a vassal, accepting my right as his superior. It was his breaking of that oath and his alliance of swords with France that began this war.' Edward's gaze came to rest on Winchelsea. 'I will bring Scotland under my dominion, your grace, and deal with every treacherous son of a bitch who defies my will, if it takes the last breath in my body.'

6

Robert entered the clearing several strides ahead of the rest of the company, the staff grasped in his fist. During their passage across the lough, the sky had lightened to an ashen grey, but beneath the tangled canopy of oak and rowan it was still dark.

Alexander Seton looked up sharply as Robert emerged through the undergrowth. Beside him, Uathach raised her head from her paws with a whine at the sight of her master. 'You have it?' Alexander stood to greet him, his eyes going to the cloth-wrapped object in Robert's hand.

Ignoring Uathach, who trotted over to nose at his palm, Robert gestured to Nes and the other squires, who had set about making a temporary camp in the glade. Blankets and cloaks had been hung from branches to air and a small fire had been lit, the smoke twisting up through the boughs. 'Pack up. We're leaving.'

As the squires hastened to obey, collecting the gear and bags of provisions, Alexander caught Robert's arm. 'What is it?'

'He heard a hound,' said Edward, hoisting his iron-embossed shield over his shoulder by its strap.

Christopher and Niall were helping the squires sling bags over the backs of the four pack-horses, while Cormac scuffed soil on to the fire with the edge of his boot.

Robert glanced irritably at Edward as Nes handed him Fleet's reins. 'You heard it too, brother.'

'It was a farmer's dog most likely. We passed a few farmsteads yesterday.'

'That was miles back,' Robert said. 'This was close.'

Thomas joined them. His fair hair curled around his brow, dampened by the moist morning air. 'We didn't hear anything.' He nodded at Uathach and the three other hounds. 'The dogs would have alerted us, surely?'

Robert took in their expressions – a mix of concern and disparagement. After a pause, he shook his head. 'You're right, it's probably nothing, but I don't want to linger here any more than I have to. We have a long journey ahead of us and precious cargo.'

Jabbing his boot into the stirrup, Robert swung up into the saddle. Shifting his filigreed scabbard, he loosened the belt a notch, enough to wedge the staff through, so it was held against him alongside his broadsword. He smiled to himself, grimly satisfied. Once back in Scotland he would offer it to Edward in return for the Stone of Destiny, which lay entombed in a coronation chair in Westminster Abbey, a symbol of England's dominion; its weight in guilt around his neck. And if the king refused? Well, Robert would have his last relic and Edward would have failed in the eyes of his faithful followers.

After Nes had tightened Fleet's girth and tethered Uathach to the crupper, Robert walked his horse to the edge of the glade. The others followed, the monks on their sturdy palfreys, the squires on rouncies, leading the pack-horses, and his brothers and the Setons on coursers. Together, they made their way out of the clearing, the vestiges of smoke from the campfire drifting in their wake.

There was no track to follow, except for the natural lines made by trees and the going was slow. As a grey light revealed the way ahead, Robert picked out the deep pocks the hooves of their horses had made yesterday. Satisfied they were headed in the right direction, he let Fleet be his guide, allowing the horse to find the best paths through the boggy ground. The land rose steadily, until he glimpsed the lough stretching away behind him, glass-smooth, the distant isle of Ibracense breaking the surface. They hadn't gone more than a mile, when Uathach began to growl.

Robert looked round to see the bitch straining on her leash, ears flat against her head. Pulling Fleet to a halt, he gave a whistle, but Uathach didn't heed it. Her gaze was fixed on a high ridge to their left, where the trees marched up, thinning as they neared the crest.

'What has she smelled?' called Cormac, turning in his saddle. 'A coney?'

Suddenly, Uathach sprang forward, the leash snapping tight. At the same time, the other hounds began barking harshly, all of them fixed on the ridge. The tension in Robert broke in a rush of anticipation. 'To me!' he roared, pulling his sword from its scabbard.

Over the ridge came an answering cry. Figures appeared on the bank – more than thirty men. Some were mounted, leaning back in their saddles as they spurred their horses down the slope. Others sprinted in their wake, wielding spears and daggers. Dogs ran with them, barking fiercely. By their mail coats and crested helms, and the great swords in their hands, the riders were knights. English knights. Each wore a red band of cloth around his upper arm. Robert had a second to take this in, then he was pricking his spurs into Fleet's sides, yelling at his men to follow as he plunged through the trees. His company of eighteen, three of whom were monks, was outnumbered and outmatched. The woods filled with the rumble of hooves as his men wheeled their horses around and charged behind him. Dimly, he heard a man's cry echo at his back as the trees closed around him.

'*I want Earl Robert alive!*'

The shock of his own name resounded through him.

The realisation that this was no random attack vanished as Robert was forced to focus his attention forward, trees and low branches whipping past, perilously close. There was a scream of pain as one of the squires caught his knee on a trunk, the force wrenching his leg back so hard his thighbone snapped. He tumbled from the saddle, disappearing into the bracken, leaving his palfrey to gallop on without him. Hearing a mad barking behind him, Robert realised Uathach was still tethered to the crupper, the bitch running frantically at Fleet's hooves. He slashed back and down with his blade, feeling the snap as the leash broke. Between the trees to the right, he caught snatched views of the lough. Thoughts raced through his mind.

They must have been watching. Following. Ulster's men? Or, worse, King Edward's?

Against his body, wedged through his sword belt, Malachy's staff had an uncomfortable solidity; more tangible with the threat that it would now be taken from him. Risking a look over his shoulder, Robert saw flashes of colour: a cloak, sky-blue, a horse's patterned trapper. The enemy was gaining.

'*Robert!*'

Hearing the shout, he whipped back round to see the hulking mass of a fallen tree blocking the way ahead, roots splayed skyward. He jerked hard on the reins, causing Fleet to veer to the right. Robert swore as he saw Edward and Thomas swerving left behind Alexander and Christopher Seton, but it was too late to change direction. He was committed to the course.

Harsh shouts rose from their pursuers, punctuated by the baying of the dogs, as the company split, Robert galloping after Niall, Cormac and Murtough. Another pained cry echoed, the sound dislocated in the tightly packed trees. Had one of his brothers been unhorsed? Or Alexander, or Christopher? Uathach was no longer behind him. Robert gripped the reins. He couldn't think about anyone else.

They were following a natural pathway of sorts, the trees thinning as the land descended into a valley, carved by a stream. Ahead, another fallen bough lay twisted across the track. Robert saw Niall kick his horse up and over, his black hair flying as he landed on the other side and urged his courser on towards the stream. As Cormac followed, the back hoof of his horse clipped the bough. The rotten wood splintered on impact, but he too landed neatly. Next, Murtough made the leap, the cowl of his habit flapping free from his head.

Even as he took the jump, Robert knew the monk wasn't going to make it. His sturdy palfrey was used to track ambling, not this reckless forest pursuit. Smaller than the swift coursers, it wasn't strong enough for the hurdle. It made a brave attempt, but caught its front hooves on the top of the bough. This time the wood didn't splinter. The palfrey pitched forward sending Murtough hurtling into the ground. There was a hideous squeal as the horse collapsed, its front leg fracturing on impact. Robert was only paces behind. There was nowhere else to go. Spurring at Fleet's sides for all he was worth, he aimed at the fallen tree, hoping against hope he could make it over the top of the flailing horse on the other side.

Fleet saw the danger and tried to veer in mid-flight to avoid the wounded palfrey. He might have made it, but the palfrey twisted instinctively away, sensing the animal bearing down on it. Fleet's hoof landed between its front legs. Robert was flung violently from the saddle as the courser buckled on top of the palfrey. The world spun, treetops wheeling in his vision, before he crashed into the mud, the breath knocked from him. His sword sailed from his grasp into the undergrowth.

Robert lay motionless, heaving the air back into his lungs, before pushing himself up. Fleet was trying to stand, the palfrey struggling beneath. Murtough was still in the saddle, being ground into the mud by the weight of both horses. The monk's scarred face was just visible. It was covered in blood. One arm was flung above his head, switching this way and that with the horse's frantic movements. Hearing hoof-beats, Robert turned to see Niall riding back.

'Hurry!' Niall drew to a skidding halt, holding out a hand. 'They're coming!'

As Robert staggered to his feet, he saw their pursuers racing towards them beyond the fallen bough. Some of the riders broke away, clearly meaning to ride around the obstacle and outflank them. He wrenched the staff from his belt, the cloth falling away as he thrust the relic at his brother's outstretched hand. 'Take it!'

Niall Bruce grasped the gem-encrusted crosier, but his youthful face filled with shock. 'No, Robert! Get up behind me!'

'Your horse cannot carry us both.' Robert glanced back. A man in a sky-blue cloak was leading the charge, his face determined. 'Go! Get it to Scotland. To James Stewart. *Go!*' He roared the last word, striking Niall's courser on the rump and sending the animal charging away.

Robert lunged for the bushes where his weapon had landed. His fingers curled around the hilt as the thunder of hooves filled the forest. He turned, swinging the blade round to defend himself as the man in the blue cloak came hurtling towards him. There was a fierce shout and a rush of limbs and red hair as Cormac swept in from the side. He lashed out with his sword, catching the man in blue in the back. It was a glancing blow that was deflected by mail, but the man had been leaning in to tackle Robert and the attack caught him by surprise. He fell forward in his stirrup and crashed against the pommel. While he was off-balance, Robert crouched and swung his broadsword, two-handed, into the front leg of the man's horse. As the animal and its rider smashed into the mud, Robert swooped.

The man reacted quickly, rolling to avoid Robert's first strike, then bringing up his sword to deflect the second. The blades clashed, the man snarling with the effort as Robert pressed down on top of him. He kicked out, catching Robert in the knee with his mailed boot. Robert staggered back, his sword going wide, giving his opponent the chance to haul himself to his feet. The man's blue cloak was streaked with mud and there was a gash down the side of his face. His black hair was matted with blood, but his gaze was focused as he came in for the attack, thrusting at Robert's side.

Robert battered his sword away, then switched back and lunged with the pommel, aiming to break his enemy's nose. The man flung his head to one side and reeled out of reach, then came in hard and fast, with a brutal cut to the shoulder. As Robert deflected it, grunting at the vicious concussion of steel, he dimly heard the squeal of a horse and Cormac's yell, but he didn't have a chance to see what had happened to his foster-brother before his opponent struck again.

Robert ducked under one blow, blocked the second, then caught the third in the shoulder. His hauberk and the padded gambeson beneath protected him from any cut, but the impact still drove him to his knees. He shoved back fiercely with his own blade, sending his opponent stumbling away, but the man recovered quickly. Swiping at his forehead with the back of his gloved hand, wiping a stroke of blood across his brow, he came in again. Pushing up from his knees, Robert launched forward, taking the man by surprise. He roared with the effort, propelling him into a tree trunk. The force knocked the breath from the man's lungs and the sword from his hand. Fear flooded his eyes, as Robert brought up his broadsword.

'*Earl Robert!*'

The sound of his name blasted through his concentration. In the periphery of his vision, Robert saw that one of the knights had hold of Cormac, one hand grasping a fistful of his hair, the other pressing the blade of a sword against his throat.

'Lower your sword,' came the knight's voice. 'Or I'll slit the bastard's neck.'

Robert paused, his gaze flicking back to the man in front of him, pinned to the tree trunk at the mercy of his blade. Even through the blood-lust that pounded in him with the desire to finish the fight, Robert knew the threat wasn't idle. The death of an Irishman, even a nobleman, would mean little to these men. The penalty for killing a native was much less than it was for the murder of an Englishman.

Slowly, he backed away, breathing hard. Lowering his sword, he placed it on the ground in front of him. The knight who had hold of Cormac didn't relinquish his grip. There were six others with him, three mounted, the rest on foot. Two of the men held mastiffs on leashes. The dogs strained at the bonds, growling.

Keeping his eyes on Robert, the man in blue bent to pick up his fallen blade. He hefted it, jaw pulsing with anger, but made no move towards Robert. Instead, he gestured to his three mounted comrades. 'Follow the others. Take the dogs. I think he gave the staff to one of his men.' He looked back at Robert. 'Who was it? One of your brothers?' He stepped forward, his sword levelled at Robert's chest. 'Tell me.'

The air filled with a ferocious barking as a grey shape hurtled out of the undergrowth.

'*Esgar!*' came a warning cry.

The man in blue turned, startled, as Uathach leapt at him, her jaws stretching wide. He just had time to thrust up with his sword, before she was on him. The blade caught the hound in mid-air, punching through the soft skin of her stomach. Uathach howled as the blade was withdrawn in a spray of red and she was sent sprawling. Robert roared in fury at the sight of his beloved hound, daughter of his grandfather's favourite bitch, curled in agony in a pool of her own spreading blood. He lunged for the man, meaning to tear him apart with his hands, but was grabbed roughly by two of the knights.

The man in the blue cloak turned on him, his blade gleaming with Uathach's blood. 'You should have stayed in Scotland, Sir Robert.'

Glenarm, Ireland, 1301 AD

Adam walked his white charger through the streets of Glenarm, between rows of wattle houses daubed with clay and peat. The horse's hooves sank in the dung and refuse packed down deep in the mud. It was market day and the town was crowded with farmers leading livestock into the square where a cluster of stalls had been erected. The clanking bells around the necks of goats and cows made a hollow cacophony. As a flock of sheep was driven in front of him, Adam slowed his horse, but kept his gaze on the young man in the russet tunic hurrying ahead of the jostling animals, a large basket carried awkwardly under his arm.

It was a bright March morning, the sea dark blue, hemmed with white along the shoreline where a river bubbled into the bay. Fishing boats bobbed on the tide, the men hauling up wicker baskets crawling with crabs and lobsters. There was a buoyant atmosphere in the little port, the inhabitants stirred by the promise of spring and the breath of warmth in the salty air. A woman pushed pale domes of dough into a bakehouse, releasing smoke fragrant with the cooked loaves inside. Above her, two men laughed and talked as they laid fresh straw on a roof. Farmers greeted one another, their Gaelic brusque over the bleating of their animals.

Adam remained aloof on his horse as he rode through their midst, an outsider looking in. It was how he spent much of his life, but while in larger towns and cities he was usually invisible, here it was impossible to remain unnoticed. His presence had already generated a great deal of curiosity, some fearful, some hostile. For a start, his charger was much bigger than the native horses, which to him looked like ponies. His navy cloak, although soiled from travel, was well-tailored and, beneath it, the fish-scale shimmer of mail was unmistakable. His dark hair had grown long these past months and his beard was full, but neither could disguise the olive tone of his skin that so distinctly marked him as a foreigner. But by far the most conspicuous thing about him was the great crossbow that hung from his back on a thick leather strap.

The composite bow was made of horn, sinew and yew, covered with leather and decorated with coloured cord that criss-crossed the stave all the way to the stirrup that was used to load it. It was the weapon of

mercenaries; banned by popes, employed by kings. Feared by all. Along
with the packs strapped to his saddle swung a basket of quarrels, each iron-
tipped head capable of piercing a knight's armour, his leg and the saddle and
horse beneath. Glenarm, under the lordship of Robert Bruce, lay in hostile
territory, for much of Antrim's hinterland was controlled by the English.
But even here, in these troubled times, people weren't accustomed to
seeing such a weapon.

As the goats crowding the thoroughfare were driven into a pen, Adam
pricked his horse into an idle trot, leaving the stares behind him. The young
man with the basket was heading for the beach, his russet tunic like a flag
against the blue sea. Adam hung back, watching as his target approached a
fisherman standing by a line of lobster pots. The two men greeted one
another, their voices faint on the breeze. When Adam had arrived he had
worried that he wouldn't be able to glean any information from the Gaelic-
speaking inhabitants, but after a fortnight watching Lord Donough's hall he
realised that quite a few of them could speak English, no doubt from living
so closely with the settlers for generations.

The youth opened the lid of his basket for the fisherman to deposit four
lobsters inside, then, hefting the basket on his hip, made for the river mouth
where a track ran alongside the estuary, following the narrowing waters
inland. Adam trailed him, keeping his distance until the wattle houses of the
town gave way to fields and animal paddocks. Lord Donough's hall appeared
in the foreground, rising from its mound above a loop in the river. Beyond,
the hills rose into rocky peaks where buzzards circled. As his target approached
a copse of trees, Adam trotted closer. The young man glanced round at the
jangle of the bridle and wandered off the track, expecting horse and rider to
pass. Adam drew nearer. The youth turned again, a frown furrowing his brow
as he took in the great horse and the armed man astride it.

'You're Lord Donough's man?' Adam called.

The young man halted at the strangely accented English. He looked nervously around, as if seeking assistance, but the track was empty. Only a few
horses grazed in the paddock that ran alongside the river. 'Yes,' he answered,
uncertain.

Adam dismounted, looping the reins over one of the paddock's posts. He
held up his hands. A gesture of peace. 'I am looking for Sir Robert Bruce,
the Earl of Carrick. I bear a message for him.'

The youth's frown relaxed a little. 'He was here, sir. But no longer.' The
English was thick in his mouth, as though his tongue were wrapped in
treacle.

'Where is he now?'

The man shook his head, too quickly. 'I know not.' He began to walk. 'I must go. My master waits.'

'Please,' called Adam. 'The message is urgent.'

The young man hesitated. After a pause, he nodded towards the distant hall. 'You must speak to Lord Donough, sir.'

Adam watched him turn and walk away quickly. The youth knew more than he was saying; that much was clear from his manner, but even if he hadn't been so furtive Adam would have known he was lying. Servants knew everything. Invisible, they waited at the edges of halls to clear the platters at feasts, ignored by kings who plotted wars and lords who schemed for power. They filled basins in ladies' bedchambers and emptied bedpans, silent witnesses to affairs of state and love: a horde of listeners, thronging every passageway. Adam could wait and find a more malleable target, but he had neither the time, nor the patience. He had already spent too long chasing a phantom.

Scotland, ravaged by war and overrun with insurgents, had proven a challenge, even for him. Forced to remain inconspicuous lest he be recognised, unable to get near the rebels – holed up in the hidden base established by William Wallace deep in Selkirk Forest – it had taken far longer than anticipated to discover that Bruce was long gone. Finally, picking up his trail from Carrick, Adam had followed him across the race – the wild stretch of sea between Scotland and Ireland. Arriving in Glenarm a fortnight ago, it had been a blow to discover the earl had moved on again. He wasn't about to spend another six months kicking his heels in this hovel.

Adam let the servant go only a few paces before he moved up behind him, drawing a dagger from the sheath on his belt. Grabbing a fistful of the young man's hair, he brought the blade up to his throat. The servant dropped the basket in shock. The lid fell open as it hit the ground, the lobsters scuttling for the river. The young man cried out a stream of high-pitched Gaelic that could have been surprise or fear, or anger for the loss of his catch, then Adam was dragging him into the copse of trees.

'Tell me,' he commanded, pushing the servant up against a trunk, one hand on his chest, the other keeping the dagger at his throat. 'Where has Bruce gone?'

The young man licked his lips. 'He left after the Christ Mass. Weeks ago.'

'Where. Not when.'

'South. On the road to Kildare.' The servant's eyes pleaded the truth of his words. 'With Lord Donough's son and the monks.'

'Monks?'

'From Bangor Abbey. The monks who took the staff from Armagh. The staff the Earl of Ulster burned our hall for. Sir Robert wants it.'

As the reason Robert had abandoned the war in Scotland and resigned his position as guardian became clear, Adam's blood was stirred. It was even more imperative that he fulfil the king's order. Bruce could not be allowed to take possession of the relic, under any circumstance. All the king had worked to achieve would be in jeopardy. 'Will he return when he has it?'

The servant shook his head. 'Please,' he murmured, glancing down at the dagger and swallowing dryly. 'It is all I know.'

'I believe you.'

Adam sliced the dagger swiftly across the young man's throat, severing his windpipe with one brutal cut. The servant dropped to the ground, where he convulsed for a few moments, then shuddered to still. Bending, Adam wiped the blade on the grass. As he did so, his mind filled with an image of a cliff-top path in stormy darkness, a thunderclap drowning the scream as Alexander sailed over the edge with his horse. Adam sheathed the dagger, musing that metal had no compunction about rank. It killed servant as easily as it murdered king. Returning to his horse, he mounted.

The hunt was on.

7

Ballymote, Ireland, 1301 AD

Robert stirred as he felt the wagon slow. Outside the thick cloth covering men called to one another, their words obscured by the hollow clopping of the horses' hooves on what he guessed was a paved road. Somewhere up ahead he heard a heavy clanking.

'Cormac,' he murmured.

His foster-brother raised his head groggily. 'Are we stopping?'

'I think we're here.'

Cormac came fully awake, frowning as he strained to hear the voices outside. The two squires hunched opposite them glanced nervously at each other. One was pale with pain and exhaustion, his leg boxed in a crude splint. The wagon's fifth occupant kept his eyes downcast, cowl low over his head, his bound hands clasped in his lap. The monk had hardly said two words since they began the trek north, the days merging into one another inside their jolting, airless prison. Robert had lost count, but guessed it was more than a fortnight since they had left the shores of the lough. The physical discomfort of the journey had only been part of the ordeal; Robert had been forced to endure hours of silent reflection, in which he was tormented by worry over the fate of his brothers and men, and what he would face at the end of the road. All he knew was what Ulster's captain, Esgar, had told him.

After he and Cormac had been disarmed, Esgar had ordered the rest of his knights to hunt down the fleeing company. Robert had refused to answer any of the captain's questions, his eyes on Uathach's prone, bloodied form. The hound wasn't the only victim of the skirmish. Several of the knights, searching the immediate vicinity, had found Murtough crushed beneath his wounded horse. Pulling the monk free, they discovered his neck was broken.

The injured palfrey they put to the sword, along with Esgar's horse, badly lamed by Robert. After ordering the dead monk to be buried in a shallow grave, Esgar had waited for his men to return.

The knights and squires came back slowly, the last rejoining the company an hour later. To Robert's relief they had been able to recover only two squires, both from Donough's household, who had been unhorsed during the flight, one of whom had a broken leg. Of the others, the knights told their silent captain, there was no sign.

Seeing the triumph in Robert's face, Esgar had made him a promise. 'We will find them, Sir Robert, and when we do your brothers will be subject to the Earl of Ulster's justice. They'll wish they hadn't run.' Ordering twenty of his men to track them down and secure the staff – for as long and as many miles as it took – the captain corralled his five prisoners. 'I'll take them to Sir Richard at Ballymote. Half a prize is better than none.'

On the journey north Robert and the other captives had only been allowed out of the wagon whenever the company stopped to rest. From the banks of the lough they ascended into mountains, travelling by drovers' roads, the peaks around them often invisible, bearded by clouds. For several days up in the heights the air was cold and sharp as if winter had returned, then slowly they descended into glades of ash and budding oak, filled with birdsong and rain. All at once, the mountains were behind them and the land stretched ahead for endless miles.

The mood of the company shifted with the change in landscape, the knights becoming silent and watchful. Fires were kept low and Esgar set four knights on guard through the nights, wary of some unseen threat. They stopped for rest where possible in forts garrisoned by vassals of the Earl of Ulster. Throughout this time, the five prisoners had not been mistreated. They had been given food, drink and blankets, and the injured squire tended to. But, for Robert, the concern over whether his men would make it safely to Scotland and unease as to what lay in store for him and his foster-brother had been torture enough.

The wagon slowed, almost to a stop, the interior darkening. The clanking had ceased and men were calling instructions, the horses jostling as the drivers urged the beasts forward. The wheel spokes scraped against something; a gateway or tunnel, then they were through, sunlight brightening their juddering prison once more.

As the wagon came to a halt, the cloth flaps were hauled back and Esgar's face appeared. 'Out.'

Robert's hands and feet were bound, but with enough slack that he could shuffle to the edge. Sliding from the back of the wagon, blinking at the light, he found himself in an expansive courtyard, enclosed by high stone walls. In places, timber structures had been erected against the fortifications: stables, kennels and outbuildings. All of them looked newly built, the thatch on the slanting roofs still being laid in places. The walls were flanked by six towers, two of which were covered with scaffolding. The towers at the four corners of the castle had open platforms at the top, each surmounted by a siege engine.

Looking past the wagon, Robert saw a double gatehouse guarding the narrow passageway through which they had entered. Hanging above the tunnel was a golden banner embroidered with a red cross, in the top left-hand corner of which was a rampant black lion. The clanking noise had come from a portcullis, which was now being lowered, its iron teeth closing over the gateway. Ballymote was a mighty castle, well-defended and heavily garrisoned. A man would find it hard to enter uninvited. He would also find it hard to leave.

A door in the gatehouse opened and three men appeared. Robert dismissed two of them as guards, before fixing on the massive figure at their centre, who came striding towards him. Robert knew, though he had never met him, that this must be Sir Richard de Burgh, Earl of Ulster and King Edward's chief magnate in Ireland. Ulster looked to be in his early forties, his face marked by battle and full of the unmitigated arrogance of a man of rank and power. He wore a sumptuous gold mantle, embroidered with a red cross.

Ulster greeted Esgar curtly, his eyes moving to take in the rest of the company. His attention came to rest on Robert. 'Sir Robert, is it? I see your father and grandfather in you. In body at least. In spirit, I judge you are quite different.' The contempt in his deep voice was unmistakable.

Standing there, devoid of armour or weapons, wearing only a sweat-stained shirt and hose, his beard and hair unkempt, Robert felt acutely discomforted by the earl's forceful gaze. Ulster reminded him of his father: the same barrel-like physique and domineering demeanour, the same condemnation in his stare. He fought away the sting the reminder provoked, meeting the earl's gaze with defiance. 'It is unfortunate we meet under such circumstances, Sir Richard. Your family and mine have enjoyed a long friendship, from which you have always benefited. It is regrettable you now jeopardise that alliance by taking my men and me prisoner. You may see my grandfather and father in me, but they are illusions. My grandfather is dead and my father in England. In their place, I am lord of our estates and head of the Bruce family. You should respect that.'

Ulster's eyes glinted. 'You lost any respect from me when you turned traitor and sided with outlaws and felons. You had everything – rich lands in Scotland, Ireland and England, the illustrious friendship of King Edward, even a claim to the throne of your kingdom. Now what do you have? Your father has disowned you from what I hear, your family's home at Lochmaben has been destroyed and your earldom is forfeit to the English crown. When King Edward takes control of Scotland, Carrick will be lost to you for good. Even your new allies have deserted you. William Wallace is abroad and the rebels founder in his absence. And here you are: a prisoner with nothing but the shirt on your back, an earl in name alone and scarcely fit to be called so. Tell me, Robert, was it worth it?'

Robert's mind filled with an image of his childhood home – Turnberry Castle – perched on the cliffs of the Carrick coastline, over the ravening sea. Following in its wake came memories of his grandfather and father, his mother, sisters and brothers. Doubt crested its head, conjured by the harsh truth of Ulster's words. But then, one image came to him, clearer than the rest: a green circlet in a web of twigs, swinging from the boughs an oak. He remembered well the night it had been created by Affraig's withered hands, the same hands that had brought him into this world. There, in her house of herbs and bones, his aim to be king had been made manifest, his destiny woven into a crown of heather and broom.

He had not given all for nothing. He had given up everything he had for everything he could be: his lands for a kingdom, his family for a people. His riches for a crown. 'Yes, it was worth it. Those things mean nothing if Scotland isn't free.'

Ulster laughed grimly. 'Wallace is not so absent after all. You have become the brigand's voice!'

'I am not the only one. James Stewart, your own brother-in-law, now leads the rebellion. There are many more voices than Wallace's and mine raised in protest over King Edward's attempts to dominate our realm.'

Ulster's eyes narrowed at the mention of James Stewart, the High Steward of Scotland and husband to his sister, Egidia de Burgh. He turned to the captain. 'Esgar, I need something sweet to take away this bitterness. I presume you have the staff?'

Esgar glanced at Robert, his face tightening. 'No, my lord.'

As the knight explained what had happened on the banks of the lough, Ulster's face clouded with displeasure.

'I wanted to escort the prisoners to you myself,' Esgar finished. 'But I sent twenty of my men after Bruce's company. They will find them. We have garrisons all the way from here to Antrim, which is almost certainly where they will head. My men have been instructed to send word as soon as they have the relic, or any information that will lead to its seizure.'

'Where will your men take the staff?' Ulster demanded of Robert. 'Lord Donough's hall?' When Robert didn't answer the earl added, 'I can burn it again. And worse.'

'And my father will build it again,' spat Cormac, his voice blistering with hatred.

Ulster ignored the Irishman's outburst, having eyes only for Robert. 'You will have plenty of time to reconsider your stance before I send you to King Edward.' As Robert continued to meet his stare, Ulster's brow creased. A flicker of something almost fatherly — a cross between consternation and concern — appeared in his face. 'Tell me where your men are taking the Staff of Malachy and in recognition of my longstanding friendship with your family, I will contemplate not delivering you to Edward. The staff is a prize I cannot give up. You, I could perhaps make an allowance for.' When there was no response, the hint of concern vanished, Ulster's grim façade closing firmly over it. 'Esgar, you and your company will leave for Antrim at first light. I imagine his men will either attempt to hide the staff, or else get it to Scotland. If the latter, they will have to procure a vessel. Track them. Question every member of Donough's family and every monk in Bangor Abbey until you discover its location.'

Esgar bowed. 'I will not fail you again, my lord.'

'Get this traitor out of my sight.'

Robert felt hands grip his arms. 'I have seen how Ireland suffers under Edward's yoke,' he shouted, as Ulster walked away. 'He is bleeding your lands dry!'

Ulster faltered in his stride, but didn't look back.

As the knights marched Robert and Cormac across the courtyard towards one of the corner towers, they passed an adolescent girl dressed in a white gown. There was an older woman with her — perhaps a governess. She tightened her hold on the girl's shoulders as the men came past. The girl followed Robert and the other prisoners with worried eyes, until they were ushered through the tower door and into the darkness beyond.

The Lateran Palace, Rome, 1301 AD

'Read it again.'

The command was strident. Pope Boniface didn't turn as he spoke, but continued to stare out of the window, hands clasped behind his back. Spread before him, Rome was a red jewel in the dusk. The glass in the windows of palazzos reflected the sunset, the crumbling walls of the ancient amphitheatres stained bloody by its light.

The papal messenger, wearied from weeks of travel, cleared his throat and read again the message from King Edward, discomforted by the defiant words issuing from his own mouth, directed at God's representative on earth.

'*Therefore,*' he finished, '*since I am rightful overlord of Scotland as confirmed and witnessed by the Scots eight years ago at Norham, I shall exercise fully my right to defend the realm from all disturbers of my peace. With respect to your holiness, I cannot abide by your request to cease hostilities against Scotland when rebels continue to make war upon my garrisons and strongholds in defiance of my sovereign right.*'

'Does he think himself above the word of the Church?' Boniface turned from the window, his great frame, robed in exquisite Venetian silk, silhouetted by the sinking sun. The white hair around his tonsure was tinged by its hue. 'For two years I have worked to reconcile him with his cousin. The ink is barely dry on England's treaty with France and I am repaid for my efforts with this brazen insolence?'

The messenger lowered his gaze at the pope's wrath. 'Archbishop Winchelsea endeavoured to make the king see reason, your holiness, but to no avail. King Edward was determined Scotland be vanquished and the rebels crushed. When we left his camp at Caerlaverock, he and his army were already preparing to advance west.'

'Would he remain so defiant, I wonder, if threatened with excommunication?' Boniface exhaled. 'Unfortunately, that is not something I can consider. The kings of England and France are the only men in Christendom in whom my hopes for a new crusade to wrest the Holy Land from the Saracens remain alive.' He turned to the chamber's third occupant, who stood half in shadow, beyond the sun's dimming light. 'It is regrettable my endeavour to intervene on behalf of your realm has not had the outcome either of us was hoping for. I know you have made many sacrifices to come here and King Philippe has spoken highly of you and your cause, but I am not certain what course of action can now be taken.'

William Wallace remained silent at the pope's verdict. A giant of a man at almost seven feet, his hands, clenched in fists at his sides, were as big as spades. His neck was thick, his torso and shoulders slabbed with muscle. He wore a well-fitted surcoat and blue mantle trimmed with silver thread, but the stately garments couldn't disguise his barbarous look, enhanced by his colossal size and by the scars that sketched their violence across his pale skin; the story of a war in one man's flesh. He looked utterly out of place in the opulent chamber of the Lateran Palace, every surface of which was glimmering gold or glossy marble, yet he maintained a stoic dignity, his sharp blue eyes revealing a fierce intensity of thought.

'There is still one course left to us, your holiness.' Wallace's voice was rough, but measured.

Boniface's eyes narrowed knowingly. 'A dangerous course, Sir William.' He shook his head. 'So soon after I have brought England and France to a truce? I cannot risk shattering that peace. If Edward abandons the treaty and he and Philippe return to war they will not be persuaded to take the Cross and turn their swords eastwards. Jerusalem will never be reclaimed while Christendom's rulers fight among themselves.'

'Does Edward's war against the Scots not prevent him from crusading? Christians are dying in Scotland, your holiness, while the infidel build mosques in the Holy City.'

A pained expression crossed the pope's face. 'I secured King John's release from the Tower through the treaty as King Philippe requested. Is it not enough that he is free of Edward's authority? I can assure you he is comfortable in my custody.'

'Not when my kingdom remains fettered by Edward's bonds and ravaged by his army.' Wallace stepped closer to the pope, his eyes reflecting the last of the sun's light, which painted his scarred face red. 'I believe this is the only way he will stop hostilities against my country. With King Philippe's aid, Edward's hand can be forced without a war. He has too much to lose by abandoning the treaty at this late stage – his son's marriage, Gascony – and too little to gain by a fight. He lost the support of his barons over his war in France. His treasury was all but emptied by it. He cannot afford another such conflict.' The strength in Wallace's voice didn't falter. 'Release John Balliol from papal custody, your holiness, and we will all get what we want. You will have peace in Christendom and my kingdom will have its rightful king upon the throne.'

PART 2

1301 AD

Therefore shall the revenge of the Thunderer show itself, for every field shall disappoint the husbandman. Mortality shall snatch away the people, and make a desolation over all countries.

The History of the Kings of Britain, *Geoffrey of Monmouth*

8

The first few days in the prison tower slipped quickly by for Robert, the danger of his situation quickening the moments, every footfall on the stairs or snap of the door bolt a potential threat. But, by the end of the first week, during which he and Cormac had mostly been left alone by their captors, the space between sunrise and sunset began to stretch and lengthen. As the days merged into weeks and the walls of the locked chamber closed in, time slowed to a maddening crawl and if it were not for the fact he could see the buds unfurling on the oak trees that surrounded Ballymote Castle and the barley growing taller in the distant fields, Robert would have said it had stopped altogether.

In these static moments, where each day seemed a week and each week a lifetime, his frustration at the incarceration and lack of information on the fate of his brothers swelled, tumour-like, until it overshadowed all else. The fact that his cell was more of a palace than a prison was cold comfort. Richly appointed with two feather beds, silk rugs on the floor and hangings on the walls, a table and stools where he and Cormac ate their meals, a basin to wash in, even a few books, the chamber was no less than Robert was accustomed to. But for all its luxury it was as confining as any dungeon and while spring ripened into summer and all his plans stagnated in his mind, the opulence only served to remind him of where he should be. And where he was not.

Robert's thoughts turned often to John Balliol in this time. The man Edward had chosen to sit upon Scotland's throne, instead of Robert's grandfather, was now wasting away in his own stately cell, himself a victim of the king's ambition to rule Britain; an ambition reinforced by the words of prophecy and by the will of the loyal young men Edward surrounded himself with. It began to seem to Robert, locked up and forgotten, over a hundred miles from his kingdom and allies, impossible — laughable almost — that he could break such resolve. Many of the king's men believed they were saving Britain by their actions. It made their struggle for control of Scotland less of a war, more a crusade. How could one man hope to fight that?

There were only two things he cleaved to in these moments of doubt. One was the faith that his brothers would get the staff safely to Scotland, where James Stewart could use it to bargain with the king. The other was the hope that there was truth in the power of Affraig's craft. But all the while Ulster's promise that he would be transferred into Edward's custody, a traitor, dangled above him like a sword on a thread.

The earl had visited Robert several times in the early days of his incarceration, offering freedom if he revealed where his brothers were taking the staff, then warning him of the consequences if he didn't. These visits had grown fewer and further between as summer bloomed. It soon became clear Ulster had more pressing things to occupy his time, a fact Robert gleaned through the endless hours spent sitting at the window, observing the coming and going of the earl's men, noting the increase in the armed companies and their movements to and from the castle. Sometimes these companies came back diminished, with some of their number wounded.

Keen for information, Robert cultivated a relationship with one of the servants who brought their meals, a loquacious man named Stephen. It was through Stephen's loose tongue that he heard rumour of the threat growing along Connacht's borders from Irish chieftains who, after years of rivalry, were putting aside old animosities to band together against the English settlers. Rumour was later followed by agitated talk of one of Ulster's frontier castles being overrun, its garrison massacred. Ballymote was on the alert, all its attention focused outwards.

During this turbulent time Stephen let slip that a feast was due to be held at the castle, in honour of the forthcoming marriage of Earl Richard's youngest daughter and a powerful local lord. Soon after, Ballymote was abuzz with arrangements for the festivities, the earl's household clearly glad to have something more heartening to occupy their minds. Robert, listening to Stephen's talk of all the lavish food that was being prepared and the honoured guests who would be coming, began to have the stirrings of a plan.

'Here's another.' Cormac turned from the window, where he was watching the guests enter the castle courtyard. Torchlight shimmered in the panes of leaded glass, setting flame to his red hair. Earlier, they had heard the port-cullis being raised over the gatehouse, followed by the hoof-beats of a mounted party, the first of many, some with wagons in tow, who had arrived for the betrothal feast. 'That's twenty companies I've counted. It looks like the earl will have a full hall tonight.'

Robert nodded from his place against the door, but kept his concentration on the conversation of the guards he could hear, muted, through the wood. Over the last hour their voices had become a little louder and their laughter less restrained. The feast was a chance for the earl's men to release some of the tension building these past months and the ale seemed to be flowing. Somewhere in the castle, down distant passageways and spiralled stairwells, Robert could hear music.

'He's late,' noted Cormac, frowning into the evening sky, which was a pearlescent blue. He looked back at Robert, his youthful face filling with worry. 'Perhaps we've been forgotten in all the excitement?'

'He'll come,' Robert assured him, though anxiety twisted his stomach at the thought.

Outside the door came a muffled burst of laughter.

The moments slipped by, the strains of music accompanied by the calls of grooms in the courtyard as more guests arrived.

Finally, Robert heard what he had been waiting for: footfalls on the stairs outside. Nodding a warning to Cormac, he crossed the room, feet hushed by the rugs. The two of them sat at the table, listening to the rattle of the bolts. The door opened and two men appeared. One, the older and stockier of the two, bore a large platter of food, the other, a pimple-faced youth, carried a pewter jug and two goblets. Once they had entered, the guards pulled the door shut behind them.

'Evening to you, Sir Robert,' said the older man, his face flushed and animated. 'My apologies for our tardiness. The cooks are in a frenzy.'

'I understand, Stephen.'

'You'll be rewarded for your patience, sir,' continued Stephen, setting the platter on the table. 'We have salmon and boar. And Ned has a pitcher of Gascony wine that's fit for a king.'

As Stephen leaned in, Robert could smell the tang of ale on his breath. 'Have Earl Richard's guests all arrived?' he asked, picking up one of the silver knives that had been set beside the plate of boar meat. Next to the knives were linen cloths for them to wipe the grease from their hands.

Ned had moved around the table, close to Cormac, and was pouring the wine.

'Oh, indeed, the revelry is well under way in the great hall.' Stephen chuckled. 'I think it will be a late night.' He inclined his head. 'Enjoy your meal, Sir Robert.'

'Bank the fire before you go, Stephen,' Robert said, digging out a sliver of meat with the knife and sliding it on to his plate.

'Of course.'

As Stephen crossed to the hearth and crouched over the basket of logs, Robert met Cormac's gaze.

His foster-brother moved quickly, while Ned still had hold of the jug and goblet. Snaking an arm around the spotty youth's throat, Cormac brought the knife he had grabbed from the table up to his face. 'Cry out and I'll stick this in your eye,' he breathed in the man's ear.

In two strides, Robert was across the chamber, knife in one hand, linen cloth in the other. Stephen, thrusting logs into the embers of the hearth, was still talking jovially, as Robert ducked down beside him, poking the tip into his fleshy side. 'Do as I say.'

Stephen froze, a log gripped in his hand. His eyes moved from Robert's face to the knife that was pushing into him.

'Tie this around your mouth,' Robert ordered, handing him the linen cloth. 'Tightly.'

Lowering the log, Stephen took the folded cloth with shaking hands. Drawing the material over his mouth, he secured it in a knot at the back. Over at the table, Cormac was instructing Ned to do the same.

'Now move.' Robert didn't allow the knife to falter as he ushered the gagged servant to the table. 'Sit. Both of you.' When they had done as bid, Robert motioned to Cormac, who hastened to his bed and snatched back the cover, revealing a twisted length of material. It was his sheet, torn and knotted for the purpose that afternoon. Robert crouched in front of the servants. He kept his knife poised over them, but it was clear neither man was going to struggle. They were terrified. A thin line of snot trickled from Ned's nose.

Cormac looped the knotted length of material around both men's wrists, securing them to each other and then to the table leg. It wouldn't hold them for long, but it wasn't designed to. Robert just wanted to make certain he and his foster-brother wouldn't be overpowered as they left the chamber. He took a log from the basket and made for the door. Cormac followed, the knife in his hand.

Robert rapped on the wood three times: Stephen's customary signal. The door opened and one of the guards appeared, grinning at something the other had just said. His expression sobered instantly when he saw them. Robert didn't give him a chance to react, ramming the rough end of the log into the guard's face. As the man staggered backwards, Cormac ducked under Robert's arm and out through the door, swiping at the second guard. The dinner knife was a feeble weapon, but it served to shock and disorient the man as it scratched across his face, causing him to throw his arms up to defend himself. As he did so, Cormac grasped the man's sword and pulled it from its scabbard. The guard Robert had struck with the log had reeled with the impact into the wall, cracking his head on the stone. With blood pouring from his mouth and nose, he tried to fend Robert off. He was no match. Robert disarmed him swiftly, tossing the log aside as he dragged the man's sword free. 'Get in,' he growled, grabbing a fistful of the wounded guard's surcoat and hauling him into the chamber.

'Sir Richard will have your balls for this,' spat the other.

Cormac snarled in answer and slammed the pommel of the man's sword into his face, breaking his nose. While the guard was grasping at his face, Cormac booted him viciously into the chamber and swung the door shut. Snapping the bolts across, he followed Robert. Down through the tower they raced, out into the pale dusk.

'Please keep still, my lady, or I'll never get this gown laced. Your father will be wondering where you are as it is. As will your bridegroom.'

'I cannot breathe, Lora,' gasped Elizabeth de Burgh, looking over her shoulder as her maid tugged in the cords of the jewel-green gown at her back. With every pull, the stiff silk bodice tightened around her ribs and chest, threatening to suffocate her. It was a mild evening and the heavy material prickled against her clammy skin. She wanted nothing more than to strip off its weight and slip into the cool gloom of the castle's chapel, where she could be alone with her thoughts and prayers. The gown's buttoned sleeves bound her arms like manacles from elbow to wrist.

'Almost done,' muttered the maid, giving one final tug to the laces. 'There we are.'

Elizabeth stared at herself in the mirror, while Lora gathered a satin surcoat and veil from the clothes perch. The gold trim on the gown glimmered in the candlelight, filling the looking-glass with its burnished glow. Her skin was pale against its radiance. Her black hair, normally hidden beneath a coif, was sleek with perfumed oil and piled up on her head, the twisted locks held in place by gem-tipped pins. Her reflection was a stranger to her. She thought of the many guests filling her father's hall, all the faces that would turn as she entered, her father and husband-to-be among them. Suddenly, the gown seemed even tighter, her breath harder to catch.

'Arms up,' said Lora, holding out the fitted gold surcoat that went over the gown. There was a black lion embroidered on the chest, from the de Burgh coat of arms.

'I can't, Lora.' Elizabeth turned to her. 'I can't.'

The maid's brow knotted as she glanced at the garment. 'Sir Richard had this made specially, my lady.' Her tone was low, worried. 'He will expect you to wear it.'

'Not the gown. The feast.' Elizabeth brought her hand to her mouth. Her voice cracked. 'This marriage.'

Lora's face filled with sympathy. As tears welled in Elizabeth's eyes, the maid placed the surcoat on the bed and clutched her mistress's arms. 'My lady, I know you are afraid, but you must have courage. You know how important this marriage is to your father, how much he needs Lord Henry's support with the troubles growing on our borders.'

'I begged him to let me enter a convent. I want to take the veil for Christ, not a man three times my age.'

'Lord Henry isn't so old,' chided the maid.

Elizabeth took her hand from her mouth, her face tightening. 'He is older than my father, Lora. His first wife bore him twelve children. She died giving birth to the last.' She twisted back to the mirror, her eyes narrowing on her reflection, feeling a hot urge to tear off the gown and rip the pins from her hair, to scratch her face until she was ugly. She had seen the way Lord Henry looked at her during that first meeting two months ago, when the marriage had been arranged. It had reminded her of the foxes that prowled around the henhouse at dusk, their black eyes intent. She remembered the liver-spots on his hands, his fingers as fat as tubers, remembered the freckled bald patch on his head and the yellowness of his teeth.

Lora sighed gently. 'This is your duty, as it was your sisters' before you. Besides, you will not be going to Lord Henry alone. I will be with you. Come, my lady,' she said staunchly, picking up the surcoat. 'Your father and his guests are waiting.'

Numbly, Elizabeth lifted her arms, allowing the maid to lower the surcoat over her head and smooth it over the gown. She thought of her sisters – of how they had loved feasts. Crowding the window of their bedchamber at Lough Rea to watch the guests arriving with their retinues of squires and servants, they had sniggered at pompous lords and blushed and cooed over strapping young knights. Elizabeth had never understood their excitement for all the heat and the noise, the fuss and upheaval, and drunken, leering eyes. She had always tried to excuse herself from such evenings, feigning fever or some other malady. Sometimes her father had permitted her absence. Tonight, there was no such escape.

Lora laid the veil over her hair and set it in place with a gold circlet. 'You look like a queen,' she murmured.

Elizabeth didn't respond. As she moved towards the door she passed the chest at the foot of her bed on which lay a small ivory cross on a silver chain. Her father had presented it to her on her tenth birthday, just weeks after she had almost drowned.

'*God will always be with you, child,*' he had told her, draping it around her neck.

She had worn it ever since, the bottom of the cross made smooth by her fingers after years spent toying with it. She paused to loop it around her neck, then headed down through the tower and out into the dusk. Horses and wagons crowded the courtyard, the stink of dung clouding the air. Feeling as though she were encased in armour in the heavy gown, Elizabeth made her way slowly towards the great hall. Clutching the ivory cross, she prayed for God to intervene in her fate.

9

Robert and Cormac were halfway across the courtyard when they saw the young woman. She was heading towards the great hall, between the rows of horses and carts. Beyond her, the tunnel led through the twin-towered gatehouse to the outside world. The portcullis was still raised to allow any last guests to enter. The two guards on watch had their backs to the courtyard and were leaning against the wall in conversation. Sprinting faster, breathless after so many weeks idle in the tower, Robert raised his hand as the woman turned; a desperate gesture of silence. Even as he did so, he realised it must look as though he were going to attack her, the blade rising in his grip.

Her scream pierced the evening. The grooms by the stables looked up, startled from their tasks, and the two guards whipped round. Robert charged, meaning to give them no time to defend themselves, but three more emerged from the gatehouse, alerted by the scream. Robert brought himself up short, taking in the line of men. As the guards drew their broadswords between him and his escape, he switched direction and lunged for the young woman, who was rooted to the spot.

She moved suddenly, coming alive with the danger, but her gown was long and awkward, and she only managed to stumble a few paces before Robert caught her, pinning her roughly to him, one arm around her chest. Her hands came up and grabbed at his forearm in fear.

'Stay back!' Robert roared at the guards, levelling his stolen sword at them.

The five men halted, looking from Robert to Cormac, who had taken up position close at his back, ready to defend him. One stepped forward, as though to test Robert's resolve, but an older man with cropped white hair and a weathered face stopped him with a barked order.

As his comrade fell back into line, the white-haired guard's gaze fixed on Robert. 'You must know you cannot go anywhere, Sir Robert.' His voice was self-assured. 'Let Lady Elizabeth go and you will not be harmed.'

At the name, Robert realised the girl, whose heart he could feel beating fiercely against his arm, must be Richard de Burgh's youngest daughter. Stephen had spoken of her often; the feast this evening was in honour of her betrothal. His fleeting triumph at the value of his hostage was quickly dampened by the reality of his actions. He had seized a lady, bodily, against her will. He made himself no better than a brigand. But he couldn't let go. Not if he wanted to see his kingdom again. 'You wouldn't harm me.'

'I wouldn't, sir,' agreed the guard. 'But if you hurt one hair on the lady's head, Earl Richard will rip your guts out through your mouth.'

Robert turned on Cormac. 'Get two horses.'

Cormac backed towards the stables, his eyes on the guards.

Robert remained where he was, the girl's shoulder blades digging into his chest, the two of them poised in a pool of shifting light from the torches that burned around the walls. Music and laughter echoed from the hall, the merry sounds strange in contrast to the scene in the courtyard. Robert guessed the noise would have masked the girl's scream from the revellers, but it wouldn't be long before someone happened upon their frozen tableau.

He glanced over his shoulder to see Cormac gesturing roughly at the grooms by the stables. They were young lads, clearly terrified by the armed, wild-looking Irishman. Sensing movement in his periphery, Robert looked back to see the white-haired guard advancing slowly. 'Don't,' he warned, bringing the edge of his blade round to Elizabeth's neck.

'*Please.*'

The faint whisper came from her.

A voice in Robert's mind – it might have been his mother's – harangued him, but he silenced it, steeling himself to the fear in the girl's voice, refusing to allow the barbarity of his actions to weaken his resolve. These men in his way, this terrified girl: they meant nothing when set against Scotland's throne.

The white-haired guard had paused twenty yards away, his four comrades ranged behind him, blocking the gatehouse tunnel. Robert saw the older man's eyes flick past him. The guard's expression changed, something expectant rising in his face. Robert jerked round to see a brawny man in a dusty tunic moving up behind his foster brother.

All Cormac's attention was on the lad leading out the horses. Robert yelled a warning, but before his foster-brother could turn, the man was on him, punching up under his ribs. Cormac curled over the blow. He managed to keep hold of his sword, but his attacker gave him no chance to swing it at him, bringing his knee crashing up into his down-turned face. Robert shouted fiercely as his foster-brother hit the ground and the man dropped down on top of him, wresting the sword from his grip.

Seeing the white-haired guard daring another step towards him, Robert dragged Elizabeth to a cart, one of many that crowded the courtyard. Two muscular horses were harnessed to the front. Climbing on to the back, he pulled her up roughly behind him. She weighed next to nothing. The horses shifted, walking forward expectantly. The cart was full of cushions and blankets, with a whip left lying down the side. The guards were edging closer, ringing the cart in a semicircle. 'My brother for the lady!' Robert shouted at the white-haired man, releasing Elizabeth to grasp the whip, but keeping the blade pointed at her as she cowered beneath him.

Cormac was struggling under the weight of the brawny man, trying to fight him off. Before the guard could answer, out of the doors of the great hall raced six more men. In their wake came Richard de Burgh, his face a mask of fury. Behind him was a balding man in his fifties, his expression incredulous as he saw Elizabeth huddled in the cart.

'*Run, brother!*' yelled Cormac.

Spitting a curse, Robert cracked the whip over the backs of the horses as the earl and his men charged towards him. The beasts took off, galvanised by the sting. The white-haired guard leapt desperately at the cart as it lurched past. Managing to grab hold of the side, he clung on as the tunnel loomed up, narrow and dark. Robert, pitched to his knees, lashed out with the whip, catching the man on the side of the face. The guard fell back with a cry, tumbling over in the dust of the courtyard.

'Drop the portcullis!' roared Ulster.

Ignoring Elizabeth, knocked off-balance in the heap of cushions, Robert threw himself into the seat at the front. Snatching up the reins, he flogged the beasts for all they were worth as the guards in the gatehouse tower responded to the earl's shout and the spiked iron bars came slamming down. The portcullis missed the back of the cart by inches, crashing shut behind as the horses careened through the tunnel and out on to the track. Robert heard Ulster's shouts continue, over the tumult of hooves, before the cart rocked around a bend in the track and plunged into the woods.

Robert maintained the reckless pace for as long as he dared, the cart reeling over rocks and ruts. It was dark beneath the trees, dense with summer growth. Faint in the distance, he heard a bell begin to clang. Judging he had very little time before the earl's men came for him, far faster on their chargers, he slowed the horses. Spying a natural break in the trees,

Robert steered the beasts off the track, twigs and bracken snapping and tearing beneath the cart's wheels. When he could go no further, he pulled the horses to a stop and jumped down. Behind, through the web of trees, he could still see the road. His only hope was that it was sufficiently shadowy for the cart to remain concealed from his pursuers, at least for a while.

His fingers fumbling in haste, Robert unbuckled the harness straps. The horses were agitated, tossing their heads and snorting. Neither had saddles, but he could ride them well enough without. He glanced at the earl's daughter as he tugged free the last strap. She was still in the cart, grasping the sides, her eyes wide and her breaths coming fast. The gold circlet she had been wearing had slipped off and her veil was dishevelled. 'I'm sorry, my lady,' he told her. 'I had no choice.' Looping the harness strap around his waist, Robert wedged the sword he had taken from Ulster's guard through the makeshift belt. 'Stay by the road. Your father will come for you.'

As he moved to mount one of the horses, Elizabeth pushed herself from the back of the cart. 'Wait!'

Robert glanced round. Her expression was less one of fear, more of desperation.

'Take me with you.'

Robert stared at the girl, for a second dumbfounded by the request, then he grasped at the horse's mane and rump to pull himself up. From the road came a rumble of hooves.

Elizabeth's face knotted in anguish. 'Then I shall tell them which way you're going.' Her voice trembled with the threat, but she pushed through the undergrowth, making her way towards the track, one hand hitching up her skirts, the other swiping branches out of her way.

Cursing, Robert slipped from the horse and went after her, leaping the tree roots, his shirt ripping open on the thorns of a briar. The hooves were louder, the forest floor trembling with the impact of a score or more riders. Grabbing Elizabeth, Robert forced her down in the undergrowth, just as the earl's men thundered past, illuminated by the gusting flames of the torches they held. He clamped a hand over her mouth, but he needn't have worried. She didn't even struggle. In a cloud of dust, the riders were gone.

Robert waited a few seconds, insects skittering over his skin in the darkness, Elizabeth's breaths hot against his palm, before he got to his feet, pulling her up roughly.

The veil had slipped from her head and her braided black hair had snagged free of its pins. 'You'll go to Scotland, won't you?'

'You can walk to the castle from here,' he told her, striding back towards the cart. Ulster's men must know they would catch up to him quickly. When they didn't they would surely double back and start searching the woods. Robert halted. The cart was where he had left it, but the horses had bolted. Fury flooded him. *'Damn it to hell!'* he hissed, rounding on Elizabeth as she came up behind him.

She shrank back from his anger, but her face remained set. 'Take me with you and I'll send a message to my father, asking him to let the other man go unharmed. He's your brother, isn't he?'

Robert looked towards the road, hearing another company riding hard along it. He glanced back at Elizabeth, taking in her determined expression and desperate eyes. She was clutching a small ivory cross she wore around her neck, twisting it between her fingers. If he left her here there would be nothing to stop her shouting to alert his pursuers. Swearing, he grasped her by the wrist and slipped into the shadows of the trees. Behind them, the forest filled with the drumming of hooves.

Picardy, France, 1301 AD

Storm clouds clotted the sky, changing the gold of the evening light to bruised copper and throwing huge shadows across the meadows of the Somme valley. From the high vantage point of Bailleul Castle, raised on its massive earthworks above the pastures and villages that surrounded it, John Balliol watched the first pulse of lightning illuminate the landscape of his birth. Behind him, servants hastened about the shadowy room, throwing fresh linen across the bed, coaxing a fire to life in the hearth, pouring water into a basin so he could wash the road dirt from his face. The rest of the castle was occupied by the family and garrison of his vassal, but this room had been kept free for its long-absent lord. It had a dusty, forgotten air.

The evening was heavy with heat and, for a moment, Balliol thought about telling the servants to leave the fire, but the cheery light blooming in the dark chamber gave him a sense of homecoming that he didn't want to extinguish.

Home.

It was a foreign word. Not since the years of his lordship in Galloway following the death of his mother had the word had true meaning to him; a careless meaning at that, one he had taken for granted. After three years in the Tower of London and two years in the papal custody of Malmaison Castle, he now understood it. Home was freedom. Freedom for a man to come and go as he pleased, to summon his vassals as he saw fit. Freedom to eat and sleep, and go hunting with his son when he wanted. He felt the word like a shudder, whether of excitement or unease he wasn't sure.

There was a rap at the door. Balliol turned as his steward entered.

'Sire, the men you have been expecting have arrived. Do you wish to eat first?'

'No, Pierre, show them up. I will see them now.'

As the steward left, Balliol looked back to the window, the apprehension building inside him, crackling like the storm. He still didn't understand why, three days ago, he had been let out of his chamber at Malmaison, without a guard for the first time in years, and led to where papal officials had been waiting to escort him to his castle in Picardy. He had been told very little except that messengers from Paris would meet him here. Maybe now he would get some answers. Freedom was his. But he wanted to know at what price.

A short time later the door opened and Pierre appeared again, leading two men dressed in blue surcoats, adorned with gold fleurs-de-lis: the royal arms of France. Ignoring the servants still bustling about the chamber, Balliol waited for the men to greet him, feeling stiffly suspicious.

'Sir John,' said one, inclining his head. He had a neatly forked beard and pointed features. 'I am Sir Jean de Reims, a knight of the royal household. I bring greetings from King Philippe in Paris. He trusts you find your new lodgings more agreeable?'

The first answer to his many questions surprised Balliol. So the King of France was responsible for his freedom? The revelation brought more questions on its heels. He knew his liberation from the Tower and transfer to Malmaison had come at the pope's behest and had been part of the negotiations between England and France, but he had not been able to fathom why his fate had been bound up in a treaty between the two countries. The French king's intervention seemed even less understandable. 'I thought the order for my release came from the papal curia?'

'In part. A supporter of yours, Sir William Wallace, arrived in Paris two years ago to present the case for your release. Philippe, your friend and ally, felt moved to intervene. He recommended Sir William and his cause to the pope. His holiness made the final decision, but your release was determined by my lord, the king.'

Balliol moved to the window, where the setting sun had vanished in the face of the coming storm. Lightning tore the sky. He had turned to the French king six years ago for help against Edward; their alliance had caused the English king's invasion of Scotland. But where was Philippe when the war had begun? Where were the soldiers the king had promised when Edward marched his army across the Tweed and slaughtered Balliol's subjects, overran his cities and seized his castles? Where were the French when Edward led him to the Tower?

'I am surprised King Philippe is taking such an interest in my affairs after all this time. I thought he and Edward were now friends?' Balliol turned back to the royal knight. 'The pope's treaty, I'm told, specifically excluded Scotland.'

'I understand your frustration,' answered Jean, his tone mollifying. 'King Philippe wishes your release could have been secured long before, but the war with England forced him to turn his attention to his own borders. Now a truce has been agreed, he can extend his hand to you once more. He intends to return you to your rightful place. On the throne of Scotland.'

Balliol's chest tightened at these words, but he exhaled that clenching hope quickly, his mind refusing to believe such a bold statement. It sounded ridiculous. 'How could he do such a thing?' His voice was quiet, weary now, revealing something of the broken man behind the stiff façade.

'A permanent peace between England and France has yet to be agreed. Gascony is still in my master's possession. He could continue to withhold the duchy, unless Edward agrees to end his war against your kingdom and allows you to return to your throne.'

'Why would Philippe do this? I do not understand.'

'In honour of your former alliance and so that he may once again have an ally on the throne of Scotland. An ally who could help him keep the ambitions of his English cousin in check.'

Trust for Balliol had become a hard-won thing: a pearl, only moulded by time and grit. He had trusted Philippe once before. Just as he had trusted King Edward, godfather to his nineteen-year-old son, who was named after him. Edward had chosen him to be king over the Bruce and all other claimants; had watched him sit upon the Stone of Destiny, the crown set upon his head. Four years later, Edward had forced him to stand upon that platform at Montrose erected for his humiliation. Balliol could still hear the sound of cloth ripping as two of Edward's knights tore the royal arms of Scotland from his surcoat, followed by the cheer of the mob. Toom tabard, they had called him. King Nobody.

He looked out of the window as lightning lit the landscape. Long before the Balliol family acquired rich estates in England and Scotland, they had lived here, amid the soft green of Picardy's meadows and vineyards. It was from this northern edge of land, which looked ever towards England, that the Conqueror had first set out, Balliol's ancestors with him. This was the birthing place of conquest. Perhaps it could be again.

Slowly, John Balliol dared to hope.

10

In the cramped, fire-lit room the rasping words whispered over the grinding of stone on stone.

'*In the name of Lady Moon and Brigid of the flame I adjure thee, cleave to my will.*'

The stifling air was choked with smoke from the fire, its bitter tang in contrast to the sickly odour of mould that rose from the straw covering the earth floor. Pots and pans crusted black from years of use hung down from the rafters, along with sprigs of liverwort, cloudberry, mandrake root and heather. Over by a pallet bed heaped with furs, things scurried in the shadows. A small pile of books teetered nearby, the boards and bindings loose. The words scored in the covers were faded, the edges of the pages mouse-eaten and green with damp, the names of the authors all but vanished. Pliny. Aristotle. Ptolemy. Galen.

'*By the power of the sacred horn and the midsummer sun I adjure thee, cleave to my will.*'

As she ground the stone pestle into the mortar, Affraig felt the twinges in her wrist and arm that afflicted her often these days, the joints seeming to knot and fuse beneath her paper-thin skin until it felt as though her limbs were on fire. Inside the bowl the desiccated liver, heart and genitals of the male coney she had snared a month earlier were slowly pulverised into a pinkish grey dust with each painful movement.

'You have the wine?'

'Yes,' came the breathy female voice behind her.

Affraig turned as Bethoc, the young wife of a fisherman from Turnberry, stepped keenly towards her, holding out a glazed jug, stopped up by a yellow wedge of wax. Affraig took it impatiently, intent on finishing the concoction as quickly as possible. She was glad of the business, but Bethoc's frequent appearances had begun to grate on her nerves; last month a cure for her son's toothache, the month before a charm for her baby daughter's rash, which she said had been caused by a hex from a jealous neighbour who was barren. Setting the jug on the worm-rotten table by the mortar, Affraig tapped the ground organs into the wine, frowning with concentration as her hands trembled. 'Have your husband drink this two days before the moon is full. No later. You will find his potency returned soon after. Make sure he drinks it all.'

Bethoc, usually so attentive to her every word, hadn't responded.

Affraig looked round irritably. 'Do you hear me, Bethoc?'

The young woman was standing at the door, which had swung open in the breeze. She was looking out, her arms hanging limp at her sides, her body stiff and unmoving. 'What *is* that?'

Putting down the mortar, Affraig shuffled across, the hems of her shabby brown dress trailing threads of straw in her wake. Standing beside Bethoc, the summer wind breathing warmth on her face, she saw a pall of smoke rising in the distance. It gusted high above the woods that surrounded her house, painting the blue sky black. It was coming from Turnberry.

'Is a house burning?' Bethoc asked, looking at her for answer.

'No,' murmured Affraig, her skin tight and cold. The fire was far too large for that, the plumes coming from too many places at once, forming a dense cloud. It wasn't one house. It was many. 'The English have come.' The impact of the words hit her a few moments after she uttered them.

For months, rumours of invasion had been spreading wild about Carrick, sowing seeds of fear and panic in the people. Affraig had heard them all from the men and women who came to her for their cures and charms. Caerlaverock Castle had fallen, they told her first, in hushed voices. Some said the English were heading north to Glasgow, others were convinced they were advancing west towards them. The people of Turnberry and other settlements along the Carrick coast seemed braced with fear, but rooted, like coneys frozen under the shadow of a hawk. Unwilling to leave homes and livestock, or let wheat wither in the fields, most had stayed put, saying the Scots under the guardians, John Comyn and William Lamberton, would turn back the English before they could get far. Now, it seemed, their faith had been misplaced.

Bethoc, who had paled at Affraig's words, stepped outside, her eyes fixed on the dark, drifting clouds. 'I must get to my children,' she said, wrapping her arms about her. Sweat beaded her brow and lip, but she was shivering. 'My babies.'

'It is too late. You should stay here. I doubt the soldiers will come this far.'
Affraig could smell the smoke now, a faint reek of burning timber, thatch
and straw.

Bethoc didn't seem to have heard. She hastened away towards the woods,
the jug of wine containing the cure for her husband's impotence forgotten.

Affraig watched her disappear into the trees, above which a flock of
seabirds came flying, their escape from the flames enviably easy. Moving
back inside the house, she wished her dogs were still with her, but the last
had died, old and blind, two winters ago. She paused in the doorway, her
watery eyes fixing on the broad oak that towered over her dwelling, adorned
with its webs of twigs. There were scores of them, the branches clouded
with destinies, hopes and prayers. Most were for love, or money or health,
each lattice of bound twigs containing a symbol of the person's desire held
there by a thread: a red ribbon around a lock of hair, a frayed silk purse, a
sprig of vervain. Affraig's gaze sought out one, hanging high amid the green,
a crown of heather, wormwood and broom spiralling slowly in the centre.

'Where are you, Robert?' she murmured.

Turnberry, Scotland, 1301 AD

Smoke wreathed Turnberry in a black shroud, billowing from the homes,
storehouses and workshops that clustered the shoreline between the
wooded hills and the sea. Flames surged up the sides of buildings, the heat
cracking open the mud-daubed walls. Over the crackle of fire came the
groaning creak and crash of timbers as the roof of a barn collapsed, a shower
of sparks erupting from the centre. Squeals echoed from within. As one of
the doors buckled inwards, a white horse burst out of the inferno, eyes
mad, mane and tail alight, flesh blistered. It galloped away down the street,
a monstrous thing cloaked in smoke and flame, past burning houses and the
bodies that scattered the ground.

There was a young man lying on his stomach, a knife still gripped in his
fist. His head had been cleaved from his body and lay a few feet away, linked
by a dark wash of blood. Nearby, two women were sprawled together over
the threshold of a flaming house, their mouths and nostrils stained black
with smoke, the air around them rippling with heat. Other corpses, most
of them men, displayed gaping wounds made by the hack or stab of swords.
Some had weapons in their hands and were on their backs, fallen in the
place where they had made a stand, but many were unarmed, cut down in

the act of fleeing, carrying sacks or armfuls of possessions that were now littered about them. Everywhere, the dusty ground was scuffed by the iron-shod hooves of horses.

Out in the fields, huge swathes of wheat were aflame. It had been a dry summer and the fires spread quickly, devouring the crops. Sheep and cattle in the pastures were fleeing. There was fire too on the beach, coming from a row of fishing boats that had been set alight. Beyond, the white waves continued to rush at the shore, as unheeding of the disaster unfurling before them as the sun in the blue sky or the cormorants that wheeled over the rocky mass of Ailsa Craig, far out in the bay. Above the golden crescent of sand, where cliffs climbed to a grassy headland, the walls of Turnberry Castle rose through veils of smoke. The fortress stood untouched on a precipitous promontory above the foaming sea, gates shut.

Beyond, just out of bowshot range, Humphrey de Bohun eased off his great helm, decorated with a spray of swan feathers. The padded coif he wore beneath was sodden with sweat and tinged black by smoke. He could taste its bitterness. Handing the helm to his squire, Humphrey swung down from the saddle. He accepted the skin of wine one of his pages offered to him and rolled his shoulders, strained by the burden of mail. Around him, spread out across the bluffs in front of the fortress, knights and squires were doing much the same. After the day's ride and in this sapping summer heat, the sack of the settlement had proven thirsty work. The torches borne by many of the infantry had been thrust into the dry soil, flames swirling in the breeze that rippled through the coarse grass.

'Sir Humphrey.'

He turned as a band of his men trotted their horses up the shallow slope towards him. He had set them to work burning the crops.

The knight at the head pulled his charger to a halt. 'It's done, sir.' He smiled grimly. 'The villagers won't be threshing any grain this harvest.'

Humphrey nodded as he tossed the wine skin back to his page. 'Good work, Aleyn. Have the men water their horses and stretch their legs. But stay close. We have more work to do today.' He looked back at the castle, which thrust from the cliff-top: the birthplace of Robert Bruce. How best to crack open its stone shell? he wondered.

As he was pondering the options, Humphrey's gaze was caught by a tall figure striding towards him. It was Thomas, Earl of Lancaster, nephew of the king and one of the most powerful barons in England. He still carried his sword, the blade of which gleamed with a smear of blood. A fearful opponent on the tournament ground, the young man, heir through marriage to the great earldoms of Leicester and Lincoln, was proving just as dangerous in war.

Thomas's usually good-humoured expression was tight with anger. 'Have you spoken to my cousin?'

'Not since we entered Turnberry.' Humphrey scanned the men, searching for Edward. 'Why?'

'He plans to move on to Ayr this afternoon.'

Humphrey's brow furrowed. 'But the castle hasn't—'

'He doesn't intend to take it,' Thomas cut across him. 'He believes Ayr will be the better target.' His gaze fixed on the king's son, who Humphrey now spotted, standing in a crowd of young men.

At Edward's side was Piers Gaveston. The Gascon youth was as dark as the king's son was fair, his black surcoat trimmed with silver. The two were sharing a skin of wine, laughing and talking as though it were a feast day.

'I believe it to be a poor excuse,' continued Thomas. 'My cousin has other targets on his mind. From what I hear, Gaveston has convinced him to hold a tournament before we take the next town. He says it will be good training for him and his friends. It appears they have become bored of burning crops and raiding villages.'

'I will speak to him.'

As Humphrey crossed the field towards Edward, his jaw clenched. After the fall of Caerlaverock, the king split his army in two, personally leading one half north towards Bothwell Castle near Glasgow, while his son led a campaign in Galloway and Carrick. Under young Edward's banner, this second force had marched across the south-west, torching settlements, leaving a land blackened and devastated. But, over the course of the past weeks, the king's son seemed to have become less and less interested in his command, until Humphrey found himself planning much of their strategy and issuing orders. He had endeavoured to guide the king's son back to the task in hand, but the newfound freedom away from his father's eye seemed to have gone to his head. This, coupled with the influence the wilful Piers exerted over him, meant Humphrey was finding it increasingly difficult to rein him in.

'My lord Edward.' Humphrey's anger sharpened at the derisive look Piers gave him as he entered the ring of men, some of whom were Knights of the Dragon, as Humphrey had once been, before he was inducted into the king's Round Table. 'I hear you plan to lead the men out from Turnberry today.'

'That is correct, Sir Humphrey,' answered Edward, sweeping back his blond hair with a gloved hand. 'We do not have siege equipment. The castle is too well-defended to take.'

'Look over there,' said Humphrey, nodding towards the woods, visible through the clouds of smoke rising over the crop fields. 'What do you see?'

'Trees,' said Edward, shrugging in question.

'Trees that can be cut down to make a battering ram. Turnberry's gates won't hold for long with a sustained assault. We need to remove the threat of its garrison attacking us from the rear while we continue north.' Out of the corner of his eye, Humphrey noticed Piers smile at something one of the other knights murmured. Forcing back the desire to slam his mailed fist into the Gascon's mocking face, he steered Edward away from his friends. 'The king said it was imperative we strike hardest at Carrick on this campaign. Now Lochmaben has been destroyed, Turnberry is Bruce's last major fortress in Scotland. It isn't enough to raze the lands of his tenants. We must take away all safe havens for him and his allies. We cannot leave such a stronghold for him to return to.' Humphrey exhaled at the youth's sullen expression. 'Besides, its capture will please your father. Imagine his pride when you tell him how you destroyed the birthplace of his greatest enemy.'

At this something flickered into life in Edward's pale eyes and Humphrey knew his words had at last hit their mark.

'Very well,' murmured Edward. 'I will order the men to make camp. We will lay siege to the castle.'

'It is a wise decision.'

Edward went to head back to his comrades, then paused. 'I find it fascinating, Sir Humphrey, to see the depth of your hatred for a man you once called brother.' His tone had a sardonic ring to it.

As he walked away, Humphrey's gaze drifted to the castle's battlements, his mind clouding with the face of Robert Bruce.

West Smithfield, London

1294 AD (7 years earlier)

*L*ong before they reached Smithfield, riding up the road from Newgate, they could see the rows of stalls strung with coloured flags, hear the music and smell the roasting meat coming from the spits. It was the third day of the August fair and the evening's revelry was well under way. The sun, sinking over the plains that stretched from the banks of the Thames at Westminster to the great darkness of the Middlesex Forest, cast a sultry glow across the fair, which spanned the expanse of ground between the Fleet River and the graveyard of St Bartholomew's. Cooking fires made constellations in the dusk.

Humphrey felt excitement bubble up. It was a feeling so closely attached to memories of coming here as a boy that, for a moment, he was eleven years old again riding at his father's side, the people on the road eyeing the earl's entourage of knights and pages with curiosity. It had been years since the two of them had come here together. Now his father was preoccupied with the war against France, they wouldn't be doing it again any time soon.

Humphrey glanced over at Robert Bruce, riding beside him on a dappled palfrey, several hands smaller than Storm, Humphrey's charger. The young earl's gaze was fixed on the crowded fields, a broad grin splitting his face. Humphrey smiled, pleased by his evident eagerness. 'I thought this would impress you,' he called, over the growing din of the crowds.

Henry Percy, riding ahead on a richly caparisoned courser, twisted in his saddle before Robert could answer. 'Do you not have fairs like this in Scotland, Sir Robert?' The Lord of Alnwick's fleshy face was mottled with heat, his blond hair curling around his forehead. His blue eyes glinted coolly as he spoke.

Robert met his gaze easily. 'We do, Sir Henry. Very similar. Only much, much bigger.'

Humphrey chuckled as Henry arched an eyebrow and turned back to the road. At his side, Aymer de Valence, heir to the earldom of Pembroke and a cousin of the king, glanced round. His was a more hostile look, but Robert didn't seem to have noticed, *his attention caught by three girls walking along the verge towards the fair, arms linked as they laughed and talked.*

'Don't get snared by the first bait you see, my friend,' Humphrey warned him with a grin. 'There are women in those fields whose beauty would knock a monk from his habit.'

'Is that so?' said Robert, shortening the reins. 'Well, I will be sure to mention you to them in passing.'

'Make way, fair maidens,' yelled Humphrey, as Robert pricked his spurs into the sides of his palfrey and set off at a canter. 'Make way for the Earl of Carrick! A man from the frozen, barbarous land of the Scots, where women grow beards to shield them from the cold!' Laughing at Robert's roar of protest, Humphrey kicked his charger after him.

The young men with them followed one by one: the royal knights, Ralph de Monthermer and Robert Clifford, then Henry Percy and Guy de Beauchamp, heir of the Earl of Warwick. Aymer de Valence brought up the rear, not bothering to steer his horse closer to the verge, forcing the commoners thronging the road to hasten out of his way to avoid being trampled.

Once in the fair grounds, the seven noblemen left their horses with their squires and moved about on foot in the milling crowds, sampling the wares from various stalls. There was dark rye bread and roasted pork, crimson cherries, moist honey cakes and sugared almonds. There was also cloudy yellow cider and sweet ale.

Humphrey paid for two tankards and gave one to Robert. 'Drink it slowly,' he shouted in the earl's ear, as they passed a ring of men bellowing at two squealing cocks that were pecking one another bloody. 'It's stronger than it tastes.'

Robert grinned. 'No stronger than my grandfather's apple wine.' He set the tankard to his lips and tipped the foamy liquid down his throat.

After a pause, Humphrey followed suit, wiping the scum from his mouth with the back of his hand. 'Another two then?'

'My turn,' said Robert, opening the pouch that swung from his belt alongside his dirk. The loop of leather where his scabbard usually hung was empty.

Swords were forbidden in West Smithfield on fair days and at tournaments, after one too many altercations had turned into full-blown riots. There was little love lost between Londoners and their noble neighbours at Westminster.

'Keep your hand on that,' warned Humphrey, nodding to the purse as Robert passed him another drink. 'You'll find few gentlemen here.'

Sipping at the ale, they headed deeper into the fair, keeping their five comrades in sight. Here were scores of stalls displaying all manner and colour of cloth: linens from Flanders, wool from Berwick, silks from Venice and damask from the Holy Land. Local mercers and those from neighbouring towns haggled with the traders. Beyond the *stalls, the fields opened out, filled with pens of animals and men selling saddles and farm implements.*

Humphrey explained to Robert that it wasn't just cloth that brought people flocking to the August fair. 'My father bought most of his stable here over the years,' he added, eyes moving appreciatively over pens of Arabian stallions and glossy Castilian broodmares.

As well as the expensive breeds there were cumbersome plough horses and ponies from Exmoor, spirited colts, rouncies and hobbies. The stink of dung and the noise of the traders were overwhelming, but for Humphrey, warm and dizzy from the ale, it was sweet with memory. It felt good, too, to be away from the oppressive atmosphere at court, where tensions had been running high all summer, since war was declared with France. King Edward had left for Portsmouth two days ago to oversee the assembly of his fleet, due to leave for Gascony in a few weeks' time, filled with an army to win back the duchy duplicitously seized by his cousin, Philippe. They would all soon be called to serve abroad and this might be the only opportunity they would get to enjoy themselves for a while.

'How much for him?' Robert was asking a trader, standing with a handsome roan charger that was being groomed by a boy.

'For you, sir, eighty marcs.'

The sum raised Robert's brow. 'Eighty?'

'Too much,' said Humphrey, coming to his side. 'Fifty.'

The trader laughed and shook his head. 'He's called Hunter,' he said, looking at Robert. 'Sired by a Persian stallion. There's fire in him, but it's tempered. He'll see you right. In the joust, or on the field of war.'

While they were bartering, Aymer pushed past, knocking Robert's ale from his grip. 'Isn't that more your style, Bruce?' he said, nodding to an old man standing nearby with two bow-legged mules on a rope.

Humphrey caught Robert's arm as he went after him. 'Leave it be.'

Robert shook ale from his hand, riled. 'I don't understand why you're friends with that whoreson.'

'He's one of us.'

'One of you?' Robert studied him intently, ignoring the crowds that jostled around them, people shouting to clear the way as a small black bear was led through the throng on an iron chain towards a staked pen where two mastiffs waited, drool dripping through their teeth. 'You mean one of you with the dragon on your shields?'

Before Humphrey could answer a group of rough-looking men forced their way through in the wake of the bear. One pushed aside a beggar boy who was proffering his bowl at the crowd. He didn't look back as the boy hit the dust, the few coins he'd collected scattering about the feet of the people who walked on over him.

Grateful for the interruption, Humphrey pointed to a group of riders, visible above the heads of the masses. 'Look! The races are about to start.' He nodded to the trader. 'We'll return and you'll accept sixty.'

'If he's still here,' called the trader, as Humphrey led Robert over to where a starting line had been set up under a string of flags.

A score of horses were gathering, most of them ridden by boys bearing whips. Before them the field stretched empty to a gibbet which rose from a patch of bald earth in the distance. As well as a ground for royal tournaments and fairs, West Smithfield was a place of execution. The cheers of the expectant mob swelled as one of the riders punched his fist into the air, his horse rearing beneath him.

Humphrey caught sight of his comrades, their silk mantles and feathered caps making them stand out like jewels amid the drab Londoners. 'Over there. Come on.' Behind him, Robert shouted something. Humphrey looked back. 'What?'

'I need to piss.'

As he moved off through the crowd, Humphrey followed. 'Wait. You'll never find us again.'

Walking in silence, Humphrey led the way towards a row of elms near the Fleet where the latrines were usually set up. He thought about offering Robert an explanation as to why he wouldn't speak about the dragon shields they carried, or rather the meaning that lay behind them, but with the ale fogging his brain and the mayhem around them he couldn't think how.

The latrines were a ditch dug behind a length of canvas strung between two poles. Men filed in on one side, before heading out the other, tightening the cords on their drawers and smoothing down tunics. Humphrey and Robert went in together. The ditch was murky with sewage and reeked in the humid evening.

Robert whistled as he relieved himself, staring into the deepening blue of the sky between the elms. 'The women grow beards?' he said suddenly, looking at Humphrey.

The two of them began to laugh. Humphrey was still chuckling as he laced up his braies. 'What's tickled you, my lord?' came a harsh voice.

They turned to see four men entering behind the screen. Humphrey recognised the barrel-necked one who had spoken. He and his rough comrades had passed them moments ago, back by the bear-baiting pen. All wore coarse clothes and looked like they were used to hard labour.

'Perhaps his beau, John?' volunteered one, grinning unpleasantly at Robert. 'They look like a couple of bawdstrotes in them silks.'

'Aye. That they do.' John, clearly their leader, nodded to the purse on Robert's belt, his smile vanishing. 'Give us it. And yours, little lordling,' he added to Humphrey.

'Come and take it, you turd,' said Robert, switching into English, his face flushed with anger.

'Would be my pleasure,' responded John, whistling sharply through brown teeth.

Robert and Humphrey looked round as two more men came into view at the other end of the canvas screen, blocking their escape. In front of them was the ditch filled with sewage and, beyond it, the river. Hands trembling with fury, Humphrey untied his purse and tossed it at the barrel-necked man, who caught it.

'Now you,' said John, fixing on Robert.

Robert had already removed the purse from his belt, but, as he lifted his left hand to throw it, Humphrey caught a glint of steel in his right.

John's eager eyes were on the purse. He only saw the dirk when Robert hurled it at him. Ducking, he threw his arms up to shield his face. The blade missed, but even as it was in flight, Robert was charging forward. He barrelled into John, who was blinded by his own raised arms. The momentum sent the man straight into the ditch. Robert leapt over him as he fell, landing deftly on the other side. John went down heavily on his back in the narrow trench, black sludge swelling up around him. Before he could struggle up, Robert put a foot on his chest, pinning him down. John bellowed in rage as he sank, but shut his mouth promptly when the greasy water surged over his chin. His companions were looking on, dumbfounded by Robert's sudden attack. One of them went at Humphrey, who pulled his food knife from its sheath and brandished it at him.

'Tell your men to back away,' Robert ordered John. 'Or I'll drown you.' He put more weight on his foot, so the sewage oozed over John's lips and into his nostrils. 'Tell them!'

John struggled, straining to lift up his head as he spluttered and retched. 'Back, you whoresons! Back!'

His men backed away slowly.

'Give me my friend's purse,' said Robert, reaching down with his free hand. In the other, he still had hold of his own.

John raised his shit-splattered hand, from which dangled Humphrey's purse. Robert took it, then jumped across the trench and snatched his dirk from the mud, eyes on the man's comrades. Leaving John to haul himself up, he joined Humphrey. Together, they slipped quickly past the two men lingering uncertainly at the edge of the screen.

As they entered the crowds, Robert handed Humphrey his soiled purse. 'We'd better join the others,' he said, leading the way back to where their companions were watching the horse races. 'Those brigands won't dare take us all.'

Ralph de Monthermer turned as they approached. 'Where were you? You missed the first race.' The royal knight, who was a few years older than them, grimaced. 'Did one of you step in shit? Something stinks.'

'You should smell the other man,' Robert said, causing Humphrey to burst out laughing.

As his mirth subsided, Humphrey watched Robert cheering on the boys who whipped their horses down the field towards Smithfield's gibbet. The man was grinning as if nothing had happened. By God, but he had moved fast, without fear or compunction. After a pause, he put a hand on Ralph's shoulder. 'What do you think?' he murmured. 'Could Robert be a Knight of the Dragon?'

Ralph stared at him, taking in the question. 'He's been in the king's company less than six months. It's too soon. Besides, it isn't your decision, Humphrey. It's the king's.'

'I could speak to my father. King Edward will listen to a knight of the Round Table.'

'Give it a few more months,' Ralph advised. 'We need to get his measure. The campaign in France will show his colours. When he has proven himself in war, we will see if we can trust him.'

'I trust him now,' said Humphrey. But his words were lost in the roar of Smithfield's crowds.

11

Ulster, Ireland, 1301 AD

Darkness came swiftly on the hems of clouds, sweeping low across the evening sky. A north-easterly wind buffeted the crop fields where weeds grew tall among the barley. In the freshening air, Robert smelled rain. He pressed on through the rustling sea of gold, intent on finding shelter. They had left the great forest behind them several days ago. Now, out in the open, they were at the mercy of the elements.

Over the rushing barley, he heard a jangle of bells. Ahead, a wooden cross rose from the crops. Approaching, Robert saw cowbells strung from the arms, presumably to scare off crows. There was something fixed to the top. Looking back as he walked beneath it, he realised it was the horned skull of a goat. It hung lopsided, its empty eye sockets staring down across the sloping field towards a road that snaked its way north through gold and brown fields towards a distant settlement.

The sight of the road caused relief and unease to rise in Robert at once. His instinct was to sprint down and follow it, racing for the sea he had glimpsed from the ridges of the iron hills they had come down from that morning. Beyond that sea lay Scotland. Trepidation held him back. He had avoided the road for weeks, ever since he had seen the patrols two days out from Ballymote, the scarlet bands of cloth on the arms of the riders marking them as Ulster's men.

As he scanned its length for signs of life the rain began to fall, soaking his shirt. At a rustling behind him, Robert turned to see Elizabeth struggling through the barley. For the first few days she had tried to keep pace with him, seemingly as keen to put as much distance between them and her father as possible. Now, after weeks trudging through dense forest, skirting vast loughs and the endless folds of hills, living on bitter berries and tiny, bone-filled fish, she lagged behind, wretched and reluctant. The determination he had seen in her face when she demanded he take her with him had vanished many miles ago. Her black hair hung down her back, lank with rain.

It was falling harder, stinging Robert's face as he glanced into the racing sky. 'We need to take shelter,' he told her, nodding to a line of trees at the other end of the field. The changing season had coloured the leaves, but the cover was thick enough to shield them from the worst of the wet.

Elizabeth stared at him, shivering as she clutched her bundle of clothing to her chest. The surcoat and gown she had been wearing when they left Ballymote were soiled and torn, but she refused to be parted from them, even though she now wore the tunic and belt he'd stolen from a farmstead, which had also provided them with two chickens and a sack of apples. The tunic was too big and he'd had to make a new notch in the belt.

'Here,' said Robert, crossing to her and swinging the sack from his shoulder.

She watched as he pulled out a blanket, also taken from the farm. It was filthy and smelled of horse. Her nose wrinkled, but she let him drape it around her shoulders.

As he took her clothes and stowed them in the sack, Robert realised how pale Elizabeth was. Her cheeks were the colour of bone, her eyes shadowed. She looked much younger than her sixteen years; a girl in an oversized tunic that swamped her thin frame. Her pace had been dragging over the course of the day and in his impatience to cover the last miles to the coast Robert had ignored her pleas for him to slow. Now, he feared she was sickening.

Concern crept level with his frustration as the rain lashed them and the wind blew ragged through the barley. If she had a fever this wet could be the death of her. Not for the first time, Robert wished to God he'd left her by the roadside that night, a mile from her home. She had slowed him down considerably, but despite the fact he'd wanted to be rid of her weeks ago, he knew she wouldn't last a day in the wild. Cormac was in Ulster's custody because of him and no doubt much less comfortable now. Robert wouldn't let his foster-brother rot away in the earl's dungeon and, since the best hope he held for his release lay in Elizabeth's safe return to her father, she remained his burden. 'Come,' Robert said gruffly, taking her arm, 'there's a village down there. We'll find somewhere to stay tonight until this has passed.'

As they headed beneath the cross with the goat's skull and clanking bells, Elizabeth stared over her shoulder at it. The thing gave off a distinct feeling of menace. It was a feeling that seemed to stretch before them as they trudged through the rain to join the road. At first Robert couldn't put his finger on it, then he realised what it was. The barley in the fields wasn't ripe: it was overripe, weeds tangled among the stalks. It should have been harvested by now. Ahead, beyond a stream, the village was blurred by rain and the growing dark, but even at this distance he could see no firelight in the windows and there wasn't a trace of wood-smoke on the wind. 'It looks abandoned,' he murmured to Elizabeth, stumbling along the overgrown highway beside him.

There was a bridge over the stream leading into the settlement. It was broken in the centre, timbers trailing in the flowing waters. Further downstream, the wheel of a mill groaned round. Robert stood there frowning as he took in the strangely familiar surroundings. He knew this place. He remembered passing through it earlier in the year, heading south with his men. Realising he was only a few days, four at most, from Glenarm, he felt a surge of elation. On the back of this came the question of what had happened here. The answer confirmed the rumours he had heard of settlers deserting homes and livelihoods to return to England, as the Irish pressed in.

Grasping Elizabeth's hand, Robert led the way downriver to where the banks were shallower. 'Climb on to my back and I'll wade across. It doesn't look deep.' When she drew away, Robert turned to her. He had noticed her fear of water before. 'I won't let go.'

Half coaxing, half pulling her on to his back, where she clung like a wet limpet, he strode into the swirling river, flinching at the cold rush of it around his legs. In the centre it shelved beneath his feet, taking him up to his waist. As he stumbled, she gasped and held on tighter, almost strangling him. Robert ploughed on, staggering up the muddy slope on the other side, where he gently prised her arms loose and deposited her on the bank.

Together, soaked to the skin, they entered the settlement where empty houses, workshops and barns rose around them. Many of the structures looked as though they had been looted, doors kicked in, the litter of people's lives strewn across the floor inside. Scraps of clothing and other material trailed from trees. Robert had spied various abandoned structures on their way north: castles and a few churches. But nothing like this – a whole town. Who had decided to leave first? Had it been a trickle, or a flood?

He saw a fire pit under the eaves of one building. The blackened circle looked fairly fresh. People had been here since the exodus, that much was clear. The dark windows of buildings seemed to stare down. A door banged in the wind, making Robert wince. The looted settlement and proximity to his estates made him wary. Ulster must know he would try to make it to Antrim. Robert had no doubt there would be men posted somewhere along this road, waiting for him to appear. The arduous journey was at its most dangerous. Feeling exposed, he led Elizabeth into a two-storey house on the edge of the town.

After climbing over broken stools and around a table, he ushered her up a set of rickety stairs to the room above. Through air grey with cobwebs and dust they made out three pallet beds beneath the slanting beams of the roof. A piece of sacking sagged in the window, letting in a draught and the last of the evening light. Rainwater dripped steadily from a hole in the roof, the boards beneath green and slimy. It smelled of rot.

While Elizabeth stood there shaking, Robert picked through the blankets on the beds, grimacing at the fur of mould growing on them. 'There's nothing useful here.' He opened the sack bag and drew out her old gown. 'Here, put this on. You can't stay in those clothes and I can't risk a fire.'

She stared at him, until he turned away to give her privacy, listening to the click of the buckle as she undid the belt and cast it on the floor. There was a rustle followed by a wet slop as she dropped the tunic beside it. Robert kept his eyes fixed on a beam in front of him, where a spider was industriously binding a fly in its threads. In Scotland, he'd spent months in the Forest living rough with his men, but that had been in the cause of war and he'd had his squires and servants, cooks to make his meals and a tent to sleep in. Even William Wallace, whom he'd once denigrated as a brigand, would be more recognisable as a nobleman. *It is the man that makes the king*, his grandfather had told him years ago. If that was so, then how could a king be made of the man he had become? How had his pursuit of kingship led him to be standing soaked and filthy in this hovel with the daughter of an earl?

'I'm finished.'

Robert looked round to see her in the jewel-green gown she had been wearing the night they escaped, the night she fled her betrothal feast. It was dirty and frayed around the hems and wrists, but mostly dry. She looked older in the dress; a bedraggled princess, her hair hanging in a tangled mass over one shoulder.

'We ate the last of the apples this morning. I'll find us something to eat. There might be a few fish in that stream.'

Her face fell. 'No more fish,' she implored. 'Please.'

Robert's frustration at the delay erupted. 'You'll eat what I find, my lady, and be thankful! I was only ever intending to feed one mouth on this journey. If not for you, I'd be in Scotland already.' Now the anger was coming he didn't want it to stop. 'Your father thinks I abducted you. If he harms my foster-brother because of you, I'll—' He halted, realising his voice had risen to dangerous levels.

Elizabeth had pressed her lips together at his outburst. She now spoke quickly into his silence. 'I've told you I'll write to my father, explaining why I ran away. That I'll tell him it wasn't your fault. I'll beg him to let your foster-brother go, I swear.' She was clutching at her ivory cross, worrying it between her fingers.

'You think he'll listen? You said you begged him to let you enter a convent rather than marry. He didn't listen then, did he?'

Elizabeth's brow furrowed at his tone. 'You'll keep your promise, won't you, Sir Robert? You'll take me with you to Scotland?'

He took a moment to answer. 'Yes. But we have to move quicker. I need to get back to my kingdom.'

When she gave a small nod, Robert headed down the creaking stairs, slightly mollified. Elizabeth seemed to accept the lie. Hopefully, she would push herself faster come morning. Then, when they reached Antrim, he would deposit her with his foster-father so that she could be exchanged for Cormac. Ulster could do what he wanted with her and that would be the end of that.

Leaving the house, Robert headed out into the rain, adjusting the sword that was strapped to his hip. Perhaps there were unsoiled stores of food in some of the buildings: salted meat or oats? As he moved purposefully down the street, where puddles reflected the darkening sky and rain hammered on the rooftops, those last words he'd said to Elizabeth repeated in his mind. *I need to get back to my kingdom.* The words had come forcefully with the strength of feeling behind them.

Until now, his intent to claim the throne of Scotland had been bound up almost completely in a sense of personal legitimacy. It had been his grandfather who, by blood and endorsement, was the rightful claimant after the death of King Alexander. Since John Balliol had been deposed, who else but Robert, to whom the old Bruce had passed his claim, should seize it? The flame of such convictions, kindled within him by the ambition of his grandfather and father, had been fanned by his supporters in the years since: powerful, influential men like James Stewart. But somewhere on his journey north, in the oppressive hush of this impoverished land, something had begun to wake in him, something that now manifested itself in this ghost of a town.

Ireland, bled dry by an absent lord to fund wars abroad, was a sobering vision. Might this forsaken town be the future of Turnberry or Ayr under Edward? The English king had no love of Scotland or its people, that much had always been plain. What was it he was said to have remarked as he crossed the border into England after the first invasion, leaving bureaucrats to run the kingdom? *A man does good business when he rids himself of shit.* If Edward succeeded in crushing the rebellion and took control, might Ireland's fate one day be theirs? Might he bleed Scotland of revenues and grain to fund another war in Gascony if the peace talks with King Philippe failed, or in Wales if another rebellion erupted?

He was so lost in thought as he wandered through the narrow back streets towards a row of barns that Robert didn't notice the horse until he was almost upon it. He stopped dead, eyes focusing on the animal, standing only yards away. It was a large white charger, the horse of a knight or man of means. It had no saddle, but a cloth was draped over its back and it was bridled. The reins were looped around a tethering post outside a barn, the doors of which were partially open. The horse snorted as it saw him and stamped. Iron rang on the hard ground.

Moving quickly, Robert pressed himself into the shadows of an open doorway, his fingers tightening around the hilt of his sword, heart racing at the unexpected evidence of another human after so long in the wilderness. The horse snorted again and a few seconds later a figure emerged from the barn. It was a tall, muscular man dressed in a dark cloak. His hair hung to his shoulders and he had a full beard. It was the weapon in his hands, however, to which Robert's gaze was drawn. The man carried a crossbow. As he scanned the dark street, his gaze sweeping the doorway, Robert's chest tightened. After a moment, he moved back inside the barn and was gone from view.

Robert slipped out and hastened down the street towards the main thoroughfare. He tried to pass off the man as a traveller seeking shelter from the rain, or an Irish bandit, one of the looters perhaps? But neither fitted. A warhorse, a crossbow? He felt uneasy, but couldn't place what threat the man posed, so long as he stayed out of his way.

He was almost at the edge of the town, where the road continued on across a river, much broader and deeper than the stream. Memory reminded him that there was a ford here, which he had crossed on his way south. He saw the ford at the same time as he saw the men. There were two of them standing under the eaves of a large building, which might have belonged to a burgher. Robert halted out of sight at the corner of a dilapidated house, fixing on the red strip of cloth around their arms.

As he watched, a third man moved out of the building to hand his comrades a wine skin. Resting his head against the damp wood of the house, Robert blinked into the arrows of rain. Of course they would be here. How else would he cross the river and make it to his estates other than by the ford? Far faster on their horses than he was on foot, Ulster's men could have been camped here for days, weeks even, just waiting. Robert cursed. He had no idea how long the river was, but he might have to travel many miles before he found another crossing. He could swim, but Elizabeth couldn't. He could leave her here; let her father's men find her. But then Lord Donough would have no leverage with which to secure Cormac's freedom.

Robert hastened back through the shadows towards the house where he had left Elizabeth. He was almost there when he heard the screams.

12

Elizabeth stood listening to Robert's footsteps on the stairs. When they had faded and all she could hear was the wind moaning through the window and the steady drip of rain through the hole in the roof, she sat heavily on one of the pallet beds. For the last miles, she had ached with every step, but she had tried to keep up with Robert, fearing to anger him lest he abandon her somewhere in the wilderness. She knew he had thought of doing so; had seen it in his eyes. Just as she had seen the lie when he said he would keep his word.

Pushing aside the mouldy blankets, Elizabeth lay down and stared at the broken roof, the ruptured timbers open on to the rain-dark sky. Her skin felt hot and tight, and her head was pounding, but she fought off the weakness that was dragging at her, forced herself to think. What was Robert planning if not to take her with him to Scotland? Would he attempt to exchange her for his brother? Was this why he had kept her at his side all this time? She breathed in deeply, feeling this was right. He had been troubled by his foster-brother's fate throughout the journey; angry at himself for not saving him and at her for ruining the escape.

Elizabeth closed her eyes as she thought of being delivered back to Ballymote; back to face her father and Lord Henry's bed. The thought of her father summoned quick tears that threaded coldly down her cheeks. He must be so worried. She imagined his fury when he discovered she hadn't been abducted, but had run away. She dishonoured him with her actions. But guilt only went so far. Deeper inside Elizabeth was a knot of defiance. She wouldn't let these past weeks of hardship be in vain. She had prayed to God, the night of her betrothal feast, to save her from her fate and He sent her Robert. This ordeal in the wilderness was a trial of faith.

Elizabeth sat up, fighting a wave of dizziness. She would keep to her plan and go to Scotland. There she would enter a convent and, once she had taken the veil, would write to her father and explain herself. Determination fired her limbs. She stood, snatching up the blanket, and made her way downstairs in the gloom. She had seen the sea from the hills that morning. It wasn't far. She could make it to the coast and surely there find a fisherman who would row her across the race?

Elizabeth paused in the doorway, clutching the frame. Rain came down in sheets before her. She shuddered at the thought of that expanse of water. She had heard her father's men speak of the race: the whirlpools that roared and could suck a boat down, the giant creatures that dwelled in the depths, the mountainous waves. She felt sick just to think of it. Maybe she could stay in Ireland – enter a convent here? 'No,' she breathed, pushing herself out into the downpour, wincing at the needles of rain. Her father controlled much of these lands. If she stayed, he would find her.

As she was crossing the street, Elizabeth caught sight of movement between two houses ahead. She froze, thinking it was Robert. Seeing three figures approaching through the rain, she turned and fled back to the house, plunging into the darkness. Breathing hard, she stood stock-still, hearing rough voices. Had they seen her? She inched to the doorway and peered cautiously out. The three men had stopped in the street. One seemed to be looking right at her. Recoiling, Elizabeth dropped the sodden blanket and backed away to the stairs. She climbed them quickly, flinching at every creak. Upstairs, she crossed the slimy boards and crouched behind one of the pallets, her heart thumping.

Dear God, don't let them have seen me.

The voices came again. She strained to listen, but the words were low. There was a splash of feet through a puddle, then nothing for a few moments. Hearing a creak below her, Elizabeth gasped and ducked down, pressing her cheek to the floor. There was a gap beneath the pallet, looking across to the stairs. More creaking sounds followed, coming closer. Suddenly, a man's head appeared in the hole. Elizabeth felt the tight shock of terror grip her as she saw the thick, matted fringe of his cúlán. He was a young man, clad in a woollen tunic and carrying a wicked-looking dagger. When he was all the way up the stairs, she could only see his feet. He was followed by his two companions. The three of them stood there in the cobwebbed gloom.

She began to tremble as the first man walked slowly around the pallets. His shoes were caked with mud. She wanted to slide under the bed, but there was no room. Nowhere to hide. As he appeared behind her, Elizabeth scrabbled to the wall, pressing herself up against it. The young man dropped into a wary half-crouch at the sight of her, the dagger poised in his fist. He had scars on his forearms, his bare skin slick with rain in the half-light. His expression changed from caution to curiosity as he stared at the girl, huddled against the wall. He glanced over at his two companions and spoke.

Elizabeth recognised the language as Gaelic, but understood little. Despite having been born and raised in Ireland, she had never learned to speak the native tongue, hearing only snatches of it outside her father's fortresses and the towns she had lived in, filled with English. Four years ago, the parliament at Dublin passed a law forbidding the English of Ireland to wear Irish clothes, grow their hair in the cúlán, or speak the native language. All her life it had seemed as if the Irish were another race entirely; a barbarous race at that, given to immoral excesses and animal appetites, who lingered always on the borders of her world, a dark and threatening force.

The scarred man spoke again, this time addressing her, his voice rough with question. Elizabeth didn't answer. Her eyes were on his companions, who now joined him at the foot of the pallet. One was a lanky, auburn-haired youth. A smile twisted his mouth as he saw her. The other was an ogre of a man with hunched shoulders and a slack jaw, who had to duck beneath the roof beams. He stared at her with unblinking eyes. He carried a club spiked with rusty nails and was somehow far more disturbing than his smirking comrade.

The scarred young man moved towards her, the dagger in his grip. He made soft, shushing noises as though she were an animal he was trying not to scare. Slowly, he crouched before her and reached out his free hand. She could smell his breath, sour and strong. Elizabeth wanted to fight, but her body wouldn't obey. Instead, she remained frozen against the wall. As he gently took hold of her wrist and coaxed her up, her eyes lingered on the blade in his hand, transfixed by it. Her legs felt like liquid. Her eyes darted, seeking escape, finding none. What would they do with her? The answer came as a sensation way down in the pit of her stomach: a deep, curdling fear.

The man was speaking to her in hushed Gaelic, but she didn't trust the look in his eyes as he led her by the wrist towards the stairs, past his two comrades. The ogre was still staring at her, the club dangling from his fist. He said something, his voice thick and slurred, either from drink or a defect of the tongue. The young man replied, his tone full of scorn. They were almost at the stairs when Elizabeth caught a sudden motion beside her.

The huge man moved quickly, the club rising in his fist. It whistled through the air to strike the scarred man in the side of his face. There was a crunch on impact and the young man flew sideways. Elizabeth landed on top of him, her face inches from his. Through the bloody pulp of his cheek, raked open by the nails, she could see the bone of his jaw. Rolling away, she screamed as the ogre turned on his auburn-haired comrade, who tried to tackle him. The club slammed into the man's head, sending him reeling across one of the pallets. Elizabeth lunged for the stairs. Before she could reach them, a hand grabbed a fistful of her hair.

As Robert raced into the house he could hear crashing and banging on the wooden floor above him. There was a grunt of pain followed by a girl's terrified cry. When he'd first heard the screams his instinct had been to flee, fearing Ulster's men would be alerted. That impulse had vanished as he'd recognised the terror in those cries.

He took the rickety stairs two at a time, sword in hand. The first thing he saw as he came level with the floor was the face of a man, staring at him out of dead, bloodshot eyes, a splintered mass of bone for his right cheek. The second was the great brute pinning Elizabeth on her stomach, one massive hand planted on her back, the other grasping a spiked club. Her face was turned away, but Robert could hear her gasps as the man bore down on her, pressing the breath from her lungs. He wielded the club high, as if about to bring it crashing down on the back of her skull. There were red scratches on his cheeks and his eyes bulged, full of madness. Robert launched himself at him.

The brute was fast, surprisingly so. He veered away, dodging the blow aimed at his neck. With the weight gone from her back, Elizabeth scrabbled to her feet and stumbled to the stairs. She ran down the first few, then turned as Robert lashed out at her attacker. The man tossed his matted fringe out of his eyes and countered, forcing Robert to duck as he swung the club at his head, skimming his scalp by a hair's breadth. While Robert was hunched over, the Irishman kicked him in the stomach. The force propelled him into one of the slanting roof beams, the impact causing him to drop to his knees, his sword striking the floor beside him. Slurring something incoherent, the man lumbered towards him.

Robert was curled over. His stomach felt as though it had been turned into a band of iron, stopping up his breath. As Elizabeth screamed at him to get up, the Irishman turned, distracted. He didn't look where he put his foot down and stepped heavily on the slimy patch where water had been leaking through the hole in the roof. There was a crack as the wood, rotten with months of rain, gave way beneath his weight. He went down suddenly, grunting in surprise as his foot disappeared. It gave Robert the chance he needed. Heaving air through gritted teeth, he pushed himself up. While the man bellowed in rage, struggling to free his foot, Robert swept in.

He shouted as he ran the man through, powering his sword through the thick muscle of the man's throat. The brute dropped his club and gripped the blade with both hands, spewing a gout of blood. His bulging eyes rolled back to the whites as he convulsed, tongue protruding as he gargled around the length of steel that had severed his windpipe. Robert withdrew the sword with a fierce twist and the man collapsed, his huge body twitching as the blood pooled.

Robert crossed to Elizabeth, who was staring at him half in horror, half in relief. 'Go,' he commanded, ushering her down the stairs.

Leaving the three dead men in the room above, they made their way around the broken furniture towards the door, him gripping his sword, her silent and shaking.

Robert stepped out into the street, the rain washing the blood from the blade and cooling his scalp. He turned to face her as she reached the threshold. 'Are you hurt?'

'W . . . what?'

'Did they hurt you?' he demanded, gripping Elizabeth's shoulder, forcing the dazed girl to look at him.

'No,' she breathed. 'No.'

'We need to go. Your father's men are here.'

'My father?' Elizabeth looked hopeful and anguished at once. She opened her mouth to speak, then stopped, her eyes on something behind him.

Robert watched her expression change, saw her face flood with fresh alarm. She shouted his name. As he was turning to see what had startled her, something slammed into his shoulder. He reeled into the doorframe where he hung, breathless, staring at the bloody iron tip of a bolt, which had gone clean through his left shoulder, tearing a red hole through his shirt. A second later he felt the pain; a wrenching, driving agony, the like of which he'd never experienced. He could scarcely get a breath into his lungs so crushing was the force of it. Half turning, the doorframe the only thing holding him up, he saw a figure striding towards him. Through the sickening waves of pain, Robert recognised the man from the barn with the crossbow.

The man paused in the wet. Unhurriedly, he lowered the great bow and drew another quarrel from the slim basket at his hip. As he put his foot in the crossbow's stirrup and pulled back to reload it, Elizabeth screamed another warning.

'Run!' Robert shouted at her. He tried to push her with his free hand, but the pain of moving his arm almost brought him to his knees. '*Run!*'

Elizabeth fled down the street, the man letting her go.

Robert staggered into the house, just as the assailant raised the bow and aimed. There was a mighty thump as the bolt punctured the doorframe where he'd been standing a second before. Robert leaned against the wall inside, sweat and rain streaming down his cheeks. The front of his shirt was dark with blood. Outside, he heard the creak and snap of the crossbow being loaded again. The man would have to come inside to use it. His only chance would be to disarm or kill him as he entered. Robert summoned the last of his strength. Moments later, a shadow darkened the doorway. As the man stepped through, Robert struck, crying out with the agony as the bolt moved deep inside his flesh.

Neatly dodging the blow, the man smacked his sword away with the crossbow. As the blade fell from Robert's grasp, he stumbled into the centre of the room, clutching his shoulder. The man raised the crossbow.

'Who are you?' Robert hissed through his teeth.

The man said nothing. His bearded face, olive-skinned, was hard in the gloom.

As Robert sank to his knees he thought the man must have shot him, but he realised the crossbow bolt was still there, aimed at his chest. His vision darkened. Pain was a raging current, carrying him into oblivion. Slipping back, hardly feeling it as he struck the floor, he heard a distant thrumming of hooves. Death, he thought, riding in to claim him. In the wake of the hooves came shouts. Robert saw the man turn, point his crossbow through the open door and shoot the bolt. He heard a girl's cry, more shouts, then a crashing sound as something heavy hit the ground beside him.

Robert's last thoughts were of his daughter. Marjorie's sweet, smiling face overwhelmed him as the world dimmed.

13

'Turnberry surrendered after two days, my lord. We took all those inside prisoner.'

Humphrey paused in his report, noting that the king hadn't looked up from the table he was seated behind. Edward's brow was creased, his pale eyes glinting in the buttery glow of the lanterns as he scanned the letter he held. The canvas sides of the pavilion undulated in the breeze streaming in through the flaps, carrying sounds of music and laughter.

The king raised his head at Humphrey's silence. 'Go on.'

'Having razed the castle we moved on to Ayr. After he burned the town three years ago to prevent us from securing it as a base, Bruce ordered its reconstruction. Under your son's command we sacked the settlement and destroyed the new fortifications. I can assure you, my lord, that these raids, combined with the slaughter of livestock and burning of crops, mean the people of Carrick will find it hard to sustain themselves through the coming winter.'

'Good,' murmured the king. He was looking at the letter again.

A gust of wind billowed the silk curtains that partitioned the royal pavilion, offering Humphrey a glimpse of the four-poster bed that accompanied Edward wherever he went. It was heaped with pillows and covered with linen coloured red with insect dye. On a cushioned chair close by was Queen Marguerite, her delicately beautiful face profiled above the cloud-soft ermine cloak draped around her shoulders. The garment couldn't quite conceal the swell of her second pregnancy. As Humphrey watched, the queen leaned forward and moved a rook made of crystal across the chessboard in front of her. One of her maids, seated opposite, countered the move with a jasper pawn. Through another set of curtains came a wailing cry as Edward's infant son, Thomas, woke for a feed from his wet nurse.

Humphrey's gaze switched back to the king. 'Have you had any word on Robert Bruce's whereabouts, my lord?'

At the question, the king looked up abruptly, his eyes at once focused. He set down the letter. As he did so, Humphrey saw the seal of the King of France attached to the bottom.

'I was hoping you might be able to shed more light on his location, having spent the past month in his earldom.'

Humphrey was accustomed to hearing the steely displeasure in the king's tone, but was still unused to the acute discomfort a man could feel when it was levelled at him. 'I questioned the Constable of Turnberry at length, my lord, but he swore he had no idea where Robert had gone, only that he left Carrick over a year ago.'

'You believe him?'

'We have no real way of knowing.' As the king's gaze bored into him, Humphrey added, 'But I cannot imagine he will remain hidden for ever. Sooner or later, Bruce will surface, of that I am certain.'

Something thoughtful, almost knowing passed across the king's face. 'Perhaps.' He waved away a page who came to refill his goblet. 'And what of my son's performance? How did he fare with his first command?'

At once, Humphrey understood why he was giving the account rather than young Edward himself. They had arrived at Lochmaben earlier that afternoon, but except to glean the bare facts of the campaign, the king hadn't requested a full report until now. 'He maintained good order, my lord,' Humphrey began carefully. 'The siege of Turnberry and the sack of Ayr were efficiently conducted. Our men sustained few injuries and there were no fatalities. We lost only five horses on the entire campaign.'

'Interesting,' said the king, lacing his long fingers beneath his chin. One of the rings he wore caught the lantern light, the ruby at its centre flashing. 'My nephew gives a different report.'

Humphrey's discomfort increased as he saw the trap he'd been caught in. He had no idea the king had already spoken to Thomas of Lancaster. He cursed himself for being so inattentive. A man did not do well to drop his guard under Edward Longshanks.

'Thomas tells me if it wasn't for you, Turnberry would not have been captured at all. He said my son was more interested in cavorting with his friends than in making war on my enemies.'

'He needed direction, my lord, that is all. Sir Thomas is not fond of Piers Gaveston. I fear his judgement in this matter may be coloured by that dislike.'

Edward took up his goblet, running a finger around the base. 'Was I right, Humphrey, to make my son Prince of Wales? My hope was that in rewarding him with such an honour he would grow to befit that mould.'

Humphrey was struck by how old the king looked, his jaw sagging beneath the frost-white trim of his beard, his skin tinged grey with fatigue. He thought of England under his son and felt a stirring of unease. It was up to men like him to help mould Prince Edward into the man needed to fill his father's place. 'Yes, my lord,' he said determinedly. 'I believe your son is ready for such authority.'

But the king was staring at the letter again.

'Word from France?' Humphrey ventured.

'While you were in Carrick I received tidings from my spies there that John Balliol had been released from papal custody on the orders of King Philippe.' Edward held out the parchment for Humphrey to take. 'This came last week, delivered from Westminster. My cousin recommends I make a truce with the Scots as a first step towards Balliol's restoration.' The king's ire stripped years from him, adding colour to his cheeks and vigour to his posture. 'It is clear that, should I refuse, there will be no treaty with France and Philippe will continue to occupy my duchy of Gascony.'

'What will you do, my lord?' asked Humphrey, glancing up from the parchment, his mind clouding with the prospects of this twist of events. 'Another war cannot be an option, surely?'

Edward looked at him sharply. 'The struggle for Gascony stripped me of my money and the support of my men – even your father and others of the Round Table stood against me.' His tone was flint. 'So, no, another war is not an option. Not yet at least. But neither will I allow Balliol to return to the throne. My plan is to offer the Scots a temporary truce, as Philippe requests. I did not intend to campaign through the winter so such agreement will not affect my plans. What it will do is buy me time. There will be a way through this – without war, without the loss of Gascony and without the return of that snake, John Balliol. I have the winter to find the answer.' The king rose. Even with the slight stoop in his broad shoulders, he towered over Humphrey. 'We will speak more of this matter in council tomorrow. For tonight, we celebrate. Go, join my daughter, Humphrey. France will wait a day.'

With a bow, Humphrey left the royal pavilion. Ducking through the flaps, past guards standing sentry, he strode into the chilly evening where scores

of campfires illuminated the compound. The king's newly built fortifications at Lochmaben — which he had retired to after a victory in the north
with the fall of Bothwell Castle — were ringed by earthen ramparts topped
with a palisade. Lookout platforms had been erected either side of the main
gates and the shadows of sentries moved against the sky. The compound
was dominated by a timber fort that rose like a tall ship above a sea of tents.
The place was alive with music and conversation. Men crowded the spaces
between tents, carts and horses, gathering around fires to share wine and
ale. Smells of meat rose from cooking pots, summoning in Humphrey an
ache of hunger.

He caught a glimpse of the king's son, in whose honour the celebrations
were being held. The newly titled Prince of Wales was standing with Piers
Gaveston, watching two bare-chested men wrestle. One of the combatants
had a bloody nose, the other a split lip. Gleaming with sweat, they circled
one another, before coming in to lock in a fist-pummelled embrace. Prince
Edward, resplendent in a mantle of gold, turned as Piers passed him a wine
skin. The Gascon leaned in as he took it and whispered something in his ear.
Humphrey saw the prince smile, his face flushed in the torchlight.

'Sir Humphrey!'

He turned to see Ralph de Monthermer.

The royal knight lifted a goblet in greeting. His yellow mantle, decorated
with a green eagle, shimmered. 'Come. Join us!'

Humphrey caught sight of Aymer de Valence and Henry Percy in the
throng. No doubt the other barons would be close by, but he had somewhere more inviting to be than with the men of the Round Table. 'In a
while,' he called to the knight, who shrugged amiably.

Humphrey headed on through the crowds towards the timber fort, side-
stepping a drunken soldier, who fell into one of the tents which collapsed
beneath him, raising a cheer from his companions. Others reeled about,
arms slung around one another's shoulders. The festivities might be for
their new prince, but all the men here were celebrating their own triumphs
at the end of a campaign that had seen the fall of three mighty castles and
the burning of the west; a campaign that had scarcely been challenged by
the Scots. The rebels, it seemed, had lost the will to fight. One more
summer like this and the English would wrest control of Stirling Castle,
fallen to the enemy last year, then the north of Scotland would be open to
them. If, that was, King Philippe's demand didn't stop them in their tracks.

They had been at war with Scotland for five years and had suffered terrible losses as well as victories in that time. Humphrey thought of all the coin

diverted from England to fund the king's cause, all the months spent away from their estates and families, all the lives wasted on the blades of swords, his father's among them. His hunger pangs and eagerness to see Bess faded with the ache of that loss. Three years since Falkirk and he still saw that moment as if it were yesterday: his father's horse up to its neck in a bog, the earl slipping from the saddle, lanced by a Scottish spear, to be claimed by the mud. Determination rose in Humphrey like a slow, prickling heat. He would do whatever was necessary to help Edward prevent John Balliol returning to the throne and the Scots reclaiming their kingdom. If they allowed that to happen such sacrifices would mean nothing. He couldn't live with that prospect.

Nodding to the men who guarded the entrance to the fort, where the prisoners and plunder they had conveyed from Turnberry were being housed, Humphrey climbed the external stairs that led up to the battlements. The fort was the first stage of the king's fortifications, which he planned to turn into a fortress of stone using material gathered from Lochmaben's old castle, destroyed in their last campaign. Once on the battlements, Humphrey had an extensive view across the surrounding land. The compound was built on a promontory that jutted into the waters of a loch. A flock of birds flew low across the surface, their reflections gliding beneath them. On the landward side, woods stretched north towards the ruins of the old castle, former home of the Bruce family. Its keep was a broken tooth of stone rising from a motte, visible against the purple, cloud-stippled sky.

Ahead on the walkway, looking out over the loch, was a young woman dressed in a silvery-blue gown. A padded net scattered with pearls covered her hair. Humphrey smiled as he saw her, his spirits lifting.

Bess turned. 'You're late.'

'I was with your father.' Humphrey halted a few inches from her, wanting to kiss her, but aware of the guards on the battlements behind them. He was Constable of England, she was the king's daughter. There was decorum to be observed.

Bess didn't share his compunction. Bridging the gap between them, she looped her arms around his neck. Like all of Edward's children she was tall, almost as tall as Humphrey. She only had to tilt her head back to meet his eyes. 'You are forgiven.'

Bess gave him a breath-soft kiss. The sentries forgotten, Humphrey pulled her to him, opening his mouth over hers. She responded and for some moments the two of them were lost in their own dark world of breath and desire. Humphrey drew back and looked into her eyes, which were a

pale grey, ringed with violet. Queen Eleanor had left a Castilian legacy in
her beautiful, black-haired daughter. He smiled at her, but the release from
the kiss had allowed his mind to wander back to the king's revelation.

Bess touched his cheek. 'A cloud just passed across your face. What is it,
my love?'

'John Balliol has been freed.' Humphrey paced the battlements, Bess falling into step beside him. They headed round the fort to the landward side,
where the woods spread into a wind-tossed darkness. 'The King of France
is threatening to withhold Gascony unless your father agrees to a truce with
Scotland.'

Bess nodded. 'I heard my father talking to Bishop Bek.' As Humphrey
halted, she leaned against the battlements beside him. 'He believes Balliol's
transfer to France, agreed in the treaty, means Philippe was planning this all
along. Now the war is over, it appears the French king favours a return to
his old alliance with Scotland, flanking my father on two fronts.'

Humphrey was sometimes surprised by the ease with which she discussed
political matters, given her youth. At nineteen Bess was six years younger
than he was, the same age as her father's new wife. He had wondered if
she'd become accustomed to such talk in the hall of her first husband, the
Count of Holland, but they had been married only a short time before he
left her a widow. 'Philippe cannot be allowed to hold your father to ransom.'

'But if my father refuses, he stands to lose permanently a duchy he spent
years fighting to secure – a duchy that comprises some of his richest lands.'

'And if Balliol returns all will have been for nothing.' Humphrey's face
tightened, the memory of his father lingering at the edges of his mind. 'Our
sacrifices have been many, but we pay the high price for victory. We must.
For only united, one kingdom under one king, will Britain be saved. We
will make them see that. All of them.'

Bess studied his taut expression. 'Do you not want an end to the war,
Humphrey? An end to the campaigns and the bloodshed?' When he didn't
answer, she sighed and looked out over the crowds of men drinking and
revelling below. 'Perhaps a truce will be the best course.'

He looked at her sharply. 'You don't know what you're saying.'

Her grey eyes flashed, something of her father's steel within them. 'I am
the king's daughter, Humphrey. I know as well as most of those drunken
sots down there the price of war. My childhood was spent with my father
always on campaign. I was moved with my sisters from one castle to the
next, never knowing if he would come home again, seeing the pain it caused
my mother when she wasn't with him and feeling the same pain whenever

she was. She rarely left his side. I grew to girlhood with her absences, knowing that his desire for victory and her desire for him were greater than their
love for me. Don't tell me I do not know.'

He touched her shoulder. 'Bess, I'm tired and these tidings weigh heavy
on me. Things will be clearer tomorrow, after the—' Humphrey stopped,
his gaze caught by scores of tiny points of fire winking into life on the edges
of the trees beyond the palisade.

As he watched, they flew into the air as one, arcing silently, gracefully up
and over like comets. They came to earth quickly, stabbing down around
the compound. Several struck tents, others stuck fast in the ground, or
skidded along it trailing traces of fire. Some found human targets, plunging
into chests and backs. Screams of pain rose above the music.

Grabbing Bess's hand, Humphrey hauled her along the walkway towards
the steps that led down the outside of the fort. The guards up here were
running, shouting instructions to one another and those below, as beyond
the palisade another crescent of lights winked into being. One man began
pulling the cord of the bell mounted on the fort's battlements. A loud
clanging smote the air above the chaos breaking out across the compound
as the flaming arrows rained down. Several struck horses, one of which
reared with a squeal, breaking its tethers. The fiery barb protruding from
its side, the beast galloped madly through the crowd, knocking down men
as they ran for cover. As more missiles caught in the sides of tents fires
began to bloom, fanned by the wind.

Humphrey was halfway down the steps when the third wave of arrows
came. He shielded Bess with his body as they thumped into the timber fort
around them. When the thuds ceased, they raced down the last few stairs,
Bess holding up her skirts. Once on the ground, he steered her into the
entrance of the fort, where two guards were watching the turmoil unfold-
ing before them, swords drawn against an invisible enemy.

'Stay here,' he told Bess, who nodded, her face pale. 'Guard her with your
lives,' he ordered the men.

'Keep safe!' she urged, grabbing his arm briefly.

Humphrey hastened towards the royal pavilion, past grooms racing to
put out fires springing up in sheaves of hay. For every little patch of flame
they extinguished another sprang up somewhere else. The air was full of
smoke and the bell's mad clanging. Humphrey saw one of the bare-chested
wrestlers lying on his back in the dust, an arrow in his face. The sky filled
with lights as another hail came in. 'Wait!' Humphrey roared at the men
racing around him. 'Watch the sky!'

Only a few listened, following his lead as he dived behind a cart loaded with barrels. An infantryman, tankard still in hand, was forced to his knees, his back arching as an arrow punched into his shoulder. The man yelled, grasping at the shaft.

'Help him,' Humphrey instructed a squire, before pushing himself to his feet.

The king was outside his pavilion, barking orders to the men around him, whose number swelled as more converged on his position. Humphrey saw Ralph, Henry and Aymer among them. He approached to hear one of the guards from the gate's lookout platform yelling down to the king. He and his comrades were crouched behind the palisade.

'*There are men in the woods, sire! A hundred or more!*'

'Saddle Bayard,' snapped Edward, turning to his squire. His grim face was lit by the glow of the fires. 'Where is my son?'

'Here, Father!' Prince Edward came sprinting towards the king, Piers at his side. The Gascon had a shield strapped to his arm. An arrow was embedded in it, the flames flickering around the painted wood.

'We ride out and take these churls!' the king shouted to the knights gathered around him. 'Mount your horses!'

Humphrey pushed through the jostle of men, spotting Hugh, his squire, and several of his knights.

Hugh had already saddled Storm and was holding his sword. The squire's face filled with relief as he saw him coming. 'Sir.' He held out the weapon. 'Shall I fetch your mail?'

'No time,' said Humphrey, taking the naked blade and sliding it through the loop attached to his belt. 'Just my gambeson and helm. Mount up,' he said in the same breath to the rest of his knights, as Hugh ducked inside the tent.

His squire reappeared, holding his gambeson. Shrugging off his cloak, Humphrey pulled on the quilted tunic, which was padded with felt. It was still damp with sweat from the day's ride. Donning the padded coif Hugh handed to him, Humphrey pulled on his great helm, decorated with the plume of swan feathers. Storm was stamping, agitated by the flames and commotion, but he calmed as Humphrey mounted and took up the reins. Around him, the knights of his household hauled themselves into their saddles.

King Edward was already astride his charger, Bayard, as Humphrey led his company to join him. Together, the king, his son and several hundred knights and sergeants rode towards the gates. More arrows poured down, most landing some distance behind them, where flames were spreading among the tightly packed tents. Part of the fort was burning, smoke billowing into the sky. Through the slits of his helm, Humphrey's vision was channelled into a narrow world of smoke and fire. He glimpsed the bright crests and mantles that marked his companions, all in faceless helms. He feared for Bess, but he could only hope the guards would protect her. The guards were hauling open the massive timber gates.

Beyond, between the backs and rumps of comrades and horses, Humphrey saw a fringe of trees stretching into darkness. More fires sprang to life in the shadows, illuminating the outlines of men among the trunks.

'Ride! Ride!'

At the king's roar, Humphrey drew his sword and jabbed his heels into Storm's sides. The destrier lurched forward at the same time as the others around him, all of them moving swiftly from trot into ground-shuddering canter. He let out a furious war cry, the sound echoing around the steel chamber of his helm. Others took up the shout, urging their steeds into a gallop. As the king and his men poured out of the gates flaming arrows lanced towards them from the trees.

Humphrey saw one horse wheel madly, struck in the head. Pitching its rider from the saddle, it crashed into another, sending charger and knight sprawling. Flailing limbs and hooves disappeared as those behind rode on over them. Humphrey saw a flash of fire, coming straight at him and jerked out of the way. The arrow shot past, but the sudden movement caused him to wrench on the reins, jamming the bit painfully in Storm's mouth. The horse stumbled, knocking against Henry Percy's charger. Humphrey recovered quickly as Percy veered sharply away. Ahead, the trees loomed up quickly.

Men were moving beneath the boughs. Some turned and ran as the knights charged them. Others stood their ground, reloading their bows and aiming at the horses. Humphrey saw the king kick Bayard up and over a clump of briars, his broadsword flashing in his hand as he came crashing down on the other side to smash the blade into the neck of an archer who had shot at him a second earlier. A spray of blood splattered the trees behind as the archer, head sagging back on his shoulders, crumpled to the ground.

Humphrey fixed on two men sprinting away ahead of him. They carried bows and were wearing green tunics and hose, the sort of clothing a man would don for a hunt. Blood hot in his veins, he pursued, ducking low branches, hearing the cracks as twigs lashed across his helm, dimly feeling the impacts against his shoulders and knees. Raising his sword as he rode up behind one man, Humphrey brought it swinging down in a brutal diagonal cut as he passed. The man fell with a gurgling scream, a wide red gash opening across his chest.

Humphrey slowed Storm, looking around for the other man, his vision hampered by the helm. He spotted Aymer de Valence riding in to his left, going after the quarry. Roaring savagely, the king's cousin leaned far out in the saddle to plunge the point of his sword through the back of the man's neck. Screams rent the air as the knights found more targets. Humphrey urged Storm on, but the trees, which quickly became more densely packed, soon forced him into a walk. The rest of the enemy archers had fled deep into the woods, where the knights on their cumbersome chargers could not follow.

A horn blew, summoning the scattered knights back to the king, who had ridden Bayard out on to the fringes of the trees. The night sky was amber with the fires billowing beyond the palisade. The fort was alight, flames racing up the sides of the timber structure. Sparks crackled into the air, like hundreds of glowing insects. Shouts echoed as men struggled to contain and extinguish the blaze. Humphrey wrenched off his helm, praying the guards had taken Bess to safety.

'It was John Comyn's forces,' shouted Aymer de Valence, ducking as he rode out under the low-hanging branches of a pine. 'There were others further back in the trees, on palfreys and coursers. I knew my brother-in-law by his colours, but he fled before I could reach him.'

'Do we follow, sire?' questioned Ralph de Monthermer, trying to calm his skittish mount. 'My lord king?' he called, when Edward gave no response. 'Shall we pursue them?'

Humphrey looked over at the king, who had pushed up the visor of his helm. He was staring at his burning fortress, his face thunderous in the hellish glow.

14

John Comyn urged his sweat-soaked palfrey up the last few yards of the wooded slope, the trees around him swaying in the rushing dark. As he crested the bald crown of the hill, he saw the sky was dusted with stars. Their phantom light shone coldly on the helms of those men who crowded the hilltop. More were appearing through the trees every minute, some riding, others on foot, panting with the effort of the climb. Several were wounded. One man, his face contorted with pain, was being dragged into the clearing by two comrades, a jagged cut across his forehead streaming blood down his cheeks.

Hauling his horse to a stamping halt, Comyn pulled off his helm and coif, breathing hard. His dark hair, recently cropped short, was plastered to his head, making his lean face appear even more gaunt. The blazon on his black surcoat – three white sheaves of wheat on a red shield, the arms of the Red Comyns – was mirrored in the trapper of his horse. Sweat prickled on his skin, the salt taste of it mixing with the metal of his ventail, which he unhooked and pulled from his jaw. Seeing his squire, Comyn tossed his helm to him, then slid from the saddle, his muscles aching. 'Dungal!' he called sharply, seeing a familiar face in the crowd.

Dungal MacDouall, former captain of the army of Galloway, forced his way through the press. His hard, humourless face was bone white in the starlight, matching the lion on his surcoat.

'Did they follow?' Comyn asked, as they met in the milling throng.

'Not for long. Their horses were too large to make it far through the trees. I heard the king's horn summon them back.'

Comyn nodded grimly. 'I imagine they had more pressing things to concern themselves with. The fires spread quicker than I could have hoped.'

'Their new fort will be ashes come dawn,' agreed Dungal, satisfaction in his eyes.

Catching sight of the tall figure of his father, Comyn strode over, sprays of pine cones crunching beneath his boots.

The Lord of Badenoch was talking to his cousin, the Earl of Buchan and head of the Black Comyns. An imposing, well-built man, Buchan had the same long face and dark eyes as Comyn's father. He carried his great helm under his arm, his surcoat billowing in the wind. Three sheaves of wheat decorated the garment, this time embroidered on a black shield. Between them, the two cousins ruled the dominant branches of the Comyn family, whose power and authority ranged across the kingdom from the glens of the Borders to the mountains and plains of the north-east. Standing with them were Ingram de Umfraville, a kinsman of John Balliol, and Robert Wishart, Bishop of Glasgow.

'We lost twenty men at most, your grace. All in all it was a success.'

'Success or no, the loss of life is to be mourned, Sir John.' Wishart's squat, bulky body lent him a bullish stance.

'And your prayers will benefit our dead, as our arrows benefited the living. After a summer of loss our people needed a victory. We have provided them with one.'

'But we must do more,' said Comyn, approaching. As the men turned, he noticed how drained his father looked, his skin blanched by a malady that had afflicted him for some weeks. The assault on Lochmaben appeared to have sapped the last of his vigour, although his voice seemed unaffected, abrasive as ever.

'Your plan worked better than I could have expected, my son. You are to be commended.'

'Thank you, Father,' replied Comyn stiffly. 'Still, I would have liked to see their camp destroyed completely. King Edward will be able to rebuild what we burned tonight.'

'That rebuilding will hamper his plans for any new campaign. Lochmaben was the main stronghold from which he would have launched more attacks. Now he'll be forced to concentrate his limited resources on reconstruction.'

Ingram de Umfraville cut keenly into the conversation. 'Indeed. It will buy us time in which to gather more men and train them for—'

'We have gathered enough soldiers.' Comyn saw Umfraville's face tighten at the interruption, but he didn't care. The man had recently been elected as a third guardian of Scotland and with himself and William Lamberton now made a triumvirate. For Comyn, it had been galling enough that the nobles felt it necessary to select yet another man for the high position. He was adamant Umfraville would not take away any of the authority he had gained over the past two years. 'We need to employ our strength.'

'What do you suggest? A raid on England?'

At the forceful question, Comyn turned to see John of Atholl. The earl's strong-boned features were sharply contoured in the starlight, his curly hair slick with sweat. With him walked his son, David, a younger reflection of him, and Neil Campbell, a knight from Argyll, one of William Wallace's staunchest supporters. Comyn felt a needle of dislike at the sight of the earl, who kept his intense gaze on him as he approached. He noticed that some of the men close by had heard Atholl's question and were looking at him expectantly, waiting for his answer.

'Perhaps,' Comyn replied defensively. 'We have the men.'

'Men we have,' agreed Atholl, halting before him. 'What we lack are generals.'

Before Comyn could respond his father spoke. 'Your contempt is unwarranted, Atholl. My son has just led us to our first victory this year. Can you claim such honour?'

'With respect, the victory was small and comes too late. I have been calling for us to take action all summer, but my words fell on deaf ears. We allowed the English to ravage the west and take castles, without contest.'

Bishop Wishart's brow puckered. 'Sir John—' he began.

Atholl ignored him, raising his voice as other men around them quietened to listen. 'Edward and his army were given free rein, leaving our people to his mercy. You can be sure he has shown none. We have all heard of towns and villages being put to the torch, men butchered, women despoiled, their children maimed. The English king has a hide of leather. What we have done tonight has stung him only.' The earl punched his fist into his palm. 'We need to pierce him!'

Comyn heard the mutters of agreement. Atholl's son, David, was staring at his father, pride naked in his face. Comyn's dislike swelled to rancour. For months, Atholl had been a thorn in his side, questioning his every decision. What was more, the man's continued support for Robert Bruce was flagrant, keeping Comyn's hated rival a palpable presence among their company, despite the fact the whoreson seemed to have vanished off the face of the earth since resigning the guardianship. Comyn dearly wanted to eject Atholl from their company, hoping that in doing so he would exorcise the last of Bruce's influence in Scotland, but Atholl commanded the support of a large number of men, whose force of arms the beleaguered rebel host relied upon.

'I say we do not give Longshanks pause,' Atholl continued. 'Caution has become our enemy. Aggression should be our ally. Let us mount a raid into England while the king and his men are still licking their wounds!'

As the mutters became calls of unison, Comyn and his father both tried to speak, but the men, fired by the night's triumph and by John of Atholl's belligerent speech, shouted over them.

'We should summon William Wallace home!' cried one, brandishing his spear. 'Have him lead us to victory against the English dogs!'

Comyn's anger boiled over. 'Wallace?' he spat contemptuously. 'He resigned as guardian precisely *because* of his inept leadership. Falkirk cost the lives of ten thousand Scots!'

As the clearing erupted in a storm of protest, Comyn realised his mistake. William Wallace may have been gone from their midst for three years, but the rebel leader still cast a long shadow. That his had been the first blade raised against the English, his savage triumph at Stirling, his ferocity on the battlefield, even his exploits as an outlaw in the early days of the insurrection: all lived on in the minds of the insurgents, in spite of his defeat at Falkirk. It riled Comyn that a man like Wallace, a second son from a modest family, managed to command more respect in his absence than he himself had won in two years as their guardian. In the tumult of voices that rose to harangue him, he saw John of Atholl staring at him, satisfaction plain in his face.

'The failure of Falkirk was not Wallace's,' Neil Campbell injected fiercely. 'But that of the nobles who left the field without striking a blow, led by the Lord of Badenoch!'

Comyn's father and the Earl of Buchan stepped forward at the Argyll knight's insult to their family's honour. Spitting an oath, Comyn gripped the hilt of his sword.

'*Peace!*'

The strident voice blasted across them. The crowd silenced, shifting to allow a short, wiry man dressed in black robes through. William Lamberton, Bishop of St Andrews, had blood on his hands, a result of administering prayers to the wounded and last rites to the dying. His face was implacable, his strange eyes – one ice-blue, the other as white as a pearl – burning coldly. He came to stand between Neil Campbell and Comyn, who had drawn his sword part way from its scabbard. 'How swiftly we go from fighting the English to fighting each other. When will we learn that strength comes from unity, not division?' His voice held all the passion of one of his fiery sermons. 'We had a victory tonight, Sir John,' he said, turning to Atholl. 'Do not forget that in your haste for the next. Come.' He motioned to the earl. 'Shake the hand of the man who gave us that victory. Your countryman.'

Atholl's jaw pulsed with reluctance, but under Lamberton's unyielding gaze he stepped forward, extending a stiff hand.

Comyn stared at the earl for a long moment, before shoving his sword forcefully into its scabbard. The two men grasped hands briefly, eyes locked, before stepping back.

Lamberton looked around at the others, all of them tense and uncertain. 'The destruction of Lochmaben has bought us some time, in which we can plan our next move. Wisely,' he added to Atholl. 'John Balliol's restoration is far from set. Bishop Wishart and I have sent word to Paris to ascertain what our king will need in order to return to the throne. Let us wait for his response before making rash decisions. The outcome may well change the direction of this war.'

Wishart and others were nodding, but Comyn noticed that Atholl looked pensive, as if the news wasn't at all welcome to him. It was strange to see they might have something in common.

As the gathering began to disperse — John of Atholl moving off with Neil Campbell, Wishart turning to talk to the Lord of Badenoch — Comyn headed to where he had left his horse and gear, ignoring the calls of some of his men. There were still a few stragglers making their way up the hill, but most had reached the clearing now and had fanned out to rest and tend their horses before the Scottish host prepared to move deeper into the Forest, making for the safety of their base. Comyn passed a company of archers huddled in a group, counting arrows. Hardy men from Selkirk Forest, they had been trained by William Wallace when he was sole guardian of the kingdom.

Wallace. Balliol.

Since word of the king's impending return had spread like wildfire through the ranks, those two names had begun to haunt him. In the absence of the former rebel leader and dispossessed king, he, John Comyn, had become virtual ruler of Scotland, a position he had cultivated with the support of his family. Now, even his ambitious father was talking with eagerness of the restoration of his brother-in-law, the king. The Comyns, he had always said, worked best behind the throne. *The king is an instrument, we are the musicians.* But Comyn liked the light that had bathed him in this position and did not want to step back into another man's shadow.

He paused on the edges of the trees where the land fell away into darkness. Several miles to the south, he made out the amber glow of fire over Lochmaben. As the face of John Balliol filled his mind, Comyn felt a surge of anger. His uncle had been a weak king who refused to stand up to Edward's demands, leaving nobles like his father to take control of the kingdom and rise against the English. Balliol had fled the battlefield during Edward's first invasion and had spent weeks on the run, before surrendering. He had stood there, as meek as a lamb, allowing the great seal of Scotland to be broken and the royal arms to be ripped from his tabard. Had these men, all so hopeful for his return, forgotten this? His father saw the limits of Comyn ambition as being the control of the throne and had never once mentioned the fact that he himself had a claim to it.

It was a fact his son had not forgotten.

15

His dreams were strange worlds of fire and ice. In them, he was pursued by a shadowy figure whose face he could never quite see. Often he was trapped, sometimes in the halls and passages of a castle he did not recognise, or else out in the open, but on his back, soaked to the skin, held down by invisible hands. Always, the figure found him. The crossbow would rise and pain would follow; the agonising violation of flesh as the iron tip punctured skin and the bolt was driven through tissue and sinew, vein and muscle. Tearing. Searing.

Sometimes he cried out, but his voice never sounded like his own. He tried to wake, to break the dream, but every time he surfaced pain would be waiting for him, a malignant beast that sank its teeth in deep, sending him fleeing back into the darkness.

Robert.

His name was a new sound in the black, familiar but unexpected, like a friend he hadn't seen for years. He stirred and glided towards it.

'Robert.'

Behind his eyes, he sensed a soft glow. Pain bared its teeth, but he pushed on, struggling towards the source of his name. That voice; he knew it belonged to someone he desperately wanted to see. The glow transformed itself from nebulous amber into the definite outlines of a bedpost, the edge of a table and a distant door, all bathed in candlelight. Someone moved into view. Panic seized him at the sight of the hand rising towards him. He tried to sit up, but the beast in his shoulder woke and howled, almost sending him reeling back into oblivion.

'Don't try to move.'

That familiarity again. Gritting his teeth against the waves of pain, he opened his eyes. The face of a man swam before him, then slowly came into focus. It was James Stewart, the High Steward of Scotland.

Robert tried to speak, but all that came out was a surprised croak.

'Here,' said James, taking a cloth and goblet from the table. When he dipped the material into the vessel it came out red. 'Wine and honey,' explained the older man, squeezing the sodden end over Robert's mouth.

The taste was a sweet shock. He swallowed, feeling the sting in his parched throat. 'James?' he murmured. 'Where am I?'

'Dunluce Castle.'

Robert went to sit up again at the name. Dunluce was one of the Earl of Ulster's strongholds, an imposing cliff-top fortress that dominated the northern coastline of Ireland. Sweat broke out coldly on his skin. 'How did I get here?'

James moved in to help, pushing pillows behind his back to support him. 'What do you remember?'

The steward was frowning as he sat back in the chair Robert now saw was placed by the bed. From his slightly elevated position, he could also see two men standing just beyond the sphere of candlelight, to either side of the door. The red bands of cloth around their upper arms and the cross-guards of their swords were the brightest things about them.

'I . . .' Robert trailed off. 'I'm not sure.' He glanced down, seeing a square of material placed over his left shoulder, held in place by bands of cloth that felt tight across his back. It was brown with dried blood. He could smell something bitter. Herbs perhaps? The bare skin of his arm and chest was livid. He remembered the rain and the blood on his blade. He remembered the man and the crossbow rising. 'I was attacked. But I cannot tell you by whom. Or when, or how I came to be here.'

'Some of those answers I can give you. Earl Richard's men brought you here four days ago. They tell me you almost died on the journey.' James's tone was grave. 'Sir Richard's physician saved your life. When I arrived the day before yesterday, he told me your wound was starting to heal. He believes he was able to remove the bolt without causing further damage and is confident you will be able to use the muscles again, given time.'

Robert felt his throat tighten; constricted by relief. The steward was studying him. His face, usually so composed, appeared grim. A host of questions rose in Robert, welling through his exhaustion and confusion. 'My daughter?' he said suddenly.

'Marjorie is still in Scotland, with my wife. She is well.'

Robert let out a breath of gratitude. 'And my men? My brothers? We were attacked in the south by Ulster's knights. I haven't seen them in . . .' He shook his head. 'It must be months.'

'Niall and Edward came to me at Kyle Stewart. They told me what happened. I crossed the race as soon as I could. It didn't take long to discover my brother-in-law was holding you prisoner at Ballymote. I was in the process of trying to secure your release when it emerged that you had escaped, with his daughter.'

Robert's gladness at the news of his brothers' safety was replaced by concern. He sat up, grimacing. 'Elizabeth, is she . . .?'

'My niece is unharmed.' James's tone roughened. 'Ulster's men heard screams and were searching for the source. Elizabeth alerted them to your attacker. Sir Richard's knights killed the man when he turned his crossbow on them.'

'He is dead?' Robert swore and collapsed back against the pillows. 'I don't even know who he was. Or why he tried to kill me.'

James didn't seem to have heard. 'What in God's name were you thinking? Dragging Elizabeth across Ireland? She could have been killed!' The high steward, whose calm in the face of all storms was one of the traits Robert admired most about him and whose poise as a politician had defined his role as one of the first guardians of Scotland after Alexander's death, stood and began to pace.

'I didn't drag her, James, she wanted to run.'

'You think that excuses it?'

'Does Sir Richard know I didn't abduct her?'

'Elizabeth told her father why she ran,' said James after a moment, his voice losing some of its force. 'She said you weren't to blame. I cannot say my brother-in-law agrees,' he added grimly.

'I thought, if Lord Donough delivered her back to Ballymote, I would be able to secure Cormac's release.' Robert met James's gaze. 'Ulster is here at Dunluce? Has he said anything about my brother?'

'Through my mediation Lord Donough has agreed to pay Sir Richard a tribute for his son's pardon. Cormac is on his way back to Glenarm.'

Robert let relief wash through him.

'Your actions have seriously compromised Sir Richard's position,' James continued into his silence. 'The marriage he arranged for Elizabeth has been called off. Her bridegroom deemed her to be sullied. You are going to have to face the consequences of this, Robert.' The steward frowned. 'Do you hear me?'

Robert wasn't listening. He still had one pressing question. After the unexpected good fortune he had been granted, this one was heavy with hope. 'I need to speak to you alone,' he said, his eyes moving to the two guards by the door.

James looked round at them and nodded. The men hesitated, but after a moment turned and left.

When the door closed, Robert's gaze shifted back to the steward. 'Did Niall bring a staff to you at Kyle Stewart?' When James answered, Robert couldn't help the smile that cracked his dry lips. He closed his eyes in prayer. It was worth it – forsaking his place as a guardian, leaving his daughter and men, the hunt for the relic, his capture and escape – it was all worth it. 'I did what I set out to do, James. What I told you I would do when I resigned after the council at Peebles. I found what King Edward needs to complete the prophecy. The Staff of Malachy is the key to Scotland's freedom.' The steward was shaking his head, but Robert ignored this, taking it for doubt. 'We can bargain for new terms. Terms that may grant us our liberty.'

'Cease, Robert,' murmured James.

'We might compel him to return the Stone of Destiny for a coronation.' Robert paused. 'My coronation.'

'I said cease!'

At the command, Robert fell silent. He frowned at the steward; at the lines of worry that creased his face, at the defeat in his brown eyes.

'Things have changed in your absence,' began James. His voice was quiet now. 'King Edward launched a campaign in the summer. A campaign that targeted your lands. While he continued work on his new fortifications at Lochmaben in place of your grandfather's hall, his son led a force into Carrick. Crops, cattle, whole settlements were put to the torch. Turnberry has fallen and Ayr has been razed.'

'Dear God.' Robert thought of his earldom, his home in flames.

'That is not the worst of it. Shortly before I came here, I heard that John Balliol has been released from papal custody. The King of France is set to help him return to the throne.'

Robert pushed himself upright, pain needling him. 'He cannot. Edward wouldn't allow Balliol to set foot in Scotland!'

'He may have no choice. Philippe is still in possession of Gascony, which Edward desperately wants back. There is great confidence in Scotland, Robert, that Balliol will soon be coming home. If he does, you and your family will no longer have a place there. Neither will your estates here in

Ireland, or England offer safe haven. Not with your current allegiance to the Scottish cause.'

As the words sank in, Robert thought fleetingly of Norway, where his older sister, Isabel, was queen, but he dismissed the prospect immediately. He would not run and hide under her skirts.

James got slowly to his feet. 'The only thing you can do is ally yourself with the one man who will do everything in his power to prevent Balliol from recovering his throne. The one man who can offer you sanctuary until such time as, God willing, this storm has passed.'

The reality of what James was saying seeped through Robert as an icy tide. 'You cannot mean what I think.'

'You must submit to King Edward. Ally yourself with the enemy of your enemy. It is the only way to safeguard your lands and family.'

'This is madness! Even if I agreed to such lunacy, Edward would throw me in the Tower the moment I crossed the border!'

'He may not,' replied James, 'if you take him what you tell me he desires most.'

Robert stared at him in stunned silence.

The steward continued, his tone adamant. 'You must surrender yourself to the king's mercy, beg his forgiveness for your trespass and give him the Staff of Malachy.'

Rage towered like a storm in Robert, billowing and ugly. Helpless with pain, he could only lie there, impotent, as it coursed through him. He wanted to strike out, but he couldn't even sit. Instead, he jerked his head towards the steward. 'Give up the only leverage I have with which to free my country? What I risked all for? By God, I will not!'

'If Balliol is restored it will no longer be your country, Robert. He and his supporters know you have designs on the throne. They will not allow you to threaten them again. You will be a hunted man, landless and power-less. What use will the staff be then?'

Robert closed his eyes, breath shuddering from him. The truth of James's words could not be denied. Even as he railed against them, they settled coldly within him. His family had put themselves in direct conflict with John Balliol when his father and grandfather had attacked his chief strong-hold in Galloway fifteen years ago and with that assault revealed Balliol's weakness to the men of the realm, crushing his early ambitions to take the crown. Years later, when, as king, Balliol commanded the Bruce family to raise arms for him against England, Robert's father declared he would rather die than fight for the pretender on the throne. But strong though the rivalry with Balliol was, worse still was his family's enmity with the Comyns; a deep-seated hatred that spanned decades.

Forged in blood and betrayal between his grandfather and the Lord of Badenoch, it was a hatred that flowed through both families, passing from Robert's grandfather to him and from Badenoch to his son, culminating in that stormy day during the council of Peebles when John Comyn had held a dagger to his throat; the day Robert resigned as guardian. If Balliol was restored to the throne of Scotland and the Comyns regained their power in the realm, he and his family would never be safe.

'I broke my oaths, James. Oaths stronger than fealty and homage. Unbreakable oaths. Edward will never trust me again.'

'He might, if you were vouched for by one of his chief vassals. Dire times called me to take dire measures. I told Ulster of our intention to set you on the throne.' The steward raised a hand as Robert cursed bitterly. 'It was a risk, yes. But Richard de Burgh has been an ally of your family for a long time, almost as long as he has been an enemy of Balliol, whose people sailed often from Galloway to terrorise and raid his strongholds. My brother-in-law may be Edward's man, but he is ruled by his own ambitions. If you were to become king, he would stand to gain a great deal.'

'And in the meantime – while I'm languishing in Edward's court waiting for that fantasy to come true – what will Ulster gain? What in Christ's name will prevent him from telling Edward of our plan and gaining much greater favour from a king who already wears a crown?'

'My brother-in-law has a condition for his help getting you back into Edward's trust.' James shook his head when Robert went to question him. 'We will talk through such things when you are healed. For now, both Sir Richard and I simply need to know that you are willing to make this sacrifice.'

Robert's hopelessness closed over him like black water. He had been hated once by his countrymen for fighting under Edward's banner. It had taken years of effort and war to prove his cause was theirs. This would destroy all of that. And what of England, home of the father who despised him and the men who had once trusted him: Humphrey de Bohun, Ralph de Monthermer and the rest? To be back in their company – a hated pariah? His eyes closed in despair.

'There is no other way, Robert,' James said quietly, watching the emotions shift across his face. 'If Balliol returns you lose everything. At least, this way, you have a chance to make sure you and your family are protected. Our best hope is that Edward will be able to keep Balliol from the throne. If he succeeds, God willing, you may one day still claim it.'

PART 3

1302 AD

One shall come in armour, and shall ride upon a flying serpent . . . With his cry shall the seas be moved, and he shall strike terror into the second. The second therefore shall enter into confederacy with the lion . . .

The History of the Kings of Britain, *Geoffrey of Monmouth*

16

The procession filed in a slow-moving column along the King's Road, which cut a path through waterlogged fields. Mist hung in ribbons above the marshes and the shallow banks of the Thames, where birds piped in the reeds. It was early morning, mid-February, and the land seemed hushed, still waiting under the held breath of winter. The hooves of the horses crunched through films of ice into pockets of mud, the wagon wheels churning up a black slush. The rising sun was a copper disc, suspended in a sky the colour of parchment.

Ahead, Westminster rose abruptly from the plain, dominated by the towering edifices of the abbey and the hall, which, with all their attendant buildings, stood facing one another on the Island of Thorney, formed between two veins of the Tyburn that flowed into the Thames. This was the beating heart of Edward's realm, all its weight of Kentish stone and Purbeck marble, Sussex oak and elm thrusting from the frozen marshes and streams that surrounded it. The sight filled Robert with a foreboding that grew with every stride of his horse. Once such a familiar, exhilarating prospect, those sheer white walls and towers now seemed to stand before him in judgement. Trapped within the column of Ulster's knights, he found scant comfort in the presence of his brother, Edward, who rode tight-lipped at his side.

Five months ago in Dunluce Castle, after he agreed to James Stewart's plan, Robert had demanded two things. The first, that James would continue to take care of his daughter and the second that his brother would accompany him to London. He had told the steward he would need someone to watch his back, but in reality the demand was born more from a desire to have one man with him who knew the truth. Without that, Robert thought he might lose all trace of his fragile hope that this bleak act was not the end of his ambition, but merely a pause in its attainment. Now, as the first of Ulster's men crossed the wooden bridge over the Tyburn, the hooves of their horses hollow on the boards, he wished to God he hadn't brought Edward with him. For the sake of his own solace he had endangered both their lives.

'No going back now.'

His brother had caught his stare. 'No,' Robert agreed soberly, the clop of hooves masking his words from Ulster's knights. 'For what it's worth, I'm sorry I involved you in this. I should have come alone.'

'And let me miss all the fun? I hear the Tower's lovely this time of year.' Edward's mirth faded quickly. 'I know we didn't always see eye to eye when we were last here, but I believe you're doing the right thing now. You have to, for the sake of our family. There will be no future for you, for any Bruce, in a Scotland ruled by Balliol and the Comyns.'

'There may be an even shorter future here,' responded Robert tightly.

Edward shrugged, grimly pragmatic. 'Imprisonment is the worst we'll face and half the men we know have suffered the discomfort of an English cell. Sooner or later, the king released most of them. Except John of Atholl, who released himself.' Edward grinned. 'I can't imagine anyone managing to keep that firebrand locked up for long.' He frowned when Robert's expression didn't change. 'Come, brother, the English king is many things and I'll be the first to name them all, but even in his cruellest moments he's still bound by chivalry. Who ever heard of the execution of an earl?'

Robert didn't respond as he was forced to walk his horse on ahead of his brother, following the knights across the bridge, under a grand stone archway. Could he himself say that imprisonment would be the worst that awaited them after what he had discovered the night he came round from unconsciousness to find the steward beside him? He fingered the piece of iron that hung around his neck on a strip of leather, hidden beneath his mantle. His brother could be doughty about their fate because he didn't know the whole truth. He didn't know what Robert had seen that night in the bowels of Dunluce Castle.

To the right, the white façade of Westminster Abbey stood stark against the sky. A shudder of anticipation went through Robert at the proximity to the Stone of Destiny that lay within those walls, encased in Edward's coronation chair. He stared over his shoulder, eyes lingering on the abbey's colossal doors, as the English knights who had accompanied them from the border escorted them towards the palace. Ahead, over the lead rooftops, loomed Westminster Hall. Passing the Queen's Chapel, the Painted Chamber and the White Hall, they came to a windswept courtyard where robed clerks and courtiers stared at their company. The hall housed the Courts of the Exchequer, King's Bench, Chancery and Common Pleas.

Dismounting, Robert gave the reins of his palfrey to Nes, who had led his destrier, Hunter, on the road from Scotland. The roan charger, conserved for tournaments and war, was a symbol of Robert's intention to make England his temporary home, as were the men of his household who had accompanied him and the wagon filled with his worldly belongings – mostly clothes, coins, armour and equipment brought over from Antrim, the rest a few personal effects handed to him by James Stewart: a jewelled dirk and a tapestry from his grandfather's hall at Lochmaben, a silver necklace he had given to his first wife, Isobel, a ring that had belonged to his mother and a motley collection of goblets, plates and furniture. It was perverse how the fortune of his family, acquired over centuries to encompass rich estates across the span of three nations, had been reduced down to a cartload.

Seeing the Earl of Ulster talking to a man in a regal blue robe who had come out to greet them – a steward perhaps – Robert headed over. His porters were unloading the cage that housed his hound from the back of the wagon. The pup, the only one of Uathach's litter he had brought from Glenarm, was just eighteen months old, but already showed signs of being a keen hunter like his mother. Robert had named him Fionn after the legendary Irish warrior whose deeds he had learned by heart as a boy in Lord Donough's hall. Fionn barked in expectation as he caught his master's scent. Beyond the cage, rolled up against the side of the wagon, Robert could see his banner. He had resigned himself to wear the white surcoat and mantle decorated with the red chevron of Carrick, but couldn't bear to have that standard raised above him as he prepared to yield to the man who had destroyed his earldom.

'The king will grant us an audience?' Robert asked, coming to stand beside Ulster, his eyes following the man in the blue robe, who was walking purposefully back towards the hall.

Richard de Burgh turned to him. His face, uncompromising in the wintry light, offered no comfort. 'They received my messengers, so King Edward is expecting us. For now, we wait.' The earl held Robert in his stare. 'You will remember our terms.' It wasn't a question.

'I'll keep my word,' Robert told him tersely, meeting the challenge in the older man's eyes. He wanted to ask him the same question – well aware of the danger in Ulster's knowledge, but he didn't have to. The devious earl had made certain his keeping of Robert's secret would be worth his while.

The tension between them was broken by a clatter and a curse. They looked round to see one of Ulster's men bending over a long wooden box that had slipped from his grasp.

'Careful with that, damn you!' snapped the earl, heading over.

Robert stayed where he was, his eyes on the box. Inside that unadorned casket was the Staff of Jesus, wielded by St Patrick, restored by St Malachy. Stolen by him. Less than a month ago, James Stewart had given the relic to him on a deserted beach on the Carrick coast.

Shortly after Ulster had written to King Edward to inform him that Robert wished to surrender and he would personally escort him to London, the high steward had left for Rothesay, his castle on the Isle of Bute. When Robert's shoulder had begun to heal, he boarded Ulster's galley and crossed the race to join him. He had wanted to meet the steward at Rothesay where his daughter and brothers were lodged, but James had refused, fearing the temptation for him to explain himself to his family would be too great.

'It is imperative your surrender appears genuine,' the steward had told him before leaving Dunluce. 'The fewer people who know the truth – that you do not intend for this to be permanent – the tighter the ruse will be. King Edward is no fool. Even if outwardly he accepts your submission, I guarantee he will use everything at his disposal to ascertain your loyalty behind your back. We know he has spies. We need every word that comes out of the mouths of Scots about you to be damning; to speak of your betrayal and infidelity to the cause.'

These words had echoed painfully in Robert as he landed on Carrick's shore, where James was waiting with his brother. From there, under cover of darkness, they had ridden south to the border in the company of Ulster and his knights. Scarcely had Robert set foot upon the soil of his homeland before giving himself up to the king's officials in Annandale and crossing into England, with barely a blade of grass bent to show he had been there at all.

Robert watched as Ulster's man righted the unadorned casket, which contained so much more than the precious Irish relic. Inside, lay King Edward's triumph and his defeat. He waited in silence, standing apart from the others, the cold seeping through him as the bare branches of the trees in the royal gardens rattled like bones in the wind. Foremost in his mind was his grandfather. Things had been so simple when the old lord was alive, his path in life so sure. Now, all the world seemed built upon sand.

At last, the king's steward re-emerged and bade Ulster's company to follow him. As the box was passed to him, Robert thought of gruff, scar-faced Brother Murtough, who had given his life in the protection of the staff. His shoulder ached as he hefted the casket and began to walk behind Ulster across the windswept courtyard, through the towering doors of the hall and into a cavernous gloom.

Westminster Hall, built by the Conqueror's namesake son, was two hundred and forty feet long. Rows of thick, moulded pillars supported the vast roof and divided the hall into three aisles. Doors led into enclosed areas that housed the various courts, while stalls selling parchment, quills and ink to the clerks and lawyers were ranked along the north wall. King Edward couldn't have chosen a better setting in which to hear his submission than this place of trial and judgement. Robert had to fight the intimidation he felt as he walked the central aisle towards a grand, carpeted dais set against the south wall.

Upon the platform stood a throne, illuminated by the pallid light slanting through the arched windows. A crowd of men was gathered there. They parted as the company approached. Robert was behind Ulster, his view blocked by the earl's broad-shouldered frame, so he heard King Edward's voice before he saw the man himself, that familiar steel tone, summoning the earl to approach. As Ulster ascended the steps and dropped down on one knee, the way ahead became clear.

Edward Longshanks was seated on the throne, as stiff and straight-backed as the carved chair itself. He looked older, more haggard, his cheeks gaunt and the droop in his eyelid more prominent. But despite this he seemed as formidable as ever, remarkably tall and erect even when seated, his long limbs swathed in a scarlet surcoat emblazoned with three lions and a gold crown ringing his head.

Robert felt the ache in his shoulder deepen as the casket's weight pulled on his arms. While the king and Ulster greeted one another, he became acutely aware of many eyes upon him from the crowd. His gaze moved over the faces of the men. There was Anthony Bek, Bishop of Durham, and John de Warenne, the aged Earl of Surrey whose army had been destroyed by Wallace's forces at Stirling. Beside them were the royal knights, Ralph de Monthermer and Robert Clifford. Once his comrades, both were grim and silent in their appraisal of him. Close by was Henry Percy with his cold blue eyes and Thomas of Lancaster, his face, more manly than boyish now, rigid with dislike. Beside them stood the rangy, red-haired Guy de Beauchamp, Earl of Warwick. Robert had duelled with him outside the walls of Conwy

Castle over an affair with the man's sister. By his expression, Guy's enmity seemed not to have diminished in the slightest.

As Robert locked eyes with a tall man standing by the dais, a jolt went through him. It was Aymer de Valence, cousin of the king and heir to the earldom of Pembroke. With the shock of recognition came hostility. His mind filled with an image of the black-haired knight coming at him in that dusty hovel in Llanfaes, his sword levelled at his chest. Aymer's lips curled back in hatred and Robert saw the glimmer of wire that bound two teeth taken from another man's mouth to his incisors. His own had been knocked out by Robert's mailed fist in the fight at Llanfaes. Aymer took a step towards Robert, but a hand grasped his shoulder. It belonged to Humphrey de Bohun. Those green eyes, full of calm antipathy, were the hardest for Robert to meet. The others he had once called brother, but more in a formal sense, through their shared allegiance as Knights of the Dragon. With Humphrey he had meant it. How treacherously those sands had shifted beneath their feet, taking them from brotherhood to battlefield.

'Come forward.'

The king's voice brought Robert's focus back to the dais. Seeing Ulster had stepped aside, he approached, passing through the hostile crowd. Up the steps he went, the carpet muffling his footsteps. Edward's pale grey eyes were fixed on him. As the king shifted forward, his lean body taut, he reminded Robert of a snake, poised to strike.

Robert placed the wooden casket on the floor at the king's feet and went down on one knee. 'Lord king, I have come to pay homage and swear my fealty anew, begging your forgiveness for my part in the Scots' rebellion. I hereby surrender myself and all my worldly possessions to your authority. All pledges made to my countrymen and their uprising I now rescind. All alliances with rebels who seek to disturb your peace and plot against you, I revoke. As a token of my faith, I beseech you, accept this gift.'

As Robert opened the lid of the casket, Edward leaned closer to study the contents. Triumph glittered in his eyes, before his gaze flicked back to Robert. 'Sir Richard informs me that his men captured you in Ireland, trying to take the relic to Scotland.' His tone was acid. 'Pray tell me why you now present it as a gift?'

Robert heard James Stewart's voice in his mind.

Tell the truth, as much as you can. It is the only way to convince a man like Edward. Shrouding yourself in truths will make it harder for him to see the lie.

'It is true, I did try to take the staff. My intention was to use it to bargain terms for Scotland's freedom. I sought an end to the war. But in Ireland I learned John Balliol was set to return and my purpose changed. I want my kingdom to have peace, but not under him. No matter the discord between us, I know we have this one desire in common: not to see Balliol take the throne. In bringing you the staff and asking that you accept my homage, I pledge to aid you in the prevention of this.'

The golden lions on the king's surcoat shifted as his fingers gripped the throne's carved arms. 'What is in this for you, other than Balliol's defeat? What is it you desire from such an alliance?'

Now, Robert didn't hesitate. 'I wish to have my lands and titles guaranteed, and assurances that my tenants will be spared life and limb. Furthermore, if Balliol's restoration can be halted, perhaps – when I have proven myself worthy – you might consider granting me some position of authority in Scotland, in which I can act as a mediator between our nations to prevent further rebellion.'

There were scattered mutters of contempt from the crowd. Neither Edward nor Robert took their eyes off one another.

Finally, the king inhaled sharply through his nostrils and held out his hands. 'I accept your surrender. Your lands will be guaranteed and your tenants spared.'

Robert, still on one knee, reached forward and grasped the king's hands. Edward's skin was cold, but his grip was strong. As Robert spoke, pledging homage and swearing fealty to his lord, the words were heavy with reality. This might all be a lie in his heart, but he would not be able to maintain the falsehood in practice. Edward would demand he act upon his allegiance. There were battlefields ahead, he knew, upon which he would be expected to spill Scottish blood for the sake of his deception. Cruel fate had shoved him back to the start of a journey, which had already taken so much strength to complete. When he'd last fought for the English, part of him had wanted to believe in their cause. How could he do it again now – given what had changed in him? And, worse, given what he feared was true?

When the act was done, Edward sat back. 'Give the staff to me.'

Robert reached into the box. The gold sheath that covered the crosier was icy. Slowly, he withdrew the staff of the King of Kings, a symbol of supreme authority. According to Merlin's vision, the relic, united at Westminster with the Sword of Mercy, the Crown of Arthur and the Stone of Destiny, rendered Edward ruler of all Britain. Robert thought of what had been uncovered in that dank cellar in Dunluce Castle and had to force himself to hold out the staff, every fibre of his being resisting.

Edward took the relic eagerly. Rising to tower over Robert, his scarlet robe pooling around him, he thrust it high to show his men. The gems that encrusted the staff flashed in the morning light. As applause erupted from the crowd, Robert's heart thudded like a drum.

As the cheers faded, the king looked coldly down at him. 'You may rise. My steward will show you to lodgings. As to Sir Richard's proposition, I will consider it.'

'Thank you, my lord,' murmured Robert. He got to his feet, the blood rushing back into his limbs. As he did so the fragment of iron around his neck slipped from the folds of his mantle.

'What is that?'

Robert met Edward's sharp gaze. Anticipation crackled through him. He heard James's voice, warning him to beware, but he pushed it aside. He hadn't meant for this to be revealed yet, but now that it had been he wasn't about to waste the opportunity. 'It is the head of a crossbow bolt, my lord, that I was shot with in Ireland.'

Edward's mouth twitched; an involuntary tic of surprise. It was there for only a second before that steel façade closed in again, but just for a moment Robert swore he saw something new in the king's face.

He was certain it was fear.

17

J ames Stewart watched through the window of his private chamber as the riders funnelled into the courtyard beneath the raised spikes of the portcullis. The horses snorted plumes of steam into the morning air and their hooves rang on the frost-bitten ground, echoing off the weather-stained walls and towers of Rothesay Castle.

The riders were wrapped up against February's chill in fur-trimmed cloaks, their hoods pulled low, but James knew well enough the devices on the surcoats and trappers. He felt no surprise at the recognition, only weary resignation.

There was a rap at the door. James turned as it opened to see his steward.

'Visitors, my lord. Will you see them?'

'Bring them straight to the hall.' James looked back to see the riders dismounting, met by grooms from his stables. 'And summon the others, Alan. It is time.'

After his steward had gone, James stood at his table, which was cluttered with documents. The fire in the hearth spat as it devoured the logs his servants had stacked in the grate. Closing his eyes, he drew in a breath.

He had known this day was inevitable, but he wished to God it hadn't come. He allowed himself a moment of grief for the way things had gone; for the plight of his kingdom and its people, weakened by the fist of war, which had squeezed blood and life, wealth and faith from them these past years. Fortune had not favoured the Scots since the day his vassal, William Wallace, had won them glory at Stirling. Now, by James's own hand, the last of that faith might well be crushed. Only he knew the secret: that hope might yet spring again from that tiny seed planted deep in the heart of England.

Bracing himself, he crossed to the door and opened it into the shadowy expanse of his hall. The fresh straw covering the tiles dulled his footsteps as he went to the dais. In the heat buffeting from the hearths the straw's grassy smell reminded him of a damp, summer afternoon. How such a simple thought brought sorrow these days. It felt as though there would never be any more summer afternoons, only seasons of English campaigns followed by the hard bite of winter with the harvests burned and ruined in the fields, and fewer sons to sow the ground for more. Wan morning light slanted through the windows, dust motes swirling. As James climbed the dais steps to stand behind the hall's head table, the double doors swung open and seven men entered, their mail coats and sword pommels glittering in the bronze light from the hearths.

The tall man at the front pushed back his hood as he approached, his boots heavy on the floor. John of Atholl's face was grim, his eyes on James. Behind came his son, David, with Alexander and Christopher Seton. After fleeing Ireland with Robert's brothers, bearing the Staff of Malachy, the cousins had remained with the high steward at Rothesay for a time, but as the weeks passed without word from Robert, they had grown increasingly restless. Frustrated by the lack of action, they had finally left, intending to join the rebels in Selkirk Forest. It was no doubt where they had met up with the earl.

'Sir James,' Atholl greeted curtly, coming to stand before the dais. 'Is it true?'

There was no point in pleasantries. None of them could afford the luxury of small talk when everything had come down to a matter of victory or defeat, life or death. Still, Atholl's abruptness took James aback.

'Is it true?' the earl demanded again. The fact he was several feet lower than the steward on the platform diminished none of his authority. 'Has Robert surrendered?'

'Surrendered?'

At the youthful voice, James's eyes moved from Atholl to Niall and Thomas Bruce, who had entered the hall with his steward. The question had come from Niall.

Ever since James returned from Antrim, the young man had pressed him as to why his brother hadn't travelled with him, despite the high steward's mollifying promises that Robert would return as soon as he had recovered from an injury. It was as if Niall had known he had been lying. James felt a twinge of regret, knowing in a few moments the upright, earnest young man would probably never fully trust him again.

'We heard rumours in Selkirk,' Atholl continued. 'Word came saying Robert had given himself up to English wardens on the border; that he had in his possession the Staff of Malachy and was planning to deliver the relic and himself to King Edward's mercy.'

'That can't be true,' said Thomas, as he and Niall came to stand with Atholl and the Setons. 'The staff is here with Sir James and my brother hasn't yet returned from Antrim.'

James caught Niall staring at him, the young man's brow furrowing as the lie was exposed, no doubt visible in his face. It was ironic that the two brothers were the last to know given their proximity to the truth, but they had remained isolated on Bute, far from the rebels' camp, where rumour spread fast. The steward had relied on that fact. The sooner the rebels discovered Robert's desertion, the sooner they would damn him for it and his surrender to Edward would appear all the more genuine. 'What you have heard is true. Robert sailed from Antrim with the Earl of Ulster a little over a month ago. I met him in Carrick with your brother,' he told Thomas and Niall. 'The two of them crossed into England with the staff.'

'Edward said he was going to visit our sister in Mar,' said Thomas flatly, still looking as though he didn't believe any of this.

'I advised him to keep the truth from you. I was afraid you might try to convince him and Robert to stay. I thought it would make it easier for them to do what they had to do.'

'What happened in Ireland?' Atholl urged. 'What made Robert do this? And why in God's name did you let him?'

Alexander was looking wrathful. Christopher seemed stunned as if, like Thomas, he couldn't reconcile this revelation with the Robert he knew.

'Robert has his own mind, John, and I think you know him well enough to understand he would not have done such a thing lightly, or without good reason. You will have heard by now that Balliol is set to return to the throne with the help of King Philippe. If this happens, Robert will have no place in Scotland. He had no choice.'

'No choice?' Alexander's voice rose to echo through the hall. 'He had the same choice we all had: to give up our lands and fortunes to fight for the freedom of our kingdom, no matter the cost. To see a rightful king upon the throne.' His tone roughened. 'He swore he would be that king. Did he think so little of our sacrifice in supporting his cause that he could not make his own?'

'Cousin,' began Christopher, grasping his shoulder. 'Robert must have had his reasons. I cannot believe he would do this without good cause.'

Alexander jerked from his grip. 'Reasons? He had them aplenty. Reasons to save his own skin when he saw the ship was sinking and damn all those of us left on board!' He stepped towards James. 'How could you go along with this?'

James stiffened, but held his poise. 'By submitting to Edward, Robert has made the ultimate sacrifice. If fate had offered any alternative, he would have taken it, believe me.' James hesitated. He hadn't planned to tell them anything more, but the shock and fury on their faces compelled him to throw them a crumb of hope. 'It is always possible, if Balliol is prevented from taking the throne, that Robert may be able to return to Scotland.'

'As the English king's puppet!' responded Atholl hotly. 'Meanwhile, the rebellion hangs on a thread in the hands of John Comyn. One meagre victory at Lochmaben was all he was able to offer us after the English onslaught this summer. Another campaign and I swear that thread will snap. Robert has taken the one thing we could have bargained with and delivered it into the hands of our enemy. I fear you have damned us all.' With that, John of Atholl turned and strode from the hall. His son followed as did Alexander, with a last furious look at the steward. Christopher lingered for a moment, then moved after his cousin.

James watched them go. He spoke to his steward. 'Alan, offer my guests food and drink before they leave. If they will not eat at my table pack it for their journey.' He looked at Niall and Thomas. 'I hope you can forgive my lie. I pray in time you will see it was the only way.' Turning from their silence, he stepped down from the dais and crossed the hall to his chamber.

Closing the door behind him, James's eyes alighted on the embroidered map that covered one wall, showing his lordships of Bute, Renfrew and Kyle Stewart. He had inherited the vast swathe of western lands from his family, High Stewards of Scotland for generations. The English had captured Renfrew, which the king had granted to the Earl of Lincoln. He wondered how long it would be before the rest of that map fell into their hands.

James thought of Robert, no doubt in Westminster now. Had their plan been effective? Had Edward accepted his surrender? Or had that seed of hope already shrivelled and died in the cold stone of London's Tower?

18

Westminster, England, 1302 AD

The steward shouldered open the door. 'Your lodgings, sir.'

Robert entered the chamber off the main room. Located on the upper floor of a building in an older part of the palace precinct, the lodgings granted to him and his men were cramped, but comfortable enough. The private chamber was crowded with a bed, a stool and a table on which stood a glazed basin and jug. The hearth was full of ash and the room was chilly, an icy draught filtering through the window.

'I'll have one of the servants light the fire,' the steward assured him. He turned away and spoke to one of the pages who had accompanied the party from the hall.

Leaving his brother and Nes to deal with the arrangements, Robert closed the door. Forcing the bolt in place, he wrenched off his mantle and struggled out of his gambeson. His undershirt was soaked with sweat. All the way from the king's hall to here, he had quelled his thoughts and emotions. Now, they surged through him like a fever, causing more sweat to break out on his brow and his whole body to shiver with suppressed energy. Grasping the glazed jug, Robert sloshed water into the basin and splashed his face. He stood, letting the water drip through his beard, as the heady concoction of relief, despair and anticipation coursed through him.

On the one hand he had gained back his beleaguered lands in Scotland and been accepted into Edward's peace. On the other, there was no going back; no chance to abandon the steward's plan, or renege on his promise to Ulster if the king now agreed to the earl's proposal. He was here to stay, under the command of his new lord, to whom he would be expected to prove his loyalty with service. But even when faced with this reality, anticipation still crackled inside him as he thought of that expression on Edward's face. Had he really seen it? Or was he just looking for it? No. He was certain. It was fear he had glimpsed in the king's eyes when he had spoken of the crossbow bolt.

Dunluce, Ireland

1301 AD (6 months earlier)

*R*obert *staggered along the narrow passageway, teeth bared in agony, one arm locked tight around James Stewart's shoulder. Down in the bowels of Dunluce Castle, the dank air was sickly sweet with the perfume of incense, beneath which was an unpleasant odour of decay. Half in delirium, he felt as though he were entering some polluted underground church. Water ran in slimy rivulets down the rough walls, hewn out of the basalt. The torch held by one of the two guards in front of them guttered in draughts as they passed openings into storerooms. The boom of waves against the cliffs was ever present, as though a giant was pounding his fists upon the castle.*

Sweat trickled into Robert's mouth and stung his eyes, despite the fact it was freezing in the labyrinth of cellars. Since he'd struggled from his bed and stumbled through the castle at James's side the linen over the wound in his shoulder had slowly turned a dark, slick red. The blood was now seeping through his shirt.

'This is madness.' The steward's voice was strained with the effort of holding him upright. 'We can wait. The coroner won't arrive for another day or so. You'll be stronger then.'

'No,' gasped Robert, the torch flames burning in his pupils. 'I want to see him.'

'How far?' James asked the guards, cursing as he lurched into the passage wall.

'Just past the ale cellar, sir. Ten yards.'

'Won't rats have got to him down here?'

'Ranulf, one of Sir Richard's huntsmen, has been guarding the body, sir.'

After passing a dark opening through which came a whiff of stale ale, another aperture opened, where the bloom of torchlight gleamed on the wet floor, spreading as their own light bled into it. Here, the incense was stronger, as was the odour of decay, a sweet, meaty smell that made Robert turn his head. The guards cupped hands over their mouths and nostrils as they ducked through the low opening. James followed, guiding Robert inside.

In the store beyond were several battered crates and barrels stacked against one wall. A torch sputtered in a bracket and smoke coiled through the holes of a censer set on a crate. On one of the barrels sat a burly man, whose mouth and nose were covered with a cloth mask. A black lymer lying on the floor next to him raised its head and growled. Ranulf the huntsman stood, eyes squinting in question as he saw James and Robert enter behind the guards.

As Ulster's men crossed to speak with him, Robert saw a trestle by the far wall. On it was a long object wrapped in sackcloth, tied at one end. The stench of something rotting was pervasive, worming its way into his nose, filling his mouth and throat.

'Well, you'll see him if Earl Richard has allowed it,' called Ranulf to Robert and James, his voice muffled through the cloth. 'But, I warn you, the stink could bring the devil to his knees. He should have been in the ground days ago.'

James helped Robert limp to the trestle as the huntsman took a knife from his belt.

'I'll have to cut the shroud,' Ranulf said testily. Pinching a handful of the sackcloth at the head of the body, he jabbed the blade through the material. 'The flies got to him when he was being brought here on the cart,' he added, splitting open the sack, 'so the maggots are already feasting.'

As the sack was torn, the reek flooded the small chamber. Half blinded by the pain in his shoulder, Robert sagged against James, bile stinging his throat.

'Mother of God,' murmured the steward, twisting away from the foulness.

Ranulf stuck his knife back in his belt and parted the sack so the corpse was visible. Breathing only through his mouth, Robert stared at the man who had tried to kill him. His beard obscured the lower half of his face, but the olive tone of his skin was still notable, although it was now more of a sallow hue with liverish patches at the sides of his neck where he had lain on the cart in rigor. His lips were parted by his engorged tongue and Robert made out the movement of fat, creamy maggots inside. There were more worms feeding around the eyes.

Robert swallowed thickly. He felt nothing other than nausea. No pity, no anger, certainly no recognition. He wasn't sure what he had been expecting, only that he had desperately wanted to see the body when James had told him it had been brought here by Ulster's men. 'How did he die?'

Ranulf pulled the sack down to reveal a hole in the throat. 'A fine shot by one of Earl Richard's knights.' His tone was full of admiration.

Maggots had infested the arrow wound, the skin around it seeming to shift and flutter with their crawling. Robert swallowed again. His legs were shuddering, the bloodstain on his white shirt spreading.

'That's enough,' James insisted. 'I'm taking you back.'

But Robert had caught sight of the crossbow placed at the end of the trestle below the dead man's feet. A pile of clothes, a mail coat and two leather bags were next to the weapon. 'Did you find anything to identify him?' he rasped, moving from James's side, clutching the trestle to steady himself. 'A seal? A mark of arms?'

'Nothing,' answered Ranulf, following as Robert stumbled to the crossbow.

'He had a destrier,' said Robert, a memory of the animal outside the barn coming back to him.

'Our men found the horse,' replied the huntsman. 'But that was all there was,' he added, glancing at the gear.

Robert ran a hand over the bow's stave, which was criss-crossed with coloured cord. It was faded and worn as if the weapon had been well-used. Beside it was a basket of quarrels. One was lying on the trestle, the shaft broken in half. He picked up the head. It was stained with blood.

'That's what they pulled out of you.'

'I'd like to keep it,' Robert murmured.

Ranulf shrugged. 'When the coroner's been, maybe.' His brow creased. 'Don't know why you'd want to.'

'To remind me.' Robert leaned heavily against the trestle and studied the bloody piece of iron that had almost ended his life. 'To watch my back.' He put it down after a moment, feeling utterly spent. 'You're right, James. There's nothing here. I thought, with the horse and the bow . . .' He trailed off. 'But he must have just been another brigand, like you said.'

There was no answer.

Robert glanced at him. 'James?'

The steward was staring at the dead man, a strange expression on his face. He turned suddenly to the two guards. They were standing by the entrance to the store, hands cupping their mouths. 'Does Sir Richard have a barber here?'

They frowned in question. The one with the torch answered. 'Of course, sir.'

'Bring him here at once. With his tools.' When the guard hesitated, James added sharply, 'Did Earl Richard not order you to grant me whatever I need?'

The man looked to his comrade, who nodded.

'What is it, James?' asked Robert, as the guard ducked out.

The steward was staring at the corpse again. 'I'm not sure.' He shook his head and murmured, 'It can't be.' But his face remained tense.

Robert hauled himself over to one of the barrels where he slumped, clutching his shoulder. He closed his eyes, the fog of incense and smell of decomposing flesh overwhelming. He rested his head on the icy wall behind him as his skin prickled with sweat.

'Just the beard. That's all I need removed.'

Robert opened his eyes. James and the huntsman were standing by the trestle with a third man, who was hastily tying a strip of linen around his nostrils. The barber, he guessed, wondering how long he'd been drifting in sleep.

The barber drew a pair of scissors from a pouch.

'Careful now,' Ranulf cautioned him, peering over his shoulder, 'you don't want the skin slipping off. He's as ripe as bad fruit.'

Robert noticed the barber's hands were shaking as he began to trim the beard. As he worked, James stood close by, eyes on the corpse. Once the beard was cropped back, the barber withdrew a bronze razor with a curved blade and jewelled handle. He paused, his hand hovering over the dead man's stubble-rough chin. 'I'll not be able to use this again,' he said tightly. 'The Lord God alone knows what foul disease this body carries.'

'I'll compensate you for the loss,' James said impatiently.

Robert licked his dry lips as the barber went to work, the room silent except for the scrape of the razor on skin and the muffled breathing of the guards. He wanted to know what James was thinking, but he could see the steward was too preoccupied to tell him. He guessed an answer would be forthcoming. The barber paused twice during the process, turning away to retch, eyes streaming in the torchlight. The lymer barked in response.

When the beard was removed, James stood for some moments, staring at the dead man. 'I need to speak with Sir Robert alone.'

Ranulf frowned, but when the steward looked up at him something in his face must have told the huntsman he meant it, for he turned and headed to the door, the lymer following. The barber gathered up his tools and hastened after him.

When the guards left, the high steward turned to Robert. 'I know this man,' he said quietly. He had taken his hand from his mouth.

Robert tried to stand, but sank back when pain almost caused him to black out.

'Don't,' said James, crossing to him and placing a hand on his good shoulder. 'There's no need to see. You won't know him.'

'Who is he?'

'I'm certain his name is Adam. He was a servant to Queen Yolande. He came to Edinburgh in her retinue from France when she married Alexander.' James looked back at the corpse. 'He was with the king the night he died, on the road to Kinghorn.'

Robert stared up at him. 'What would a former royal servant be doing in Ireland? And why would he try to kill me? It makes no sense.'

'Unless he was sent here.'

Robert leaned against the wall, his shirt sticking to his skin. 'Sent by whom? Who would even know where I was?'

'Ulster's men knew. They guessed you would pass through that settlement. Maybe he was following them? Maybe . . .' James swept a hand through his hair and began to pace, his usual calm vanished. 'Perhaps Adam fell on hard times after the death of King Alexander, lost his position under the queen and took up as a mercenary?' His eyes went to the crossbow. 'The weapon would suggest it. Then an enemy of yours paid him to hunt you down.'

'A servant turned mercenary? James, I watched him load that crossbow. It was second nature. What if he never was a servant?'

'What do you mean?'

Robert fought to think through the fog of pain. 'From what I know of that night the king got separated from his men in the storm and went over the cliff in the darkness.'

James nodded, his face tightening.

'Suppose that wasn't an accident?' Robert looked over at the corpse. 'Suppose he had something to do with it?' He watched the steward shake his head, but saw the lack of conviction in the denial. 'You must have thought something like this when you recognised him. I saw the shock in your face.'

'To kill a king?' James closed his eyes, the gravity of the statement plain in his face. 'Why come after you? Who would want you both dead?'

'His son and heir would have been King of Scotland,' murmured Robert. 'If the boy had married Princess Margaret.'

James's eyes flicked to the open doorway where the faint voices of the guards could still be heard. They hadn't gone far. 'Robert,' he warned.

'I remember my grandfather speaking of it,' Robert continued. 'Of how quickly King Edward moved his pieces into place after Alexander died. I was there, at Birgham, when the treaty was sealed. I heard Bishop Bek read out the king's proposal. Edward claimed then that Alexander had wanted to join their houses in marriage; that he had spoken of a union between his granddaughter and Edward of Caernarfon. Of course, when Alexander wed Yolande, that proposition was rendered meaningless. Any children they had would have prevented Edward's son from gaining the crown of Scotland. When Alexander passed without issue and his granddaughter was named queen, the marriage was once again set. It was only because Margaret died on the voyage from Norway that Edward didn't get his wish. He had motive, James.'

The steward rubbed at his temple, as if his thoughts pained him. 'Alexander was Edward's brother-in-law. I cannot believe he would do it. Murder? We have no proof,' he finished tersely. 'And no chance of finding any now this man is dead.'

Robert understood the steward's reluctance to believe. One of the king's closest advisers and, indeed, a friend, he had been among the first to proclaim Alexander's fall to be an accident. It must have been a twist in the gut; the prospect he had been wrong and had allowed a murderer to go unpunished. But Robert wasn't going to let this hinder a search for answers. 'Perhaps I can find proof in London?'

James took his head from his hand, his face clearing. 'No. You must put this from your mind. We both must. By my faith, I cannot believe it. But if – God help us – you are right, Edward would not hesitate to remove the threat of you exposing this crime. Do you understand what it means? If proof was found of his involvement in the *murder of a king, Edward would be excommunicated and England placed under interdict. He came close to facing civil war when he insisted on continuing his unpopular conflict in Gascony. Imagine what his more rebellious subjects would do if this was exposed and they had to suffer the wrath of Rome because of it?'*

'That sounds nothing but good to my ears.'

James shook his head. 'I'm saying what the risk to Edward would be – why he would fight tooth and talon to keep you from exposing it. Not what you could actually accomplish. I cannot see what proof you could find to convict him before he finished you. Edward is a dangerous, volatile man even when the land lies open before him. Imagine him cornered and threatened?'

Robert held his gaze. 'If he did send this man, Adam, to kill me, what's to stop him completing the task the moment I arrive in Westminster?'

'If you surrender you no longer pose a threat to him. Indeed, it will be much to Edward's advantage to accept you. He knows you have been a leader of the rebellion since William Wallace left. Not only will your submission be a blow to our side, it will also prove to his barons that his war is working. I expect, in your usefulness, you will cease to be a target.'

Robert could see from the steward's eyes that he wasn't completely convinced by his own assertion. 'What will you tell Ulster?' he asked finally.

'I'll think of something. Not the truth. That cannot be told to anyone. Not Earl Richard, not your brothers. No one. After tomorrow he goes in the ground,' finished James, looking over at the dead man. 'And this must go with him.'

Westminster, England, 1302 AD

The water drying cold on his cheeks, Robert turned from the basin and crossed to the chamber's window. The voices of his men came to him, muffled through the door, as they conveyed the rest of his belongings from the wagon up to their new quarters. The glass in the window was slightly distorted, fragmenting the marshy landscape beyond the palace buildings. He toyed with the head of the crossbow bolt as he stared out.

Edward claimed to have discovered the *Last Prophecy* within a stronghold of the rebel prince, Llywelyn ap Gruffudd in Nefyn, the same Welsh village where the *Prophecies of Merlin* had been found over a century earlier and were later translated by Geoffrey of Monmouth. In his *History of the Kings of Britain*, Monmouth described a vision of Merlin in which the prophet foresaw the ruin of Britain, unless the relics of Brutus were reunited under one king. It was the prophecy Edward found at Nefyn that named these four relics. Soon after the discovery, he established his Round Table and the Knights of the Dragon, their purpose to help him retrieve them.

The Crown of Arthur, the Sword of Mercy, the Staff of Jesus, the Stone of Destiny: these sacred relics, whose origins were shrouded in mystery, held the essence of each nation's sovereignty, recognisable to all. By taking them, Edward executed a spiritual conquest over the physical realms he sought to dominate and the *Last Prophecy* excused him, justifying his wars as being fought for the good of Britain.

Robert had always doubted the truth of Merlin's vision, yet had found its apparently accurate prediction of Alexander's death difficult to discredit. But now, after his discovery at Dunluce, fate was no longer the only suspect. Was it the fulfilment of prophecy, or a man's intent? He closed his eyes, thinking through the dates. The timing – Margaret's recognition as Alexander's heir and his betrothal to Yolande, Edward's conquest of Wales and establishment of the Round Table – all seemed to fit. He could have sent Adam to join Yolande's retinue with the aim of killing the king and rendering the *Last Prophecy* incontrovertible, proving his righteousness to his subjects. The question that remained was whether the text itself was real and Edward had simply sought to fulfil the vision on its pages, or whether he had invented it for his own purposes. The latter had the potential to undo him.

If the men of the Round Table discovered he had fooled them all these years, what would they do? Prophecy had been the fire that had stoked their convictions; had lifted them above the hardship of the campaigns and the loss of men, the rising taxes and the depletion of their fortunes. Edward had survived the civil war in his youth, led by Simon de Montfort, and had come close to one over his struggle for Gascony. Now – with his treasury emptied and his reputation marked by the long, costly war in Scotland – would he survive another?

Robert might never prove what he feared was true: that Edward had ordered the murder of King Alexander to gain control of Scotland. But the prophecy? That might be a key he could turn to change his kingdom's fate. He had seen the Latin translation Edward claimed to have had made from the original Welsh: a beautifully bound and illustrated book containing images of the treasures and motifs from the legends of King Arthur. But the source from which these writings were taken the king kept in a sealed box, the pages he'd found at Nefyn so ancient it was believed they would crumble into dust if removed. Robert had glimpsed that black box once at the shrine of the Confessor in Westminster Abbey, the day the Crown of Arthur had been placed there.

Hearing his porters moving chests around in the adjacent room, Robert opened his eyes. He was only yards away from the abbey, where the king's secrets might be unlocked. James Stewart's warnings about any search for proof echoed in his mind, but they were faint in the face of the determination building inside him. He needed to see inside that box.

19

A s the doorward bowed and opened the doors, Edward swept into the Painted Chamber, the hems of his scarlet robe whispering across the patterned tiles. Humphrey followed, his eyes on the king's stiff back as he strode to his desk, which was dwarfed by a grand table that divided the narrow room. At the far end was a canopied bed, the green posts of which were decorated with yellow stars, a favourite motif of Edward's father, Henry III, who had lavished a fortune on the chamber. Edward paused at the desk, before turning to the stained-glass window behind. Violet prisms of light were fractured and scattered by his frame.

Humphrey stood waiting, wondering why the king had summoned only him from Westminster Hall. As the silence elongated, his eyes drifted over the vivid murals that gave the chamber its name. Muted by February's pallor, the flowing robes of the Vices and Virtues, the crowns of biblical kings and the gallant form of Judas Maccabeus, an Old Testament Arthur, seemed flat and dull. Humphrey remembered when he had first come here to attend an opening session of parliament with his father. He had stepped impatiently in behind the shuffling lords to be dazzled by the blaze of colour. Every stroke of paint on the walls – newly restored after a fire – had gleamed in the sunlight reflected through the windows by the Thames. Behind the canopied bed the Painted Chamber's greatest glory, a scene of the crowning of St Edward the Confessor, glimmered with gold.

'Leave us.'

Humphrey glanced round, seeing two pages slipping out quietly. He hadn't even noticed they were there. When the door thudded shut, the king turned to face him, haloed by the luminescence of the stained window behind. Standing there, erect, the gold crown encircling his head, he looked to Humphrey like an image in the glass itself; a king of old embedded in the fabric of the palace, set there as an example of good, or evil. The illusion was broken as Edward spoke.

'Do you believe it to be genuine?'

Humphrey knew the king referred to Robert's surrender, just witnessed in Westminster Hall. At once, he realised Edward had summoned him here because he was the one who knew Robert most; who had been his closest comrade during his time in the king's service. The realisation was not a flattering one. The fact was he should have seen Robert's betrayal coming. He often felt Edward thought this too and blamed him for the Scot's desertion.

'I smell some trick,' Edward continued into Humphrey's taut silence. 'But I find it hard to believe Earl Richard wouldn't have seen through a lie in the months Bruce spent in his custody. He vouches for the man. That much was made plain by his proposition.'

'Sir Richard was an ally of the Bruce family. Who is to say, my lord, that old allegiance isn't somehow bound up in his trust?'

The king's eyes narrowed, but he shook his head. 'I have faith in Ulster. Besides, he had nothing to gain by an alliance with Bruce, not without knowing for certain I would accept his surrender. If I had rejected Bruce, his English inheritance would have been lost to him, along with his Scottish estates. He faced going from earl to pauper overnight.' Edward paused. 'But, even discounting Ulster's patronage, Bruce freely gave up his most powerful means of bargaining with me.' His eyes glinted with satisfaction as he spoke of his new acquisition. 'The Staff of Malachy, more than anything, persuades me that his surrender may well be genuine.'

'My lord, the unification of Brutus's relics is indeed a moment to be honoured – all of us have striven for this day for years. But this aside, I believe it would be safer and wiser to throw Bruce in the Tower.'

'Perhaps. But think beyond your prejudice, Humphrey. Bruce could be far more useful to me as a willing ally, closely watched and guarded, than an embittered prisoner. His defection is a severe strike to the rebels' cause and will do great harm to their morale. Through him I will show them the futility in continuing their struggle against my dominion. In short, Bruce may prove invaluable when I begin my new campaign.'

Edward's tone sharpened on the last words. Humphrey knew it had aggrieved him deeply to seal a truce with Scotland last autumn on King Philippe's urging.

After the rebels' attack on Lochmaben, the damage of which was still being repaired, the king had wanted nothing more than to pursue the Scots into Selkirk Forest and bleed the life from every last one of them, but the loss of his base, along with the approach of winter and the improbability of finding the rebels in their secret lair, prevented him. The only thing that consoled him was the knowledge that the truce was a temporary feint. When the spring came he would lay Scotland waste from sea to sea.

Recently, Edward had been listening with interest to reports from his spies speaking of growing trouble in Flanders, which Philippe had annexed to his kingdom four years earlier. French officials were finding it difficult to keep control and there was rebellion in the air. Edward clearly felt this would keep his cousin occupied long enough for him to find a solution to the Balliol problem, for he had been speaking more frequently and ardently of a new Scottish campaign.

Humphrey was worried that the king was letting his hunger to defeat the rebels cloud his judgement. Resentment bubbled hotly under the surface of his concern as he saw that Edward sought assurance from him; reason to throw caution to the wind and accept Robert into his household if it would help him break the last of the Scottish resistance. 'What if he has come here on behalf of the Scots to spy? What if he deserts you again, my lord, taking valuable information on campaign plans back to the rebels? It is too dangerous to risk it.'

The king's craggy face remained impassive. 'That is why I want the son of a whore watched. My men in Scotland will keep their ears to the ground for any sign he is still in contact with his old allies. Any hint of deception and Bruce will spend the rest of his years in the Tower.' Edward paused. 'In the meantime, I want you to win back his trust—' He held up a hand as Humphrey began to protest. 'Bruce returned to me out of desperation. I am not fool enough to think he will willingly give up any information that could harm his people. He will offer me only what is required to keep my faith. But I want you to draw the rest – anything that might aid my forthcoming campaign – from him. Drink with him, talk to him, prove yourself a friend.'

Humphrey said nothing; he didn't trust himself to.

'One last thing, Humphrey. In seeking Bruce's friendship, I want you to find out what happened to him in Ireland. He said he was wounded by a crossbow bolt. I want to know who his attacker was and whether or not they are still alive.'

Humphrey's brow furrowed as the king moved out from behind the desk. 'Can I ask why, my lord?'

The king went to the long table to pour a goblet of wine. Above him on the wall, Tranquillity pressed her painted foot down on the hunched body of Anger, a switch in her virtuous hand as she prepared to lash the Vice.

'I simply want to know all that led him to the point of surrender,' finished Edward, taking a draught of wine. 'Do you understand?'

'Yes, my lord.'

'Who attacked him, Humphrey. And whether or not they are still alive.'

Robert followed the usher along the passageway, his brother and two squires behind him. Music and the din of conversation and laughter spilled down the corridor. He was glad of the change of scene, having mostly been confined to his quarters for the past few days while he awaited the king's decision on Ulster's proposition. With the walls closing in at the prospect of that fate, he'd had plenty of time to think, frustratingly close to the abbey and that sealed box. He was desperate to see the king again; to search his face for sign of the great sin he believed lay behind those pale eyes. Finally, that morning, when he was as taut and stretched as a thread on a loom, Robert was told he would be the king's guest at a feast that evening.

Ahead, double doors opened into the White Hall. The cacophony of voices assailed Robert, along with a welcome pulse of heat, which melted the last of the evening's chill. The chamber's walls and most of the furnishings were white. It was starkly, coldly beautiful; a winter palace of a room, adorned with tapestries in ivory and silver, depicting a unicorn being pursued by knights. The quest began with huntsmen and dogs tracking through snow, and the chase, which followed across several tapestries, ended in the death and unmaking. Here the unicorn, felled by one bold knight, became a woman, lying prone beneath snow-laden trees.

At the far end of the hall was a gallery with doorways set between carved wooden panels, through which servants came and went. The gallery was topped with a platform where the heads of minstrels could just be seen. The metallic notes of a harp and the thud of a drum were joined by the high voices of two young men. They were singing the deeds of Sir Perceval and his search for the Grail. Their words soared across the beams of the chamber, while below was a scene to rival any from Camelot.

Two long trestles faced one another across the hall, covered with white linen and flanked by cushioned benches. The benches were packed with lords and ladies attired in velvet tunics and feathered caps, satin gowns and veils. The flames of beeswax candles were reflected in the curved surfaces of silver bowls and goblets. As the last few guests entered the hall, Robert and his men among them, the servants were already bringing out dishes of lampreys swimming in juices, salvers laden with porpoise and boar, and pies crammed with the bodies of birds.

For a fleeting moment, Robert was back in his grandfather's hall at Lochmaben, enveloped by the warmth of laughter and song; smelling the roasted meat of the hart he had hunted with the old lord, listening to the rise and fall of bagpipes, seeing his grandfather's eyes sparkle with content-ment as he watched his men bask in the glow of his hospitality. The illusion was shattered as his gaze came to rest on the hall's top table. There sat King Edward, in a splendid dove-white robe, trimmed with ermine. His young queen was to the left of him, Richard de Burgh to the right.

As the usher led him inside, Robert felt the stares of several hundred men and women turn on him. In the periphery of his vision he saw a sea of flushed faces, red mouths opening as lords murmured to their neighbours, greasy fingers poised in the act of clutching goblet or bone. Among curious glances and looks of disdain were stares of hatred. The men of the Round Table, who had once been his brothers as Knights of the Dragon in appren-ticeship to Edward's inner circle, were all present, their contempt for him as flagrant as a blow.

Robert rested his hand on his belt, near to the place where his broad-sword would normally be. His grandfather's blade, returned to him by Ulster, was in his lodgings. No man was permitted to come armed into the king's hall, let alone one who, until a few days ago, was deemed a traitor. With the lords and earls were noble ladies, among them Joan de Valence, Aymer's sister and wife of John Comyn. She had borne Comyn two chil-dren while he was in Edward's peace, but when he rebelled Joan and their offspring were ordered back to England by the king. In the weave of the tapestries beyond, Robert glimpsed the faces of wolves in the woven forests.

His brother and squires were directed to a nearby trestle, as the usher motioned him to the king's table. Climbing the dais steps alone, Robert heard his brother give a sharp intake of breath, but didn't look back to see what had caused it. He came to stand before the king and bowed, the thought that all here present might have been taken in by this man's grand and gilded lie filling his mind. He wanted to shout, to tell them their beloved king might have fooled them all. 'My lord.'

Edward met his gaze, his own eyes boring into Robert, as if searching for something in his face. After a pause, he spoke. 'You may sit.'

Robert straightened and walked the length of the table to the space at the end. He passed Humphrey de Bohun, who didn't look at him, but turned instead to talk to the young woman beside him. Tall and slender, she wore an ethereal gown of pearl-white samite, the only thing of colour about her the blush of wine in her cheeks. She nodded at something Humphrey said, but followed Robert with cool, appraising eyes. It was Bess, the king's youngest daughter. She looked very different to the mischievous young princess who had stuffed the token in Helena de Beauchamp's hand and pushed her towards him years ago on the tournament field. Robert noticed one of her hands was placed over Humphrey's. On Bess's other side sat Elizabeth de Burgh.

Ulster's daughter was barely recognisable from the bedraggled girl who had trailed across Ireland with him only months ago. Slight of build in an ivory dress, her black hair bound up beneath a net of silver, she still had a fragility about her, but it was softer, less brittle. Almost seventeen, she was a girl on the cusp of womanhood. She didn't meet his gaze, but kept her head bowed as he passed. Robert felt his blood rush, thinking fate – and her father – had a merciless sense of humour. Moving on, past Bishop Bek and an old man huddled in a cream cloak, he took up his place at the table's end. As a servant slipped in to fill his goblet, Robert realised that the old man in the cloak was staring at him. The shock of recognition was a shard of ice through his heart. The man was his father.

In the six years since Robert had seen him last the Lord of Annandale's black hair had grown grizzled and thin. There was a patch of scalp visible on his crown, like a monk's tonsure. His nose was webbed with veins and his skin had sagged around his chin and neck. His once broad, muscular frame had turned to fat, the voluminous cloak scarcely concealing the paunch. But the eyes, those glacial blue eyes, were the same. In them Robert saw a hundred disappointments, a thousand regrets. His father's fist was gripped tight around a goblet of wine. His eyes narrowed on Robert, welling with resentment and accusation. He opened his mouth and went to speak, but then the king was rising and the occupants of the hall quietening, until only the footfalls of the servants and clatter of spoons could be heard. The Lord of Annandale said nothing, raising the wine to his lips instead.

'Tonight, we celebrate the betrothal of my dear daughter Elizabeth to Earl Humphrey.' King Edward paused to allow the cheers.

Dimly, Robert noticed his brother at the trestle below staring up at their father, his face frozen in shock. Picking up his wine, he realised his hand was trembling. As the king continued, Robert barely heard a word.

'We also celebrate the forthcoming marriage of Lady Elizabeth de Burgh, daughter of the Earl of Ulster, to Sir Robert Bruce.'

20

The figures drew closer, wrapped in patterned woollen hukes. The older of the two was struggling through the slush, while the younger carried two pails. Affraig stepped down to meet them, blinking in the wind that caused the boughs of the oak to creak and sigh. The branches, adorned with their slow-turning webs, were as bare as antlers. She noticed the older man glance up as he passed beneath and make the sign of the cross. There was a time when she would have challenged him, sneering at his ritual when his faith was clearly so feeble he felt the need to come to her. She had always revelled in the power she had over the village folk, desperate or resentful when pleas to their God went unanswered. Now, she let it pass. A prayer was a prayer.

'Angus,' she greeted gruffly. 'What do you have for me?'

'Milk and eggs,' wheezed Angus, his face chapped by the wind. 'And Ade skinned you three coneys, if you'll do us another charm for little Mary.' There was a beseeching look in his watery eyes. 'She's come down with a fever again. Worse than last.'

Affraig felt a spark of anger, although she didn't know why. 'Put them by the door,' she said testily to the lanky youth holding the pails. When he crossed to the house, she pulled out a pouch looped through her belt and handed it to Angus. 'Your wife's herbs.' As he took it, she added, 'Take your family back to the village. Your daughter needs the warm and dry. Charms can only do so much. The body must be cared for as much as the soul.'

Angus was already shaking his head. 'They're fools, them who've gone back there. Where's the use rebuilding homes or sowing the ground with seed, only for the English dogs to burn it all again? No,' he said firmly, his eyes on his skinny son who returned to his side. 'We'll be safer in the woods with the others. We've built shelters to keep off the worst of the wet and we're sharing the livestock we saved. There's talk of going north into the mountains when the thaw comes, where the knights and their warhorses can't follow. There's a truce now, but it won't last. The English will return in spring, sure as the tide.'

As Affraig's anger deepened she realised it was directed at herself. She could cure a headache or purify an abscess, deliver a child into the world and cause a woman to conceive. But these men and women now asked the impossible. *Make my seeds grow in the scorched earth. Fill my empty larder. Help us have victory over the English. Bring back my son.* The gods seemed crueller these days, less agreeable to her supplications. Destinies dropped from her tree unfulfilled. One man came last year, stormy with threats and cries. His destiny had been to wed his love, but she had been killed when the English stormed the village. It had made Affraig doubt herself.

'You fool,' she said sourly to Angus, plucking her cloak tighter. 'You do not know the English will return. Will you risk your daughter's life on rumour? Earl Robert will hear of the ruin of Turnberry. He'll come with an army to rebuild his fortress and defend his—'

'Have you not heard?' Angus cut across her. 'Bruce has submitted to the English king. He crossed the border two months ago and went to London. The whole village has been alive with it. We'll find no help from him.' He trailed off at her changing expression. 'I'm to be getting back.' He frowned hopefully. 'The charm?'

'Come tomorrow.' Affraig didn't look at him. Her eyes were on a web in the tree above her, in the centre of which hung a crown of heather and broom, withered by weather and time. Her gaze remained on it as the two men walked away. Then, with a hot rush through her veins and a snarl on her lips she turned and struck out through the muddy snow towards the house. The wind caught her cloak and tore it from her shoulders. She let it fall. Against the side of the house was propped a long, forked stick. Snatching it up, her cheeks mottled, Affraig returned to the oak. Grasping the stick in both hands she stood beneath the branches, eyes on the crown. Her heart pounded out the rhythm of the words in her mind.

Tear it down.

With a thrust, she pushed the forked stick up through the branches. A woman's shout stopped her. Affraig looked round, breathing hard, the pronged end of the stick hovering inches from the web. In the doorway stood her niece, her young daughter balanced on one hip.

'It's raw, Brigid,' called Affraig, her voice hoarse. 'Take Elena inside.' She turned back to the task, but her arms were burning with the effort of hold-ing the stick above her head and she had to lower them.

Brigid crossed the ground towards her, her dress whipping around her lean figure, her hip and collarbones protruding through the thin material. Crow-dark tendrils of hair streamed behind her. She was only in her mid-twenties, but looked older, her face careworn, her eyes like haunted pools. Still, there was strength in her voice. 'What are you doing, Aunt?'

'Angus says Robert Bruce surrendered to the English king. He has aban-doned us.' Affraig's eyes flicked to the web. 'I will tear his destiny down!' As she spat these words her mind filled with an image of Robert sitting by her fire five years ago, watching as she wove the broom, heather and worm-wood into a circle. The fierce light of ambition in his blue eyes had reminded her of his grandfather. The image changed, twisting into the face of Robert's father, scornful, hateful. He had come to her once, as his father before him and his son after, desiring her arts. He had been hot with temper and drink, but she had taken his coins and worked him his spell.

Later, when one of his men assaulted her, she had gone to the earl to beg for justice, the bruises still livid on her throat and thighs. The bastard had laughed in her face; said his man was worth a thousand witches. This – after she had woven his destiny and saved his son and heir at birth. Next day she had ripped apart his fate and left it in pieces outside the walls of Turnberry Castle. For this act, he banished her from the village.

Both father and son had wanted the same thing: to be King of Scotland. History repeated itself. Maybe, in destroying the first destiny, she had cursed the son without knowing it; the son she had brought screaming and bloody into the world when Mars was red in the heavens, the son who had so far followed in the deep ruts of his father's footsteps.

Brigid's voice cut through her thoughts.

'You would destroy what you made in faith before the goddess, on the word of a frightened peasant?'

'The gods mock me, girl. I cannot make a man a king. Cannot cure Elena's scars, or bring back your husband and son.'

Grief surfaced on Brigid's face at the pain of memory, like a stain soaking through cloth. Her husband had been killed in the English raid on Ayr, knocked down and trampled by the destriers of knights as he had raced home, her son hacked apart by English blades when he'd run to help him. Brigid had seen it from the window of their house. When she rushed out to gather her dying son in her arms the knights had ridden right past her, intent on throwing their burning brands on to the thatched roofs. By the time she staggered back to her house, drenched in the blood of her loved ones, she had found the place ablaze. She managed to save her daughter, but the child bore the scars. On one side, Elena's face was smooth and soft. On the other it was a horror of scar-tissue, ridges and coils of skin bubbled up like pig flesh when cooked over a hot fire.

Affraig had tried every poultice, every charm to diminish the child's disfigurement. None had worked.

Elena hid her face in her mother's neck as Affraig stared at her. 'My power is failing,' she murmured. 'Failing with this land. I fear we will lose our kingdom. It will be swallowed up by the great serpent that is England.'

'There is no one I have ever met who knows more the lore of trees and herbs,' Brigid said. 'But you do not know the ways of politics and men. What does your heart tell you of Robert Bruce?'

Affraig stared into the blank sky. 'I do not know,' she said wearily. 'There is a veil across my eyes.' As she stood there a flock of geese passed overhead, flying in a phalanx towards Turnberry. There was something determined in their flight; something straight and true. Affraig tossed the stick down in the mud.

21

Writtle, England, 1302 AD

'They're here.'

Robert, seated on the edge of the bed, looked up from pulling on his boots. Elizabeth was standing in the window, her back to him. The shutters were open and the sky was aflame with bands of scarlet, rose and amber. The spring evening was still and crisp. The bleating of lambs echoed from the surrounding pastures and crows cawed in the fields where wheat and rye were growing. On the hush rose the distant drum of hooves.

As he came to stand behind her, Robert caught the scent of almond oil and lilies. He didn't recognise his wife's perfume. *Wife*. That word still snared and tripped him, despite the fact he'd had months to get used to the idea. Elizabeth was wearing one of the gowns she had brought from Ireland, with a matching veil and circlet. The hems of the surcoat she wore over the tight-fitting kirtle were decorated with black lions from her father's coat of arms. Robert's tailor had made new dresses for her, embroidered with the arms of Carrick, but they hung unworn on the clothes perch in the corner of the room. He felt a prickle of anger, but said nothing. There was no time for her to change now anyway.

The window of the bedchamber looked out over the moat that girdled the lodge, with its chapel, hall, stables and outbuildings. Beyond the drawbridge, a track, scattered with puddles that reflected the crimson sky, stretched towards the village of Writtle, where it turned into the road that led south to London. Writtle's timber-framed houses were clustered around a green and the square-towered church where he and Elizabeth had married six weeks earlier. Robert fixed on the riders approaching along the track, the hooves of their caparisoned horses splashing through the mud. A banner was hoisted above the company, sky blue with a white band. Robert couldn't see the detail at this distance, but knew there would be six golden lions on it.

His jaw tightened. From the depth of hostility he'd seen in Humphrey de Bohun's eyes the day he submitted to King Edward, he'd have said Humphrey would like nothing more than to see him wiped from the face of the earth. The memory made him question again why the earl had requested this meeting. The only word Robert had heard from Westminster in recent weeks was talk of a massacre in Flanders where the townsmen of Bruges had risen against French occupying forces. Other than this, things had been quiet since his surrender, but he knew this couldn't last. Edward clearly expected him to prove himself in his service. Did Humphrey bear a royal order – some way for him to earn the king's trust?

Whatever the reason for the meeting, Robert wondered if it might present an opportunity to seek the answers he'd so far been kept from, the move to Writtle and his wedding taking up every spare moment. The head of the crossbow bolt sat cold against his skin, hidden beneath his surcoat.

'Shall we greet them?'

Robert glanced at Elizabeth as she spoke and saw she was twisting her wedding ring. She was always fiddling with it, as if she couldn't get it to sit right on her finger. Maybe the band didn't fit properly, or perhaps it was some show of protest at the union she had been forced into. Either way, it needled him. Elizabeth wasn't the only one trapped by this alliance. He had gone to Ireland with the hope of liberating his kingdom and gaining the throne, and had ended up surrendering to his enemy and locked in a marriage of convenience with the daughter of one of the king's most power-ful allies. He felt like a fly, trussed up tight by the threads of two spiders.

'No,' he told her. 'Edwin will show our guests in. We'll meet them in the hall.'

Down in the great hall servants were busy putting the finishing touches to the tables, decorating them with sprays of flowering hawthorn. As Robert and Elizabeth entered, she left his side and crossed the rush-strewn tiles to speak to Lora, one of the three maids who had travelled with her from Ireland, along with a laundress, grooms and porters. The hall was fill-ing up with knights and ladies, summoned from the Writtle and Hatfield estates by Robert's father. They were being ushered in by pages under the watchful eye of the Bruce's steward, Edwin. Nes and the other squires who had accompanied Robert from Scotland were also there. Far above their heads, oak beams, pitted with age, criss-crossed the ceiling.

The hall and the buildings that surrounded it had been built almost a century earlier. Formerly a royal hunting lodge, it had come into the Bruce family's possession sixty years ago through Robert's grandmother. He had never met the illustrious Isobel de Clare, who died before he was born, but his grandfather had spoken of her as a noble Englishwoman who had given him much pleasure, as well as rich estates. Writtle was one of several manors Robert stood to inherit, now he had surrendered to Edward.

His father was seated at the top table nursing a goblet of wine, accepting greetings from the guests. His corpulent frame was swaddled in a heavy mantle despite the warmth of the candle-filled hall. The old Bruce had lived at Writtle ever since the king dismissed him as Governor of Carlisle, after Robert joined Wallace's rebellion. To either side of the lord sat two men. One was Edward Bruce, nonchalantly handsome in a linen shirt and hose, eyes idly following the servants as they hurried around the trestles dealing out goblets. The other was dressed in plain brown robes, his black hair framing a solemn face. Alexander, the brother Robert hadn't seen in years, had arrived at the manor four days ago from Cambridge, where he was studying for a Masters in Divinity.

At first, Robert had been heartened to see him, realising how much he had missed his family, scattered first by their mother's passing, then by the war. Their father had recently received word from Kildrummy Castle, where Robert's sister, Christian, wife of Earl Gartnait of Mar, had given birth to a son. Robert had been pleased to hear his younger sisters, Mary and Matilda, were with her and safe, but his gladness at the reunion with his brother had been short-lived, for Alexander had barely said two words to him.

Joining them, Robert noticed with a sinking feeling that the pewter jug of wine in front of his father was already almost empty.

Alexander glanced at him as he sat. 'Lady Elizabeth seems to have settled in well,' he observed, after a stilted pause.

'Indeed,' growled their father, before Robert could respond. 'My son should bless his good fortune.' His gaze turned on Robert. 'Given your conduct these past years, you could hardly have expected such an auspicious union. And yet you look as though you're at your own funeral!' The old Bruce snapped his fingers at the page and gestured to his goblet. He watched intently as the page filled the vessel to the brim. 'You must do everything in your power tonight, Robert, to prove yourself worthy. It is only by the king's mercy that you are a free man.' As he drank, wine dribbled from his mouth. 'By God, you should be on your knees in thanks for his forgiveness of your crimes!'

'I am quite sure, Father, that you have prostrated yourself low enough for both of us these past years.'

As Robert spoke the doors were opened by the doorward, who loudly announced the arrival of the evening's guests. The disruption covered Robert's words from his father, but not from Alexander, who glared at him. Edwin went to meet the grand company now filing into the hall.

Robert drained his drink, a strong wine from Bordeaux, and motioned for the page to refill it, his gaze on Humphrey, who entered at the head. At his side, almost as tall as he was, walked Lady Bess. They made a striking couple, he broad in the chest and shoulders with a hale, ruddy complexion, she slim and long-limbed with milky skin. They wore matching surcoats and mantles embroidered with the de Bohun arms, his pulled in at the waist by a sword belt, hers girdled with a silver chain.

Elizabeth greeted the newly wed couple, dropping to kiss their hands, before Bess grasped her arms and raised her with a smile. In the short time Robert and Elizabeth had spent at Westminster, before Richard de Burgh returned to Ireland, she and Bess had formed an immediate bond of friend-ship. It was through their insistence that the meeting tonight had become a feast. Handing his sword belt to his squire, Humphrey said something that caused the women to laugh. Robert curled his fingers around his goblet.

Escorted by the steward, Humphrey approached the top table. He greeted the elder Bruce with a geniality that surprised Robert. As they clasped hands, he wondered how often the two of them had met in his absence. They were neighbours after all, one of Humphrey's castles lying only ten miles away. Robert felt a sting of regret. He and his father had never been close. The lord had clearly been envious of the affection between his own father and Robert. But the man was his blood and he had offered him nothing but cold silence these past years. Could he blame him for his contempt?

'Sir Robert.'

Robert looked up from his wine to see Humphrey standing before him. He rose to greet him. 'Sir Humphrey.'

As Edwin showed Humphrey to his place at the top table beside Robert, Bess followed. She allowed Robert to give her hand a fleeting kiss, before moving to sit between her husband and Elizabeth.

When all the guests were seated, the old Bruce thumped down his goblet, spilling wine on the tablecloth. 'It is with honour that I welcome Sir Humphrey de Bohun and his wife, Lady Elizabeth, to my home. Not since the days of King Henry has this hall been blessed with such illustrious company.'

The lord continued to the tune of a clatter of dishes as servants brought out platters of roasted swan and goose, steaming trout cooked in apples and saffron, and an enormous rabbit pie. The dishes were followed by bowls of creamy butter and custards spiced with clove and ginger. On each table was placed a silver basin of water for the guests to wash their hands in.

'My last great pleasure,' finished the Bruce, his voice slurred, 'is reserved for my dear son, who has returned home to me.' Robert stared at him. His surprise curdled when the old man grasped Alexander's shoulder. 'From Cambridge. He will say grace.'

After Alexander offered up a lengthy prayer that had Humphrey's knights shifting impatiently, the feast began. The wine flowed and the murmur of voices grew louder, the guests more flushed and animated with each passing hour.

Robert sat in silence, hardly eating, his head hazy with drink, the faces of the gathering blurring in the candlelight. He wanted to know why Humphrey had come here, but the earl seemed in no hurry to come to the point, regaling Bess and Elizabeth with a story of a peasant boy from the Low Countries who had fought and won three tournaments in the guise of a knight to win the love of a shepherdess. It sounded to Robert like nonsense, but the women were hanging on every word and when Humphrey finished, Bess pulled him close to kiss him. When she drew back, lips glistening, he came in for more and she pushed him away play-fully, laughing at his ardour. Grinning, Humphrey drained his goblet and raised it for the pages to fill.

As Robert caught Elizabeth's eye she blushed, clearly discomforted by the display of affection. He recalled their wedding night, his passion dying as he lay on her and saw the fear in her eyes. They had only consummated the marriage last week. It had been a quick, tense affair, him willing himself to react to her taut, unmoving body, her with her head turned from him, arms wrapped over her breasts. Afterwards, before he drifted into sleep, Robert thought he heard her crying. She would not, now, be Christ's virgin bride.

There was a screech of a chair as his father rose to retire. Unsteady on his feet, the lord blamed his years, but it was clear he was blind drunk. 'You will stay and entertain our noble guests,' he told Robert thickly. 'I only pray you have not forgotten how, after all the months spent living with outlaws.'

'Even among outlaws, Father, my conduct befitted my rank. I wish I could say the same for a lord too drunk to hold himself upright in his chair.'

As his words cracked out the hall fell silent. Men glanced uncertainly at one another. Others hid smirks in goblets, clearly hoping for sport, or some gossip to take back to Westminster.

The Bruce seemed to reel at the insult, causing Alexander to rise quickly and catch his arm. Robert's younger brother turned on him, his glare fit to melt steel. 'How dare you insult our father! He has maintained your inheritance all these years, while you deserted your own family to join rebels and thieves. Now you return to claim it when it suits you!'

'If you want to give lectures,' said Robert, 'then go back to Cambridge.'

'Peace, brothers.' Edward leaned in to refill Alexander's goblet. 'It's been years since we've all sat at the same table. Let's not ruin the moment just yet.'

Ignoring his brother, Alexander escorted their father from the hall. Edward shrugged and drank from the goblet himself. Elizabeth, who had half risen, flinched when Bess put a soothing hand on her arm.

Bess turned to the steward. 'Do you have any minstrels?'

'Of course, my lady,' said Edwin, looking relieved to have something he could deal with. He crossed to the hearth, where two men were sitting on a bench, sharing a mug of ale. At his command one took up a flute, the other a lyre.

As the notes drifted over the company and the hum of conversation started up, Robert poured himself more wine without waiting for the page to do it.

'You should treat him with respect.' Humphrey was staring at him coldly. 'Whatever you think of him he is still your father. The wound will be deeper than you know when he is gone.'

Robert went to retort, but stopped himself as he thought of Humphrey's own father, who died on the battlefield at Falkirk. 'Why have you come here, Humphrey?'

For a moment, the earl looked as though he wasn't going to answer, then he sat back, gripping his wine. 'I thought it good to clear the air. The king has forgiven you. I want to do the same.' He didn't meet Robert's gaze as he spoke. 'But I do need to understand what brought you back to England. Why you submitted to the king.'

'You were there at Westminster when I gave my reasons.' Robert was surprised by Humphrey's reason for coming. He hadn't expected the earl ever to want to forgive him. Edward's own forgiveness was purely political. It made sense for the king to pardon him, perhaps believing it would persuade other rebels to give up the fight. Not Humphrey, whose friendship he had so gravely betrayed.

'What happened in Ireland, Robert? What made you change your mind? You said you were attacked?'

Robert was suddenly alert. Was the king trying to find out something about the attack?

'Do you know who assaulted you?' Humphrey pressed.

'No,' said Robert, wishing he hadn't drunk so much. His thoughts were foggy. What did he want the king to think? 'No,' he repeated, more forcefully. 'My attacker was killed by Ulster's men before I could find out.' That was good; let the king feel secure. He wondered how far the conspiracy went. Was it possible Humphrey knew any of what he himself suspected – that the prophecy might be nothing more than a lie that masked Edward's naked ambition and the murder of Scotland's king? Or was he a true believer, as Robert had always thought? 'It was strange that my attacker used a crossbow. It is an unusual weapon, don't you think?' He paused to take a sip of wine. 'Though of course the Gascony regiments use it commonly. King Edward's men.'

Humphrey's face clouded. 'What are you implying?'

'I'm just making conversation.'

Humphrey set down his goblet. 'Perhaps it was a mistake to come here.'

'Perhaps it was,' Robert agreed. His voice roughened. 'You make merry in my father's hall less than a year after you and your men burned my earldom. You sit here, drinking my wine and eating my food, when months ago you were setting torches to my home, imprisoning my men, overseeing the slaughter of farmers and their wives and children!'

'You rose in arms against us. We were quelling an insurrection led by you and your men, in defiance of a king to whom you pledged allegiance. You broke your oaths, Robert. What in Christ's name did you expect? That King Edward would do nothing?'

'Humphrey,' said Bess sharply. Neither man listened.

'You stand on the border between our two kingdoms,' Humphrey continued, his face livid in the candle flames, 'hopping from one side to the next as it suits you. I say that makes you a man without conviction. A coward!'

Robert stood abruptly, his chair toppling behind him. He stumbled as the drink rushed to his head and then grabbed for his broadsword, which wasn't there. While he was fumbling for the blade, Humphrey punched him in the face. Robert rocked back with the impact, but managed to stay upright. He straightened, holding his jaw, then went at Humphrey, hands clutching around his throat.

As Bess and Elizabeth cried out and knights began to rise around the hall, the two men staggered sideways, locked together. Losing their balance, they crashed into the trestle, which broke beneath their combined weight, sending platters, jugs and goblets clanging to the floor. They wrestled in the debris, punching and kicking at one another. Robert managed to straddle Humphrey and caught him with a fierce cuff, before the earl grabbed a silver plate and clouted him round the head. Robert rolled with the blow. Feeling something wet and warm sliding down his cheek, he grasped his face, thinking the bastard had wounded him gravely. His palm came away brown with goose fat.

With a snarl, he drew back his fist. Just then, a cold shock struck him from behind. Robert swayed over Humphrey as water cascaded down his face and neck. Turning, he saw Bess standing there, as furious as a storm, holding one of the silver basins the servants had brought for guests to wash their hands in. He had got the worst of it, but Humphrey hadn't been spared. Flailing beneath him in the wreckage, he too was soaked. Pushing his wet hair out of his eyes, Robert got to his feet.

Seeing his brother, his wife and all the men and women in the hall staring at him, he felt a rush of shame. He had attacked another earl, his former friend, brawling like a common thug in a tavern. As greasy water dripped from his nose, he held out his hand to Humphrey. After a pause, the earl accepted it and hauled himself up. The two of them stood there dripping, under the baleful glare of Bess.

'Humphrey . . .' Robert began. He reached up distractedly as a piece of swan fat slid down his cheek.

The earl's mouth twitched in what might have been a laugh, but the sound didn't come.

22

Struggling across the plain came three thousand foot soldiers, black with mud and blood-splattered, soaked with sweat in the midday heat. The wounded were helped through the mire, across ditches and water-filled trenches, grunts and cries punctuating the clamour of their coming. They left a wreckage of fallen swords, axes and the bloody meat of comrades in the churned earth behind them. A roar sounded at their backs from the nine-thousand-strong horde of men arrayed in front of Courtrai Castle, who thrust spears and maces into the air, as French trumpets continued to sound the retreat.

Count Robert d'Artois watched his exhausted infantry come, paying little heed to the jubilant cries of the Flemish that rolled like a wave in their wake. A veteran warrior, a feted champion of tournaments, he had been sent here by King Philippe to crush the uprising that had consumed Flanders. The jeers and howls from the rabble of weavers, fullers and dyers did not cause him to quail. Armed with spear and club, they were clad for the most part in leather aketons, the only adequate armour among them worn by the small number of noblemen who led them. Artois smiled. The churls thought they had won. Behind him, on the marshy plain, waited two and a half thousand knights, lances held aloft, the July sun gleaming on their basinets and iron helms and flashing in the embossed bridles of their warhorses.

After the infantry had funnelled between the ranks of the French destriers, the call of the trumpets faded to be replaced by the slow pounding of drums. Artois snapped orders at his commanders, orders that were taken, echoing, down the line. Some horses reared in expectation as the knights shortened reins and shifted in their saddles, gripping their lance shafts. As he pushed down his helm, Artois's vision was narrowed to two slits of field carved by ditches, beyond which were the bristling ranks of the Flemish. The castle, where a beleaguered French garrison was holed up, rose behind over the waters of the River Lys. As he dug in his heels, the sting of his golden spurs impelled his destrier towards the Flemish lines.

With Artois came lords, counts, knights and squires drawn from Normandy, Picardy, Champagne and Poitou. They came with the snap and flutter of banner, in crested helms and billowing surcoats, their shields decorated with a blaze of arms: snarling yellow leopards and soaring red eagles, crosses and fleurs-de-lis. They came with the thudding of drums to avenge the massacre of their countrymen in Bruges and raise the siege on their comrades in Courtrai Castle. They came outnumbered, three to one, leaving infantry and archers behind them, assured in the knowledge that each and every one of them, armoured, trained and blooded, was worth ten foot soldiers apiece.

The French infantry had fought well, battering the Flemish with a determined assault. Artois suspected they might have won had he left them to it, which was why he had recalled them. No self-respecting commander would allow the honour of victory to go to foot soldiers. They had worn down the enemy. Now, he and his noble comrades would finish them.

The plain was a riddle of trenches, gullies and swampy pools, some natural, others dug by the rebels. It was unsuitable terrain for heavy cavalry. Arriving two days ago, Artois and his commanders had studied the battleground in front of the castle with some concern until, by good fortune, they found a local man willing to draw them a map of the field, with all its pitfalls, for an exorbitant sum. By use of this map, the count had employed his infantry to ford some of the deeper ditches with branches cut from trees and beams stripped from local houses. It was by these crossings that the cavalry now picked their way slowly, purposefully, towards the enemy, the knights leaning far back in their saddles as they urged their horses down muddy banks, then spurred them up the other side. The rebels' jubilant roars had faded. They were silent as they watched the French come, their ranks drawing in. Flies twitched over the opened corpses in the mud before them.

By the time the cavalry forded the last trench, the neat ranks they had started in were broken. Artois, compelling his horse across the wide ditch on to firmer ground beyond, realised, with fleeting unease, just how close the rebels were; how short a distance he and his men had to kick their horses into a charge. He forced his disquiet aside, unwilling to entertain the prospect of turning back before such low-born sons of villains. They would quail. He was sure of it. Across the last few yards of open ground, he and his men pricked their horses savagely and, with furious cries, lowered their lances and charged.

The guildsmen of Ghent, Ypres and Bruges tensed as the knights surged towards them. Steadied by the shouts of their commanders, led by the sons of their imprisoned count, they brandished long spears and iron-headed clubs, many of which were flanged or spiked. Breath hissed between teeth, along with snatches of prayer. Eyes narrowed in desperate concentration. Legs trembled and, here and there, bladders voided. As the ground before them was swallowed up by the great wave of knights, those with spears thrust forward with a roar.

The French cavalry crashed into the Flemish lines, but without enough momentum the impact, although brutal, wasn't devastating. Many guildsmen went down in those first seconds, chests, necks and faces pierced by lance tips, ribs and skulls crushed by the hooves of rearing horses. Men screamed as they fell, throats and stomachs opening to spill their contents, bowels emptying into the welter of blood and mud. But the Flemish weren't the only ones death snatched from the field. In the clash, scores of knights went down, their horses speared in mouth and eye, the squeals of the animals joining the shrieks of riders pitched from saddles into the barbed lines.

After the front lines thrust in with their spears, those behind smashed and buffeted at the French with clubs. The knights' helms were no match for these two-handed weapons that came crashing in to stave heads and break jaws, spikes and flanges ripping holes in gambesons and mail, tearing at flesh. The guildsmen used the weapons on the horses too, with terrible effect, turning the proud animals into sprawling masses of pulped bone, skin and brain. One horse, head lolling obscenely on its shattered neck, rampaged through the crowd before collapsing.

Quickly, the marshy ground grew treacherous with the dead and dying, giving the French little room to manoeuvre in the crush. The Flemish attacked relentlessly, allowing their assailants no chance to fall back. Those knights who did manage to wheel away found themselves floundering into hidden bogs. Others, caught up in the chaos, tumbled blindly into the deep, water-filled trench at their backs, dragged down by the awful weight of their destriers.

Compelled by the shouts of their leaders, fired by the scent of victory, the Flemish fought on, their ranks closing over the fallen. Exhausted and bloodied, many ravaged by wounds, they refused to tire. The French had occupied their country and these past years they had suffered the brutality of the king's men. Now, their rage was released, compelling them beyond the limits of body and mind. With every hammering blow, every arm-wrenching stab, they downed another knight. No mercy was given. No prisoners taken.

In the heart of the battle, Count Robert d'Artois, unhorsed and bleeding, found himself surrounded. Throwing down his sword and pulling off his helmet, he raised his hands in surrender, knowing he was finished. Expecting to be taken captive, his sweat-drenched face registered utter surprise as his head was wrenched back by one man and his throat took the full thrust of another's spear. As their commander collapsed, gargling blood down his surcoat, the remaining Frenchmen began to abandon the field. Those who made it across the swampy plain, to where their infantry and archers were already turning to flee, were pursued by the Flemish.

In less than an hour, the weavers and fullers of Flanders had crushed the flower of French chivalry, killing more than a thousand of the king's best men, leaving the fields outside the town of Courtrai drenched in blood and littered with golden spurs.

Picardy, France, 1302 AD

John Balliol stared down at the maps and letters spread across the table, hands splayed on the wood. The corners of parchment lifted in the warm wind coming through the open shutters. Beyond, the valley of the Somme was drowsy with summer. Cattle sheltered in the shadows of trees, the pastures baked brown.

Balliol glanced up, distracted by the faint voices of servants, stringing coloured flags around the courtyard outside. That evening he was hosting a feast for his vassals from the Picardy estates during which he would command them to join the French force he would be leading to Scotland. Edward, his son and heir, he had set in charge of one of the companies, satisfied to see the young man's enthusiasm for the coming struggle. The great hall was lavishly decorated, food prepared and barrels of wine delivered – everything had been readied for the occasion. Everything, that was, except the army.

He had heard nothing for weeks now of the men the king had promised him. Balliol knew Philippe was preoccupied with trouble in Flanders. He had tried to tell himself that once the king had put down the rebellion he would turn his attention to the matter of Scotland, but such thoughts had done little to mollify his impatience. The oppressive heat had frayed his temper further.

The maps beneath his palms traced the outline of his kingdom, which he hadn't set foot in for six years. The letters, most of which bore the seal of his brother-in-law, the Lord of Badenoch, were charged with hope, conveying the strong support for his return among the barons of Scotland. Balliol had come to France a broken man, humiliated by defeat and incarceration. But over the past year these messages from Comyn, along with Philippe's pledge, had wrought a change in him. Smoothing over the cracks in his faith, gradually they had made him whole again. He was ready to return home, eager to regain his honour and dignity; to reclaim the throne for himself and for his son.

The door opened and his steward appeared. 'My lord, riders approach the west gate.'

Balliol frowned irritably. 'I told you to deal with the guests, Pierre. I do not need to know of every arrival. I will see them all tonight.'

'I beg your pardon, my lord. These men are not guests. They bear the royal arms.'

Balliol straightened, his pockmarked face flushing with expectation. As he moved to the door the sleeve of his robe caught one of the letters. It fluttered to the floor in his wake, the red wax seal like a bright drop of blood.

Once in the courtyard, Balliol crossed quickly to the west gate, ignoring the respectful bows from his staff. Ahead, through the archway, he saw the riders approaching, plumes of dust rising from the track. Shielding his eyes from the glare, he fixed on the blue banner raised above the company, decorated with gold fleurs-de-lis. He stood there waiting, a tense smile on his face, as they rode in through the gates.

The man at their head was Sir Jean de Reims. The royal knight looked taken aback to see Balliol waiting to greet him. 'Sir John.' Jean swung down from his saddle, leaving his comrades mounted behind him. His cloak was stained with horse sweat. 'I bring tidings from the—'

'At last,' Balliol cut across him. 'It has been weeks.'

'Let us speak inside,' said Jean, looking beyond Balliol to where the servants were stringing flags over the doors to the great hall.

'First, tell me when King Philippe will send his men. I've waited long enough.'

Jean hesitated, then began to speak.

Balliol remained silent as he spoke of a battle outside Courtrai, which had seen the deaths of a thousand French knights. He heard of the outrage, raw from Jean's mouth, that had been stirred in the royal court and the retaliation Philippe had been forced to plan in response to the catastrophe. At last, Jean told him that the king was calling every fighting man in France to raise arms and, when this army was gathered, Philippe himself would lead it into Flanders to wreak vengeance upon the rebels.

'You must understand, Sir John, my king can no longer aid your return to Scotland. Not when Flemish peasants pick through the bodies of our noble comrades, stealing spurs and armour, leaving carrion to strip the flesh from their bones. He must bring Flanders under his dominion.'

'Everything is ready.' Balliol threw a hand towards the hall. 'My vassals are joining me this very evening. My kinsmen in Scotland have paved the way for my return. Now is the time to make my move!'

'I am afraid any move will have to be made without my lord's support. He bade me send you his deepest regrets.' Jean turned to his horse, then looked back. 'Perhaps in time, when Flanders is subdued . . .?' He left his words hanging, apologetic. Unconvincing.

'You came to me, damn you!' When Jean mounted, Balliol's pitch changed, becoming soft and pleading. 'I beg you, let us talk. There must be something the king can do. Some men he can spare? Anything!'

'I'm sorry.'

'Wait!' shouted Balliol, as Jean and his men kicked at their horses and sped through the gate. 'This will be the end of my *kingdom*!'

Behind, in the yard, servants and kitchen boys stared in bewilderment as the former King of Scotland snatched up a handful of grit and flung it at the backs of the fast retreating riders. As dust from the hooves billowed up around him, John Balliol slumped to his knees.

23

John Comyn watched as the walls of Lochindorb Castle drew closer. The fortress, rising dark against the dusk from its rocky island, took its name from the waters that surrounded it, which in the Gaelic tongue meant *loch of trouble*. As a boy, he had relished that name, believing it added a potent defence to the already indomitable structure; shrouding it in menace as well as stone, warning enemies what would face them if they dared to cross uninvited. Now, the omen seemed to turn against him, the black waters pressing close against the rocks. He thought of his plan and shuddered in the breeze.

Torches guttered on the battlements, glowing in the red shields that hung between the arrow loops. His father's banner swirled from one of the towers. As the oarsmen guided the boat around the island beneath the high walls, Comyn caught a whiff of sewage where the latrine chutes opened. Jutting into the water from the east wall was a landing platform, where two men in his father's livery were waiting. They grabbed the rope an oarsman threw to them and hauled the vessel in alongside the jetty. Comyn stepped on to the boards, leaving his squires to gather his belongings. As he headed for the archway in the east wall, Dungal MacDouall fell into step beside him.

The captain's face was bruised by the torch flames. 'Will you speak to your father tonight?'

Comyn glanced at him. Despite having confided in MacDouall, he was still uncertain as to whether he could rely on his full support, for the man had been a faithful vassal of John Balliol's for years. The white lion of Galloway, embroidered on the captain's surcoat, seemed to blaze in the firelight. 'I cannot delay,' he admitted, after a pause. 'The delegation will remain in France only for so long. My best hope of raising the support I need will be in their absence.'

MacDouall nodded as they passed beneath the portcullis. 'Your father will need to stand aside. Without his endorsement your plan cannot work.'

'I am well aware of that,' muttered Comyn, though the captain's words made his stomach churn. All through the journey home from the assembly in Selkirk Forest, he had thought of little else.

Entering the castle courtyard, he was greeted at once by his father's steward. The grave, officious man who had served the Red Comyn for decades was unusually animated, his steps more hurried than seemed comfortable for his stooped frame.

'Sir John!' He came towards him out of the darkness. 'Praise God, you've returned!'

'What's wrong, Duncan?' The steward's manner halted Comyn in his tracks.

'It's your father, sir. Please, come.'

Comyn followed Duncan across the courtyard into the stone and timber building that housed his father's chambers. Once inside, he overtook the steward, mounting the stairs two at a time, hastening down the passage to the lord's room. The door at the far end was ajar, candlelight and low voices spilling out.

The well-appointed chamber was stuffy, the windows covered up with drapes. The air smelled of urine and herbs. As he stepped inside, Comyn's gaze alighted on two figures standing by the canopied bed. One was a man in clerical vestments, the bald scalp of his tonsured head gleaming in the candlelight. The other was his mother.

Eleanor Balliol, sister of the exiled king, turned as her son entered. Her lined face, framed by greying chestnut hair, softened with grief. 'John . . .'

Comyn moved past her to the bed. Lying there, dwarfed by the expanse of covers and pillows, was his father. The old man's face was ashen, his eyes sunken holes. A scrawny arm, once corded with muscle, lay outside the sheet. It was bruised where the leeches had suckled.

When the message came, calling them to the urgent assembly in the Forest, his father, weakened by the malady that had plagued him for the past year, bade him go alone. But though frail he hadn't been bedridden then, let alone teetering on the very brink of life. As he groaned through desiccated lips, Comyn turned to his mother. 'The physician?'

'Has done all he can.' It was the priest who spoke. 'Your father's care is in the hands of God now.'

When the priest picked up his crucifix and a phial of oil from the bed, Comyn realised, with spreading numbness, that his father had been given the last rites. He stared at the once proud lord lying before him. How was it possible that a man who had been the iron will behind two kings could be reduced to a wizened vessel ready to crack open and spill its soul? He barely felt his mother's hand on his shoulder as she and the priest departed, leaving him alone. Their voices resumed beyond the door, joined by the steward's. They were murmuring funeral plans.

Comyn sat on the edge of the bed, staring into his father's bloodshot eyes.

The lord licked his lips. 'What happened at the council?'

Comyn had to lean in close to hear him. He could smell his breath, stale and familiar. 'King Philippe reneged on his promise, Father. Instead of sending an army to Scotland, he will lead the French into Flanders. Bishop Lamberton and Ingram de Umfraville intend to leave for Paris at the head of a delegation. Their hope is that even if Philippe cannot be persuaded to aid us militarily, he will continue to occupy Gascony until Edward agrees to Balliol's return.'

The old man's eyes closed. When they opened again, Comyn exhaled, realising he had been holding his breath.

'They leave you sole guardian of Scotland?'

'Yes.'

'Good.' The lord's eyes fluttered, but stayed open.

'I had time to think, Father,' Comyn began, his heart thudding, 'on the journey home. The events of the past year have made me question whether our hopes for King John's return to the throne are realistic. Whether, in fact, to cling to them is to ignore other paths to the reclamation of our liberties.'

A frown puckered the lord's brow.

Comyn continued, quickly now, impatient to get it done. 'King Philippe has gone back on his word before. There is scant reason to believe, whatever promises the delegation receives in Paris, that he will fulfil any pledge. With Balliol isolated and Philippe occupied, I have no doubt Edward will attack us the moment the current truce has expired. To face him with any hope of victory we need a leader who can unite the strength of the barons, a leader whose authority cannot be disputed, or undermined by others.' He steeled himself. 'Our family has a claim by marriage to the throne. It was a claim recognised by King Edward himself, during his trial to choose Alexander's successor.'

The bedcovers shifted as his father tried to move. 'No,' he croaked.

'I am Balliol's nephew. With him helpless in France and Robert Bruce turned traitor in England I am the next viable candidate.'

His father's voice strengthened. 'Balliol's son is the heir!'

'Edward Balliol hasn't led the men of the realm, hasn't worked to gain their trust as I have. I took us to victory at Lochmaben.'

'You speak of overthrowing the king!'

Comyn flinched as his father grabbed his wrist.

'I forbid you to pursue this,' rasped the lord. 'Swear to me you will not!'

Comyn tried to free his arm. 'This is the best hope for our kingdom. Surely you see that?'

The lord jerked his head away. 'I gave all I had to see my brother-in-law take the throne. I will not have that effort wasted by the actions of my own son!' He wrenched back to face Comyn, gripping his arm, white-knuckled. 'My sins will not be in vain! Do you hear me?'

'Sins?'

The old lord's eyes clenched shut. His words came in gasps. 'I sent my man across the sea – to Norway with gingerbread – for the girl. Her sacrifice for the kingdom – for Balliol's sake. All our sakes!'

'I don't understand, Father. Princess Margaret died on the voyage from Norway after eating rotten food. Father . . .?'

The Lord of Badenoch's hand slipped from around his son's wrist. A last breath rattled in his throat, then faded into silence. Comyn rose, feeling a storm of emotions as he looked down on the slack face of his father. The strongest, surging up through him, was defiance.

He headed across the room and pulled open the door. In the passage his mother, speaking quietly with the steward, turned. At the look on his face, her hand went to her mouth. She moved past him into the chamber. Her muffled cries faded behind him as he ran down the stairs, out into the evening. Dungal MacDouall was there, waiting.

Comyn pushed his hands through his hair and leaned against the wall. 'He has passed.' His voice cracked on the word.

'I'm sorry, sir.' The captain left a respectful pause, then said, 'Did you have the chance to talk?'

Comyn stared into the sky beyond the haloes of torches on the battlements. The wind rippled his father's banner. He focused on it with the numb realisation he had inherited the lordship of Badenoch and was now head of the most powerful family in Scotland.

'Sir John?'

Comyn looked back at MacDouall. 'Before he died my father gave me his blessing.' He stood up straight, his voice strengthening with the lie. 'He believed, as I, that this is the best chance for Scotland's future. But I need to prove myself. I need another victory.'

When MacDouall nodded, Comyn felt his question over the man's commitment to the cause answered. When Balliol was deposed, MacDouall and his men lost everything. It seemed his ambition to see his fortune restored was stronger than that old allegiance. Comyn had banked on this fact. 'I want you to summon your comrades-in-arms, all the Disinherited of Galloway. Raise me an army, Dungal. When I have proven myself in strength as sole guardian, there will be few able to challenge me.'

'You have my sword.'

Comyn's gaze went to the white lion of Galloway on MacDouall's surcoat. 'From now on, you will wear my arms. That symbol no longer has relevance in my realm.'

Perth, Scotland, 1302 AD

Russet leaves swirled in the water, autumn's first fall carried on the currents of the Tay. As the men hauled on the oars, some distance upriver the walls of Perth came gradually into view, darkening through the layers of fog. Smells of human settlement hung on the air: the astringency of a tannery, smoke from pottery kilns and bakers' ovens, the sweetness of overripe fruit in an orchard. Somewhere in the haze, a bell tolled from the tower of St John's kirk.

At the hollow sound, a flock of crows flew up from the trees on the far bank, wings clapping. The boat's five passengers looked in their direction, two of them resting hands on the pommels of their swords as they scanned the banks, where herons stood sentry on the mud-flats.

They were an odd group all told, their skin browned by a warmer sun than this northern land knew, fine cloaks swaddling their muscular forms, concealing the mail and the battle scars beneath. All were watchful. From what they knew Perth was still in Scottish hands, but theirs had been a long journey through hostile waters.

One of the five, seated at the prow, head and shoulders above his comrades, dragged a large hand through the river, catching a faded oak leaf. As he held it up, his blue eyes studied it with regret. 'All these seasons gone and nothing to show for it.'

'You did what you could, sir,' responded one of the others. 'You came closer than anyone to seeing the return of our king. Who would have fore-seen such a disaster could happen – a band of Flemish peasants defeating French cavalry?'

The blue-eyed man smiled wryly. 'We would, my friend. Stirling was our Courtrai.' His hard smile vanished. 'I have been away too long. In the courts of kings war is only words. Sooner or later a man must return to the arena of swords if battle is to be decided.' He drew in a breath and flicked the oak leaf back into the water for the current to claim it. 'Head in there,' he called to the oarsmen, pointing to a sandbank. 'We'll slip around the town and make for Selkirk.'

As the crew strained against the flow of the river, William Wallace watched the banks draw closer.

Westminster, England, 1302 AD

Robert headed purposefully through the press of men filing out of the Painted Chamber, all discussing the matters raised in the parliament. The most dominant topic of conversation was Edward's proposal for a new campaign in Scotland, planned for the coming year. A campaign made possible by the news from France.

Word had come of a bloody battle in Courtrai that had seen a horde of Flemish peasants destroy an army of knights. In order to avenge this humili-ating defeat, King Philippe had declared war on Flanders, turning his back on John Balliol and his hopes for restoration. Edward, forced into a truce with the Scots by his scheming cousin, had clearly been gratified by the turn of events.

Robert had listened to the news with anticipation, for with Balliol cut off in France Scotland's throne remained empty. But, despite his satisfaction at his enemy's plight and the removal of the immediate danger of Balliol's return, his own path to claiming it was still far from clear. It was known a Scottish delegation had arrived at the French court to try to persuade Philippe to keep his word and, so long as they were there, there was a chance Balliol might yet return. Patience, Robert knew, would have to be his bedfellow for a while yet. In the meantime, he had more pressing preoccupations.

Passing Ralph de Monthermer and Robert Clifford, who glanced at him but gave no greeting, Robert pushed out into the palace yard. It was a bright afternoon in late October, clouds scudding fast across the sky, a brisk breeze rustling the carpet of gold leaves that covered the ground. Ahead, beyond the royal gardens, rose the white walls of Westminster Abbey. Pulling his mantle around his shoulders as the wind snatched at it, Robert strode towards the soaring structure. This was the first time he'd been to Westminster in months and the first opportunity he'd had to seek answers to the questions that continued to burn inside him.

In the royal gardens, a group of young men had gathered with their horses and hounds. Robert looked over, drawn by their loud voices. It looked like a hunting party about to set off. Some of the men wore riding cloaks and feathered caps, horns slung over their backs on baldrics. In the centre of the group was Piers Gaveston, resplendent in a black cloak embroidered with silver birds. Standing beside him, no less tall or well-built, yet somehow overshadowed, was Prince Edward, his blond hair tousled by the breeze. As Piers drank from a wine skin and passed it to the prince, Robert saw Edward's hand clasp over the Gascon's. He kept it there for what seemed a long moment, their eyes locked, before Piers let go with a sly smile and watched him drink.

Robert was distracted by his name being called. He cursed beneath his breath, seeing Humphrey de Bohun approaching, his mantle billowing in the wind. Robert nodded stiffly in greeting. 'Good day to you, Sir Humphrey.'

'Sir Robert,' answered the earl, offering a similarly curt nod. 'You seemed in a great hurry to leave the parliament.' He smiled, the expression not meeting his cool green eyes. 'Might I ask where you are going?'

Robert turned to the abbey and continued walking, determined not to be kept from his purpose. 'To pray, if it please you, at the shrine of the Confessor.'

Humphrey fell into step alongside him. 'The patron saint of England?' he enquired wryly.

Robert's excuse came quickly. 'My wife is sick. Nothing serious,' he added at Humphrey's frown. 'But she asked me to say a prayer for her over the saint's bones.'

'If you don't mind, I will join you,' said Humphrey. It wasn't a question.

Robert said nothing, but seethed with irritation. He had seen Humphrey several times since the fight at Writtle, mostly through the insistence of their wives, but while there had been no repeat of the violence, their friendship remained strained. Clearly, it wasn't camaraderie that spurred Humphrey to join him. Robert suspected the earl had been ordered to watch him while he was here.

The king may have returned Robert's Scottish lands and freed his constable, Andrew Boyd, and the men captured at Turnberry, but it was evident he still didn't trust him. At least Humphrey hadn't asked again about the attack in Ireland and, since no more had been mentioned of it, Robert suspected his claim not to have known his assailant had been conveyed to the king and been believed. But the mere fact the question had been asked had made him more certain than ever that Adam had been Edward's man.

Together, he and Humphrey ducked through an ivy-clad archway in the precinct wall and crossed towards the abbey. Its pristine exterior was surrounded by a cluster of smaller buildings, including a watermill, its wheel clacking round in the Tyburn. Beyond, marshes and meadows stretched into the distance, the watery expanse shining like steel whenever the sun dazzled out from behind the clouds.

The dusky gloom of the interior was fragrant with incense and melted beeswax. Entering, Robert and Humphrey made their way down the nave. Westminster Abbey, re-endowed by the Confessor almost two hundred and fifty years ago, had been extensively rebuilt by King Edward's father, Henry III, but not all the works were complete. Here, the paintings were discoloured with age, the stones worn and the marble limbs of angels and saints smoothed by the hands of passing worshippers. As they moved past the choir towards the crossing of the church the structure changed abruptly, colour bleeding from every surface.

Light made dappled patterns on the gold and vermilion walls, filtering through ruby and sapphire glass in the windows. The new vault rose one hundred feet above them, lost in shadow, while on the floor intricate patterns of serpentine and porphyry glimmered, a pavement of gems. Robert glimpsed the indistinct figures of monks and pilgrims moving in the half-light through the ribbed mouldings of archways and between the gaps in carved wooden screens. Candles on altars in the chapels flickered in agitation as the air was disturbed by their passing. Heading for a carved and painted screen at the heart of the abbey, he and Humphrey came to the shrine of the Confessor.

Before they reached it, Robert's attention was caught by a chair on a stone dais that was draped with a crimson rug. The chair was painted with the image of a king surrounded by birds and trailing flowers. Its seat was suspended over a large base. Robert knew at once that this was Edward's coronation chair. The realisation stopped him in his tracks. Encased within that base was the Stone of Destiny. His breathing was loud in the hush, every fibre of his being aching with the desire to hack apart that oak coffin with his sword and free the stone from its prison.

'Robert.'

With effort, he tore his gaze from the chair to see Humphrey staring at him. Without a word, Robert forced himself forward, around the painted screen.

The Confessor's shrine, crafted by an Italian mason, had a large stone foundation with steps that rose into recesses. Three men were kneeling there, heads bowed. By their soiled travelling clothes they appeared to be pilgrims. Above them a gold feretory contained the saint's remains, over which was an elaborate canopy decorated with biblical scenes. The moment he entered, Robert was struck by memory.

He was standing with the Knights of the Dragon, newly welcomed into their order and fresh from war in Wales, watching as King Edward placed the Crown of Arthur on an altar before the shrine. The crown, taken from the head of Madog ap Llywelyn and restored by the king's goldsmiths, was set beside Curtana and a plain black box that shone darkly in the candle-light. The prophecy box.

The altar was still there, draped in cloth, but other than a pair of silver candlesticks it was empty. Robert turned to Humphrey. 'I thought the relics were kept here?'

Humphrey's face, already guarded, tightened with suspicion.

Robert feigned an air of irritation. 'I ask out of simple curiosity, Humphrey. Do not forget I helped the king retrieve three of the treasures. I played as much a part in their unification as you did.'

After a pause, Humphrey answered. 'The relics are kept in the Tower under guard. They are brought here only for ceremonial occasions.'

Robert's disappointment weighed heavily on him. All this time waiting for this moment and the object he sought wasn't even here. James Stewart might be right – he might never find any proof to confirm his suspicion that Edward had ordered Alexander's murder. But if he could prove the proph-ecy itself was a lie, the revelation might go a long way to alienating the king from the men he had bound to his cause by its power. Without their support, Edward would not be able to continue his war. Robert knew he was push-ing his luck with Humphrey, but tried anyway. 'Did you ever see the origi-nal prophecy the king found in Nefyn?'

Humphrey closed like a clam. 'I thought you wanted to pray for your wife?'

After a moment, Robert nodded. Moving past the pilgrims, he went to the shrine and knelt on the steps. As he closed his eyes, the most prominent image in his mind was Edward's coronation chair. The stone was a shard of Scotland embedded in the heart of England. Just like him. Left long enough, God willing, a splinter could infect the body in which it was buried.

PART 4

1303–1304 AD

Pleasures shall effeminate the princes, and they shall suddenly be changed into beasts. Among them shall arise a lion, swelled with human gore.

The History of the Kings of Britain, *Geoffrey of Monmouth*

24

An eagle drifted on the currents, making slow circles in the sky as it moved south from its eyrie in the crags around Edinburgh towards the great darkness of Selkirk Forest. Below, a road and a river wound like two snakes between snow-covered humps of hills. Along this highway rode a company of men, the only thing moving on the ground for miles.

As the eagle passed overhead, Sir John Segrave, the lately appointed English Lieutenant of Scotland, looked up to catch the dull glint of gold. With a narrowing of his eyes, Segrave focused on the sprawl of beech, pine and holly filling the way before him.

King Edward's order that he lead the advance of a scouting party into rebel-held territory as a prelude to the summer's planned invasion had not been a welcome one, less so given the conditions. It was almost March, though there was little sign of a thaw, winter still gripping the country in its fist. His company was less than a day's ride from the English garrison at Edinburgh, but they might as well be in another world for all the signs of life they had seen on the road. There was some comfort at least in the knowledge that the two other companies that formed the rest of the scouting party were only a few miles behind.

With Segrave rode the three other English royal officials who had been sent on the mission. They were escorted by sixty knights, the hooves of their destriers sinking in the slush, the horses' bulk increased by mail skirts and by the burden of their charges, each man clad for combat. The standards borne by the bannerets, the largest of which was Segrave's own black banner emblazoned with a silver lion, snapped in the wind, which carried on its bitter breath a trace of snow. Behind the knights came squires on palfreys, followed by two hundred foot soldiers and a band of archers. They turned the air to a soup of odours with the tang of metal and stink of sweat, leather and dung.

Bells on bridles vied with the clink of mail against wooden saddles and the harsh rhythms of hooves and tramping feet. Breath steamed in front of faces chapped red with cold. Dogs loped alongside their masters, tongues lolling, and six supply wagons rolled at the rear, hauled by teams of oxen. The drivers kept the beasts ploughing forward with lashes of the whip as the road sloped down between two shallow hills.

Conversation among the men, already subdued, grew dimmer as the Forest loomed, a dark cloud stretching as far as they could see. It had a menace, made all the more potent by what it concealed. Somewhere in those depths was the lair established by William Wallace at the start of the rebellion, its location still a closely guarded secret. Over the past six years the insurgents had used it as a safe haven, a training camp and a place to hoard supplies and plunder. They had sallied often from its green shadow, attacking English-held castles and supply lines, even raiding into England itself. It had become known, in time, as the cradle of insurrection.

Segrave had no intention of going far into that maze of trees, where noon became midnight and a man could get lost in moments, impeded by rocky rivers and hidden gorges, no room to manoeuvre his horse in the deeper parts. Instead, he and his company would skirt the fringes to check on the Borders and seek out the best routes for the king's planned march north.

All of a sudden, shouts of alarm erupted around him. Segrave caught movement in the periphery of his vision. His eyes fixed on the brow of the hill to his left. On the ridge a host of riders had appeared. His brain made a rapid calculation: three hundred, maybe more. They seemed to hang there for a second, a black mass against the sky, before rushing down the slope in a thunderous wave, heading straight for his company.

Powdery snow rose beneath the tumult of hooves. Segrave's bellowed commands were drowned by battle cries that ripped through the valley. The cries were incoherent, but for the English lieutenant and his knights — now wheeling their destriers around — the banners hoisted above the charge were enough to identify the tide of men. One in the centre, raised like a fist, was decorated with three sheaves of wheat: the arms of John Comyn, guardian of Scotland.

Roaring orders to the squires and foot soldiers, Segrave snapped down the visor of his helm and pulled his blade free from its scabbard. Kicking at the sides of his horse, he impelled it up and over the bank that bordered the road, spurring the beast across the white field towards the enemy, followed by his men. In the wake of the knights and squires, foot soldiers plunged through the snow, hefting falchions and iron-flanged maces. The dogs, straining at their leashes and barking furiously, were loosed to hurtle ahead.

On the road, the drivers hauled the supply wagons to a stop and watched in fearful expectation. The band of archers scrabbled on to the verge. Stringing their longbows, they plucked arrows from the baskets attached to their belts and took aim. They had only seconds before their own men would be in range. Two volleys were shot in rapid succession. One arrow punched into a horse's neck, sending the animal and its rider slamming into the ground in a plume of snow. They disappeared under the hooves of those who came behind. Other missiles skidded off helms or stuck fast in gambesons. Two more horses went down in a flail of limbs, one rearing and crashing into another as an arrow pierced its eye. The archers raised their bows again, but stopped short of loosing them. The two forces were almost upon one another.

Segrave was in the front line as canter became gallop. He braced for impact, teeth gritted, sword swinging round for the first strike. Around him, knights crouched into the charge, raising shields and blades. Ahead, rushing up at speed, the enemy did the same.

The sound as they met was horrendous – a brutal concussion of iron, wood and steel. Some men were heaved out of their saddles, rolled up and over the rumps of their mounts. Others were pitched forward, their horses buckling under the vicious hack and slash of swords that ripped flesh and shattered bone. The initial crack of blades meeting helms and shields was followed by the crunching, grating sounds of two armies grinding into one another. Swords clashed in the frozen air, spitting sparks. Feral cries tore from throats in the twisting thicket of weapons as armour was pierced and limbs chopped in the butchery of battle. Men squealed like animals as they were opened, undone.

One of the dogs loosed by the English infantry leapt at a Scot who was unhorsed and had lost his sword. He staggered back as it sank its teeth into his arm. Protected by his vambrace, he was saved from the bite. Pulling free his dirk, he shoved the thin blade into the dog's stomach, puncturing its guts. Leaving the animal spurting blood into the snow, the Scot turned to face a foot soldier coming at him with a falchion. He crumpled at a blow from the blade that cleaved his skull. Close by, another Scottish knight was dragged from his horse by two infantrymen and went down roaring under their swords. But for every Scot that fell, more were there to take their place.

Sir John Segrave was fighting fiercely. His black surcoat had been ripped right through the silver lion, the mail beneath snapped to reveal the felt stuffing of his gambeson. Sweat poured down his face in the tight encasement of his helm as he stabbed at a Scot crushed in beside him. His broadsword was growing heavy in his hand. The ache, he knew, would soon build to a muscle-clenching agony.

His head rang as a sword cracked against his helm. Enraged, he snarled and thrust his blade through the defences of the Scot beside him, managing to jam it partway through the eye slit of the man's helm. There was a gush of black blood as he yanked it free. As the Scot slumped in the saddle, Segrave realised the enemy had surrounded his forces. Those on the edges of the battle were punching holes through the English lines, moving to outflank them. Two wings had already split from the fray and were riding down the foot soldiers behind, cutting through them like corn. Others were impelling their horses through the chaos to the road where the wagons were halted.

Before Segrave could yell orders to his men another Scot lunged at him, forcing him to counter. He fought on, bitterly. In between the thrust of swords and shields, he caught glimpses of a giant of a man among the Scottish ranks, wearing a blue cloak over the bulk of armour. Sitting astride a muscular palfrey, he wielded a great axe. The colossus was scything this weapon through the ranks of Segrave's cavalry like a man making hay. Segrave just had time to see a fellow royal official hacked apart in a burst of blood and entrails, before his sight was cut off by a tide of red cloth that swept into his vision. The banner of the Red Comyn had been hoisted higher. As the war cries of the Scots grew stronger and the death screams of the English rose in pitch, the lieutenant spurred his horse desperately towards a man in a black surcoat and crested helm who was fighting beneath that banner. Certain it was Comyn himself, Segrave cuffed aside the sword of one man who crashed into his path, rammed his shield into the face of another, then blocked an axe that smashed in, nearly breaking his arm with the impact.

He was almost there; close enough to see the dark hanks of hair beneath the rim of Comyn's helm. The rebel leader was yelling orders to the Scots around him. He wouldn't see him coming. With blood thrumming in his temples, Segrave swept in at his target from the side. The blow, when it came, was like a thunderclap. It slammed into his back with a force that reverberated through his bones. Thrown forward, his stomach jammed against the saddle's high pommel and his sword slipped from numbed

fingers. He didn't even have time to raise himself upright before the next
strike came, this one a searing pain in his side as a sword pierced his mail.
He slipped from the saddle, falling down among the hooves and the dying,
as a horn began to call.

As John Comyn pulled off his helm the blare of horns filled his ears. More
of his men were sounding them in victory as the last of the English scattered before them. Sweat-drenched, his chest rising and falling, Comyn
surveyed the churned-up fields. Scores of bodies littered the ground, the
snow stained where the insides of men and horses had spilled out. Among
the dead, the wounded whimpered pleas into the leaden sky. The surviving
English were fleeing the battleground, but there was little hope of escape
with a large force of Scots covering the road around the wagons and only
the river beyond. Some urged their destriers towards the fringes of the
forest, swiftly pursued. Others threw down their weapons and begged for
their lives. Triumph flared in Comyn.

'Sir!'

He turned to see Dungal MacDouall approaching. The red shield on the
captain's new surcoat had spread down his chest, elongated by a bloodstain.
Comyn's gaze moved past MacDouall to two Galloway men hauling someone through the snow between them. Their prisoner was dripping a trail of
blood that pumped from a wound in his side, visible through broken rings
of mail and torn padding.

'He claims to be the leader of their company,' said MacDouall, halting
before Comyn and glancing at the captive. 'I cut him down when I saw him
coming at you. My men dragged him out from under his horse. He pleaded
for mercy.'

The prisoner's face was oily. His eyes flickered open. When he spoke his
voice was barely a breath. 'My name is Sir John Segrave. As Lieutenant of
Scotland under the authority of King Edward, I ask that clemency be
granted to me and my men.'

'You are here under no authority I recognise,' Comyn said, whipping his
palfrey with his looped reins as it tossed its head and gnashed at the bit.
'You and your men are trespassers.'

Segrave bared his bloodstained teeth, in pain or anger Comyn couldn't
tell.

'I know you, John Comyn,' he panted. 'You and your father paid homage
to King Edward. Swore fealty to him. You married his cousin and fought
under his banner in France. You rose against him. Committed treason!'

'We swore fealty under a falsehood, all of us,' Comyn snapped back, kicking his horse closer to Segrave. 'He said he would return our liberties to us when a new king was crowned. He lied. No sooner was John Balliol set upon the throne than Edward went back on his word. Now we defend our right with swords.'

'Swords you will need,' gasped Segrave, 'when the king comes for you this summer.'

MacDouall stepped towards the wounded man, raising his blade. 'Shall I finish him, sir?'

'No. Tie him up. We'll take him and the knights as prisoners. The ransoms they fetch will help fund my campaign.'

The captain gestured for his men to drag Segrave away. 'And the rest, sir?' he asked, looking to where scores of infantry, archers and squires were kneeling among their dead comrades, weapons thrown down in surrender.

'Take all their gear. Any uninjured horses too.' As MacDouall nodded and turned to go, Comyn added, 'Your men get first pickings of food and wine from the wagons. But anything of value you bring to me.'

The surviving English knights – barely half their original number and some so badly wounded they were unlikely to last the day – were rounded up and bound. Scots moved across the battleground, stripping weapons, purses and mail coats from the dead. Others tended wounded comrades, bandaging cuts with torn scraps of shirts, offering swigs from wine skins or words of comfort and prayer to those on the brink.

The men of Galloway swarmed over the six wagons, the ground around which was slippery with blood from the drivers and archers slaughtered there. There was some grumbling among the other Scots at this favouritism, but these dispossessed men, who had lost lord and land with the dethronement of John Balliol, formed the greatest part of the rebel company; larger even than Comyn's own troop of knights from Badenoch. Raised and commanded by MacDouall, his right-hand man, they were known as the Disinherited and were a force to be reckoned with. The grumbling therefore went unheeded as the men of Galloway dragged barrels of salted pork, pickled herrings, cheese and casks of French wine from the back of the wagons.

Jubilant, they set about opening the casks, splitting the tops of the barrels, looped with willow to protect the contents, and plunging in cups and skins. One man, to the amusement of his comrades, stuck in his hunting horn and, with one finger pressed to the mouth hole, upended the vessel and poured the crimson liquid down his throat. As the drink was downed, their laughter swelled, mingling with the harsh calls of the crows forming in the sky over the battleground. It was mid-morning, but the day was darkening, flakes of snow swirling in the wind.

Comyn had dismounted and was overseeing the round-up of English knights who, relieved of their weapons, were being lined up on the verge. A couple sagged against their neighbours, bleeding. 'We'll transport the prisoners to our base in two of the wagons,' Comyn instructed one of his men. 'They shouldn't see the route we take, but blindfold them in case.' He frowned when he realised the man wasn't listening, but looking straight past him, eyes wide.

Comyn turned to see a giant striding towards him, wielding a great axe. It was coated from blade to shaft in blood and matter. The man himself was covered in the stuff. It soaked his blue cloak, scraps of meat and gristle clinging to the rings of his mail coat. More splattered his cheeks and jaw, and dripped from the ends of his brown hair, matted on the scalp where his helm and coif had sat. His blue eyes stared out from all that red, his gaze on Comyn.

Comyn stiffened, a knot of displeasure tightening in his chest. 'Sir William,' he greeted curtly. His gaze moved beyond Wallace to where the man's comrades – most of them his commanders back when he was guardian of Scotland – were watching the looting of the wagons. He picked out the bald head of Gray, Wallace's second-in-command, and the lanky figure of Neil Campbell among their number. Their faces were grim with disapproval.

'We must move out, Sir John.' Wallace's voice was hoarse from battle, but carried enough strength that many turned on hearing him. 'Rein in your men. This is neither the time nor the place to celebrate.'

Comyn smarted at the condemnation in the former leader's tone, coming as it did in earshot of so many of his troops. In the five months since the delegation of nobles had left for France to request that King Philippe honour his word and aid Balliol's return, Comyn had been working hard to increase his standing among the men of the realm. Victory today was a good step and, in allowing the Disinherited first share of the plunder, he ingratiated himself further with Balliol's former army: a necessity, given his secret intent to overthrow their exiled lord. Still, he had much to do, not least in the face of William Wallace's unexpected return during the winter.

Standing erect, Comyn faced the blood-soaked Wallace, who was a good head and shoulders above him. 'I imagine your view would be different had your men won the battle. The victory belongs to Badenoch and Galloway.

They deserve the spoils. Let any man say otherwise,' he added, glaring around him.

'They can have all the spoils they want, when we return to camp. The scouts told you there were three companies set out from Edinburgh. This was only the advance. The others will not be far behind. We have lingered too long already.'

'I never thought you to be wary of facing the English.'

Wallace didn't falter at the trace of scorn in Comyn's tone. 'I pick my battles, Sir John. I have been bold, yes, and paid a high price for that daring. But I have never been foolish.'

Comyn caught sight of Earl John of Atholl standing close by with Alexander Seton. Atholl gave a cold smile at Wallace's response. At his side, Seton was nodding. Comyn felt his cheeks grow hot. As he opened his mouth to retort, a horn sounded from the hillside. Turning abruptly, he saw men on the higher ground gesturing frantically down the road. Comyn went to his palfrey and mounted quickly. As he kicked the tired animal across the field he was followed by Wallace. Even before he reached his men, Comyn heard their shouts rising over the fading echo of the horn.

'*The English are coming!*'

Reining in his horse, Comyn rose in the saddle to stare down the road. In the distance he saw a mass of riders. They were coming fast along the highway. As distant trumpets sounded, he knew they had seen his force. His troops were battle weary and in disarray, the greater part of them drunk on looted wine. They stood little chance against heavy cavalry without the element of surprise.

'You have stirred the hornet's nest, Comyn,' came Wallace's hard voice beside him. 'Now let us see if you can bear the sting.'

Cursing bitterly, Comyn impelled his horse down to the road, yelling at the men still crawling over the wagons. Many, heeding his alarm, were jumping down from the carts, pouches bulging with food and plunder, but others were too dazed with drink to understand what was happening.

MacDouall, mounted and with sword drawn, was at his side in an instant. 'Sir, the prisoners?'

Comyn stared at the row of bound knights facing the road in eager expectation, looking for the comrades they guessed were coming to their aid. His gaze went to the wagons, still full of weapons, coins and valuable equipment, ignored – on his orders – by the looters. 'Leave them. There's no time,' he spat, wrenching his horse around. '*Retreat!*'

A bear-like roar sounded above his cry. 'Back to the trees, you curs! *To me!*'

John Comyn had a moment to see how quickly the men under his command were moved to action at Wallace's roar, then he was jostled and shoved by the tide of Scots now riding for the safety of the Forest, swept up in the haphazard retreat.

25

Writtle, England, 1303 AD

Robert stood in the yard outside his father's hall, watching the wagon approach. Beside him, he felt Elizabeth shiver. His wife drew her grey mantle, lined with sable, tighter around her shoulders. He had bought the expensive pelt last month from a furrier in Chelmsford and had his father's tailor sew it on her favourite cloak without her knowledge, enjoying her surprised smile when she had taken the newly lined garment from her clothes perch. Since then he had sensed a slight easing of the discomfort that hung between them like an invisible hair shirt, chafing them both. Neither of them had wanted this marriage, but there was no use in lamenting it. Besides, the union with Ulster's daughter had helped him secure his position in England and he couldn't deny the advantages of allying himself with the powerful de Burgh family. A thoughtful gift to keep her happy took little effort.

Elizabeth's eyes, pale in the spring sunlight, were fixed on the approaching company of riders escorting the wagon. As she exhaled, her breath fogged the air.

'Don't worry,' Robert assured her. 'She will soon come to love you.' But, as he turned his gaze back to the road, he felt those words as a cold blade against his heart. Would she love him? Would she even know him?

The riders funnelled across the drawbridge, hooves clopping. The men's surcoats bore the arms of Annandale: a red banded saltire on yellow. The wagon followed in their wake, rumbling over the boards. Grooms came forward to take the horses as the drivers jumped down and dogs rushed from the kennels barking excitedly. Among them was Robert's hound, Fionn, fully grown and boisterous.

One of the riders, a thickset man with cropped grey hair, dismounted and came to Robert. 'Good day to you, sir.'

'Walter,' Robert greeted, recognising the man at once. Walter had been one of his grandfather's vassals, before Annandale had passed to his father. His weathered face provoked memories of hunts in the woods outside Lochmaben, a gratifying reminder of home. He seemed haggard, worn by more than just the journey or the years that had passed since Robert had seen him last. He reasoned it must have been hard for all his father's vassals who remained in Annandale, forced to live a strange half-life in a region overrun by the English, tolerated, but unwelcome. Memory now had a sting. He thought of Carrick, of all he had left behind. His constable, Andrew Boyd, had returned to Turnberry, but the castle was still in ruins. It would take time to plan the reconstruction and gather funds. 'I take it you had no trouble on the road?'

'None, sir.' Walter looked past Robert into the shadows of the hall. 'Is my lord in residence?'

'My father is still sleeping.' *Sleeping off last night's drink*, Robert added silently. 'Edwin will show you and your men to lodgings where you can eat and rest in the meantime.' He gestured to his father's steward, who had come out to greet the arrivals.

As Edwin escorted Walter across the yard, Robert saw that two figures had climbed down from the back of the wagon. One was a woman dressed in a green woollen cloak, a white coif covering her hair. The other was a girl. Her thin frame was swamped by an embroidered yellow mantle, fastened at her shoulder with a silver brooch and her hair, grown fine and dark like his, was braided and pinned on her head. She looked around nervously as the woman guided her to where Robert and Elizabeth waited.

Robert's chest tightened at the sight of his daughter, whom he hadn't seen in almost three years. What had happened to the toddling girl he had left in James Stewart's care? Before him stood a solemn child of seven, impossibly changed. Realising she was staring uncertainly at him, her pallid brow pinched, he forced himself to smile. His eyes went to the young woman at his daughter's side, who had also changed in his absence, though less markedly.

Judith had become Marjorie's wet nurse shortly after the passing of his wife Isobel, who died in labour during the siege of Carlisle. Back then, Judith had been a skinny, sullen creature of fifteen. Now, she was in her early twenties, with blotchy cheeks and light brown hair, strands of which drifted from under her coif. Though she had stopped nursing his daughter some years ago, Robert had kept the young Englishwoman in his pay, wanting the child to have at least one constant in her life.

'Sir,' Judith greeted, with a little bob and an inquisitive glance at Elizabeth.

Robert nodded to the nurse in greeting, then held out his arms to his daughter. 'Marjorie.' The pain in his chest sharpened when she remained rooted to the spot.

Reaching up, the girl grasped Judith's hand.

Judith smiled slightly, then slid her fingers from the child's grip and patted her back. 'Go to your father.'

Marjorie took a few reluctant steps forward. She flinched when Robert pulled her to him, enfolding her tense body in his arms.

He closed his eyes, breathing in the warm smell of her hair, before kissing the top of her head and stepping back. 'How was your journey? Did you see much of England?'

Marjorie looked back at Judith, but her nurse had returned to the wagon and was instructing one of the porters to unload their belongings.

'And Sir James and his wife Egidia? How are they? Did they treat you well?'

Still no answer.

'This is my wife, Lady Elizabeth, Egidia's niece.' Robert paused. 'Your new mother.'

The word caused little reaction in the girl. She merely nodded dutifully.

As Robert stared at the silent child, his words gumming in his mouth, he felt Elizabeth move beside him.

She went and crouched in front of Marjorie. At eighteen and with no child of her own, she was tentative. 'Would you like some honey cake? It's warm from the oven.'

The knot in Marjorie's brow vanished, a spark of life appearing in her blue eyes. When she nodded, Elizabeth took her hand and led her into the shadows of the house, leaving Judith and their belongings to be dealt with by the steward. Robert followed them, feeling an unexpected rush of gratitude towards his wife.

In the smoky warmth of the hall, a servant was banking the fire. One of the older Bruce's hunting dogs, as fat and unexercised as its master, was stretched out by the hearth, watching from under hooded eyes as more logs were stacked in the blaze. Two other servants sat at one of the trestles polishing an array of silver dishes and goblets, and Elizabeth's maid, Lora, was seated by the fire, mending one of her mistress's gowns. They all glanced up curiously as Marjorie entered at Elizabeth's side.

On one table were several objects. Marjorie, who was already showing more interest than uncertainty as she looked around the well-appointed hall, brightened considerably as she saw them. There were two felt dolls with plaited woollen hair and velvet dresses beside a cup and ball game. The most impressive object, however, was a model of a castle, painstakingly carved from ash. The girl fixed on it as Elizabeth escorted her towards the table.

'Your father had this made for you.'

Letting go of Elizabeth's hand, Marjorie slid on to the bench in front of the toys.

As his wife called one of the servants to bring honey cake and spiced wine, Robert watched his daughter peer in through the slit windows of the castle. 'Here,' he said, crossing to her. 'It opens. Like this.' He pushed up the silver catch on the side, so that the front swung open on tiny hinges.

His daughter gave a happy intake of breath as three floors were revealed, one containing a miniature wooden bed, one a table and bench, the other a carved wooden fireplace and two ivory figures, a man and a woman. Robert, drinking in the pleasure in Marjorie's face, wished he had brought her here sooner, but it had taken a year living in England before he had felt secure enough to do so. His infrequent visits to London remained tense affairs, where he was watched constantly by Humphrey or others of the king's men. Now though, watching his daughter play, Robert couldn't deny there was a deeper reason he hadn't summoned Marjorie sooner. In truth, he hadn't just been afraid for her safety. He had been afraid of the stranger she had become. He thought of his own father, the distance between them not lessened by a year under the same roof. 'Did you see much of your uncles in Rothesay?' he asked to distract himself.

Marjorie nodded, placing one of the ivory figures in the top room of the castle. 'Niall tells me stories.'

'He does?' Robert brightened at the revelation, keen for news from home. The long silence from his brothers and comrades had been unbearable, the knowledge that they thought he had betrayed them a sore in his heart. 'Well, your uncle Edward lives here and I expect if you ask he'll do the same.' He paused. 'Did Niall and Thomas speak of me?'

Marjorie's attention remained on the castle.

Before she could answer, Edwin called from the doorway. 'A message, sir.' The steward held up a scroll.

Leaving his daughter playing and his wife frowning after him, Robert crossed the hall and took the parchment. As he saw the royal seal he felt a tug in the pit of his stomach.

'What is it?' Elizabeth asked as he read.

Robert looked up. 'The Scots have attacked a company of the king's men outside Edinburgh. The truce is broken. King Edward wants to bring his plans for invasion forward. He has summoned me to arms.' Looking back at the parchment, he felt a spark of hope.

Under the veil of suspicion at court, he'd had no chance to uncover anything of the prophecy, just the maddening elation among the men of Edward's supreme victory in gathering the four relics beneath him – a fact that led many to believe the king would soon crush the last will of the Scottish rebels and take full control of Britain. Neither had Robert found a scrap of evidence, beyond his suspicion, of the king's complicity in the murder of Scotland's king. He knew, in order to get closer to the truth, he needed to win the king's faith, but to do that he needed to prove himself and there had been no opportunity, until now.

On the heels of hope, came the sinking thought of the battlefields ahead of him. Once again, he was being called to raise arms against his country.

Elizabeth looked from Robert to Marjorie. 'When do you leave?' she murmured.

'Three weeks.'

They fell silent, staring at one another.

Into the hush, Marjorie's voice came cool and clear. 'They do not speak of you.'

Robert glanced at her.

'Niall and Thomas,' said his daughter, removing one of the figures from the castle. 'They do not speak of you.'

26

While girls made hawthorn garlands for May celebrations and wheat and rye ripened in the fields, the men of England prepared for war. Tailors mended tears in gambesons, farriers shoed horses and squires whetted dull blades and cleaned rust from their masters' mail coats in barrels of sand. Bidding wives and children farewell, leaving crops flourishing under clement skies, knights donned armour and bands of cloth decorated with the red cross of St George and made their way to the point of muster, called to arms by their king.

Converging on the east coast, the train of knights and squires, infantry, archers, pack-horses, mules, carts and siege engines wound for miles, raising a pall of dust over the Great North Road. Summoned in the wake of the attack on Segrave's company, it was the largest force Edward had gathered since the campaign that had seen the deaths of ten thousand Scots at Falkirk. The sum of a king's revenge.

After pausing at York to amass supplies, Edward continued towards Scotland, crossing the border at the beginning of June, where he split his forces. The Prince of Wales was set in charge of a large company and sent into Strathearn to burn, loot and, in the king's words, raise hell, while Edward himself led the main body of the army towards the east coast, passing beneath the indomitable shadow of Stirling Castle, which the Scots held firm against him. Meanwhile, a fleet of Irish ships, under the Earl of Ulster's command, harried the west coast by sea.

By August King Edward reached the town of Brechin, where he set about besieging its castle. Built on a rocky outcrop over a river, the fortress was well-garrisoned and supplied and, after a fortnight's bombardment, the stout walls and the pluck of the men within continuing to frustrate him,

Edward was forced to bring in more siege engines by sea to Montrose. Needing heavier ballast than stones with which to counterweight these new machines, he sent a company under the command of Aymer de Valence to nearby Brechin Cathedral to strip its roof of lead.

Robert squinted up at the square tower, which was shrouded in scaffolding. Although broad, it was still only half the height of the round tower that loomed behind it, almost one hundred feet high. They brought to mind two brothers standing side by side, one tall and slender, the other short and squat. In the midday sun they cast stunted shadows across the cathedral yard and cemetery, beyond which were the manses of the canons and the bishop's palace.

A fly landed on his cheek and crawled towards his mouth, until he swiped it away. The heat had brought them out in swarms, along with the horseflies that tormented the destriers.

'What are you waiting for, Bruce?'

Robert turned at the voice, which brayed above the general hubbub of men and horses that crowded the precinct, stinking up the air. His gaze fixed on the speaker, standing in the shade of an oak, holding a pewter goblet.

Aymer de Valence's chiselled face was flushed, his dark eyes narrowed beneath the rim of his upturned visor. Around him, sheltering from the glare, stood other knights and nobles, among them Thomas of Lancaster and Ralph de Monthermer, drinking the wine Valence had commandeered from the bishop's palace. Servants continued to hurry from the palace conveying casks of the stuff, along with meat pies, bread and cheese for the invaders. A little way away, lined up in the sun, faces red with heat and anger, stood Brechin's bishop and canons. English squires paced close by, hands on swords, watching them.

'Well?' Valence gestured at the tower. 'Send them up, for Christ's sake. King Edward needs this lead tonight.'

Robert bore Valence's contempt with the same turn of the cheek he had learned to employ often on the march north. 'Get climbing,' he ordered the group of foot soldiers, whose tunics were dusty from the piles of rubble they had just cleared from the masons' trays. Beneath the bulk of his mail no one could see his rigid shoulders, or his fingers under the steel-plated gloves flexing to curl around a weapon and cleave Valence's skull. The infantry, who Robert had been ordered to raise from his Scottish estates by the king, went to work, hefting the wooden trays they had emptied.

Robert stood alone, watching as they began to ascend. He could have protested; told the son of a whore to send his own foot soldiers, but Edward had expressly set Valence in charge and any disrespect to his cousin's authority would be an affront to the king. Above all, Robert knew he must maintain the illusion of obedience and loyalty. Aymer had been watching him like a hawk since the start of the campaign. But he was not the only one. The closer they had come to Scotland, the more Robert found himself aware of everything he said or did, until he no longer felt he inhabited his own body. It was as if he were a puppet on strings, manipulated by those around him, moving only according to their expectations. The pretence had become exhausting.

The men looked awkward on the flimsy ladders that zigzagged the tiers of platforms, supported by spindly conifer frames. It was slow going, each pair struggling with the trays they carried between them, forced to climb one-handed.

'Blood and thunder, we'll be here till Judgement Day,' complained one of Valence's men.

A merciful breeze cooled the sweat on Robert's face and stirred the dead hawthorn blossom that littered the grass. On it, he caught a faint briny smell, perhaps from the lagoon at Montrose. Some miles to the east, the town had witnessed the day, seven years ago, when the royal arms had been stripped from John Balliol's tabard, the same day Robert and the Knights of the Dragon had entered the abbey at Scone to take the Stone of Destiny.

Robert was pulled from his thoughts as one of the soldiers on the ladders lost his footing. The man fell with a shocked shout to sprawl on the narrow platform a few feet below him. His comrade, connected to him by the masons' tray, kept his balance, but dropped the tray, which plummeted three floors of the square tower to shatter on the dusty ground. Aymer's knights jeered, wondering – in voices loud enough for the Scots on the scaffold to hear – how many pieces the youth would have broken into had he dropped from the same height. A wager was called as to which of them would fall first. Ralph de Monthermer was the only one who didn't join in the jests. Standing there, his yellow mantle with its green eagle garish in the sunlight, the royal knight nursed his wine in silence, observing the first of the youths as they reached the top platform, his eyes occasionally drifting to Robert.

Just above the top platform the square tower finished abruptly. The masonry there was paler than the bottom sections, only recently whitewashed. The first two men set down their tray and moved to reposition one of the ladders, eyeing the drop to the yard below. Between them, they laid it diagonally on the roof of the cathedral's nave, which rose at a slanting angle to the tower. Beyond, the round tower pointed like a stone finger to the sky. The slabs of lead were blue in the sunlight. Armed with a chisel, one of the men crawled up the rungs and began to prise up the slabs, passing them down to his comrade, who stacked them in the tray.

Soon a line was formed and they picked up a rhythm. Once a tray was filled, two men would hoist the heavy container and inch their way down the ladders to where two carts waited to take the loads to the English siege lines surrounding Brechin Castle. Each pair was panting and drenched by the time they reached the wagons. The young Scot on the roof, levering off the lead, shifted further up as the blocks around him began to disappear. His comrade, belly down on the ladder, took each slab as it was handed to him.

Robert was directing the men offloading the lead on to the carts when he heard the shriek. He turned sharply, shielding his eyes from the sun, to see the man on the roof had lost his footing and was sliding fast towards the edge. Loose rectangles of lead skittered away from under him and crashed to the ground, causing the men below to duck and scatter. As his legs shot out into sky, the man managed to twist round and grab hold of the roof. He clung there for dear life, feet kicking desperately.

'Help him!' Robert roared, cupping his hands to direct his shout at the man on the ladder, who seemed frozen by the spectacle.

There was another shriek as the young Scot slipped further, panic making him lose his grip. He was screaming something incoherent as his comrade reached out a hand.

'*Take it*,' Robert urged the screaming youth, beneath his breath. '*God damn you, take it!*'

Even the jeering knights had fallen silent. One of the canons, lined up alongside the bishop, was mouthing a prayer.

The man on the ladder shouted encouragement, stretching out his arm as far as he could. When the youth fell it was a jolt: a sudden plummeting of limbs. Robert had time for a flash of thought – *how fast we are snatched from heaven* – before the man landed with a thud on a pile of rubble. He lay there like a broken doll, one leg bent under him, arms flung wide. Blood trickled from under his head, seeping through the mortar.

'A sign of God's displeasure.' It was the bishop's voice that cut through the hush. 'More will fall in the face of His wrath.'

Aymer de Valence strode out from under the shade of the oak. 'Keep moving, you whelps!' he shouted at the youths on the scaffold and around the carts, all of whom were motionless, their eyes on the body of their comrade.

For a second, Robert's mask dropped. He stepped towards Valence, his hand going for his broadsword. Aymer, yelling at the Scots, didn't notice. Robert was brought up short by Ralph de Monthermer.

The royal knight's face was firm as he stepped in front of him, although his eyes showed understanding. 'Take four of your men from the work and have them bury him, Robert. I will replace them with ten of my own.'

Robert's rage dissolved slowly, fizzing back down inside him. Clarity drew his hand from the sword's hilt. Not here. Not now.

'Sir Ralph?' Valence questioned, as the knight began ordering his own men to help the Scots on the scaffold. 'What in God's name are you doing?'

'More hands will make this task quicker. As you said, King Edward wants the lead tonight.'

Robert allowed himself a brief, silent victory at the affront in Valence's face, before he moved to the corpse, calling four men to help him.

By the time the dead man had been put in the cemetery's ground and prayers said over him, one of the carts was full. Far above, the bare timber boards cladding the cathedral's roof showed pale through the missing lead.

Hot with temper and wine, Valence called his knights to him, telling Ralph and Thomas of Lancaster that he would escort the first load to Brechin Castle. 'Follow when you're done,' he finished, digging his mailed foot into his stirrup and hauling himself up.

The bishop watched him with resentful eyes. 'Bad enough your king wages war on Scotland. Now, he wages war on the Almighty, stealing from His temple!'

Aymer's expression changed to one of mocking indignation. 'My lord does no such thing, your grace.' He reached into his pouch and drew out a purse. 'He sent this for you.' The knight tossed the purse at the bishop's feet.

With a short laugh at the bishop's outrage, Aymer rode out of the cathedral grounds. The cart of lead rolled in his wake, churning up the grass.

Robert awoke in his tent the next morning to the air-splitting crack of stones striking the walls of Brechin Castle. He lay, staring up at the stained canvas, as the creak of the siege engines' frames and the shouts of the engineers filled the dawn. When the next strikes came there were distant splashes as masonry tumbled into the river over which the fortress perched. Robert sat up, his skin glistening. The blankets were soaked where he had lain.

Standing, he crossed to a chest, on which was placed a small basin of water, razor and beaten silver mirror. As he crouched to wet his face, the crossbow bolt dangled from its thong. The pendant was more hex than talisman, taunting him with the reminder that he was no closer to finding the truth. He stared at its reflection, wondering how long he could go on with this charade; praying Balliol would never return, waiting for some chance to look inside that sealed black box, which might or might not prove anything. Would he end up like his grandfather: kept from the throne until he died? Or like his father: a washed-up old drunk, pinned under Edward's thumb, whose only hope for the throne was in his wine-dazed dreams?

Robert felt a surge of hatred towards the English king, like acid inside him. God damn it, he was the descendant of Malcolm Canmore! He should stride out of this tent and order the fiery cross sent through the kingdom. He would don Affraig's crown of heather and raise himself an army against the conquering English. His eyes, storm-blue in his sun-darkened face, glared back at him in the silver. During the first invasion of Scotland he had been torn by divided loyalties. This time, the conflict was all one-sided. He wanted to be leading the rebels. Instead he was here, trapped in Edward's service, wearing this hateful mask of loyalty.

Robert dropped his head with a rough sigh. James Stewart's voice echoed in his mind, warning him of the futility of decisive action. The English were so close to victory. Any men he could even persuade to join him would be cut down immediately. Alone, he couldn't raise the size of army needed to counter Edward's might. *There is a season to everything,* the steward would say. *Have patience for the natural order of things.*

After dressing, Robert pushed through the flaps that divided his sleeping area from the rest of the tent. His brother was tucking into a plate of meat and cheese one of the servants had set out.

Edward nodded as Robert appeared. 'Did you sleep?' he asked, around a mouthful of bread.

'As much as I could with the din.'

In answer came another almighty crash as a stone exploded against the castle walls.

Edward raised his eyebrows. 'How long do you think they'll last?'

Robert tore off a hunk of bread, but didn't eat it. 'Not long at this rate.'

'Nes told me about the lad, yesterday,' Edward said, after a pause. 'And what Valence said.' He leaned forward, lowering his voice. 'Brother, please tell me that one day, when you're king, we'll get the chance to kick that arrogant cock and all his men into the next life.'

Robert was taken aback by the strength of feeling in his tone. Until now, his brother had been utterly convincing in the deceit. Having worried about his hot temper, believing he would not be able to hide his resentment fighting for the hated enemy, Robert had been gratefully surprised when he had thrown himself with gusto into his new role. Sometimes, he thought Edward enjoyed the charade, lording over the English knights and barons they shared campfires and rations with at night, two loyal Scots hidden among them. 'We will. I swear it.'

Edward fixed him with a stare. 'Do you truly believe if Edward conquers Scotland he will give you what you want?' He spread a hand to indicate the camp outside. 'Even after all this?'

Robert was silent. He had never confided in his brother about the identity of his attacker in Ireland, or his suspicions about Alexander's death, fearing Edward might do something reckless and jeopardise them both. The answer to the question was no. Despite James's faint hope, Robert had never believed the king would willingly give him the throne and here on the campaign, witnessing first-hand his determination to crush Scotland beneath his heel, that belief had solidified. Realising his brother was frowning at him, waiting for an answer, Robert sat back. 'We don't know anything yet. We have to be patient. For the moment.'

The tent opened and Nes stuck his head in. 'Sir Humphrey is here to see you.'

'Send him in,' said Robert, tossing the hunk of bread, uneaten, on to the platter.

Edward stood. 'I need some air.' As he headed for the flaps, Humphrey entered. They passed one another, Edward offering the earl a curt nod, before ducking outside.

Robert felt instantly wary at the smile on Humphrey's face. Over the past year, his former friend had become better at the pretence of playing the ally, all the while watching his every move. But Robert had never been convinced by his show. Being a deceiver himself, he knew the signs: the stiffness of the body, the inability quite to meet the other's gaze, the little cough Humphrey sometimes gave and that smile that didn't reach his eyes. 'Does the king require me on the siege lines?'

'Not yet,' Humphrey told him. 'But the castle is taking a hammering. I imagine Brechin will surrender before the week is out. Then we can continue our progress north.' He paused. 'I spoke to Ralph last night. He said there was an accident at the cathedral – one of your foot soldiers?'

Robert didn't have to feign the regret. 'Yes.'

'He also told me you and Aymer had a disagreement. That he thought you might . . .'

As Humphrey hesitated, Robert filled in the words. 'Attack him? Indeed I might have. The bastard was taking wagers on which of my men would fall first.' Before Humphrey could respond, Robert continued. 'You and I have, I believe, come to an understanding this past year. But Aymer?' He gave a humourless bark of laughter. 'We will never make amends.'

In the silence that followed, stones continued to bombard the castle walls.

Humphrey nodded. 'You should keep out of his way. He is waiting for an opportunity to drive a wedge between you and the king.'

Robert went and poured wine into two goblets, one of which he handed to Humphrey. 'I've heard once Brechin falls the king plans to move on Aberdeen?'

'That's true.'

As Humphrey drank, Robert thought of his brother-in-law, John of Atholl, the Sheriff of Aberdeen. 'So we might be at this for a while yet?' When Humphrey looked at him, Robert added, 'My daughter – I miss her.'

Humphrey relaxed and smiled. This time, the expression almost reached his eyes and Robert saw a ghost of his old friend.

'It gets harder, doesn't it, the more we love what we leave behind?' Humphrey took another sip of wine, his smile softening with affection. 'But Bess keeps me moving through the blisters and the marches, knowing every step will eventually bring me back to her. As I'm sure Elizabeth and Marjorie do you.'

In truth, Robert had found relief leaving his wife and daughter at York Castle with Bess and Queen Marguerite. After little more than a month in Marjorie's presence, and most of that spent in preparation for war, she remained a stranger to him. And Elizabeth – his wife? The brief thawing between them had slowed, her angst at being left to look after his estranged daughter cooling their marriage further. 'Of course,' he told Humphrey, knowing he must say what the knight expected to hear, while inside he wondered if there was any part of his life that wasn't a lie.

The tent flaps opened and Henry Percy entered. The Lord of Alnwick's fleshy face, usually full of arrogant humour, was grim.

'The rebels, led by John Comyn, have raided into England. The king has just received word from Carlisle. He will send a company to counter at once.'

Humphrey's jaw tightened, but he nodded determinedly as he set down the goblet. 'When does he want me to leave?'

'Not you,' said Percy, turning his gaze on Robert. 'Him.' The challenge was clear in his cold blue eyes.

27

Rothesay, Scotland, 1303 AD

John of Atholl jumped down into the shallows. His son, David, came after him, the hem of his cloak trailing in the foaming waves as he followed his father up on to the beach, his hair damp with spray. The waves in the firth had buffeted the little craft on the crossing.

John turned to the two fishermen who had rowed them to Bute. 'You'll wait here?'

One of them cracked a toothless smile. 'Your coins will buy our patience, sir.'

The earl dug his hand into his purse and brought out a penny. It still had the seal of John Balliol on it. He tossed the coin to the fisherman, who snatched it from the air. 'You'll get two more when we're back on the mainland.'

'Father.'

David was pointing up the beach. John followed his son's gaze past the clutter of boats and nets on the shore to the fishermen's huts and wattle houses, then to the edifice of Rothesay Castle, its four drum-like towers looming above the town. Its hulking silhouette, ringed by a moat, was stark against the milk-grey sky. Between a gap in the houses, John made out the drawbridge protruding like a black tongue from the entrance. There were many figures crossing it, some leading horses or drawing handcarts.

Gruff voices drew the earl's attention along the shore to where four galleys, each of sixteen oars, were drawn up. Long and low with their curved prows, they held echoes of the ships of the Norsemen, who had terrorised these seas and stormed the walls of Rothesay Castle seventy years ago. Men were hoisting chests and barrels into the galleys from a pile on the beach. John saw other figures heading down the main thoroughfare from the castle, carrying crates and casks. Several were wearing the colours of the steward, the blue and white chequered band bold against their yellow tunics.

'It seems our arrival was timely,' murmured John, his brow creasing. 'At least, I hope it was, or our journey will have been wasted.' He set off up the beach, boots sinking in the sand, his curly hair blown by the salty breeze. David followed.

On reaching the thoroughfare, they found themselves in a tide of people. The air was full of anxious shouts, children's wails and the bleating of animals. Doors banged as people left their homes, carrying armfuls of belongings. John passed an old woman leading two braying mules, while David found himself in a flock of geese that scattered as he hastened through their midst. He muttered an apology to the young woman herding them, who didn't respond as she gathered the geese back in with her crook. Her face, like all the others, was drawn and afraid.

Heading across the drawbridge, past lines of men carrying chests and leading horses down to the beach, they entered the courtyard, the castle buildings rising around them. Guards manned the walkways that ringed the upper part of the walls, clad in the steward's livery. Others hurried up and down the stone steps, calling to comrades. The courtyard itself was frantic with people. The air stank of sweat and smoke; of fear, thought John. Turning in a circle, he caught a glimpse of a tall, dark-haired youth. He thought it might be Niall Bruce, but before he could be sure the young man was gone, swallowed by the crowd.

'I see him, Father.'

As David caught his arm, John twisted round to see a familiar figure. James Stewart was talking intently to one of his men. The high steward looked uncommonly harried.

'Sir James!'

The steward turned, his face registering surprise and confusion as he saw them approaching. 'John? What in God's name are you doing here?' Before John could respond, the steward looked back at his man. 'Pack the last of it. I'll meet you at the boats.' As the soldier hastened off, James motioned to the hall. 'Come, both of you, I cannot hear myself think out here.'

In the hall servants were stacking barrels and sacks against one wall. The trestles and benches had been pushed back to make room, the steward's banner removed from behind the dais.

'What's happening?' John asked as they entered.

'King Edward has summoned an army from Ireland to attack us from the west – there has been burning and looting all along the coast. Last night we saw fires on the mainland and, at dawn, my scouts spied the ships. They are headed for Bute.'

John noticed two pages heading out of the steward's private chamber that adjoined the hall, carrying what looked like money chests. 'You're not going to hold Rothesay against them?'

'My men will,' said James, facing him. 'But I cannot afford to be trapped here. I'll take a small force to Inverkip then try for Paisley, unless that has fallen too.'

'What about Ulster, your kinsman? Is there any way you can parley with him, have him call off the attack?'

'Sir Richard is Edward's man. Kin or not, he will do what he is ordered to do.'

As James pushed a hand through his hair, John noticed the grey shot through his temples. He knew his looked the same. They were growing old with this war. 'If it's any comfort, the bulk of the king's army is firmly entrenched on the east coast.' He smiled grimly. 'And the son of a bitch will be forced to divide his strength further when he discovers our forces have crossed into England.'

'Comyn has led our men across the border?' When John nodded, James frowned. 'Why aren't you with them?'

John's smile faded. 'Comyn has become reckless and ambitious since he became sole guardian. Our victory against Segrave's company at Roslin was won by a hair's breadth; it was only thanks to Wallace that it was a victory at all.' John noted James nod at the mention of Wallace, his vassal. 'Comyn has grown close with MacDouall and the Galloway rabble, and since his father died he's been drawing in others of greater power: the Earl of Strathearn and John of Menteith, David Graham and, of course, his kins-man, the Black Comyn. It seems to me he intends his new position to be permanent.'

'Lamberton and Umfraville won't stand for that,' James said sharply.

'While the other guardians remain in Paris there is little they can do about it.' John paused. 'But this isn't the reason I am here.' He waited as servants dragged grain sacks past them to line against the wall: supplies for the coming siege. When they were out of earshot, he continued. 'Last year, on hearing of Robert's submission to Edward I was furious. But I've had time to think. You didn't tell me everything, did you, James?'

The steward looked away. 'I told you all I could.'

'Robert is my brother-in-law. I've known him since he was a boy and was as much of a friend to his grandfather as you were. When he first went against his father and Edward and joined the rebellion he forsook his lands. I cannot believe he submitted to the English king solely for the sake of his earldom and inheritance, not when he gave up both before. I know how strongly Robert yearns to be king. He inherited that fire from his grandfather. I cannot believe it has been doused. King Philippe has turned his back on Balliol. I, for one, do not think Bishop Lamberton and the others will be able to change his mind. Not while war continues in Flanders.' John lowered his voice. 'Surely this is the time for Robert to make his move? To press his claim?'

'We should speak in private.' The steward glanced at David, standing in solemn silence at his father's side.

'Anything you say to me can be said to him,' John assured him.

James motioned to his chamber.

Inside, a servant was hastily rolling up a map of the steward's lordships. 'Leave us.' When the man left, closing the door behind him, James turned to face them. 'Robert must retain his lands. Without them he has no platform of power, no vassals and scant authority in the eyes of the nobles. It isn't the same situation as he faced before. That was why he had to submit to Edward, or risk losing all – as I told you.' The steward hesitated. 'What I didn't tell you was that he means his submission to be temporary. As and when the threat of John Balliol is nullified and circumstance allows, Robert will attempt to take the throne. It remains his sincere intent.'

John felt hope soar in him at these words, which confirmed his suspicions. It was quickly taken over by impatience. 'Then why not now, when that threat is so diminished? Meanwhile, the greater support for Comyn grows and the more victories he secures, the harder Robert will find it to challenge his authority when he returns. I fear he will find he has scaled one mountain only to be faced with another.'

James looked troubled, but still he shook his head. 'Neither of us knows what the delegation in Paris will be able to achieve. Nor do we know how long we will survive this war.'

'Then why in Christ's name do you have Robert helping the English to destroy us?'

James was silent. His gaze drifted to the map the servant had left on the table. 'In truth, John, I do not think we can last much longer. If Scotland falls, Robert has a better chance of becoming king if he is on the winning side.'

'You want us to lose the war?' David cut in, incredulous.

'I wanted none of this. But when faced with the devil or the deep – well, a man must choose. If Robert returns prematurely to take the throne and we lose, he will face the same fate as Balliol. If King Edward hammers us into submission with his help, Robert has a hope of being offered a position of power in time. Such an outcome would neutralise the threat of Balliol and any danger to his authority that may come from Comyn.'

'James, with all respect, such an outcome would set us back ten years! Robert would be another dog on a leash, as Balliol was under Edward.'

'Edward is past sixty. He cannot last many more years. His son is not half the man he is and Robert is not John Balliol. I believe he can assert himself in time. But he needs a place of strength from which to do it. That is why he had to safeguard his lands and vassals.'

The door opened and one of the steward's men appeared. 'Sir, we need to leave. Smoke is rising in the west.'

James levelled Atholl with his gaze. 'None of us knows what will be. All any of us can do is pick a path and follow it through the darkness. I need you to trust me, John, and Robert needs you to trust him.' He held out his hand. 'Can you do that?'

John's mind filled with a memory of Robert Bruce standing in the court-yard of Turnberry Castle surrounded by his brothers and men, his face lit by torches and by an inner fire as he spoke of his right to the throne of Scotland and his intention to take it. He had seemed, to John, the very image of his grandfather in that moment – only younger and stronger – a cub who would yet become a lion.

Reaching out, John gripped the steward's hand. 'I pray to God your path is right, James.'

28

Elizabeth awoke with a start to the sound of shouting. As she sat up, the Book of Hours she had been reading slipped from her lap. Catching it before it fell, she placed the book carefully beside her on the window seat, open on an illustration of the Virgin suckling the infant Christ, the blue of Mary's robe rendered luminous with powdered lapis lazuli. Her ivory cross on its chain, given to her by her father, lay along the book's crease, marking the page. She rarely wore it these days, not since her marriage. Her neck felt stiff from the draught coming through the leaded glass that looked out over the castle's limestone walls to the River Foss. Beyond, the King's Fishpool shimmered gold in the afternoon sun.

The shouts continued, muffled through the bedchamber walls. As Elizabeth pushed open the door to the smaller adjacent room they sharpened.

'I won't tell you again, girl!'

It was Judith who had spoken. The nurse was facing a table, the surface of which was cluttered with furniture from Marjorie's model castle. Behind it stood Robert's daughter, stormy-eyed, her small fists clenched at her sides.

'What is happening here?' Elizabeth looked from the nurse to the girl.

'I've told Marjorie to put away her toys and get ready for supper, my lady,' said Judith, turning to her. 'Three times now.'

Elizabeth rubbed at her neck, feeling tendrils of pain worming into the base of her skull. It was her bleeding time and she felt fractious. Another quarrel was the last thing she needed. 'Just put them away yourself, Judith. Surely we can deal with this tomorrow.'

'She still has one in her hand,' said Judith, eyeing Marjorie, who glared balefully at her. 'And begging your pardon, my lady, but I think this should be dealt with now.'

Elizabeth stared at the stubborn child, battling the defeat already weighing heavy on her. In the three months since Robert had gone, marching north with the king's army, the girl's behaviour had grown steadily worse. Last week she had crept out of their lodgings when Judith's back was turned. It had taken three hours and all Elizabeth's staff to find her, hidden in the castle stables, even though the girl must have heard them shouting her name. The week before in a fit of temper she had ripped apart one of the dolls her father had given her, then was inconsolable for the rest of the day. She shouted and screamed when she didn't get her way, refused to do anything when told and was sullen or rude to almost everyone who spoke to her, even gentle Queen Marguerite on one occasion, which had left Elizabeth mortified.

She knew the girl's behaviour was starting to reflect on her. She had heard two of the queen's ladies-in-waiting remark on the wild Scottish girl, who needed to be tamed by a firmer hand. A rebellious seed, they had called her; so clearly the product of her father. Marjorie wasn't the only thing they gossiped about. One morning, leaving the chapel after Mass, Elizabeth had caught several women murmuring about the fact that she wasn't yet with child, even after more than a year of marriage.

As if in response to the memory, her belly gave a spasm and blood trickled warm into the wad of linen secured between her legs. 'Marjorie,' she said sharply. 'You will do as you're told.'

Marjorie's gaze flicked to her, then returned to level Judith once more, as if the nurse were the real authority here.

'Do you hear me?'

This time the girl didn't even glance at her.

Elizabeth felt a rush of heat in her cheeks, anger rising, fierce and sudden. She strode around the table and took hold of Marjorie's arm. 'Give it to me.'

Marjorie flinched, her mouth parting in shock, then tried to wrench herself free. Keeping tight hold, Elizabeth managed to wrestle the girl's hand from around her back. Ignoring Marjorie's yells of protest, she prised the child's fingers apart and snatched away the toy she had been clutching. It was the ivory man from the model castle.

For a second, bent over, out of breath, her hair straggling free of its pins, Elizabeth stared at it, then Marjorie lashed out, scratching her cheek. Elizabeth reacted, slapping her across the face, so hard she stumbled into the table. The girl hung there, one hand gripping the wood, the other coming up to clasp her reddening cheek. Elizabeth put the ivory figure on the table, not meeting Judith's eyes, and left the room.

All the way down the stairs, she could hear Marjorie's cries echoing behind her.

Elizabeth pushed out into the heat of the afternoon, taking deep breaths of air. Her maid Lora was sitting outside in the sunshine with her laundress, who was bent over a tub washing her chemise and underskirts. The women seem to have settled easily into their new lives across the water, their routines much the same as they had been in Ireland. She was the only one who hadn't seemed able to adapt.

'My lady,' Lora greeted. 'Another fine afternoon, is it not?' The maid's smile faded as Elizabeth moved on.

'My lady?'

Head down, Elizabeth hastened through the bailey, intent on putting as much distance as possible between herself and her lodgings. The castle was hectic with life, grooms leading horses to the stables, three boys laughing as they raced barrows of vegetables from the gardens to the kitchens, clerks and royal officials coming and going from the great hall. Above the bustle, rising on its high, green mound, the walls of the keep were honey-coloured in the late August sun.

Elizabeth threaded her way through a knot of serving girls, carrying buckets of water from the well. Their high-pitched voices grated in her ears and she pressed on, desperate for solitude. But where to go? York had served as King Edward's administrative seat and a staging ground for his wars in Scotland for the past five years and the city beyond the castle walls, second only to London in population, would be no less frenetic.

The maze of streets, lined with timber-framed shops and scores of religious houses, was always crowded with traders and ale-wives, fishermen and friars, while the rivers Ouse and Foss teemed with fishing craft and merchants' cogs. Elizabeth had come to know the thoroughfares and markets well in the months she had been here, but for all its familiarity it remained a foreign, transitory place where she felt squeezed out on the borders by the bustle of others' lives.

Moving on past the stables, the warm air clotted with pungent odours, she chose her direction and headed for the castle gardens. As her feet took her from the dust of the yard to soft grass and the rumble of barrow wheels and laughter faded into the thrum of bees, her pace slowed. Smells of lavender, fennel and mint rose around her, soothing and sweet. Over the bright faces of peonies, butterflies tilted at one another. Two men were digging up onions and off through the apple trees and climbing roses she saw other figures pruning and watering the herbs, their hoods up to keep off the sun. In comparison to the bailey the gardens were an oasis of calm.

As she walked, Elizabeth's guilt rose, Marjorie's cheek, scalded by the slap, filling her mind. She had seen some of the wardens of the sons and daughters of English barons being forceful with their charges, violent even. But it felt wrong to her, whose father would have whipped any governess who raised her hand. More than this, she understood how Marjorie felt. The girl wanted to be back in Rothesay with people she knew, just as Elizabeth longed for the old comfort of her father's home. The fact that they had both been abandoned in this foreign city should have united them. Instead, she had pushed the girl even further away.

Hearing raised voices, Elizabeth was drawn from her thoughts. Ahead, through the pink bells of a row of foxgloves, two women stood facing one another. Tall and dark-haired, they were a mirror image of one another, both clad in fine silks, erect and tense. Elizabeth halted as she recognised Bess and her sister, Joan, King Edward's eldest daughter.

'You told me it was over. You swore it!' Bess's tone was sharp with accusation.

'I swore it to keep you silent. I was worried you would go to Father.'

Elizabeth turned to leave, not wanting to find herself in another argument.

'You should know I wouldn't. But, Joan, you must end it with him.'

Elizabeth paused, her curiosity piqued. She hated spying on her friend; it was the kind of thing her older sisters would have done and then tattled about it. But there was something undeniably reassuring about listening in on someone else's scandal.

'If Father does find out . . .' Bess trailed off. 'I am concerned for you. He will want you to marry again soon. What suitor will want you if this comes to light?'

Joan turned away abruptly. 'You should be happy for me. You know how miserable I was married to Gilbert de Clare. The man was a beast.' She tilted her head to the sun, her pale features tightening. 'I cried myself to sleep for five years in his bed. My tears only stopped when he died.' She faced Bess. 'You don't know how blessed you are to be married to a man you love.'

'I didn't love my first husband. Count John was a stranger to me when we were wed. We scarcely became more than that before he passed away.'

'He never treated you the way Gilbert treated me.' Joan clasped her sister's hands. 'I need you to keep your silence. I beg you.'

'Imagine the cost to your lover if our father discovers your affair? It isn't just your reputation you endanger,' said Bess, removing herself from her sister's grip.

Joan backed away, shaking her head, then turned on her heel and hurried across the grass. Bess watched her go, a pained expression on her face, before she too began to walk. With a start, Elizabeth realised she was coming in her direction. She looked around for a hiding place, but there was no time. As Bess ducked under the low bough of an apple tree and came around the row of foxgloves she saw her standing there.

Bess halted, her face still taut from the conversation with her sister, then her features softened and she came forward with a questioning smile. 'Elizabeth?'

'I'm sorry,' said Elizabeth, flustered. 'I was just trying to find somewhere quiet. I didn't mean to spy. Forgive me.'

Bess brushed aside her apology. 'Nonsense, I'm glad to see you.'

'Is everything all right?' Elizabeth asked as Bess embraced her. 'I couldn't help but overhear.'

'Love's madness.' Pulling back, Bess frowned. 'But what is this?'

When the princess touched her cheek, Elizabeth remembered Marjorie lashing out. The girl must have left a scratch. 'Marjorie and I had a fight. Worse than before.'

Bess sat, her gown pooling around her. She patted the grass beside her. 'Tell me.'

Elizabeth felt the weight on her mind start to ease a little as she spoke to the princess of the argument, the setting sun warming her shoulders. 'Two years ago,' she finished, 'I was so desperate not to marry, I ran away in order to escape it. For that foolish act, I find myself trapped in a marriage my husband has no desire for and mother to a growing girl who hates me.' She hugged her knees to her chest. 'I wonder, had I consented to my father's match, would I have been happier? Living close to my family in Ireland, raising children of my own? My bridegroom was much older than me, but at least he might have loved me.'

'Love can take time to grow.'

'Maybe, if I had Robert's child, things would be different between us,' ventured Elizabeth. 'But what with the war . . . Well, we have not had much chance to make one.'

'Humphrey and I are the same,' confided Bess. 'Though not for want of trying.' She touched her stomach with a silvery laugh. 'But nature is capricious, so my mother used to say.'

Elizabeth blushed as she thought of the times she and Robert had shared a bed. She could count the uncomfortable occasions on one hand. Was it her? Did she repulse him? Or did he not think she wanted him to? She supposed she had not given him many signs. Lora had talked a lot about signs when Elizabeth had confided in her back in Writtle. The maid had even, to her deep embarrassment, given her a powder of dried rosebuds, laurel and cloves, which she quietly instructed her to rub on her breasts and between her legs before lovemaking to entice her husband better.

To deflect the conversation, Elizabeth continued. 'Robert is so distant. Even when he's with me I feel he is somewhere else.' She stared at a beetle crawling across the grass, remembering his long silences during those weeks on the road in Ireland. The few times he had spoken of anything beyond their miserable day-to-day existence it had been about King Edward, the hated invader of his homeland. He had spoken with such hostility. Now, he was in Scotland fighting for the man. It made no sense. 'I don't know him,' she finished, absently fingering her wedding band. The ruby embedded in the gold flashed in the sun. 'Not at all.'

Bess caught her gaze. 'There was another thing my mother used to say. Men are like seasons. You just have to learn when he moves from one to another and dress accordingly.'

Elizabeth nodded, but inwardly she thought Robert only had one season. The cold silence of winter.

29

Under the dead light of a half-moon, the figures threaded wraith-like through the long grass. The shadows of broad oaks thronged the field, the swell of their branches haloed black against the sky. Other than the wind in the leaves the only sounds were the distant noise of sheep in a pasture and the shrill call of an owl. The men moved silently with practised ease, their cloaks making them one with the darkness, shrouding the glint of mail and blade.

Reaching the crest of a shallow hill they dropped to the ground, pressing down in the grass. Though the air was balmy, the earth was cool with night. A damp smell rose from the soil. Rye fields stretched away before them, recently harvested, the ground stubble-coarse. Beyond was a ring of thirty or so thatched houses, barns and animal pens clustered around a small stone church. The men's eyes gleamed, catching the moonlight, as they fixed on the settlement, where the faint glow of nightlights flickered in several windows. A tang of smoke hung in the air, not from the town, but from the men themselves. Echoes of other, less pleasant odours lingered on their clothes, stained with the rust of dried blood.

Lying belly-down in the centre of their line, his weight crushing the grass beneath him, William Wallace surveyed the moon-washed vista. After counting the houses and barns, his gaze roved over the blackness of a meadow to the River Eden that carved its way through the countryside to the south-west. He studied the ghost-grey channel of water, eyes narrowed in thought. There was movement behind him; soft footfalls on grass.

'Sir,' came a whisper, as the squat form of Gray hunkered down beside him. In the half-light, the commander's bald, scarred head looked like a boulder perched on his thick neck. 'Comyn is getting ready to move.'

'He hasn't even looked at the town.'

'I don't think he intends to, until he's riding through it.'

Wallace cursed beneath his breath. He stared down the line of men, past the familiar silhouettes of Gilbert de la Hay and Simon Fraser, then Alexander and Christopher Seton. The cousins had been Bruce's men for years, but with the Earl of Carrick turned traitor in England they had pledged themselves to him soon after the battle at Roslin. Despite the fact Christopher was a Yorkshireman by birth the young man had fought as fiercely against the English as any Scot in his service. As Wallace's keen eyes fixed on the hawkish profile of Neil Campbell, lying just beyond the Setons, he gave a low whistle. When the Argyll knight turned, Wallace raised his fist. Neil nodded, knowing he was now in charge.

Edging back through the grass, rising only when he knew he would be hidden by the incline of the hill, Wallace strode towards the copse of trees he and his men had come from, his huge frame towering over Gray, who marched steadily beside him. His broadsword, strapped to his back beneath his cloak, rattled in its scabbard. Wallace swore again as he saw the glow spreading from the thicket.

'What does the whoreson think he's doing?' seethed Gray. 'Lighting a beacon? Christ on His cross, we're less than twelve miles from Carlisle. The garrison will be on us!'

Pushing through the undergrowth, Wallace entered the haze of torch-light. A crowd of men were spread out through the trees, some sharpening weapons and adjusting armour they had taken from the English dead at Roslin, others sharing wine. It was a smaller force than the one Wallace had led down into these hills and valleys six years earlier – his men still bloody from the battlefield at Stirling – but these fifteen hundred foot, commanded by a hundred mounted noblemen under John Comyn, had done ample damage on their way south nonetheless.

After assaulting the English garrisons at Dumfries and Galloway, depleted by King Edward's call to arms, they had crossed the border ten days ago. Giving the walled town of Carlisle a wide berth, they had busied them-selves burning villages and farmsteads across Cumberland, meeting little or no resistance.

Around three hundred of the infantry gathered among the trees were under Wallace's command, but the majority were from Galloway. Most still bore the white lion on their tunics, although their captain, Dungal MacDouall, had forsaken Balliol's arms in favour of his new master's. The captain was standing in a circle of men, arms folded, no trace of humour in his hard face. Beside him, John Comyn was swigging wine and chuckling at something his kinsman, the Earl of Buchan, was saying. The Black Comyn cut a formidable figure, his powerfully built frame enlarged by a coat-of-plates beneath his mail. With them were Edmund Comyn of Kilbride, head of the third branch of the family, David Graham, John of Menteith and the barrel-chested, white-haired Earl of Strathearn, who was married to the Black Comyn's sister.

Close by, their squires shortened stirrups and tightened girth straps. Even as Wallace headed for them, John Comyn tossed the wine skin to one of his knights and moved towards his horse.

'Sir John.'

MacDouall looked round sharply as Wallace loomed up, his hand going to his sword.

Comyn was slower to turn. 'Sir William.' His tone was stale.

'You're planning the assault?'

'We've planned it. We mount up. We ride in. We sack it.' Comyn's mouth curled. 'What more is there to it?'

The contempt in his voice was mirrored in the faces of the men around him. Wallace was used to that look; had seen it often during the early days of the insurrection, levelled at him from men like these – lords and earls – who had tried to keep him in his place. He had seen the look change after his victory at Stirling when thousands of peasants and freemen alike had flocked to his banner roaring his new name to the sky. *William the Conqueror*. In some, it became grudging respect. In others, fear. Fear that he, second son from a minor family, could wield more power than they.

'I've surveyed the terrain,' he told Comyn. 'The Eden flows close to the south of the town. We risk getting trapped if challenged.'

'And who will challenge us, pray tell, Sir William? Farmer Edgar with his pitchfork?' It was John of Menteith who had spoken, his red hair flaming in the torchlight.

Menteith, himself a second son, of the well-respected Earl Walter who had died some years earlier, had only recently latched himself to Comyn's band, but already he had become one of his most vocal allies. Wallace knew his type: a leech, who fed off the success of others. His older brother, the Earl of Menteith, had disappeared into English custody after the Battle of Dunbar at the start of the war, leaving him in charge of the earldom and its estates. It was known Menteith liked a wager. Cock-fighting, bear-baiting, horse-racing and the dice had all helped him squander his family's fortune these past five years. Looting had been his primary concern since they crossed the border.

Ignoring the others, some of whom were smirking at Menteith's derision, Wallace fixed him with his gaze. 'You seem to have forgotten our reason for being here is to draw the king's fire – to split his forces so our countrymen in the north have a better chance. We should beware of taking unnecessary risks, when we expect to be challenged by the enemy.'

Menteith's freckled face coloured under the intensity of Wallace's stare. He looked away first, glancing at his new ally for support.

John Comyn came to his aid. 'Indeed, the longer we waste time with debate, the sooner the enemy will arrive.' He met Wallace's blue eyes. 'My men and I will take the settlement. I thought I saw a few grain stores to the north, back the way we came. Take your company and burn them.' Comyn headed to his horse. He looked back before mounting, a smile creasing his face. 'Feel free to keep anything you find.'

Wallace stood in silence as the rest of the nobles moved to their horses and swung up into their saddles, faces flushed with wine and anticipation. Pulling on helms, shortening their reins, they walked their horses out of the copse. Menteith rode his charger directly at Wallace, who sidestepped neatly. The Disinherited followed in their wake, laughing and joking as they hefted weapons and flaming torches, for all the world as if they were embarking on a feast-day hunt, rather than the rape and sack of a sleeping community.

Under Comyn and his plunder-hungry comrades the men of Galloway had grown careless, used to easy victories assaulting undefended villages. Many bore trophies taken from their victims: an ivory-handled dagger, a silver brooch pin, a silk purse, a soiled veil. Some, he had noticed, had taken to wearing locks of female hair around their necks on thongs. As one, a bull of a man, with a black beard, stalked past, Wallace counted at least six different coloured hanks of hair knotted together to hang down the front of his aketon.

He couldn't berate them for these tokens; he who had worn a necklace of human teeth in the early days of the rebellion and who'd had a belt fashioned from the skin of the hated English treasurer, Hugh de Cressingham. Still, he found them distasteful now. Maybe the courts of Paris and Rome had tempered him, or maybe it was just the abandon with which these men wreaked havoc that troubled him. Wallace had no compunction about killing English on the field of battle. But the homes split open by axe blades, the women and girls dragged out into the streets for the pleasure of the infantry, farmers pissing themselves as they were lined up and beheaded, boys screaming like animals as they burned to death in a barn: these things lingered in his mind. His own forces had been driven to similar excesses when he had led them here after Stirling, but he hanged the worst offenders. Blood-lust made a man careless. An ill-disciplined army was a useless one.

'Bastard sons of bitches all,' murmured Gray at his side, as Comyn and the others disappeared through the trees. 'And Menteith? I wouldn't give that mincing whoreson the sweat of my arse crack if he was dying of thirst.' When Wallace didn't speak, Gray glanced at him. 'Burning grain? You should have rammed his order up his—'

'He's guardian of Scotland, Gray. The men of the realm have given him that authority. We must respect that. The last thing Scotland needs is more division among its defenders. Come,' Wallace said, moving off through the trees to where they had left their own horses. 'Gather the rest of our men. We'll play our part. For now.'

30

They could see the flames a mile away. Strangely silent, the tongues of fire curled into the sky revealing the outlines of houses and barns. The thatch on many of the buildings was ablaze, smoke rolling thickly. Figures – some riding, more running – were illuminated in the streets. Although the fire itself could not be heard at this distance, the faint screams were unmistakable.

As Robert looked across the dark fields towards the burning town, a memory awoke in him. Anglesey, eight years earlier. He was riding through filthy, snow-mottled streets, men scattering before him. Llanfaes had been bloody, the English breaking through the town's palisade in moments, but its inhabitants had at least been defended, if ineffectively, by Madog ap Llywelyn's forces. What was happening in this settlement tonight was butchery.

They had seen similar scenes as they'd ridden into England, but only the aftermath; smoking ruins of buildings under ashen skies, corpses strewn across the streets, flies already swarming, survivors dead-eyed with shock. It was by this trail of devastation that they had followed the rebels down through Annandale and across the border, always a day or more behind the Scots, until that evening when monks from an abbey they passed said they had seen a large band of marauders moving south along the River Eden. The English company, made up of three hundred horse and two thousand foot, headed by Aymer de Valence and Robert Clifford, had pushed on through the night in pursuit.

Above the harsh breaths of foot soldiers struggling up the hill to join the knights on the ridge, the sound of hoof-beats rose. Two figures emerged from the darkness and hauled their horses to a halt before Valence.

'Scots have overrun the place, sir,' panted one.

'Have they formed a perimeter?' Aymer questioned. 'Any defence?'

The rider's teeth flashed in the moonlight. 'No, sir. The churls have left themselves wide open. The river cuts off their path to the south. If we ride now, we can block their escape.'

Robert, staring down at the blazing town, wondered just who was in those streets. No more faceless castles, manned by unknown garrisons; there might be men he knew, comrades even, down there.

Valence drew his sword and nodded to Robert Clifford, mounted beside him. 'You and your men take the town. I'll secure the periphery and keep the whoresons penned in. Remember, brother, the king wants as many ringleaders brought to him alive as possible. He wishes to deal with John Comyn personally.' The knight's tone roughened as he spoke his brother-in-law's name.

Robert watched as Valence swept the company with his stare, his face shadowed by the raised visor of his helm, his eyes like pools of pitch beneath the rim.

The knight fixed on him. 'You will join him, Bruce.' Leaving Clifford to summon his men, Valence pricked his destrier closer to Robert. 'If you hesitate to confront, kill or capture any one of your countrymen I will know of it.' He leaned in, hefting his broadsword. 'I'm going to ram my steel into the gut of every Scot I find down there.' The wire in his mouth gleamed as he bared his teeth, before wheeling away with a shout. 'We ride!'

'What did the bastard say?'

Robert turned to see his brother looking at him. Edward, whom he'd set in charge of the knights of Annandale, wore their father's arms, his yellow surcoat divided by the red saltire. He had taken off his helm and his face glistened with sweat in the moonlight. 'Just follow my lead,' Robert told him.

As Clifford and his men set off at a canter down the hillside, Robert snapped down his visor. He couldn't think about who he might meet in those streets. If he faltered, the sacrifice he had made in submitting to Edward would be in vain. He had to seize this moment, no matter the cost. Had to prove he was one of these men. Kicking at Hunter's sides he followed Clifford, his brother and Nes to either side of him. Around them rode knights and squires of Annandale and Carrick, summoned to arms by Robert. The men of Annandale had seen the devastation wrought in their lands by the rebels under John Comyn, whole towns ravaged by sack and slaughter. They now showed no compunction about confronting fellow Scots. They were out for blood.

The flames grew in the slits of Robert's visor and smoke tainted the air as he and his men plunged through a harvested field. Clods of soil were kicked up, stones skittering off helms and shields. Spurring their horses over a bank, they joined a track that led into the settlement. Canter became gallop as they approached the town, their blades and the bosses on shields burnished by the glow of the fires. In their wake came Valence and his knights. Behind, the foot soldiers hastened to form a barrier on the outskirts.

Clifford didn't slow as he neared the first houses, the roaring flames masking the hoof-beats. In the street, two men were bent over a chest. There was a body on the ground close by. A third man was watching his comrades open the chest. He had a cask in his hands, which he upended and guzzled from, wine dribbling down his tunic. On lowering the vessel, he looked straight at the knights cantering towards him. His mouth widened, the cask slipping from his hands. Staggering back, he turned to run, a shout tearing from his lips.

The Scot only made it a short distance before Clifford caught him. As he swung his sword down, the blade hacked through the running man's neck, beheading him. His body continued for a couple of seconds, before he crumpled in the dust. His two comrades were cut down where they stood, one taking a slash of a sword that split his face, the other stabbed through the throat. Clifford and his knights swept on into the burning streets.

Robert led his men through the buffeting heat. Above the thudding hooves, he caught jubilant cries and anguished shrieks. The streets were strewn with debris. Through his visor he glimpsed dozens of corpses among the wreckage. Here, a half-naked woman, split from groin to throat, there another whose face had been staved in. A man burst from the door of a burning house and lumbered into the street, skin and hair flaming. One of Clifford's knights rode him down and, with a chop of his sword, ended his screams.

Beyond, the thoroughfare was filled with Scots, mostly infantry. Here, looting continued, as did rape, judging by the tortured screams coming from the few buildings not yet on fire. Shouts filled the air as the Scots saw the English coming, but half of them were too drunk on pillaged ale to form any adequate defence. Few wore mail and many of those with helms and shields had discarded them, the better to drink and pillage. Clifford's knights rode right through them.

As swords swung in, blood splattered the walls of houses and strangled howls were lost in the clamour of hooves. Many Scots turned and ran, but a few defended themselves, roaring and wild-eyed as they leapt at the riders, or hacked axe blades into the legs of horses. Now, the first English went down, knights hurled from tumbling mounts, or grappled and pulled to the ground. The crack of blades meeting shields echoed in the confined streets. One of Clifford's men lost control of his horse as its neck was split open by a Scot's falchion. The destrier careened into the side of a burning house, causing the roof to collapse inwards with a burst of sparks that showered the men in the street.

The charge of the knights was quickly brought to a stop, choked by the press. Scots were running away down side streets, shouting the alarm. Among them, Robert caught sight of tunics emblazoned with the white lion of Galloway. The symbol of John Balliol fired his blood. With a shout, he led his men off between the buildings. A huge man with a black beard lurched out of a doorway in front of him. He had a dirk in one fist and something long and wispy trailed from the other. Robert just had time to see it was a hank of blond hair, before he brought his sword down in a cut of wrath that cleaved through the man's leather aketon and into his shoulder. Wrenching the blade free, he cantered on, the forty-two inches of Damascene steel christened in the first blood of the battle.

Heart pumping furiously, he drove Hunter on into a market square where the Scottish force was concentrated. Among the foot soldiers were knights, sprinting for their horses as Robert's men rode into their midst. Fleeing Scots were falling prey to their own devastation, stumbling over strewn furniture and sacks to be trampled by the brutal charge of iron-shod hooves that could burst a man's skull or snap his spine. Some darted to the houses for cover, but were faced with fires they had set. Smoke choked the air.

Outside the church, from which the invaders were carrying coffers and candlesticks, Robert saw a knot of red surcoats. Glimpsing the Comyn arms illuminated by the flames, he kicked Hunter towards the looters. Somewhere, a horn began to call. One man, foot already in his stirrup, turned at the sound. Robert, plunging towards the group, caught sight of his face. His heart gave a fierce leap. It was John Comyn. Robert spurred Hunter harder. By capturing the rebel leader he could prove his loyalty to Edward and rid Scotland of his greatest obstacle to the throne in one move. Comyn had mounted, but his back was to Robert. In the chaos he hadn't seen him.

Robert's concentration was so intently fixed on his enemy that he only saw the rider rushing up on his left at the last moment. With barely a second to spare, he dropped the reins and raised his shield to block the sword that came crashing at him. The impact was brutal, the concussion jolting all the way up to his shoulder, weakening the nerves in his hand and arm. The momentum of his charge carried him some distance past his attacker, before he could veer Hunter round with a jab of his knee to counter. As they came together again, swords arcing above the heads of their horses, Robert realised he knew him. The man, whose white surcoat bore the arms of the Red Comyns, wore a conical helm with a nasal guard, the ventail of which hung loose, exposing his mouth and jaw. It was Dungal MacDouall; the man whose father had been killed by his in the Bruces' attack on Buittle Castle.

As Robert cut in at him, the captain smacked the blade away with a cuff of his shield, then rammed his sword towards Hunter's head. Robert reacted quickly, jabbing his spur into the horse's flanks, causing the destrier to rear up. He was rocked back against the cantle as Hunter's hooves pummelled the air, one of them catching MacDouall's palfrey on the side of the head. The palfrey stumbled, crashing into Hunter's side, causing the destrier, still up on his hind legs, to lose his balance. The palfrey, stunned by the kick, went with him as he toppled.

Luck jolted Robert from the saddle, throwing him sideways out of the way of Hunter's massive weight. He rolled as he struck the floor, his gambeson absorbing most of the impact, mail crunching on the hard-packed ground. Somehow, he managed to keep hold of both sword and shield, but his helm had been knocked out of place, meaning the slits no longer lined up with his eyes. Robert pushed up the visor to see MacDouall struggling to his feet a few yards away. The captain's shield strap had broken in the fall and the shield was hanging off his arm. Between them, the horses untangled their limbs and thrashed upright. All around, the clash of battle continued. Robert's brother and knights were engaged in fierce fighting with men in the colours of Badenoch and Buchan. More horns were sounding, both near and distant.

Tossing the shield aside and grasping his broadsword two-handed, MacDouall strode in through the smoke. Recognition sparked in his eyes as he saw Robert's face. He came in fast, bringing his sword swinging down. Robert, still on his knees, hefted his shield to block. The blade bit into the wood, scoring a deep gash through Carrick's red chevron. Robert stooped under the strike, then heaved upwards, forcing MacDouall to reel away. Once on his feet, Robert moved quickly. Their swords cracked together, splinters of metal flying from the blades in sparks. Robert had lost sight of

Comyn, all his attention now focused on the captain, who clearly intended to kill rather than capture him. As the two of them hammered and thrust at one another, men streamed past.

The English knights under Clifford had overrun the town. Though greatly outnumbered by the Scottish infantry, they far outmatched the disarrayed and drunken soldiers. Many Scots not yet caught up in the fray ran down the streets bearing whatever loot they could carry as the horns continued to sound. Those running south would be faced with the river, those heading north would find themselves in Valence's killing ground.

The timbers in the house beside Robert collapsed inwards with a groan, a wave of heat gusting out of the doorway and windows. He ducked out of harm's way as smoke and sparks billowed towards him. MacDouall wasn't so fortunate. A clump of blazing thatch fell from the roof on top of him, causing him to lurch away. While his defences were open, Robert barrelled into him with his shield. The captain, caught unawares, was rocked backwards, his arm flung wide. Thrusting his sword up under the edge of his shield, Robert punched the tip through MacDouall's mail coat and gambeson to pierce the flesh of his armpit. Snarling with the effort, he rammed the blade home.

The captain roared, his sword falling from his fingers to clang in the dust, but he managed to kick out, catching Robert above the knee. As Robert stumbled back his sword pulled free of MacDouall's body. His foot caught on a grain sack discarded by the looters and he went down, dropping the weapon. Mad-eyed, MacDouall wrenched a dirk from his belt with his left hand. His right was clamped to his side where blood pumped, staining his surcoat. Robert reached out, his fingers curling around the grip of his fallen sword. As MacDouall thrust towards him with the dagger, he brought the sword up and round in a mighty arc. The blade came down on the captain's wrist, cleaving mail and flesh, its momentum halted only by bone. MacDouall's mouth stretched in a hideous scream. He dropped to his knees, his hand, still in its mail glove, now hanging at a sideways angle, dangling from the wrist. Blood spurted from the wound.

Hauling himself to his feet, Robert stepped towards MacDouall, meaning to finish it.

'Earl Robert!'

He turned, distracted, to see Robert Clifford riding towards him with a score of knights.

The knight pulled his horse up sharp. 'Sir Aymer's men are being attacked from the rear. Come,' he ordered, slamming his spurs into the flanks of his destrier.

Lungs burning from the exertion and the smoke, Robert looked around for Hunter. The destrier, well-trained, hadn't bolted. He was close by, stamping in agitation, eyes reflecting the flames rippling up the sides of the buildings. Shouting to Nes and his brother, who had despatched three Galloway men between them, Robert climbed into the saddle. Leaving Dungal MacDouall curled over his bleeding hand, he and his men rode away across the market square into the corpse-strewn streets.

On the edge of the town, fierce fighting had broken out. In the red glimmer of fires, Robert saw the white and blue striped surcoats of the knights of Pembroke. They were clashing with a motley crew of mounted men. Many of the English foot soldiers had forsaken their positions and were engaged helping Valence and his men tackle this company, creating a breach in the perimeter through which scores of Scots were fleeing. Some Scots, dazed by the darkness beyond the flames, or slowed by injuries, blundered straight into the mêlée, but many more escaped thanks to the efforts of this new force.

Clifford was riding ahead. As the royal knight entered the fray, Robert caught sight of a massive figure, scything an axe into the crowd around him. There were few men so impressive in height and size. Robert, still some distance away, knew instantly that it was William Wallace. A jolt went through him. He slowed his horse, letting other men ride on past him, his eyes fixed on Wallace, who roared as he hacked into an English foot soldier, sending the man flying backwards in a mist of blood. An English knight charged in at him from the side. Wallace turned, moving with surprising speed and fluidity for such a large man, and, with a savage arc of his axe, took the top off the man's helm as if he were slicing open an egg. Half the knight's skull went with it. He fell forward, spilling his brains as he slipped from the saddle. Robert had not been on the field at Stirling or Falkirk. Although he had watched Wallace in training and often heard tell of his prowess and fearlessness during his time in the rebel army, he had never actually seen the man in the heat of battle. It was an awe-inspiring sight.

More of Valence's men were closing in, moving to surround Wallace. Robert had a mad impulse to shout a warning. He caught himself in time, but he needn't have worried. All at once, Wallace veered away, his men following at his shout. It seemed they had only engaged in order to give as many Scots a chance to escape from the town as possible. All who could were now withdrawing, turning and riding into the night after the rebel leader, leaving hundreds of wounded and dead behind them. To his left,

Robert glimpsed a group of horsemen moving fast out of the town. Several were wearing the red and black surcoats of the Comyns. Seeing Clifford gesture to him, Robert forced Hunter in pursuit. His brother and several Carrick knights, seeing him break away, followed swiftly.

The horsemen had a good lead, but Robert managed to compel Hunter to a last burst of speed. Fixing on a man at the rear, a knight judging by his trappered horse, he galloped up on him. The knight turned, too late. As Robert smashed his sword into his back, the man was pitched from the saddle and caught up under the hooves. Edward Bruce rode up behind another who bore John Comyn's arms. With a sideways swipe he hamstrung the man's horse, which went down, crushing its charge.

Sensing motion behind him, Robert turned and came face to face with a snarling Scot, bearing down on him. It was Alexander Seton. Time seemed to slow. In the few seconds it took for them to pass one another, the swing of their blades faltering and going wide, Robert saw the shock of recognition reflected in Alexander's face. Then, his friend was galloping on past to be swallowed by the darkness. As the Carrick knights tackled the last few riders, Robert brought Hunter to a shuddering stop. Removing his helm and letting it fall to the mud, he collapsed back against the cantle, taking great gasps of clean night air. Smoke coated his mouth with its acrid tang and it burned when he swallowed. Sweat ran into his eyes.

'Did you see Comyn?' His brother came up alongside him. Edward had removed his helm and his nostrils and mouth were stained black. With his bloodshot eyes, it gave him a demonic look. 'Bastard just rode right by me. I couldn't get to him.'

'William Wallace was with them,' Robert told him between breaths. 'I think he made it out.'

Edward's eyes widened. 'Wallace? He's back in Scotland?'

Robert nodded. For a moment, they stared at one another, the surprise of this sinking in through the numbness of battle.

Clifford rode over, his surcoat, sword and horse all slathered in blood. 'Comyn?'

'Gone,' Robert answered. He nodded to where the Carrick knights were rounding up the Scots they had managed to bring down in the pursuit, checking the bodies for signs of life. 'We took six.'

Clifford cursed. 'We would have got them all if not for that company. They came out of nowhere.' He wiped sweat from his forehead with the back of his arm, leaving a smear of blood across his face. 'I think it was William Wallace leading them.' He cursed again, bitterly. 'More men and we could have taken both him and Comyn. The rebellion would have been done for.'

'No matter. We have done them great harm this evening.'

Clifford nodded after a pause and gave a hard smile. 'That we have.' He gestured to the fallen Scots. 'Make sure your men secure them. The king wants prisoners.' Clifford paused, before riding off, his eyes lingering on Robert. 'Well fought, Sir Robert.'

Dunfermline, Scotland, 1303 AD

After Brechin Castle surrendered, its commander killed on the walls by a stone shot from a trebuchet, King Edward led his army north. Like a plague, they laid waste to everything in their path; razing castles, destroying towns, burning barns of grain and scorching the earth. Seeing the telltale smoke of their coming on the horizon, many Scots fled before them into the mountains and moors, driving livestock and saving what they could carry. The old and sick remained, locked behind the flimsy barricades of wattle and daub houses, listening to the rumble of hooves, supply wagons and siege engines roll in.

In the last days of summer, the king marched through Aberdeen into John Comyn's lordship of Badenoch. After laying siege to the Red Comyn's chief stronghold at Lochindorb, which he captured in a matter of days, he remained here for some weeks, hunting stags on the moors and enjoying the wine in the castle's cellars. The victory, though sweet, coming as it did after Comyn's assault on the advance party at Roslin, was soured somewhat by the knowledge that even as he was drinking his enemy's claret, the knave himself was busy despoiling the north of England.

Daily, Edward waited for tidings of the company he had sent south to counter the Scots, impatient with the silence. Just as autumn was turning the leaves to gold and the days were drawing in, the news he had been waiting for came. Aymer de Valence had bested the rebels near Carlisle, killing several hundred of their infantry and sending the survivors scattering back into the depths of Selkirk Forest. The king, satisfied by these tidings, moved south, winter descending through the mountains in his wake, bringing the first flurries of snow to lace the higher peaks.

At Perth, close to Scone Abbey, his army joined the force commanded by his son. Prince Edward and his men, among them Piers Gaveston, had been busy pillaging the earldom of Strathearn and the prince was keen to show his father the plunder they had gathered during the campaign. The king, pleased to see his son seemed to be taking his martial responsibilities more seriously, organised several days of jousting and feasting in reward, at the end of which Gaveston was crowned champion, to the irritation of some in the Round Table.

But Edward presided over the celebrations a king preoccupied. Although he had succeeded in progressing unchallenged to the far north of Scotland, devastating the lands of his enemies and severely weakening their resistance, it had not been a complete victory. Stirling Castle – the capture of which was essential to the control of Scotland north of the Forth – remained in Scottish hands. In the west Ulster's men, after seizing several castles including the high steward's stronghold on Bute, had foundered. Despite Ulster's allegiance, many of his troops, unpaid and starving, had deserted and sailed home. But more troubling still for Edward were the tidings that had come with the news of the rebels' defeat.

The report from Aymer de Valence stated that among the Scots fighting under John Comyn's banner was William Wallace. Aggrieved that the infamous outlaw had somehow managed to return unchallenged from France, slipping through the blockade of ships in the Channel, Edward found himself deeply agitated by Wallace's arrival. The rebel leader appeared like a comet or other bad omen late in his day of triumph, auguring disaster. More than ever, he wanted to hunt down the beast in its lair and drag it from the shelter of Selkirk.

The one thing that appeased Edward came on the fourth day of his sojourn in Perth in the form of a message bearing the royal seal of France. It was a letter from King Philippe, formally ratifying the peace between England and France. The truce, which excluded the Scots, restored the Duchy of Gascony to Edward and his heirs and granted approval for the marriage of his son to Lady Isabella. Philippe, who sent greetings to his sister, Queen Marguerite, and gifts for his nephews, Thomas and Edmund, said he no longer wished to be at war with his brother-in-law.

Edward knew it wasn't familial sentiment, but rather the expense and difficulty of the continuing war in Flanders that provoked the French king's peace, but the reasoning was immaterial. What mattered was that he was once again in possession of Gascony and the Scots no longer had a hope in hell of placing John Balliol on the throne. Leaving Perth somewhat lighter of heart, Edward took over the impressive monastic precinct of Dunfermline Abbey on the banks of the Forth, to winter and to reward his commanders.

*   *   *

In the nave of Dunfermline's church, where grand circular pillars carved with bold motifs flanked the aisles, the captains of the English army gathered before their king. A clear November sky filled the arched windows of the upper storey, blue and brittle. The men wore fur-trimmed cloaks to ward off the chill, surcoats mended, swords cleaned of the blood and rust of the campaign.

Robert stood among them, his gaze on King Edward, who was seated on a cushioned chair in front of the altar in a scarlet mantle trimmed with gold. Behind the king was his dragon banner, first raised on the tournament fields of France when he was a prince in exile, later hoisted in his wars; a symbol that there was to be no mercy. The great standard was patched in places and frayed around the edges, but the winged serpent at its centre was still vivid, wreathed in fire. As Robert watched, Clifford was called before the king.

The royal knight crossed the floor and went down on one knee. Edward's voice rang imperiously through the nave as he granted him estates in Roxburghshire, adding to the knight's already considerable awards of Caerlaverock Castle and the lands of Sir William Douglas, who fought alongside Wallace early in the rebellion. When Clifford rose, the men of the Round Table applauded, Guy de Beauchamp and Thomas of Lancaster smiling and grasping his shoulder as he returned to their ranks.

'Sir Robert Bruce.'

As Robert walked forward, his footsteps loud in the falling quiet, he caught the gazes of Humphrey de Bohun and Ralph de Monthermer. Both were nodding their approval. After the victory in Cumberland the frost in some of these men had begun to thaw. They had seen him throw himself into the battle; seen him kill his countrymen without compunction and celebrate when it was done. Clifford, in particular, had spread word of Robert's part in the slaughter and capture of Scots to the others.

Behind King Edward, a carved rood screen separated the nave from the monks' choir. Beyond were the shrines of King Malcolm Canmore and his wife Queen Margaret, who founded the abbey two hundred and thirty years ago. The nearness of the bones of his ancestor set a fire inside Robert. Dunfermline was the royal necropolis where many of Scotland's kings lay entombed, among them Alexander III, who had plunged to his death not fifteen miles from here. Now, the man Robert suspected may have been responsible sat above his corpse; a conqueror, on a throne of adamant.

Robert thought of his grandfather who had spoken of the Bruce line as a mighty tree, with roots stretching back to the Normans and the ancient kings of Ireland, and he, Robert, a new shoot sprung from those great boughs. The blood of dead kings ran like sap in his veins. He could feel their will working within him, demanding that he fulfil the promise of his line: that he drive out this tyrant and claim his destiny, by any means. No more waiting. No more.

Coming before Edward, Robert forced himself to one knee and lowered his head.

'Sir Robert,' said the king. 'For your part in the defeat of the rebels in Cumberland, I confer upon you a new position. Henceforth, you will be Sheriff of Lanark and Ayr.'

Robert remained motionless staring at the flagstones, but his mind was racing. Edward's shrewdness in his choice of gifts was not lost on him. Word was out that William Wallace had returned to lead the rebellion – the court had been humming with the news since Aymer de Valence delivered it – and the king was clearly disturbed. Before the war, Wallace's uncle had been Sheriff of Ayr and it had been the rebel leader's home. Later, after the occupation, the English Sheriff of Lanark had been responsible for the death of Wallace's wife and daughter. By putting him in these positions, Robert knew Edward was setting him against the outlaw, physically and symbolically.

'Your brother, Sir Edward Bruce, will have the honour of serving my son and heir in his household, and to Alexander Bruce I grant the deanship of Glasgow.'

Robert barely listened as the king continued. William Wallace filled his thoughts, as he had often these past weeks, since the bloodbath in the town. He had thought Scotland's fate sealed with this campaign, the resistance too weak to withstand Edward beyond another summer of war. He had feared his own fate would be sealed with it, trapped in Edward's court – his only hope to change his fortune the faint chance he would yet find that elusive proof. Now, he wondered.

The threat of Balliol's return was finally over and William Wallace had come home at the eleventh hour to lead the rebellion. This changed everything. Second son of a minor knight who had risen to become guardian of Scotland, Wallace had gathered the greatest force of men the kingdom had seen in centuries and had bested an English army at Stirling. He was a general with a celebrated reputation, who had drawn thousands of men – peasants and earls alike – to his banner. Robert knew Edward's weaknesses; knew where to hit him hardest: the supply depots at York, the diminished garrisons at Edinburgh, Dumfries and Lochmaben. Together, their strength combined, might he and Wallace have a chance to turn the tide?

'Arise, Sir Robert.'

Robert looked up as Edward finished. 'Thank you, my lord, for the great honour you do me.' Standing, he met the king's pale gaze. 'I am, as always, your loyal servant.'

31

Dunfermline, Scotland, 1304 AD

The prisoner cowered against the wall when they came for him, daylight flooding the stables where they had kept him and the others for weeks. He cried out in protest, his dry lips cracking blood into his mouth, as they seized him.

'Silence, turd!'

While two guards held him upright, the one who had spoken punched him in the stomach, knocking the cries from him. With the prisoner doubled over, the guards dragged him from the stables, where the moans and pleas of other captives echoed in the stinking gloom.

As they hauled him through the snow across a deserted yard, the man raised his face to the grey sky and opened his mouth, desperate to catch the mist of drizzle in the air. The breath of the guards steamed as they bore his weight between them, their boots crunching through the drifts. The snow had come late, only falling in earnest a fortnight ago, shortly after the Christ Mass. The roof and towers of Dunfermline church were slabbed with white. The prisoner squinted up at the abbey, mouthing a prayer.

The guard who had punched him glanced back and saw. His mouth curled. 'Talking to God again, Scot?' The smirk vanished. 'Only I am listening today, understand? You'll talk to me.'

As the man the others called Crow turned away, the prisoner hawked a wad of bloody phlegm into the snow and gritted his teeth, but as he saw the ruined barn looming black at the end of the yard his courage failed him. It was a place of pain and nightmare that haunted his dreams and waking delirium. He threw back his head and howled at the sight of it, though the disused barn and stables were well out of the way of the other buildings in the precinct and even if someone heard him who would come to his aid?

The English king and his army had taken over the abbey for their winter quarters, ousting the monks. It didn't stop the man roaring himself hoarse as Crow pushed open the barn doors.

Inside the shadowy space were various farming implements and equipment: harnesses, ropes and whips, buckets and nails. All ordinarily innocuous, to the prisoner they had become instruments of torment. There was a trestle in the centre stained with fresh blood. Its coppery smell sharpened the air. He arched back as the two guards marched him towards it, over patches of snow that had fallen through the barn's broken roof. But it seemed they weren't using the trestle today for they passed it without stopping. The prisoner, breathing hard, looked wildly around, searching for a sign of what they would do. They had already gone past the trough where they had all but drowned him on occasion. The dark water had a sheet of ice over it. He could taste it just looking at it.

'Here,' said Crow, motioning to a hook that dangled from one of the rafters.

The prisoner winced as the guards hoisted his arms and looped the rope that bound his wrists over the hook. They stepped away, leaving him dangling like a piece of meat.

The whip, he thought to himself. They will use the whip today. It surprised him. They had used the whip early on, stripping the tunic from him and baring his back to its sting. The pain had been ungodly, but other things they had done to him since had been worse. The whip, at least, was unlikely to kill him.

Crow stood before him, studying him with an unpleasant, knowing expression. It was different to his usual look and disturbed the prisoner.

'The time has come, Scot, for you to tell me where that son of a whore William Wallace is hiding.'

The prisoner shook his head weakly. 'I cannot tell you what I don't know.' His voice was raw. 'Why won't you listen?'

Crow smiled. 'You've known all along that's not the truth. Now, we both know.' He drew a dagger from his belt, sheathed beside his sword. 'One of your friends, some Galloway scum we scraped off the field in Cumberland, told me this morning. You were the man to talk to, he said, about Wallace's base in Selkirk.'

'I know nothing of the camp. I only joined Wallace's company in Annandale just weeks before we crossed into England. He was lying.'

'I recognise the truth when it comes from a dying man's lips. It was the last thing he told me, before he bled out.' Crow cocked his head to the bloodstained trestle. 'Right there.'

The prisoner knew this wasn't pretence. In the weeks since they had been taken, after the disaster at the town, several captives hauled away for Crow's interrogations had not returned to the stables. He knew their deaths didn't matter to these men, or the master they served. They were all peasants, or lowly tradesmen like him, a tanner's apprentice, not worth any ransom, unprotected by the rules of chivalry.

As Crow came towards him, the prisoner found himself fixated by the dagger. The blade was thin and keen.

'Now I know not to waste my time with the others. That you're the one to concentrate my efforts on.'

'No,' breathed the prisoner, twisting away as far as his bonds would allow.

'I'm going to keep you here, alive and in torment, until you talk. Do you understand, Scot? Until you talk.' Crow nodded to his comrades. 'Hold him.'

The prisoner shouted and pulled away, but the guards held him firm between them, crushing his head with their hands. He could smell their breath. Ale for breakfast.

Crow stepped up, dagger in hand. He placed the tip at the corner of the prisoner's eye. 'First, I'm going to put out your eyes.' He scraped the tip down the side of his right cheek. 'Then your ears. Fingers. Toes. By the time I'm done, you'll be half the man you are now, but I promise you will still be alive.'

The prisoner was panting, spittle flecking from his mouth. He yelled as the blade returned to his eye. This time, Crow jammed his thumb into the corner and pushed up the skin, so the white was fully exposed. Then, slowly, he began to push the tip in. There was a tiny spurt of blood and fluid as it punctured the first layer of jelly. The prisoner's yell became a tortured scream. '*I'll tell you! Dear God, I'll tell!*'

Crow removed the blade. Blood trickled a red tear down the Scot's cheek. He was gasping, hanging limp from his bonds. 'I know where the camp is.'

'Where?'

'I cannot say. *Wait!*' shouted the prisoner, as the dagger rose. 'I cannot say, but . . .' He faltered, hanging his head. In the end, fear was stronger than shame. 'I can make you a map.'

King Edward stood in the window, staring at the vista that stretched from Dunfermline's walls. The land, white with snow, folded down to the Firth of Forth, the wide waters dark under the sullen sky. In the distance, across the estuary, he could make out the black cliffs that flanked the city of Edinburgh.

Edward felt the chill of that frozen landscape in his bones. He was more affected by the winter these days, his joints sore when he rose in the mornings, his chest tight. On the outside, despite his frost-white hair and the creases in his skin, he still cut an impressive figure, his frame taut and muscular from years of training and war. But, inside, he could feel himself weakening.

At a burst of laughter, he turned to see his three-year-old son Thomas come racing into the chamber closely followed by his toddling brother, Edmund. They ran to their mother, who was reading by the hearth. Shortly before the Christ Mass, Queen Marguerite and the rest of the womenfolk had travelled up from York with an escort of knights. Scotland was almost conquered and Edward wanted his family with him when he crushed the cause of eight years' woe beneath his heel. He watched Marguerite plant a soft kiss on the boys' tousled blond heads, before their nurse came hurrying in.

'Begging your pardon, my lady. My lord,' she breathed, bobbing her head to Edward. 'They are too quick for me.' She shooed the boys out of the room, closing the chamber door and muting the sound of their laughter.

Edward's gaze lingered on his wife as she settled back with her book. Sister of King Philippe, she had been seventeen when he married her in Canterbury. They had called her the Pearl of France, a shy, delicately beautiful girl with milky skin. Now, at twenty-one, after the birth of two children, her fragile features had filled out into supple curves. Her youth made Edward feel older still; more aware of time passing, more aware of what he wanted to achieve before his body failed him and the earth rose to claim him.

His great-uncle, King Richard, had been called the Lionheart. His uncle, King Louis of France, had been canonised. Crusader and Saint: that was how they were remembered. He wanted his own legacy to stand as tall. The man who brought Britain under his dominion, a kingdom united. A man they would speak of as a new Arthur. The greatest warrior king who ever lived.

Marguerite caught him staring at her. 'You look lost in thought, husband.' Her French was silvery.

Edward inhaled. 'I am thinking of the coming campaign. Stirling Castle will prove a challenge, I fear.'

'Can you not cut off their supplies? Isn't that what you have done before, with success?'

He half smiled, enjoying her interest in his strategies. 'It will take too

long. Stirling is well stocked and even better defended.' Edward held out
his hand to her.

Marguerite put down her book and crossed to him, the hem of her gown
rustling across the rug. She allowed Edward to guide her in front of the
window, while he stood behind, his hands on her shoulders.

'Like Edinburgh,' he said, stooping so his face was level with hers and staring
towards the distant crags that loomed over the city. 'A rock too high to scale
with ladders. Only one road in. Walls too lofty and too thick for most engines.'

'What will you do?'

'I am thinking of using something I saw in the Holy Land, employed by
Sultan Baybars.'

Marguerite turned and laid her palm above his heart. 'The one who tried
to kill you?'

Edward had an image of a cloaked man and a dagger rising. His brow
pinched at the memory of the blade punching into his chest and of Eleanor's
screams as he collapsed. While his guards had tackled the Assassin Baybars
had sent, his wife had thrown herself down on him, the blood washing hot
over his chest as she removed the dagger and put her lips to the wound to
try to suck out the poison.

Edward put his hand over Marguerite's and removed it from the scar that
riddled the skin beneath his shirt. His second wife was everything he could
have hoped for in a queen: quiet of voice and gentle of nature, lovely of face
and studious of mind, and she had borne him two sons. But she wasn't
Eleanor. She hadn't touched his soul.

'My lord.'

Edward turned to see Aymer de Valence standing in the main doorway of
the chamber. He looked grim.

'What is it, cousin?'

'I've just learned that you've granted Robert Bruce permission to return
to Turnberry Castle.'

As Edward let go of her hand, Marguerite went to the chair to pick up
her book.

Aymer nodded curtly as she passed him. 'My lady.'

Edward waited until his wife had disappeared into the room his sons had
been taken into, before answering. 'He wishes to oversee the reconstruction of his castle and to assess the state of his new sheriffdoms.'

Aymer entered the chamber fully, pushing the door shut. 'I think this is
unwise, my lord. Unwise and dangerous. When you are so close to conquering Scotland? I implore you to deny his request.'

'The defences at Ayr need rebuilding and garrisons must be re-established in both towns.' Edward crossed to the hearth and held out his hands to the flames, feeling warmth seep into the tips of his icy fingers. 'My campaigns have focused on the destruction of the west these past years. If I am to profit from my conquest, I must look to restoring peace and prosperity across the realm. If no harvests are growing, no cattle or sheep reared or trade routes opened, my coffers will not be filled.' He turned to Aymer. 'This is no whim, cousin. I need what Bruce can provide in this.'

'Then allow me to accompany him. Keep an eye on him.'

The king studied Aymer's expression. Almost thirty, the man was very much in the mould of his formidable father, William de Valence. The truculent Frenchman, Edward's half-uncle, had been one of the only members of his family who hadn't turned his back on him when his father sent him into exile. Like William, Aymer was well-built with dark, strong-boned features, though his good looks were somewhat marred by the wire that now kept his front teeth in place. The injury, sustained at the Battle of Llanfaes, had been caused, so the knight maintained, when several of Madog ap Llywelyn's men attacked him, but Edward had seen the way he had looked at Robert Bruce that day, with murder in his eyes, and had wondered.

Aymer, his father's son, was also given to violent outbursts of temper and excesses in battle, but he wasn't as strong a leader and the king saw he found it difficult competing with men like Humphrey de Bohun, a natural commander whom others liked and respected. Edward guessed this was in part because Aymer wasn't yet titled as his peers in the Round Table were. Despite the fact his older brother had died in the Welsh wars and his father in Gascony, he hadn't yet inherited the earldom of Pembroke, still held by his mother. The king had seen the knight come into his own in the last year's campaign, but his suspicion of Robert Bruce was fast becoming an unwelcome obsession. It irritated Edward, as if Aymer thought he could see something he himself could not. After the initial fear that Bruce knew something of Adam had been allayed, Edward had watched him settle, quietly and obediently, into the role of humbled servant. Just as the man's father had, years earlier. Over time, his suspicions had faded in the face of Bruce's continued loyalty. 'I need you here, Aymer, when I plan my next campaign.'

'My lord, please tell me what Bruce has done to earn your trust? He has done little I can see other than fight John Comyn – and his enmity towards my brother-in-law is well known. He has given us only the barest scraps of information on the rebels, talking about weakness in castles we already know about, seemingly unable to give us information about their encampment in the Forest.'

'He told Humphrey all those outside Wallace's inner circle were met on the boundaries and led to the camp blindfolded.'

'And you believe that?'

'Sir Humphrey does. That is enough for me.'

Aymer scowled. 'Humphrey was wrong about him before.' He went to the king and stood before him. 'My concern is that Bruce might use this moment to slip away and warn the rebels of our plans. Surely that is a concern worthy of an escort, if nothing else?'

'Warn them of what, exactly?' Edward demanded, anger cutting through the tolerance he had towards his cousin. 'That I intend to batter the last life out of their insurrection this coming summer? That I will take Stirling and hunt down that dog, Wallace? John Comyn and his merry band will be well aware of my intentions, I can assure you. Indeed, I pray they are. I want the whoresons to know what is coming.'

Aymer pressed on, despite the king's displeasure. 'My lord, you must know Bruce only returned to your service because he knew he would lose everything if John Balliol came back. Not out of any loyalty.'

'Of course I know this.' Edward took up a goblet. 'Robert Bruce first rebelled against me because he wanted to creep from under his father's shadow, not for any real love of his kingdom. He proved that by returning to me with the Staff of Jesus when Scotland needed him most. I admit I thought him a treasonous wretch on a par with Wallace himself, but now I see he is just like his father; an ambitious toad, happy to sit and grow fat on a lily pad so long as he is rich and comfortable, and has a little power in his pond.

'The authority I have bestowed upon him will keep him loyal. He may also prove very useful in keeping the population under control. A familiar face.' As Edward paused to take a sip of wine he saw his own face reflected in the goblet's gold surface. The droop in his eyelid was his most prominent feature these days. 'In the end,' he murmured, 'we are all made in the moulds of our fathers, Aymer.' At a knock on the chamber door, he looked up irritably. 'Enter.'

The door opened and Richard Crow, the man he'd set in charge of questioning the Scottish prisoners, entered. There was a piece of parchment in Crow's hands and his face was lit with triumph. 'I have it, my lord. The location of Wallace's encampment.'

Edward set down his goblet and went to Crow. He took the parchment, his eyes darting over a roughly drawn map. A dark ring clearly indicated the perimeter of the Forest. Inside were various jagged lines and triangles, circles with crosses in and a larger cross near the south-west of the ring. 'What are these symbols?' he demanded, stabbing at the parchment with his finger.

'Rivers, hills, ruins of buildings,' said Crow, at the king's side. 'The Scot who drew it explained it all to me. There are markers on the trees the nearer you get to the camp.'

Edward stared at the black lines, his heart quickening as he realised he might be looking at a map to victory.

His reign had been a long road with much lost and gained along the way. He had crusaded in the Holy Land, conquered Wales and survived civil war, defeating Simon de Montfort, one of the greatest generals in England. He had reformed the realm left to him by his father, providing strong government, regular parliaments and new laws. He had fought his cousin for Gascony and had finally won, had fathered eighteen children and endured the grief of burying eleven of them. And he had done what he set out to do all those years ago on Gascony's sun-baked soil, when the taunting songs the Welsh had sung of his first defeat against them still echoed in his mind. He had brought Britain under his command.

But though the *Last Prophecy* had been fulfilled and the four relics gathered, his victory was not complete. Scotland still defied him and the one man who was the symbol of that defiance remained at large.

William Wallace was a blight on Edward's record of strength. There had been other opponents, more noble and distinguished, who had sought to destroy him, but he had bested them all. De Montfort, his own godfather, he had torn apart at Evesham, his remains fed to the dogs. The head of the Welsh prince, Llywelyn ap Gruffudd, had long since rotted away on London Bridge. Edward had no intention of letting Wallace, the brigand behind the defeat at Stirling – the greatest military disaster of his reign – escape the same fate. Edward had murdered his own brother-in-law in pursuit of his legacy. He would not stop until it was complete. 'I will send a company at once.' The king looked at Crow. 'Tell the prisoner if this map doesn't lead us to the camp, he will face the worst punishment I can conceive.'

'Oh, he knows, my lord,' said Crow with a smile, turning and heading from the chamber.

Aymer stepped in quickly. 'My lord, send Robert Bruce with this force.'

Edward's pale grey eyes narrowed. 'Why?'

'For one, blindfolded or not, he knows the Forest far better than any of our men and far better,' Aymer added, 'than I suspect he has admitted. Second, it will be a good opportunity to test his loyalty, once and for all.'

Edward couldn't deny there was sense in this. 'Very well.'

Aymer smiled, surprised, but before he could speak the king continued.

'Sir Robert Clifford and Sir Ralph de Monthermer will lead the expedition.'

32

Dunfermline, Scotland, 1304 AD

'When?'

As Robert crouched by the chest that contained his sword, he glanced at his wife. Elizabeth had risen abruptly from the window seat at what he'd just said.

'When are you leaving?' she repeated.

Robert opened the chest and removed the blade. Pulling it part way from its filigreed scabbard, he was satisfied to see Nes had cleaned and whetted it. Rising, he pushed it through the loop in his belt. 'As soon as my men have loaded the wagons. This afternoon at the latest.'

'Why didn't you tell me sooner?'

Robert faced her resignedly, knowing the look he would be greeted with. There it was: the narrowed eyes and furrowed brow of her displeasure. 'I found out only yesterday that King Edward granted my request. He informed me after vespers. When was I supposed to tell you?'

Discarding the book she had been reading, Elizabeth turned to the window, wrapping her arms about her. Her pale blue gown, belted under her bust with a plaited girdle of navy silk, was creased where she had been sitting. The hem of her fur-lined cloak was stained from the mud that swamped the abbey grounds, the first snows already trampled to slush by the host of men wintering there. The king, taking up residence in the abbot's lodgings, had granted the earls use of the monks' dormitory, lay quarters, laundry and stores. Knights and squires had taken over barns, or else pitched tents in the gardens and cloisters.

Like a web, with the king at the centre, the greater part of the army radiated outwards, infantry and archers setting up camp in the fields surrounding the precinct. Many had erected wooden huts in which to shelter from the worst of the winter. The boggy site, haunted by hopeful quacks, mummers and whores, had become a breeding ground for lice and infections of the lungs, and the men were suffering with January's plummeting temperatures. The cacophony of coughing and phlegm hawking that accompanied their waking each morning could be heard in the abbey itself.

'You could have told me last night.' Elizabeth looked over her shoulder at him. 'But how could you when you were with Humphrey and Ralph? Bess told me at chapel this morning that you were drinking and playing dice until dawn.'

A girlish shriek sounded from the adjacent chamber where Elizabeth's maids were billeted with Judith and Marjorie. The door to the room, which had served as a linen store for the monastery's laymen before the king commandeered the abbey, was ajar. Over the chatter of the women, Robert heard Judith telling his daughter to play quietly. The accommodations were cramped and sparse and Robert had found being cooped up with his wife and her maids unbearably claustrophobic after the months on the road. It had been a relief to spend last night in the company of men. 'I would have thought it would please you and Bess that Humphrey and I have begun to make amends. You've both petitioned for it enough.'

'You have no idea how hard it is when you are gone, Robert. I'm moved from one town to the next, all the while trying to take care of your daughter.' Elizabeth lifted her hands. 'You do not see what she becomes. Now you are with us, Marjorie is an angel. When you're gone – well, the devil himself would find it hard to keep pace with her.'

'King Edward has ordered me to check on my sheriffdoms and has given me licence to rebuild Turnberry. I cannot refuse my duty to him or my tenants just because you find it difficult dealing with a child. You have Judith to help you.'

Elizabeth lowered her voice further so the women in the next room couldn't hear. 'Marjorie is too old for a nurse. She needs a governess. When I was her age I could read scripture, play chess, sing and embroider.' She continued quickly as he went to speak. 'Lady Bess knows a woman, the wife of one of Humphrey's squires, who has taught children in several noble families. She can read Latin and French. Judith can stay as Marjorie's nurse, but your daughter needs someone to teach her. And a firm hand.'

There was a knock at the door. As it opened, Robert saw two of his porters.

'Sir, the wagon is ready,' said one. He nodded to the chests stacked against the wall. 'Shall we start loading these?'

Robert nodded. As the porters hefted the trunk that contained his mail and carried it out of the room, he looked back at Elizabeth. 'I don't have time to discuss this now. We'll talk when I'm back.'

'When will that be? Two weeks? Two months?'

Robert crossed to the bed where he'd left his marten-trimmed riding cloak – a wedding gift from her father. He noticed Elizabeth had folded it neatly for him and felt an unwelcome stab of guilt. 'I need to oversee the reconstruction at Turnberry, then check on the defences in Lanark and Ayr.' He shook out the garment and swung it around his shoulders. 'I'll be a month at most.'

'Then let me return to Writtle. Marjorie seemed to like it there. My squires are more than capable of escorting us.'

'No,' said Robert, more roughly than he'd intended. The last thing he wanted was his wife and daughter back in England.

The real truth behind his request for the king to grant him leave to travel to Turnberry was his desire to make contact with James Stewart. Rothesay had fallen to Ulster's forces during the summer campaign and the whereabouts of the steward were currently unknown, at least to the English, but Robert thought his family's old allies in the west, the MacDonalds of Islay, might be able to help track him down. These past weeks in Dunfermline, the snows banking up against the abbey walls, he had become increasingly impatient to begin his search. His hope, if Wallace could raise an army like the one he'd summoned for Stirling and if he could add his vassals to such a force, was that they could make a stand and turn back the English. Now the threat of Balliol's restoration was ended, it was the moment for action. Caution had only got him so far. It was time to throw it to the wind.

Wallace was the steward's vassal and if anyone could persuade the man to work with him to this end it would be James. But, the moment Robert made any such move, the lies he had built around himself would come crashing down and the king and his men would see him for what he was: a traitor, who had betrayed them twice. Elizabeth and Marjorie could not be in England when his deception was revealed. Nothing he cared about could.

Elizabeth moved towards him. 'If not Writtle, then take us with you to Turnberry.'

'You expect me to take my wife and daughter through the heart of a land at war?'

At this she drew herself up. 'You've done it before.'

Robert stared at her, his brow knotting in question. When he realised she was referring to their flight across Ireland, his anger boiled over. 'Your memory fails you, Elizabeth. You forced me to take you that night. What choice was I given?'

She seemed to want to retract what she'd said, holding up her hand, trying to speak. Robert wouldn't let her. He had wanted to say this for a long time.

'You trapped us both in this marriage. As your father told you, you made this bed for yourself. You'll damn well lie in it!'

Elizabeth's pale cheeks coloured. 'I try to, but you keep that bed so cold.' Her voice rose. 'And I'm not the only one to blame for this sorry marriage. Lest you forget, husband, you held a sword to my throat that night. You used me to get away, just as I used you. My father was punishing us both.' At this, the fire seemed to go out of her. She slumped on the window seat. 'My father was angry, yes, but he wouldn't have arranged our marriage unless he believed such an alliance would benefit both our families.' She glanced up at Robert. 'I want to prove him right. Make amends for what I did. But I cannot do it alone.'

How little she knew, thought Robert, looking down at her. The ambitious Richard de Burgh had agreed to the marriage, not because Robert would make a good husband, but because one day he might make her queen. He felt some of his anger towards her drain, replaced by weariness. He didn't want to make her unhappy, but until he gained the throne, his wife and daughter had to come second. As long as they remained safe and ignorant, that was all that mattered. He went to speak, meaning to tell her he would find a governess for Marjorie, but there was another knock at the door. He turned sharply. 'Come!'

When it opened, Robert, expecting to see his porters, was surprised to see a young page. His tunic bore the blue and gold chequered arms of Robert Clifford.

'I bring a message from my master, sir,' the page ventured, glancing from Robert to Elizabeth, who had her head in her hand. 'He says you are hereby ordered to undertake a royal mission with him and Sir Ralph de Monthermer.'

'What mission?'

'My lord said to tell you that you weren't to leave for Turnberry as planned. He will speak to you himself in due course.'

Unease unfurled in Robert as he wondered why he had been chosen for another assignment when the king had already granted him leave. 'Very well.' He held his temper until the page had closed the door, then thumped his fist into his palm. 'Damn it!'

Elizabeth started at his shout. Lifting her head from her hand, she watched as he paced.

After a moment, Robert stopped. If Ralph was going on this mission, he probably knew more about it. He was certain the knight would tell him if pressed. 'I must attend to this.'

Elizabeth nodded in silence.

Robert turned down the passage that led to the room Ralph had been billeted in. Reaching it he knocked, determined to get what he could out of the knight. There was no response. He knocked again. Still no answer. Frustrated, he went to move off. As he did so, he heard a muffled laugh. His suspicion piqued, Robert tried the door, which opened at his touch.

In the room beyond, a pallet bed covered with crumpled blankets stood against one wall. Chests were piled on top of one another and a candle flickered on a stand beside two goblets and a jug. In the centre of the room were two figures. One had his back to him, but Robert knew Ralph by his dark curly hair. The other, a woman, took him a moment more to recognise. It was Joan of Acre, the king's eldest daughter. She and Ralph were locked in an embrace. At Robert's appearance they pulled apart as if wrenched by invisible hands.

'*Christ – Robert!*' hissed Ralph, moving in front of Joan.

The princess was wearing only a gauzy chemise, through which Robert could see the swell of her breasts. In her mid-thirties, like Ralph, she was a tall, statuesque woman with the same long limbs as her sister, Bess. Her black hair was loose around her shoulders, undressed and unbound.

'What the hell are you doing?' Ralph's face was red.

Behind him, Joan moved to the bed and snatched up an ermine-trimmed mantle which she wrapped around her shoulders, pulling it close against her chest.

Robert lifted his hands. 'My apologies, Ralph. Lady Joan,' he added, glancing at the princess, who levelled him with her stare. 'I knocked, but no one answered.'

Joan said nothing, but slipped past Ralph and headed for the door. When Robert moved aside she hastened away down the passage, clasping the mantle over the chemise.

'Close the door, for God's sake,' growled the knight, turning and going to the stand, where he took one of the goblets and drained its contents. His undershirt was open at the neck and the skin of his chest glistened with sweat, though the bare room was chilly.

Closing the door, Robert watched as Ralph poured another measure. He was stunned. He had known the royal knight for years and would never have guessed he was involved in such a dangerous affair. A knight of the royal household, swiving the king's daughter? Edward would flay him alive for the dishonour.

'Swear to me you won't tell a soul,' said Ralph, when he'd finished the wine.

'How long has this been going on?'

The knight shook his head. 'A few years now,' he said finally. 'Since the death of Gilbert de Clare.' He tossed the empty goblet on the rumpled bed and pushed a hand through his hair. 'I love her, Robert.'

'You're out of wedlock.'

Ralph scowled. 'That doesn't stop half the men in this court. Most of the earls of England have illegitimate children tucked away on a manor somewhere.'

'I doubt any of the mothers are the king's daughters. Joan isn't just some wench, Ralph. She's one of Edward's prized possessions.'

Ralph exhaled and looked him in the eye. 'What will you do?'

'I'll keep my mouth shut is what I'll do.' As Ralph's face filled with hope, Robert held up his hand. 'If you'll tell me what this mission the king is ordering me on is. I'm being sent somewhere with you and Clifford. I take it you know of it?'

'Of course.' Ralph looked surprised, his shoulders slumping in evident relief at such a trifling condition. 'One of the prisoners taken in Cumberland gave up the location of Wallace's base in Selkirk. The king wants us to lead a mounted raid into the Forest. We are to hunt down and capture the rebel leaders, Wallace and John Comyn, then destroy the camp.'

Robert fought to keep his emotions hidden. 'Then an end to this war may not be long in coming?'

'God willing.' Ralph paused. 'There's one thing you should know. I'll give it to you in return for your pledge of silence. It was Aymer's idea that you be in this company. From what I heard, he petitioned the king to be allowed to lead it himself with the intention of testing your loyalty. The king denied his request; he, as the rest of us, is becoming irritated by Aymer's obsession with you. But King Edward will expect you to hunt down your countrymen with as much ferocity as the rest of us do.'

Robert nodded. 'Thank you.'

'You swear it?' called Ralph, as Robert turned to go.

'I swear it.' As he opened the door, Robert realised he had one of the king's men in his debt. And he was no longer the only deceiver in this court of wolves.

*   *   *

Aymer de Valence strode along the passageway, rigid with anger. The king's decision to send Clifford and Ralph into Selkirk had infuriated him, especially since it had clearly been done just to spite him. How the king could not understand his intentions were in the best interests of them all, he could not fathom. Robert Bruce was a snake in the grass, a wolf in a lambskin. A Judas. Why could no one see this but him?

Bruce might have gone up against Comyn's forces in Cumberland without compunction, but it had not been a true test of his loyalty, since Wallace had fled the field before Bruce had time to engage. In Selkirk he would be pitted against the rebel leader – a man whose company he had joined when he first deserted, a man he had subsequently knighted with his own sword. In short, a friend. Faced with capturing Wallace and destroying the rebels' base, Aymer had no doubt Bruce would reveal his true colours. He had wanted to be there to watch for the slip of the mask he felt certain the bastard was wearing, but since Edward had refused him, he would have to try the next best thing.

Ralph had been a comrade of Bruce's when they were Knights of the Dragon and was clearly beginning to trust him again. Aymer knew he would have to tread carefully in order to convince him to watch the earl, would have to keep a rein on his hatred so Ralph would see him as well-meaning. It was going to be difficult. But he had to do something. He wouldn't sit idly by and allow Bruce to betray them again. Aymer flicked his tongue over the wire that held his front teeth together. He would see the bastard hang before that happened.

Reaching a fork in the gloomy passage, he turned around it. A figure was outside the door to Ralph's lodging. The devil himself. Robert Bruce. Cursing beneath his breath, Aymer stepped back around the corner. After a pause, hearing the creak of a door, he peered round to see Bruce entering the room. He thought he heard an exclamation from within. Wondering whether he should interrupt the meeting, he was surprised when a second figure hastened out moments later. It was Lady Joan.

Edward's daughter was wearing a mantle that she clasped at her breast. As she hastened towards him, she pulled up the hood, but Aymer had time to see her hair falling loose around her shoulders. Time, too, to catch the swish of a gauzy chemise beneath the cloak. He slipped around the corner as she approached, pressing himself against the wall, but he needn't have worried. Joan had her head down as she passed by. He caught a brief glimpse of her flushed cheeks and then she was gone. When Aymer looked back, Ralph's door was closed.

33

The East Coast, Scotland, 1304 AD

The moon hung low over the coast of Scotland. For James Douglas it was a lantern, guiding him home. With his gaze, he traced the cliffs and the white swell of the snow-clad hills beyond, eyes shining at the sight of his homeland, which he hadn't seen for seven years.

Back then he'd been a whip-thin boy of twelve summers, barely able to wield a blade. Now, at nineteen, his body had lengthened and thickened into that of a young man, his arms and chest were corded with muscle from the strict martial training his uncle had given him and his chin was shadowed with a beard, the same crow-black as his hair.

'Is it how you remember?'

James forced his eyes from the cliffs to see William Lamberton looking at him. The Bishop of St Andrews was wrapped in a black cloak, the hood pulled over his tonsure. His eyes gleamed in the dawn, one icy blue, the other pearl white.

'No, your grace,' replied James, his French clear and strong over the splash of oars. 'It is even more beautiful.'

'Do not get your hopes up, Master James.' The caution came from Ingram de Umfraville, who sat stiffly on one of the benches between the oarsmen, his breath fogging the air as he spoke.

James's gaze flicked to him. Umfraville, along with Lamberton and John Comyn, was one of the three guardians of Scotland. James had been introduced to him back in Paris, when they boarded the boat on the banks of the Seine. He hadn't liked him then and the fortnight's crossing – navigating around the English blockade in the Channel – had done nothing to alter his first impression.

'It is not the Scotland you knew,' continued Umfraville morosely. 'The years of warfare have changed it beyond recognition.'

'It looks much the same to my eyes,' observed Lamberton, his gaze on the coastline.

James moved to sit beside the bishop. He had known Lamberton less than three months and felt he had his measure as much as he had Umfraville's. He was a man of few words, but all of them were keenly weighed. He was young for a bishop, James guessed not much more than thirty, quick as silver and twice as bright, with a voice that forced men to listen when he spoke. James had liked him immediately. Not least because Lamberton was the one man who had vowed to do what no other had. He had pledged to help him get his lands back.

James's father, Sir William Douglas, former governor of Berwick, had been the first nobleman to join the insurrection. A tower of strength and fiercely patriotic, he had been there when Wallace had risen to surge across Scotland, bringing fire and sword to the English. He had fought at Wallace's side, hounding King Edward's justiciar out of Scone and battling the enemy during the sack of Berwick. But, for all his might, he had been unable to resist when the English had taken him in chains to the Tower of London.

James had been in Paris when he learned of his father's passing. The year before Robert Bruce had arrived at the family's castle in Douglas to abduct James and his mother on behalf of King Edward, who had wanted to use them to persuade the lord to forsake his alliance with the rebels. As it turned out, Bruce had disobeyed the king's command and let them go free, but James's mother had sent him to Paris to live with an uncle, until the danger passed. On hearing of his father's death in the Tower, James learned that the lands of Douglas, to which he was heir, had been granted to a man named Robert Clifford, one of the king's favourites.

James had raged against Edward, cursing him and all who served him, but finally his fury subsided to a cold hatred and one morning, sitting on the banks of the Seine, he made a solemn promise to his father's memory that he would return to his homeland and reclaim what was rightfully his. That opportunity had presented itself in the late autumn when his uncle introduced him to Lamberton, who had been part of a delegation at the French court, hoping to restore John Balliol to the throne, a hope now crushed by the treaty agreed between England and France. Unbeknown to James, his uncle had been in contact with the bishop, speaking about the possibility of Lamberton taking him on as his ward, a proposition to which the bishop had agreed.

James had packed little in the bag he took from his uncle's house. Just some coins his uncle gave him, some spare clothes and his sword, now strapped to his hip beneath his cloak, the pommel digging into his side. He was a lord in name, but felt like a vagabond. Still, there was a freedom in his rootlessness that was appealing. He was the adventurer, in search of riches, glory and redemption.

'Do you think I'll get the chance to fight, your grace?' James kept his voice low, so Umfraville and the knights escorting the two guardians wouldn't hear.

Lamberton's face was clearer with the advancing dawn, a rosy hue now tinting the horizon. He looked thoughtful. 'The messages we received in Paris were ominous. The king and his son conquered much of Scotland during the summer. Instead of returning to England when the campaign was ended, he chose to winter at Dunfermline. I believe he means to end us this coming year, when the snows thaw.' The bishop's gaze drifted to the cliffs, whose scarred faces were rust red in the breaking dawn. 'There is a belief among my comrades that surrender is the only viable option left to us.'

James studied the bishop's expression. 'But you still have hope?' He half smiled. 'You wouldn't have promised to help me win my lands if you didn't.'

Lamberton met his gaze, those strange eyes burning in the fire of the rising sun. 'There is always hope, Master James.'

Dunfermline, Scotland, 1304 AD

Ralph de Monthermer lay awake, one arm propped behind his head. As he breathed in, he could smell traces of olive oil and herbs on the cover; Joan's scent caught in the weave. Ralph closed his eyes, the darkness behind them filled with visions of her lustrous hair tumbling over her shoulder as she leaned forward to kiss him, her skin honeyed by candlelight.

The door opened, banging back against the wall. Ralph sat up, startled from his reverie, as four of the king's men burst into the room. 'What in God's name are you——?'

'Sir Ralph, on the king's order you are hereby charged with the crime of rape. We are to take you into custody.'

Ralph swung his legs over the bed and stood. He was naked except for his braies. 'Rape? Is this some jest, Martin?'

'No jest,' replied Martin grimly. He took a pair of hose and an undershirt that were draped over a chest and tossed them at Ralph, who caught them. 'I suggest you put these on. The stables are cold.'

'Stables?' murmured Ralph. He stared at the knight. 'Where the outlaws are?'

'I'm sorry, my friend. I petitioned the king for you to be housed some-where appropriate until this matter can be judged, but he was adamant.' Martin's brow creased. 'Why did you do it, Ralph? The king's daughter?'

Ralph's thoughts tumbled off a cliff in his mind. Shock at the exposure of his secret was followed by fear.

'I didn't believe it when the king told me,' Martin continued, 'but he said Lady Joan's tears confirmed it.'

Ralph knew, without any doubt, that Joan would not have accused him of any such thing. Rape was the king's charge because he'd discovered the affair, of this he was certain. It was a harsh charge at that, punishable by castration if he was found guilty. On the heels of his shock came rage at the realisation that Robert Bruce must have betrayed him. 'The son of a bitch gave me his word!' With a shout, Ralph battered aside the stand with the goblets and jug on it. Red wine sprayed as the table toppled, the vessels clanging on the floor. '*I'll kill him!*'

At Martin's nod, the knights came towards him. Ralph lashed out, punch-ing one of them in the face, but even as the man staggered away, clutching his bloodied nose, his comrades came in. Between them, they wrestled Ralph's arms behind his back and marched him from the chamber.

34

The horses ploughed through the snow, the tremor of their passing bringing more flakes scattering down through the trees. Bare branches of ash and pine webbed the sky, where bands of copper fire glowed in the west. Outside in the world the sun was setting, but in the depths of Selkirk Forest it had been twilight for days.

Yesterday morning, following the course of a river whose breadth had been matched by a wide channel of sky, they'd had a brief respite from the gloom, but before long the train of three hundred knights and squires had veered south-west away from the river, deeper into the Forest. Thorny bushes and briars snaked across the uneven ground, where steep banks rose only to fall sharply into bracken-filled dells, riven by networks of frozen burns. It was an endless, monochrome expanse of white snow and black trunks, punctuated by the odd shock of red from holly berries.

'Recognise any of this, Bruce?'

Robert, riding a piebald palfrey that was several hands shorter than Hunter and thus better to navigate through the dense woodland, didn't have to look round to know it was Valence who had spoken.

As the knight tried to manoeuvre his horse up alongside him, one of the Carrick knights accompanying Robert kicked his mount in between them.

Valence laughed. 'No need to be concerned. We are all friends here.' He leaned forward in his saddle to peer around the man at Robert. 'Aren't we, Bruce?' His mirth faded. 'And it was a simple question.'

'I was blindfolded on the few occasions I was led into the camp,' replied Robert. 'As I think you already know.' In truth, he didn't recognise any of the Forest on the route they had taken, coming south from Dunfermline through a land bleak with winter. He had almost always entered Wallace's base from the west.

'No doubt the closer we come to the viper's nest, the clearer things will become.' Pulling the reins tighter, the steel plates on his gloves clinking, Valence pricked his courser through the trees to join his own men.

Robert looked round, hearing the crunch of hooves. Seeing Humphrey, he nodded to the Carrick knight, who kicked his horse ahead allowing the earl to ride at Robert's side.

'Sir Aymer seems to be vying for the position as your shadow,' observed Humphrey. 'Every time I look round he's at your side.'

Robert's gaze lingered on Valence, riding erect in his saddle, his white and blue striped cloak swept back over one shoulder to display his mail and broadsword. 'I wonder how he managed to persuade the king to let him come on this raid. From what I was told, King Edward refused him until the business with Ralph came to light.'

Humphrey's face clouded at the mention of Monthermer's transgression. 'I still cannot believe it. I've known Ralph for years. I was there when he was inducted into the Knights of the Dragon. There when the king welcomed him to sit at the Round Table. Rape?' He shook his head. 'I would never have thought him capable of such an act.'

'What if it wasn't rape?' Robert ventured, careful to keep his tone questioning. 'What if Ralph and Joan were lovers and the king found out? He would be furious, understandably. Maybe he levelled the charge at Ralph to punish him?'

'That certainly sits better with the man I know. But if Ralph was engaged in an affair with Lady Joan, he kept it close to his chest. I never suspected it.'

Robert said nothing, but his eyes strayed to Valence. He was certain the knight had something to do with it. Not only was he now under Aymer's constant watch, but Ralph, imprisoned in Dunfermline, must think he had been the one to betray him. Worse still, every stride of their horses was taking them closer to Wallace.

The rebel leader always had patrols on the perimeter, who would hear them coming, but Humphrey and Aymer, both ordered to lead the raid in Ralph's place, had anticipated this and had sent their own men on ahead to scout out their positions. Robert's hope hung in the balance. If Wallace and the last of the resistance fell during this raid, he would have no chance to face the king head-on – to turn back the English and lay claim to the throne, in defiance of Edward's new laws. The rebellion would be ended and the most Robert could expect – if he never found the proof he sought – would be that the king would make him governor, or perhaps guardian in time. The thought he would have to continue living this lie indefinitely was unendurable. He would rather go down fighting than face another year in Edward's service.

Robert wished his brother were here, but Edward had been posted in his new role in the household of the Prince of Wales. He wondered if the king had intended to isolate him with that move; keep him corralled and in his place. His gaze drifted to Nes, riding close by. Humphrey's voice broke through his thoughts.

'I realise this is a strange moment to bring this up, Robert, especially in light of the business with Ralph. But I cannot keep it to myself any longer. Bess is with child.'

Thrown by the sudden shift in conversation, Robert gathered himself. 'Bess? Expecting?'

'Well, she tells me we must wait and see, but, yes, she believes so.'

Through his tension, Robert felt an unexpected pleasure at the pure delight in the earl's face. From Elizabeth's talk, he knew the couple had been hoping for a child for some time. Humphrey's smile was infectious. Robert found himself laughing with him. 'I'm overjoyed for you. Truly.'

Humphrey's grin broadened. 'Thank you, my friend.' He faltered, seemingly also caught unawares by the heartfelt exchange.

Clifford's voice cut through the moment. 'Here!'

Humphrey and Robert urged their horses up a shallow bank towards the knight's shout, closely followed by Valence. It had been growing dark while they were talking and the sun had set, the woods sinking into a purple dusk.

Clifford had dismounted on the edge of a large clearing. 'Look,' he said, pointing to a structure that thrust from the tangled undergrowth. 'We must be close.'

Robert, sliding from his saddle, saw the skeletal frame of a siege engine between the trees. It looked abandoned, the lower beams strung with ivy, the timbers rotten and stippled with hoarfrost.

Behind them, the train of knights and squires pooled to a stop, men seizing the opportunity to relieve themselves, or flex their stiff muscles.

Clifford took the map from one of his knights. He looked from the crumpled parchment to the clearing. 'See, here. I think this place is marked.'

Valence had come to stand beside him, barring the view of the map from Robert. He was nodding. 'Three days from the river. Yes. You're right.'

'Sir!'

Several of Clifford's knights had spread out into the clearing, their boots trailing lines through the snow. One had stopped and was motioning between the trees on the far side.

Clifford and Valence made their way towards him, Robert and Humphrey falling into step behind them. The knight, they soon saw, was pointing to something painted on a tree. In the encroaching shadows it was faint, but still apparent: a white circle with a cross inside. Robert's heart sank as he recognised Wallace's mark. There was another in the distance on the gnarled trunk of an oak.

Clifford smiled. 'If the Scot was right, we're no more than half a day's march away.'

Less, thought Robert. Two or three hours at most.

'I suggest we make camp here for the night,' said Humphrey. 'Then move in at dawn. It should give our scouts time to return with locations of any enemy patrols.'

Clifford nodded. 'I agree.'

'We'll set up a perimeter of our own,' added Humphrey, looking between them. 'We don't want the bastards coming on us unawares. This is their territory, remember.'

'Don't worry,' said Valence, his eyes on Robert. 'My men will be watching.'

Robert headed back through the snow to where his men were waiting. As the voices of the commanders echoed, relaying orders, the knights dismounted. Any talk was subdued, the men wary now they were so close to the enemy.

Squires unpacked blankets and sheets of waxed canvas to lay on the ground, while others fed horses and fetched water from a nearby burn. In all the activity, no one took any notice of Robert talking quickly and quietly to Nes. When the young man unhooked a bucket from his saddle strap and headed into the trees, it was assumed he was going to fetch water with the others. Even Aymer de Valence, who saw him go, didn't pay the young man, who was so beneath him he was scarcely worth notice, much attention. Night was soon upon them and the faces of the men huddled around the clearing faded to indistinct patches of pale. No one noticed one missing squire.

'I will not do this.'

The voice of William Wallace rose over the crackle of flames. His face was illuminated by the campfire, the scars that carved his cheeks contoured by the flickering glow. His blue eyes raked the company of men who stood or sat around the clearing, the boundaries of which were defined by soaring pines, the cloud-like branches laden with snow. 'How can any of you consider it?'

'Have you not heard a word we have said, Sir William?' said Ingram de Umfraville. He motioned to Lamberton, standing close by, the cowl of his black robe shadowing his face. Beside the bishop was James Douglas, eyes keen as he surveyed the men around him. 'His grace heard the same words as me from the mouth of King Philippe. The king has chosen to make peace with Edward in order to concentrate on his Flemish war. Any hope we had of military or political support is gone. Balliol could no more hope to return from France and take the throne now, than he could rise from the dead. Surrender is our only chance for survival.' Umfraville frowned at Lamberton, seeking support. 'You agreed this, your grace, even before we knew the state of things here. Now, well . . .' He shook his head. 'It is futile to consider further resistance. Edward has all but won.'

'With respect, you haven't been here,' answered Wallace. He turned his gaze on Lamberton. 'Do you want to bow down before a tyrant, your grace?'

Lamberton's eyes glinted in the firelight. 'You know this is not what I wanted, my friend. But, I admit, I can no longer see a way through this disaster. The king does not want a protracted war in Scotland, any more than he wanted one in Wales or Gascony. I believe we may be able to convince him to offer us decent terms of surrender. That way, most men here might just come out of this with their lands and lives. The same cannot be said if we refuse to yield.'

'Look at what King Edward has taken this past year,' said Umfraville, nodding emphatically at Lamberton's words. 'He has hacked away at our army and our territories reducing us to this.' He spread his gloved hands to take in the ragged company of men gathered in the glade. Beyond, through the trees, a few figures flitted between other fires, but the Forest encampment, once the home of thousands, was mostly quiet. 'We have to admit defeat. Lay down our arms and pray the king will be generous.'

A few murmurs of agreement rose from the circle, the loudest from Robert Wishart, hunched on a rotten trunk, his huge frame mantled in furs. The Bishop of Glasgow, crippled by gout, had spent much of the year barricaded in his manor near Peebles. 'Sir James Stewart isn't here to add his voice, but I believe he would agree with the sentiment of my good brother,' he said, nodding to Lamberton. 'Do not forget, Sir Robert Bruce has become a trusted man of Edward's. The Earl of Carrick may prove a useful bridge between our sides when negotiating terms.'

There was much murmuring at this suggestion, particularly from Gray, Neil Campbell and Simon Fraser. Alexander and Christopher Seton, standing with these men, remained silent at the mention of their former friend. Alexander's face was grim. Beside him, Christopher stared into the flames.

Wallace fixed on John Comyn. 'And you, Sir John, I would have thought, of all here, you would not go along with this. All your grand plans? Your determination to lead our army to victory? Do you now wish to yield?'

Comyn met Wallace's gaze, his own eyes hooded from lack of sleep. Over the past few months living rough in the Forest his beard and hair had grown long and unkempt, making him look far older than his twenty-nine years. His skin had a sallow tinge in the firelight and his face was hollow from the meagre diet they had all been forced to subsist on. 'I no more want to bow down before the English king than you do. To give up my guardianship?' His brow knotted, the strain clear in his face. 'To give up my hope of ever . . .?' Comyn fell silent, then shook his head and turned away. 'Edward's campaign took everything. What point is there in being free if we cannot live the life we choose? Lochindorb Castle has been taken from me, my lands raided and burned. What do I fight for now?' His eyes scanned the men around him, among them the Black Comyn and Edmund Comyn of Kilbride, John of Menteith and Dungal MacDouall. 'What do any of us fight for without hope of victory?'

None of his comrades answered. All had been tested by the hardships of a winter in the Forest. Accustomed to feather beds and armies of servants, a diet of Bordeaux wine, venison and boar, they had been reduced to this frozen half-life, living hand to mouth on what their squires and footmen could scavenge, plagued by lice and fevers. All the while growing more frustrated as reports filtered in of their lands and castles falling to Edward's forces, their cellars and coffers plundered, walls torn down, vassals captured and killed. None of them was born to be an outlaw.

'We cannot hope to win,' John of Menteith agreed. 'Not after we lost so many men in Cumberland.'

Wallace's eyes flashed with fury. 'And whose fault was that?'

Menteith drew himself up in the face of Wallace's accusation. 'How dare—'

'What was it you said when I told you we were in danger of becoming trapped in that town?'

Menteith flushed in the firelight. 'I was not the only one!'

'*Who will challenge us, pray tell?*' Wallace continued, doing an uncanny mimicry of Menteith's high-pitched, haughty tone that had Gray and others smirking. 'You thought of nothing but lining your own purse. Your greed cost us the lives of those men. All of you,' he snarled at Comyn and the other nobles. 'You cost us this war, damn you to hell!'

'I will not stand trial by this brigand!' shouted Menteith, but his voice was drowned by others.

'By God, you insolent cur,' the Black Comyn growled at Wallace, wrenching his sword from its scabbard.

Dungal MacDouall did the same, although the movement was awkward for the captain, his right arm not fully healed from the injury Robert Bruce had inflicted upon him. That was nothing compared to what had happened to his left hand. Delirious with pain and blood loss, he'd been pulled out of the burning town alive, only to face the removal of his half-severed hand. One of the Disinherited had done it, while four others pinned him down. MacDouall had felt both the severing of the limb and the fire as they cauterised his flesh, before slipping into unconsciousness. Now, all that remained was a livid stump swaddled in dirty linen, and a fading ghost of sensation.

Gray and Neil Campbell moved swiftly to counter, pulling free their own weapons. Lamberton and Wishart were shouting to make themselves heard, but no one was listening.

It was James Douglas who first saw the figures emerging from the darkness beyond the campfire. Two patrolmen, dressed in the customary green and brown of Wallace's infantry, were leading a third man between them. His face was covered with a hood and he was stumbling blindly in their grip, his hose and tunic soaked with snow. Another two foot soldiers followed, scrabbling through the undergrowth, dirks in their hands.

'Your grace,' said James, catching Lamberton's attention.

Lamberton's eyes narrowed as he caught sight of them. The rest of the company were still arguing over one another. Gray and MacDouall were up in one another's faces, weapons hefted, spittle flying as they snarled threats. Any moment, it would come to blows. 'Silence, all of you!' roared Lamberton.

'Sir William,' called one of the patrolmen. 'We caught this spy trying to enter our camp. He says he has a message for you, from the Earl of Carrick.'

Wallace pushed through Gray and MacDouall to see the captive better. 'Who is he?'

One of the men removed the prisoner's hood. The young man whose face was revealed stood blinking in disorientation at the crowd of people staring at him. His cheeks were scratched from branches and briars, his skin chapped with cold.

'Nes!' exclaimed Christopher Seton.

'You know him?' Wallace asked the Yorkshireman, not taking his eyes off the captive.

'He's Sir Robert's squire,' answered Christopher, unable to disguise his pleasure at seeing the young man.

Alexander was frowning. John Comyn had moved forward and was looking at Nes in a mixture of dislike and fear.

'What message?' Wallace demanded.

'The English are less than three miles north-east of here. They will be coming for you at dawn.'

Wallace raised a hand to silence the host of voices that erupted. 'Sir Robert sent you?'

Nes nodded. 'My master is with the English, but he ordered me to warn you.' He faltered under Wallace's hostile gaze, then steeled himself and added, 'He takes a great risk in doing so.'

'How large is the force?'

'Around three hundred on light horses led by Aymer de Valence, Robert Clifford and Humphrey de Bohun.'

There was another outburst at the names of these feted commanders, all well known by the Scots. James Douglas stiffened at the mention of Clifford, the man who had taken his lands.

'They plan to destroy the camp,' finished Nes, 'and take the leaders of the rebellion alive.'

'Why would Sir Robert warn us?' Lamberton wanted to know.

'It could be a trap,' ventured Neil Campbell.

'I cannot say, your grace,' answered Nes.

'Cannot or will not?' burst out Alexander Seton. 'Christ, Nes! Speak! What is the truth here?'

Nes wiped sweat from his forehead with his arm. 'Please, Alexander, do not ask me what I cannot tell you. Just know this is no lie.'

'Take him away while I consider this,' Wallace ordered his men.

Nes's eyes lingered on Christopher and Alexander Seton, as if he wanted to say something more. Then the hood was pulled over his head and he was marched off by the patrolmen. Wallace waited until they were out of earshot, before turning to the others. 'We can use this to our advantage. We—'

'We move out,' John Comyn cut across him.

Wallace turned on him. 'What?'

'I will not be hauled before Edward in chains. I'll go to the bastard of my own free will if that is my only choice. If we surrender, we may win back our lands,' he added to his comrades.

'We know the English are coming, you fools!' roared Wallace, beside himself at the thought of surrender to the men who had taken so much from him – his home, his father, his wife and daughter. 'We can make a stand here! Set an ambush!'

But Comyn was already walking away. He was followed by Ingram de Umfraville, the Black Comyn, MacDouall and the Disinherited, Menteith and a host of other nobles, proving to Wallace that while he might be able to command men on a battlefield, he was not a politician. He could do nothing but watch as more men began to hasten from the clearing, shouting at squires to saddle horses, kicking snow on to campfires, grabbing supplies.

Robert Wishart hobbled to Wallace's side, the hems of his furs caked with snow. The bishop was too short to place his hand on Wallace's shoulder, but he made an attempt at it. 'My friend, you know I will always stand beside you in spirit. In body, alas, I am too old and fat.' He waddled in front of Wallace when the rebel leader tried to move away. 'Maybe we should lay down our arms, William?'

'I would rather die.' Wallace levelled the bishop with his stare. 'I raised an insurrection against Edward before. I can do so again.' He called Gray and the others to him.

Wishart exhaled in resignation. 'What about our informer?' He gestured in the direction the patrolmen had taken Nes.

'If we keep him,' Lamberton intervened, 'and the English arrive to find this camp deserted, their suspicion will fall on Robert.'

'What if he's spying for them?' growled Gray. 'You'll send him back with our numbers and location.'

'Neither of which will matter if we're gone,' answered Lamberton. He looked at Wallace. 'Until we can hear an explanation from Sir Robert himself, I say we have faith in him.'

Wallace nodded to one of his men. 'Tell them to take him back to the perimeter and release him.' He turned to Wishart. 'I pray we meet in better days.' The rebel leader's voice was strained. Taking the leather pack one of his men handed to him, he slung it over his shoulder.

'I'll make sure he gets to safety, Sir William,' Lamberton promised, moving to the side of the older bishop.

James Douglas nodded in confirmation, resting his hand on the pommel of his sword.

Head down, Wallace strode away through the trees, followed by Gray, Neil Campbell, Simon Fraser and around two hundred foot soldiers and archers, many of whom had been with him since the beginning of the rebellion.

Christopher Seton went with them. He paused, glancing back when Alexander remained in the pool of firelight. 'Cousin?'

'Perhaps we should save our own skins like Comyn and the rest.'

Christopher walked back to him. 'You heard Nes. There was obviously more going on than he could say. Robert sent us this warning. We should heed it.'

'It's easy for him to tell us what to do when he sits at the king's table eating his meat, drinking his wine. Maybe we should surrender, Christopher. Gain back our own lands like he did.' Alexander's face tightened. 'I can no longer see hope for victory.'

'We don't know what is happening in court, or what Robert is planning. John of Atholl thought James Stewart hadn't told us everything, didn't he?'

'And where are Atholl and the steward now? Maybe they've already surrendered.'

'Please, cousin,' implored Christopher, looking through the trees where Wallace's men were still funnelling. Comyn and the others were already gone. 'We cannot stay here.'

Alexander looked up and met his gaze. After a pause, he began to walk. As the cousins followed Wallace's company, the last men gathered up their belongings and slipped into the trees.

Less than an hour later, other than the crackle of flames from a few fires, the rebels' camp was silent.

35

The English first knew something was wrong when the patrols their scouts had spied a mile from the perimeter were nowhere to be seen. The situation became increasingly clear as they approached the outskirts of the rebel encampment.

Here, the snow had been churned to slush by feet and hooves. The ground was littered with refuse, some of it old and packed down deep in the soil: animal bones and threads of rope, splinters of firewood, a rotten bucket half buried in ice and the charred stub of a torch. Other items had clearly just been discarded: a bag with a broken strap, a pewter goblet on its side with a red stain colouring the snow, a sword in its scabbard propped against a trunk and blankets around the ashen remains of a fire where smoke still curled.

As the English company urged their horses deeper into the camp past a broad river, the shallows of which were covered with a film of ice, the sense of abandonment became more apparent. Among the debris of dropped wooden bowls crusted with food and fire pits with embers glowing at their hearts were tents with flaps hanging open in the frigid air. Inside, furs and blankets lay crumpled on empty pallets beside chests, piles of clothing and other belongings. There were even a few oil lanterns burning low in some.

The knights at the vanguard slowed their horses as they entered a large clearing in the trees. Beyond, tents and makeshift shelters stretched into the woods as far as they could see, along with more substantial dwellings of timber with turf roofs mottled with snow. There were even staked areas for animals with stalls and troughs. But despite all the evidence of habitation, there was not a soul to be seen.

'What is this?' demanded Clifford, bringing his mount to a halt and pushing up his visor. He fixed on the scouts they had sent out yesterday. 'You said you saw patrols?'

'Yes, sir,' answered one.

'Then where in God's name are the Scots?'

Valence walked his courser on into the clearing. Leaning out in the saddle, he stabbed his broadsword into a pile of blankets near a fire pit, as if hoping there were a body inside. Calling his knights to him with a harsh command, he began flicking aside tent flaps with the flat of his blade.

Humphrey turned in his saddle as Robert rode up behind him. 'Is this Wallace's base?' he asked sharply. His face was taut.

'It is,' answered Robert, careful to keep the relief from his voice. 'That's Wallace's shelter over there.' He nodded to a timber structure set between two soaring pines. Outside were several carts loaded with barrels and sacks of grain.

'Search it,' Humphrey ordered two of his men. As they dismounted, he stared around him. 'Remember Wales?' he murmured.

Robert thought of the ambush Welsh rebels had set for them in the deserted settlement on the road to Conwy. He and Humphrey had only just escaped with their lives. He wondered for a moment if Wallace – having been told the English were coming – had set a trap. He looked over at Nes, sitting quietly on his palfrey.

That morning, he'd been worried to see the telltale scratches on the squire's hands and face, but most of the men here had been caught unawares by stray twigs and briars. The squire's absence through the night didn't seem to have been noticed, but there had been no chance, with Aymer on his tail, for him to glean anything except Nes's brief acknowledgement that he had successfully delivered the warning. In alerting the rebels, Robert had exposed himself to them, but he'd had no other choice.

He scanned the trees. To all appearances the Forest was eerily peaceful, the only sounds the chatter of birds and the steady drip of snow melting from branches. If the desertion was a ruse, it was a highly effective one.

Several of Valence and Clifford's knights had dismounted and were spreading out, becoming more forceful in their searching, kicking in doors, tossing blankets and furs aside, pushing their way into tents. Others, who had ridden deeper into the camp, now returned.

'There are footprints leading in all directions,' called one of Valence's knights. 'No way of tracking them all.'

'There!' shouted Clifford, pointing through the trees to their left.

Following the knight's gaze, Robert saw a dark figure standing in the mist. As Clifford, Humphrey and Aymer kicked their horses towards it, swords raised, he followed, heart thudding. Was it Wallace? Emerging through the undergrowth behind the knights, he realised the figure was, in fact, hanging from a branch. It was a target made of straw and sacking in the shape of a man, crudely painted with a gold crown and a red tunic with three gold lions on the front. There were several arrows sticking out of it.

'Bastards!' seethed Aymer. He rode up to it and, with a slash of his broadsword, severed the rope that tethered it to the branch. The target sagged into the snow.

'How the hell did they know we were coming?' said Humphrey, pulling off his helm and hooking it over the pommel of his saddle. He dismounted, his boots crunching in the snow as he turned in a circle, staring up at the tower-like pines rising all around. 'Did they see us?'

Robert slid down from his saddle and joined him. 'They must have.' He lifted his shoulders, feeling an overwhelming urge to grin. 'Perhaps there was a patrol our scouts didn't see? Wallace always made sure there were many men on the periphery. He never took chances.'

'You!' Aymer swung himself from his saddle and strode towards Robert, pointing his sword at his chest. 'You warned them.'

Robert laughed. 'I'm flattered you think I'm so impressive as to be in two places at once. Perhaps I can fly as well? Or turn water into wine?' His mirth vanished. 'You were watching me all night, as always.'

'One of your men,' snapped Aymer, jerking his head at the Carrick knights, the red chevrons on their surcoats making bold patterns between the trees. 'You sent one of the whelps to warn them we were here!'

'Aymer,' cautioned Humphrey, moving in front of Robert. 'This isn't the time for your obsession.'

Aymer was brought up short. 'I shouldn't be surprised at your defence of this serpent. After all, he tricked you once before.' He glowered at Humphrey, his sword now aimed at the earl like an accusatory finger. 'You're a blind and trusting fool to be taken in again.'

Humphrey grasped his own sword, his green eyes flashing with anger.

'Brothers . . .' warned Clifford, moving to intervene.

Aymer pushed past Humphrey, fixing on Robert. 'We never should have let him into our circle. He was never one of us.'

Robert hefted his blade, facing him. 'How quick you are to count yourself a brother among these men. But I wonder just how readily you would betray any one of them in pursuit of your mad obsession?' Robert nodded as Aymer stopped, mid-stride, some new emotion flickering in his eyes. 'You found out about Ralph and Lady Joan, didn't you?' Robert turned to Humphrey. 'I'm sorry, I kept the truth from you yesterday. I discovered the affair by accident in Dunfermline. It wasn't rape. They're lovers.' He continued before Aymer could speak. 'Ralph said Aymer petitioned the king to come on this raid with the intention of spying on me. He was angry when the king refused to indulge him. Come, Valence, admit it, you informed on Ralph so you could be my shadow. Indeed, I wouldn't be surprised if *you* warned the Scots, just to blame me for their disappearance!'

'Madness!' spat Aymer, looking at Clifford and Humphrey for support. Both men were silent, staring at him. Beyond, a crowd of knights had begun to gather. Aymer laughed in disbelief. 'Please tell me you don't believe the whoreson?'

'You never liked me,' Robert went on, 'that much you made plain from the start, but since I battered you in Wales you've loathed me. How does it feel, Aymer? Knowing the man you hate gave you that smile?'

With a roar, Aymer launched himself at him. Before Robert, ready and willing, had the chance to counter, Humphrey lunged. He caught Valence on the jaw, the steel plates in his gloves lending a vicious force to the punch.

Aymer reeled with the blow, blood spraying as his lips tore on his wired front teeth. He staggered upright, spitting blood, and turned on the earl. Several of Humphrey's men came forward, swords drawn in a protective ring. Aymer's eyes flicked to them, then back to Humphrey. Slowly, he lowered his weapon. 'He'll betray you again,' he rasped, hawking another glob of blood into the snow. 'I'll stake my earldom on it.' He threw a last look at Robert, who had come to stand beside Humphrey. 'And when he does, Humphrey, I'll remind you of this.'

As Aymer walked away, one of his knights came towards him, but he pushed him roughly aside.

36

D ay was drawing to a close as Robert and his men took the track that led
to Turnberry. To either side, boggy fields studded with blackthorn
stretched to the fringes of woodland. Beyond the tangle of ash and wych elm,
the Carrick hills rose into the dusk, the higher slopes still glazed with snow.
Ahead, the sea filled the horizon, the humped dome of Ailsa Craig looming in
the distance. The rush of waves came to Robert on the wind. Already, he
could taste the salt tang. At the end of the track, rising from a promontory of
rock above bluffs stippled with thrift and mayweed, was the castle of his birth.

Other than the brief landing on the deserted shore where James Stewart had
handed him the Staff of Malachy it was four years since Robert had set foot in
his earldom. Now, approaching the village where he'd spent his childhood, it
felt as though he'd never left. The sense of homecoming – of belonging – was
deeply affecting. The landscape seemed to breathe memory from every rocky,
sandy pore.

There were the cliffs he and Edward once climbed as boys to escape the
incoming tide, and the beach where his instructor, Yothre, trained him with
sword, lance and shield. There were the woods he played in with his brothers and sisters, and where he first met Affraig. Within the castle's sea-stained
walls he learned of King Alexander's death and sat at his grandfather's side
as the Bruce men and their allies planned the attack on John Balliol in
Galloway to end his hope of succession. Years later, standing on those lofty
battlements, he had tossed the blood-scarlet dragon shield into the foaming
waves, breaking his oaths to his brethren and King Edward. That same night,
the night Affraig had woven his destiny in a crown of heather, he had stood
in the courtyard before his men and pledged to be king.

As Robert approached the castle's walls, the cries of gulls hanging on the
wind, one of all the memories came clearest to his mind.

Turnberry, Scotland

1284 AD (20 years earlier)

Robert stood outside the bedchamber's door, listening to the low voices of his mother and father. Firelight glowed around the edges where the frame had warped with the change from winter to spring. He found, by pressing his face to it and closing one eye, he could make out a small section of the room beyond, dominated by the large, canopied bed.

His father was sitting on the edge of the mattress, a fur-trimmed mantle draped over his hulking frame, a goblet of wine gripped in his fist. He had removed his boots, which lay on the rug in front of him. Not yet properly cleaned, though the Bruce had been back for over a week, they were caked with a year's worth of the mud and dust of foreign soil. Robert's mother stood close by, her long black hair hanging loose down her back. As Robert watched, she placed a hand on his father's shoulder.

'You cannot dwell on their deaths, Robert. Your men were doing their duty, serving you.' She tried to prise the goblet gently from his grasp, but he pulled back and glared up at her, eyes glazed with drink.

'They took Donald and his son Alan alive, after a surprise attack on our company near Conwy.' The Bruce's words were thick and slurred. 'We tracked them to a camp on the lower slopes of Snowdon. Llywelyn's rebels were long gone, but they left us a token. Staked out in the snow were the bodies of the men they had captured in the raid. Their stomachs had been cut open with long, thin cuts. Not enough to kill. Not instantly. Just enough to lure the wolves. Some were still there, eating when we arrived.' His face twisted in memory. 'They'd grown bold that winter with all the carrion. Our archers shot a couple before the rest fled.' He put the goblet to his mouth and tipped it back to drain it. 'Alan's face — I'll never forget it. I fear he and his father were still alive when they began to feast.'

Robert felt himself grimace. His mother had pressed her hand to her mouth.

'Do you want to know what my compensation was?' The Bruce fumbled for a small chest that was partially sticking out of a bag on the bed. He held it up for a moment, then tossed it aside, the coins inside rattling. 'Lincoln, Surrey and others got lands and castles for their sacrifices.' Glowering, he tossed the purse aside. 'I heard King Edward plans to found a new order of men, an elite brotherhood, in honour of the victors of his conquest of Wales. But he spoke no word of it to me. I lost fifteen men in his service. Where is my reward?'

Marjorie reached forward and, this time, managed to remove the goblet from his hand. 'Edward is an English king, my love. He will reward his own first and foremost. Didn't your father always say that?'

He looked up at her, his brow furrowing. 'I wish you hadn't summoned him. The last thing I need is his interference.' Now the drink had left his hand, his shoulders slumped. He looked at his boots, lying on the rug, his eyes seeming to stare right through them. 'Alan was sixteen, Marjorie.' His face crumpled and, suddenly, tears were streaming down his cheeks.

Marjorie clasped her husband's shoulders, pulling him close, as he pushed his head against her stomach and wept.

Robert straightened abruptly, stepping back from the door as his father's sobs seeped through the wood. In all his ten years he had never seen the man cry. It was an awful sight. One he felt ashamed and frightened to have witnessed.

'Robert.'

He jerked round to see a huge figure looming in the passage, a mane of silver hair haloed by the light of a single torch on the wall behind. His grandfather raised a finger and beckoned to him. Grateful to leave his father's hoarse sobs behind, Robert headed down the passage. The old lord said nothing, but placed a firm hand on his shoulder, steering him past the room he shared with his four younger brothers and through the archway that led up a spiral of steps to the battlements. The chill evening air was filled with the cries of gulls. Far below, waves crashed against the cliffs, the waters foaming and boiling.

Robert glanced uncertainly up at his grandfather, as the old man rested his arms on the parapet wall and stared out towards the loaf-shaped dome of Ailsa Craig. 'Grandfather, I—'

'Spying is an ugly habit, Robert. A man's business is his own.'

Robert nodded after a pause. 'I just wanted to know why he is sending me away.' His eyes narrowed as he followed his grandfather's gaze to Ailsa Craig, then beyond the fairy rock, south to where the horizon line darkened imperceptibly, marking the northernmost tip of Ireland. 'Am I being punished?'

'Punished?' The old lord turned to him. 'Fosterage isn't a punishment, Robert. It is the time-honoured custom of your kin. The sons of your mother's family would all have taken this rite of passage over the years. Besides' — he looked back at the sea — 'your father didn't arrange it. I did. It is long past time you saw some of the lands you stand to inherit. Lord Donough is one of your father's vassals in Glenarm. He is a *good man. You will be a page and serve his table, put into practice the hunting skills I have already taught you. And you will be instructed in the arts of war — learning to ride and to wield a sword. It will be the first step in your training for knighthood.'*

Robert stared at his grandfather. He felt a bubble of excitement at the thought of being trained to fight. But, still, Ireland seemed a long way from the only home he knew. 'Why Antrim? Can I not be fostered to a family in Ayr, or somewhere closer?' He brightened with an idea. 'Or to you in Lochmaben, Grandfather?'

'In time, perhaps. For now, your path is set. Lord Donough has sons of his own. One, Cormac, is around your age I believe.'

Robert looked away with a frown, not ready to be mollified.

But his grandfather grasped his shoulders and turned him to face him, fixing him with his dark, hawk-like eyes. 'Your mother's line stretches back to the O'Neill kings of Ireland and mine through my grandfather, the Earl of Huntingdon, to King David and his father, Malcolm Canmore. The blood of kings runs in your veins, Robert. This you know. But what I have not told you before is that our king's father, Alexander II, named me as his successor.'

Robert stared up at him in astonishment. 'But his son . . .?'

'It was before our king was born. Alexander, at that time, had no heirs.' The old lord took his hands from Robert's shoulders and leaned against the parapet wall. His mane of hair blew wild about his head in the breeze. 'The king had organised a stag hunt in the royal park at Stirling. I went with him along with many nobles from the court. During the chase the king's horse took a fall. He landed badly, crushed beneath his destrier, breaking several ribs. It could have been much worse and he knew it. In severe pain, Alexander insisted — before any of us could ride to the castle and fetch him a litter — that he name a successor. It was me.

'In the dust of that forest track he made all the nobles present go down on one knee and recognise me as his heir. I was eighteen at the time.' He inhaled sharply. 'Two years later, Alexander had a son — our king — and his line was secured, but I have never forgotten the sense of purpose and pride I felt that day. It was as though . . .' He frowned, searching for the words. 'As though my blood awoke. I was aware of my part in the world and of the great line of men I belonged to, aware of the legacy each one had passed from father to son, down through the years to me. You, Robert, are now part of that line. In time, your father and I will die and you will inherit not only our fortune, but our place in this world, our . . .' He smiled slightly, his eyes taking on a strange, faraway look. 'Call it destiny if you will. You must be ready for that burden.'

Robert nodded, inspired by the old man's story. 'I will be, Grandfather.' He paused, looking out over the churning sea towards Ireland. 'And I'll make you proud.'

'I know you will, my son.'

The old man turned to watch the waves, not seeming to realise his mistake. Robert thought of his father crying into his mother's gown, but didn't correct him.

Turnberry, Scotland, 1304 AD

As Robert's company neared the castle, the devastation caused during the English raid became apparent. Turnberry's walls were blackened with smoke and damaged where timber beams had been burned away. The gates were long gone, the walls to either side tumbled down. In the gaping hole that was left the courtyard beyond was revealed. His constable, Andrew Boyd, had done as ordered, for the site had been mostly cleared of debris, piles of broken masonry heaped up outside the gates. Still, the place looked utterly forlorn.

Looking at the village that stretched down the windswept bluffs to the shore, Robert saw signs of rebuilding, though there were far fewer houses than he remembered. Burned-out shells jutted like blackened teeth between newer buildings. He could see some villagers going about their business, shutting up chicken coops, pushing shutters to, setting muddy clogs outside the door and calling children in from the evening chill, but although Nes held the banner of Carrick hoisted above the company no one rushed to greet their earl. Robert's return was met not by a fanfare, but by suspicious stares and closing doors. The men who had served in his company this past year might have come to forgive his long absence in England, but he had given the men and women of Turnberry no such reason to pardon him.

Passing the piles of rubble and charred timbers outside the castle's entrance, Robert noticed a splintered tree trunk looped with chains. It looked like it had been used as a battering ram. He imagined Humphrey standing here with an army, shouting orders as men heaved it against the castle gates. The thought brought the memory of the earl stepping in front of him and striking Aymer. Robert had played out that scene often since leaving the Forest, Humphrey telling him to continue to Turnberry as planned, while they returned to Dunfermline. The earl's defence of him came loaded with guilt. Bastard though he was, Valence had his measure. And Humphrey he betrayed again.

In the courtyard, carts and wagons were lined up beside a makeshift stable. Of the old stable and kennels, or any of the wooden and thatch outbuildings, there was no sign. There were a few other temporary structures around the courtyard. When Robert and his men approached the gates, two guards emerged from one of them. Seeing their lord had returned, one hastened into the castle.

As Robert was dismounting, Andrew Boyd, Constable of Turnberry, came out to greet him. 'Sir Robert, it is an honour to welcome you home.'

'The honour is mine, Andrew,' answered Robert, clasping the man's outstretched hand. 'I am glad to see you.'

'I was expecting you sooner, according to your message. Did you encounter trouble on your journey?'

'I had an unexpected detour – a mission for the king. But I'm here now and anxious for us to begin.' Robert scanned the courtyard with a sense of determination. He had come here with the aim of seeking James Stewart, his plan to draw Wallace into his confidence back on track since he'd sabotaged the Forest raid, but now he was here he was eager to start the reconstruction the king had permitted him to carry out.

'As you can see we are ready for the rebuilding.' Boyd's gaze drifted up the smoke-stained walls to the battlements. 'The structure is still mostly sound. Turnberry will be as new in no time.'

'Is there somewhere for me and my men to bed down? It has been a long journey.'

'Of course. The great hall is mostly intact. But first, there is someone here to see you.'

'Who?' asked Robert, feeling a surge of hope as he wondered if the high steward had pre-empted him.

'Your brother, sir.'

As Boyd said this, Robert realised there was a man standing in the castle's arched doorway. Alexander Bruce merged with the shadows in his plain brown robes and black hair.

'I'll see to your men, sir. You should talk with your brother alone.' Boyd's tone was grave. 'As I said, the great hall is warm and dry.'

Leaving the commander to direct the weary knights, Robert headed across the rubble-strewn yard to where his brother was waiting. He felt unease stir in him at Alexander's solemn face. His brother was supposed to be at Cambridge, completing his Masters. He wasn't due to take up his position as dean of Glasgow – as granted by King Edward – until later in the year. 'Brother,' he said, embracing him briefly. 'What brings you?'

Alexander returned the stiff greeting. 'I've been waiting for you. I arrived at the king's court a fortnight ago. They told me you would be coming here.' His gaze remained hard, accusatory, then he shook his head and turned down the passage. 'Come.'

Robert gritted his teeth, knowing his younger brother liked to hold the power and would only stretch the waiting further if pressed. He followed in a taut silence along the dim passageway to the great hall.

The hall was a sorry sight. The whitewashed walls were black with smoke. Gone were the trestles and benches that had once filled the grand chamber, now a dingy shell; an echo chamber for the sea's muffled boom. The floor was covered in piles of blankets and sacks of belongings, the hall clearly having become a barracks for Boyd and his men. A few torches burned low in sconces on the walls.

Seeing a ragged scrap of material hanging from one wall, Robert crossed to it. As he lifted a frayed and burned edge, he realised this was all that was left of the tapestry that depicted the moment Malcolm Canmore killed his rival, Macbeth, and took the throne, beginning the dynasty from which the Bruce family were descended.

Alexander watched him for a moment, before speaking. 'I bring tidings, brother.' He drew in a breath as Robert turned to him. 'Our father has passed away.'

Robert let go of the burned tapestry, which drifted back against the wall.

'He had a sickness of the lungs over the winter, from which he never recovered. He died shortly after the Christ Mass.'

Robert leaned against the wall. He had a flash of memory: this hall filled with music and firelight, his father standing behind the head table, drink in hand, watching as Marjorie danced with their infant daughter Christian in her arms. As his wife spun in time to the rhythm of pipes and drums, Christian squealing with delight, a smile had played about the man's lips.

The wall was cold and damp against Robert's back. He could smell charred timbers, mouldering stone and the bitter sea.

'I have sent word to Isabel in Norway and Christian, Mary and Matilda in Mar,' continued Alexander, his tone stilted. 'I presume you can get word to our brothers?'

'Thomas and Niall I haven't seen in some time. The last I knew they were with James Stewart. Was he at peace?' Robert asked suddenly, looking over at his brother.

Alexander stared at him, then looked away. 'Yes,' he said quietly. 'He died in his sleep. He made his confession the day before. The last rites were able to be observed in full.'

'You took them?'

'No. But I was there.'

'Thank you, brother.'

Alexander looked surprised. His frown lines disappeared and he seemed at once like the boy Robert remembered, standing there in his sombre brown robes. He made a move towards him, his face filling with tentative compassion. 'Robert, I—'

The sound of raised voices came to them from outside.

Robert glanced round, frowning at the interruption, but when he looked back Alexander had straightened, his face closing in. 'I should see what the commotion is,' he told his brother.

Alexander nodded in silence, letting him go.

As Robert reached the door to the courtyard, Nes almost walked straight into him. Over his squire's shoulder, Robert saw two men standing with horses by the gates. Andrew Boyd was with them, surrounded by a group of knights. Their voices were raised in question, men shouting over one another to be heard.

'What is it?' Robert asked Nes.

'Two of Sir Andrew's men have come from Ayr where they were recruiting more labourers. A company arrived there, fleeing the Forest. They say John Comyn and his army will surrender to King Edward. Sir, they say the war is over.'

37

The nobles of Scotland crowded into the great hall of St Andrews Castle, their sodden cloaks dripping on the flagstones. Smells of damp fur and stale sweat mingled with the tang of armour. Men coughed and sniffed in the dank air. Outside, rain came down in sheets, obscuring the town and the windswept sands that stretched in a vast crescent from the outcrop of rocks the castle was built upon.

King Edward looked down on the damp and miserable host from the raised height of the hall's dais. His officials stood to either side of his throne. As he waited for the last men to file in, he let his eyes drift across the company. Few, he was satisfied to see, could meet his gaze. There in the front row, head bowed, rainwater dribbling from the ends of his hair, stood Ingram de Umfraville, alongside John of Menteith and Robert Wishart. Close by was the Black Comyn with his nephew, the fourteen-year-old Earl of Fife. One or two did lock eyes with him, William Lamberton among them, but these little acts of defiance meant nothing to the king. His victory was plain to see in the downcast stares and grim expressions of the majority of the Scots gathered before him.

As the doorwards pulled the great doors shut, Edward fixed on John Comyn, standing before the dais. The Lord of Badenoch was rather more salubriously dressed than he had been last week when he came before the king to present the Scots' terms of surrender. He had shaved and his dark hair, long and unkempt from a winter living rough in the Forest, had been clipped and washed. Despite appearances, the young man had conducted himself well when delivering his conditions. So different, Edward had mused, to the wretched submission the man's uncle, John Balliol, had made eight years earlier. He could respect him for that. As to the terms themselves, they had been rather expansive, but Edward was feeling magnanimous. He could afford to be.

'Welcome, men of Scotland.' The king's voice resonated in the crowded chamber. Any murmurs or shuffling of feet faded into a hush. 'I am pleased to see so many of you standing before me today in peace. None of us wished this war to continue unchecked. The terms of your surrender, as put forward by your guardian, Sir John Comyn of Badenoch, I hereby accept.' The king nodded to Sir John Segrave, who was standing beside the throne, holding a roll of parchment.

As the English Lieutenant of Scotland walked to the edge of the dais his limp, caused by the injury sustained in the attack at Roslin, was apparent. Unrolling the parchment, he began to read. 'Edward, by God's grace, illustrious King of England, Duke of Gascony, lord of Ireland, conqueror of Wales and overlord of Scotland, in accordance with the surrender of the people of Scotland, agrees that no man, including those involved in rebellion against him, will be disinherited. Nor will any face imprisonment for his actions, although a list of those who are to be exiled for a period of time has been drawn up and will be enforced. It is conceded that so long as any Englishman imprisoned in Scotland is released immediately, without penalty, the same freedom shall be awarded to any Scot currently in captivity in England.' Segrave paused to clear his throat, the sound harsh in the dead silence.

'Those who have forfeited estates will be able to gain back their lands, at a cost of between one and five years the value of the holding, depending on the severity of each claimant's part in the rebellion. Scotland will benefit from the liberties, laws and customs enjoyed under King Alexander III. But King Edward no longer recognises the kingdom of Scotland. Henceforth, it will be a land and he will draw up a new set of ordinances for its government. To this end, he takes into his care Earl Duncan of Fife.'

Edward stiffened at the murmurs of discontent that rippled through the hall, but he was pleased to see John Comyn turn to rake the assembly with a glare that soon silenced any dissatisfaction. This was one of his most important terms: one he would not compromise on. The Stone of Destiny might be entombed in Westminster and John Balliol powerless in France, but he wanted the Scots to see, once and for all, that there would be no new sovereign on their throne. The fourteen-year-old earl, whose hereditary right it was to crown a king, was the last glimmer of that hope. Fife would remain in England.

The king watched, satisfied, as two royal knights marched unchallenged to where the young earl was standing with his uncle. The Black Comyn appeared furious, but he stepped aside all the same, allowing the knights to escort his nephew, who looked pale and shaken, to the front of the hall, where all could see the symbolism of the act.

John Comyn's face had tightened, but he didn't contest. Faced with the choice of losing Fife, or gaining back his vast possessions, even at a cost, it was clear where his priorities lay. As Segrave finished, rolling up the parchment, Comyn bowed to Edward. 'My lord king, on behalf of the men of Scotland, I accept.'

'There is one last thing,' said Edward, rising as Segrave returned to his place. 'One man to whom I will not extend my peace.' His voice rang imperiously. 'William Wallace has refused to submit himself to my mercy, therefore he shall be shown none. I want him hunted down and brought to me.' The king's gaze roved across the men in the front row, fixing last on the three guardians, John Comyn, Ingram de Umfraville and William Lamberton. 'Whosoever captures him will be freed from any of the obligations laid out in the terms. That man will serve no exile and will face no reparations for the return of his lands.'

Edward didn't miss the spark of interest in John Comyn's eyes.

When his officials declared the parliament closed and the Scots began to troop out slowly, directed to an adjacent chamber where they would set their seals to the surrender, the king sat back in his throne. After eight long years, Scotland had finally bowed before him. His rule of Britain was almost complete. Two loose threads remained, in the form of Stirling Castle whose garrison still held against him, and William Wallace, on the run with a ragged band of outlaws. One good tug and both would be pulled. Edward smiled, feeling an unfamiliar sense of calm.

'My lord.'

He looked round, surprised by the woman's voice, to see his eldest daughter Joan had appeared on the dais.

'I did not know you were present, my dear.'

Joan nodded, although her eyes remained downcast. 'I didn't want to miss your hour of triumph.' She hesitated, then crossed to the throne and crouched before him. 'Father, I've watched you pardon your enemies here today – men who have raised fire and sword against you. Ralph de Monthermer's only crime was in loving me. Can you not extend the same forgiveness to a man who has served you faithfully for so many years?'

Edward sat back with a long exhalation. He closed his eyes, feeling his daughter's cool hands clasp over his. He had been beside himself with rage when Aymer de Valence had told him of the affair, but in the weeks since, seeing his daughter's grief, that fire had cooled.

'I love him, Father.'

Opening his eyes, Edward saw the tears streaming down her face. After a moment, he laid his hand over hers. 'Peace, daughter. I will send the order for Sir Ralph's release today.' As Joan gave a sob of relief, he continued. 'When he arrives we will discuss marriage terms.'

Joan's cries strengthened. She kissed his hands, now laughing through her tears. Finally, managing to collect herself, she rose. 'Thank you, my lord.'

As Edward watched his daughter go, his gaze was drawn to his son. Now the crowd was clearing, he could see the prince was leaning against the far wall with Piers Gaveston. The two were deep in conversation, their heads close. The prince smiled at something Gaveston said and clasped his shoulder. The king's eyes picked out the movement of his son's thumb, moving in slow circles on the velvet of Piers's mantle. Edward's calm faded. For a time, he had noticed, with growing concern, the closeness between the two young men, but he had been too preoccupied to deal with it. Now the war with Scotland was over, he would turn his attention to a matter he had left too long unattended: the marriage of his son and Isabella of France.

PART 5

1304–1306 AD

The brightness of the sun shall fade at the amber of Mercury, and horror shall seize the beholders. Stilbon of Arcadia shall change his shield; the helmet of Mars shall call to Venus.

The seas shall rise up . . . and the dust of the ancients shall be restored. The winds shall fight together with a dreadful blast, and their sound shall reach the stars.

The History of the Kings of Britain, *Geoffrey of Monmouth*

38

The sun was rising over the scarred ridges of the Ochil Hills. As the first crimson rays touched the battlements of Stirling Castle a bell began to toll, the echoes rolling down from the craggy heights on which the fortress stood, before fading across the marshes and meadows that bordered the banks of the River Forth. The encampment stirred to life, the low voices of waking men lifting over the crackle of flames as fresh logs were tossed on to fires that had burned to embers during the night. As cooks went to work at cauldrons and spits, smoke thickened into a haze over the English army, sprawled across the slopes between the castle and the royal burgh.

Robert walked through the camp, shielding his eyes as the sun poured its gold across the castle rock, blazing in the banners hoisted above the sea of tents. Men emerged from their billets bleary-eyed, stretching and yawning as they set about their business. A few nodded as he passed, but most ignored him, preoccupied with their own routines. The bell had ceased its tolling and the clanking of chains now took its place as the siege engines were readied for another day of violence.

On the edges of the camp, past the tents, animal pens and supply wagons, stood carts loaded with stones and lead stripped from the cathedrals at St Andrews and Perth. Beyond, sixteen engines rose from points around the hillside, their frames dark against the red dawn. Already there was much activity around their bases, the engineers making any necessary repairs or adjustments while the crews heaved stones into the slings of trebuchets and the spoon-like beams of the mangonels. The whole area was protected by wooden screens covered with bundles of twigs lashed together to deaden the impact of any incoming missiles.

After three months, the machines were as familiar to Robert as the faces of the men who manned them. The Parson, the Thunderer, the Conqueror, the Bull: each one shipped or hauled from across Scotland for the last siege of an eight-year war. Beyond, the walls of Stirling Castle were bathed in the sunlight, revealing every crack and scar. From the siege lines a path wound steeply up grassy plateaux to a bridge, which spanned a ditch below the castle's outer walls. The stone walkway ended abruptly in mid-air, several metres from a massive gatehouse, the drawbridge shut up over the entrance. The bridge and path were strewn with rubble, as was the hillside. Arrows protruded from the banks of the ditch and snatches of cloth switched in the breeze where bodies lay half buried in the debris. Robert scanned Stirling's walls, searching for any new damage done since he'd last looked. It had become a routine; something to mark the passing of days while he waited, his impatience running high like a fever inside him. Four months gone and he'd heard nothing.

His attention was drawn to a group of men gathered beside two twenty-foot mangonels – the Victorious and the Thunderer. Among them was King Edward, standing head and shoulders above the crowd. His surcoat was blood-red in the dawn light, the three golden lions shimmering. The king was talking to one of his chief engineers. Close by was Humphrey de Bohun, who raised a hand on seeing him. Crossing to the earl, Robert sensed an air of excitement, the men talking animatedly as they drank wine the king's pages had conveyed from the burgh beyond the camp. Approaching, he realised three new carts had arrived in the night, two of which still had oxen harnessed to the front. Globe-shaped clay pots were being unloaded from one. Wads of material were stuffed into their necks. From the back of another cart, men were hefting off large wooden barrels.

'A fine morning,' Humphrey greeted with a smile.

'What's this?' Robert noted how carefully the men were handling the pots. Once unloaded the clay containers were being stacked up next to the Thunderer.

'The king's surprise.' Humphrey motioned to a page, who came over bearing a jug of wine and a goblet that was filled and handed to Robert.

Robert had heard of the surprise Edward had planned for Stirling's garrison, but other than the rumour it was something the king had discovered on crusade, he'd been told nothing more. Whatever it was, he knew Edward had been impatient for it, increasingly so, the engines, although impressive in number, managing only to chip away at the castle's walls. Stirling, perched on its precipice guarding the only bridge over the Forth, had remained impervious.

The castle was defended by a small garrison of Scots, captained by a man named William Oliphant, who had stayed defiant in his refusal to surrender, stating during negotiations that he held Stirling for John Balliol and would give it up only when ordered by him. Well-supplied, he and his men had dug in deep. Believed to be sheltering through the worst of the bombardment in caves hidden within the bedrock, they would slip out between onslaughts to shoot arrows at their attackers, picking off unwary engineers. Robert had witnessed, with grim satisfaction, Edward's growing frustration as the siege had worn on without sign of end. The king was so close to victory. Most of Scotland's magnates had surrendered, new ordinances for government were being drawn up and Edward had control of many of the kingdom's castles. But Stirling and William Wallace – missing since the failed raid on the Forest – continued to defy him. Both were vital to his dominion over Scotland.

'Careful!'

The shout had come from the chief engineer. Two men hoisting one of the barrels off the cart had lost their grip, letting it crash to the ground. Robert saw a fine, yellow-grey powder gushing from a split in the barrel's side.

Leaving the king, the engineer crossed to them. 'Get every grain of that picked up. Christ on His cross, do you want this whole camp to burn? My lord,' he called, turning to Edward, 'I suggest you move back a distance.'

As the king and the assembly of earls and knights retreated, Humphrey fell into step with Robert. 'Greek Fire,' he murmured.

Robert looked at him, surprised. He'd heard of the substance from his grandfather, who had seen it employed in the Holy Land. Greek Fire, favoured by the Arabs, was a volatile mix of oil, saltpetre and sulphur, which would burn on almost anything and was said to be only extinguishable with sand or urine. The old lord had spoken of its awesome power – thunder of God he had called it. 'A Saracen weapon? Here in Scotland?'

'Needs must,' answered Humphrey. As they came to a stop a safe distance from the siege engines, he nodded to the barrels. 'God willing, this siege will be over by the end of the day.' He turned to Robert, his green eyes alight with passion. 'Then, that will be the end of it. Our kingdoms are united, as they once were under Brutus. Now, we can start to rebuild its former greatness – all of us. In time, Britain will be the stronger for it, you will see, my friend.'

'Warwolf is ready.'

Robert and Humphrey looked round at the voice to see Ralph de Monthermer behind them.

'The king intends to have it drawn up this afternoon.'

Thomas of Lancaster, overhearing, turned with a keen smile. 'Once the Scots get a taste of the beast they'll be out on bended knees, begging for mercy.'

Only a few months ago, Robert knew these men would have weighed his response to such talk, searching for any sign of loyalty towards his country-men. No more. After two years, he was one of them, even trusted by the king to be involved in negotiations with the Scots for the new government. Humphrey treated him like a brother and Ralph, recently engaged to Lady Joan and due to inherit the earldom of Gloucester, had sworn he was in Robert's debt after learning he had exposed Aymer de Valence's betrayal. For his part, Valence had left Robert well alone. The knight, standing with Henry Percy and Guy de Beauchamp watching the engineers, hadn't spoken to him or Humphrey since the Forest raid.

'To victory,' said Humphrey, raising his goblet.

As Thomas and Ralph lifted their cups, Robert joined them.

A horn was blown, sounding across the encampment. The crews manning the trebuchets heaved on the winches, the chains grinding round, drawing up the great baskets filled with lead. The other end of each engine's beam seesawed to the ground, where the sling could be loaded with a stone. Those at the mangonels – all except the Victorious and the Thunderer – levered stones into the spoon-like beams pivoted over the frames.

One by one the siege engines began to move, like giants coming to life, their wooden arms groaning up and round to fling their loads towards Stirling's walls. Stones smashed into the battlements and corner towers, mortar and masonry exploding. After the last missile hit there was an eerie pause, the only movement the clouds of dust drifting into the air. Then, the beams were arcing back round and the engineers shouting orders as more stones were rolled forward to be loaded.

This time the crews at the Victorious and the Thunderer joined in the preparations, placing several of the clay pots in the hollowed-out bowls of the two beams. Men wielding burning brands stepped up to each engine. As they touched the flames to the wads of material in the necks of the pots fire sparked, dull against the sun's glow. The skyward end of each beam was hauled down through a complex system of ropes, causing the loaded end to arc upwards and slam against a padded crossbar. The flames brightened in the rush of air as the pots were hurled over the castle walls towards the buildings beyond. Each one shattered as it struck with a burst of fire that seemed to gush like liquid over everything it touched, while all around stones shot from the other engines crashed and pounded against the outer walls. Smoke billowed beyond as Greek Fire surged across the rooftops. Robert, watching with the others, understood why some believed the substance to be sorcery. It was disturbing – fire behaving like water, against its nature. Many of the noblemen standing with the king began to clap, awed by the sight.

Edward gave a nod to his chief engineer, who turned to bark orders at the crews of the Victorious and the Thunderer. Now, instead of the clay pots, the barrels were loaded on to the mangonels. Once again the men with the brands came forward, this time lighting a short piece of rope that protruded from the side of each barrel. Stones from the trebuchets began to hammer the walls in rapid succession. The beams of the two mangonels were released in unison, the barrels sent hurtling towards the castle, ropes flaming behind like the tails of comets. One of the barrels missed its mark and slammed into the ditch. For a few seconds nothing happened, then there was an almighty bang that resounded around the hilltop, soil and rock blasting into the air. The second barrel sailed over the parapet and impacted with the roof of the castle's chapel. There was another thunderous explosion, accompanied by sounds of crumbling masonry.

Robert, standing with his cheering comrades, gripped his goblet and forced his face into a jubilant expression.

'Like taking a hammer to a turtle's shell,' observed Thomas of Lancaster. The king's nephew shook his head, impressed. 'God curse them, but the Saracens know how to break down a castle.'

'Where is my son?'

Thomas turned at the king's sharp question. 'I believe he is practising for the tourney, my lord. I saw him heading down to the meadow just after sunrise. With Gaveston.'

Robert noticed Thomas's face tighten as he spoke the name. There was no love lost between him and Piers. He had once heard Lancaster speak in a low, disgusted tone, after a little too much wine, of the unnaturalness of the friendship between his cousin and the Gascon.

'He should be here to witness this.'

'I will summon him, my lord.'

As Thomas moved off, Robert caught sight of two men approaching, flanked by royal guards. One was short and slender, dressed in black robes trimmed with silver, his tonsure gleaming with sweat from the stiff climb up to the camp. Robert recognised him with a thrill. It was William Lamberton, the Bishop of St Andrews. The tall, athletic youth beside him was James Douglas, confident in his stride despite the armed escort. The young man, whom Robert once spared from King Edward's clutches, had been with Lamberton at St Andrews four months ago, when the bishop and most of the magnates had submitted to the king. On learning of the mass surrender, Robert had returned to Edward's court to ascertain what the unexpected events would mean for his plan. It was there that the bishop had sought him out.

Lamberton took no notice of Robert as he was led before King Edward, his gaze going briefly to the beleaguered castle. 'My lord,' he greeted, raising his voice over the din as more stones and barrels were catapulted into the walls with ear-splitting explosions, followed by cheers from the watching English. 'I bear a message.' Closely observed by the royal guards, the bishop reached into a leather bag he carried and pulled out a roll of parchment. 'The High Steward of Scotland, Sir James Stewart, wishes to enter your peace. He has set his seal to this surrender.'

Robert listened keenly to this news. So, Lamberton had done as promised and found the steward? Robert hadn't expected James's surrender, but it made sense: keep the king appeased and his gaze turned from any possible danger. He felt a surge of impatience. Did the bishop bear the news he had been waiting for?

Edward unfurled the parchment and scanned it. After a moment, he handed it to one of his knights. 'I will consider this. As you can see, I am otherwise occupied.' The king gave a thin smile. 'Stirling's commander does not have the sense of his countrymen. He will rue that today.'

The king turned back to watch the onslaught, leaving the bishop standing alone. As explosions continued to rock the mountainside, Lamberton's gaze settled on Robert.

The two horsemen faced one another on the meadow. Dew glimmered beneath the hooves of their horses as the animals stamped and shifted. One of the riders was gripping the reins tightly, struggling to hold his horse steady, while a page stood close by waiting to hand him a red lance. He wore a quilted gambeson, greaves on his legs, vambraces on his arms and a plain iron helm. A curved red shield covered the left side of his body.

At the other end of the meadow, the second rider sat at ease, leaning back against the cantle as his courser champed at the bit. The reins were looped in his gloved left hand over which a black shield, painted with a white swan, was positioned, his arm pushed through the strap at the back. He wore mail chausses on his legs and a black leather aketon studded with silver, drawn in at his waist by a belt. A helm crested with swan wings covered his face. Seeing his opponent wrestle his horse into position and reach for the lance, the man held out his hand to his own page, who passed him his weapon. His fingers curled around the ash shaft, gripping the black lance just beneath the steel disc of the vamplate that protected his hand. Pricking the courser's sides with the barbs of his spurs, he goaded the animal into a gallop.

Away across the meadow, Edward Bruce watched as the two men hurtled towards one another. He could feel the pulse of hooves in the soil beneath his feet. Around him, the men of the prince's household – most of them sons or grandsons of knights and earls – cheered them on. On the periphery, pages and squires waited, bearing the burdens of shields and helms so their young masters could pass around wine and enjoy the sport unencumbered. Shielding his eyes against the gold of the rising sun, Edward observed the lances swinging down to level at one another, the gap between the horses closing rapidly. The black lance was straight as an arrow, the red bouncing with the tumult of the charge. Behind him he heard a couple of men exchanging coins, but most didn't bother. The outcome was clear.

As they came together, the rider with the black lance thrust forward in his saddle, jabbing savagely at his opponent's red shield. He caught it dead centre. These were lances of peace crowned with coronels, the three-pronged iron heads spreading the force of impact. Even so, the strike managed to shatter the shield as well as the lance. The splinters flew up into the face of the rider, who was tumbled back out of his saddle. As the rider in black galloped on past, his opponent went slamming into the grass, his horse continuing without him. He rolled to a stop and lay still among the shards of his shield, his pages running to help him. At the other end of the field, the winner brought his horse to a prancing halt, lifting his broken lance in triumph.

'Excellent, Piers. Truly excellent!'

Edward Bruce looked round at the shout to see the prince applauding.

The prince caught his eye and grinned. 'You look worried, Sir Edward.'

'On the contrary, my lord, I am eager to face such a worthy opponent.'

The prince laughed. 'Well said.' Tall and well-built like his father, he cut an imposing figure in his polished mail coat. His scarlet surcoat was emblazoned with the same three gold lions, the only difference the blue indented band across the top. His face was gentler than the king's, a blond beard softening the lines of his cheeks and jaw. His blue eyes gleamed in the sunlight as they followed Piers Gaveston, trotting his spirited courser back to the starting line. 'When this war is over, I intend to take my company to France. With Piers as our champion we'll win any tourney.'

'I do not doubt it.'

After seven months in the prince's household Edward Bruce had learned many things, the foremost of which was always to agree when it came to the Gascon. Employing this rule early on, he had quickly won the prince's affection, hoping this would allow him to get closer to the king's son and glean valuable knowledge that might help Robert when his brother finally broke these hateful bonds of loyalty and turned on the English. But he had soon discovered that with Piers around there was little room for anyone else at the prince's side.

The distant call of a horn broke his thoughts. It was followed by the faint thud of stones striking Stirling's walls as the day's assault began. The echoes sent a couple of crows flying up from the woods that bordered the meadow. Beyond the treetops the castle rock thrust into the sky, the standard that hung from the battlements just a speck of gold at this distance.

'Until then we will have to content ourselves with my father's planned contest,' mused the prince, passing Edward a gem-studded wine skin.

Edward took a swig, his gaze on the fallen rider who was being helped up by his pages. The young man shook them off after a moment. Grabbing the new red shield that was handed to him he staggered to his horse. The watching men applauded his resolve. Piers Gaveston waited at the starting point, flexing his arm, before taking the fresh lance his page passed to him.

'My father held a tournament for his new Round Table when he conquered Wales.' The prince didn't take his eyes off Piers. 'At Nefyn. I don't remember it of course. I was just born. But men still speak of it – the jousts, the prizes. Not my father though. All he recalls is the conquest.'

An explosion resounded from the heights of Stirling's rock, this one sending a black mass of birds scattering up from the woods. The young men on the meadow turned, staring up at the distant fortress. Edward saw plumes of smoke rising and wondered what new devilry the king had devised with which to torment the garrison.

Only the prince seemed to take no notice, staring across the meadow as the riders steadied their agitated horses, a faraway look in his eyes, as if he were looking out over another vista, or time. Beneath his blond fringe his brow furrowed. 'I wonder, if Stirling falls today, what my father will do next. His whole life has been spent in war. I don't think he knows anything else.' The prince seemed to come back to himself as Piers surged into a gallop, spurring his courser fiercely across the meadow. 'I find it interesting,' he said suddenly, turning to Edward with a curious smile. 'How we're both named after my father, yet neither of us are firstborn sons. It's as if they thought we could never live up to the expectation of that name.' He laughed, though the sound had little humour in it. 'My brother Alfonso, my father's first heir, died just months after I was born. But I sometimes think, even now, I am still the second son.'

Across the field, Piers Gaveston shattered his third lance against his opponent's shield.

Edward stared at the prince, surprised by his candour. 'I know what it means to be in a brother's shadow.' He frowned, feeling the sting of the truth. 'I think it was easier for Alexander, Thomas and Niall; they never expected to inherit. Me – I was always that much closer to the promise. Now my father is dead . . .' He faltered. 'Well, I see how great the gulf is.'

The prince nodded and grasped his shoulder. 'You're in my household now. We will make our own fortunes.'

'Are you sitting this one out, Sir Edward?'

Edward Bruce looked round at the sour enquiry. Piers Gaveston had spurred his horse over to them while they were talking. He had removed his helm and his face was hard with question.

'I'm ready whenever you are, Master Piers,' retorted Edward, enjoying the flash of anger in Piers's coal-dark eyes. It had become a petty, yet pleasing pastime, reminding the arrogant young cock that he wasn't yet a knight, like himself.

The prince released his hand on Edward's shoulder and smiled approvingly. 'Come then,' he said, gesturing to the field, 'let's have it!'

As Piers turned his courser, Edward crossed to Euan, his squire. The young Annandale man held his grey mare steady as he dug his foot in the stirrup and swung up into the saddle. Euan passed him his helm, which he pulled down over his coif, smelling the tang of the iron. Taking his shield, decorated with the arms of Annandale, Edward pushed his arm through the strap on the back and looped the reins in his hand. Digging his spurs into the mare's sides, he urged her across the meadow. Euan followed in his wake, bearing three yellow lances.

Piers turned in his saddle as Edward rode up alongside him. He had donned his swan-winged helm, but the visor was lifted. 'It would seem my prince has taken a liking to you.' His French was different to that of his English comrades, Piers having spent his early years in Gascony. He had been taken into the royal household in adolescence, shortly after his father, a favoured knight in King Edward's service, had died. 'I hope you can

forgive him for showing you what might appear to be genuine affection.'
Piers smiled and looked away. 'Edward just has a weakness for ruffians.
Boorishness amuses him.'

Before Edward could respond, Piers roused his courser into a canter,
heading for the other end of the meadow. Edward trotted his mare to the
starting point, then took the first lance from his squire. 'I'll give you rough,
you son of a bitch,' he murmured.

As Piers took a new black lance, Edward kicked at the mare's sides,
impelling her to flight. Full of fire she was and ready for the race. Though
there was little breeze today, the air seemed to rush and buffet against him
with the speed. Edward leaned forward as the mare's hooves drummed the
ground. He went with her, rolling his body in time with the motion, as he'd
first learned to do under Lord Donough's tutelage in Antrim. As he swung
the lance down his eyes narrowed behind the slits of his helm, all his concentration focusing on Piers Gaveston coming fast towards him.

Edward bared his teeth for the blow, driving the lance towards the centre
of the black shield. He knew it was a perfect strike at the moment of impact;
felt the sharp release as the lance broke upon the wood. Piers reeled sideways, dropping his own lance and only just managing to stay in the saddle.
As the Gascon came to an ungainly halt, Edward wheeled his mare around,
punching the jagged shaft into the air. Across the field, the prince and his
men cheered.

Breathing hard with exhilaration, Edward Bruce rode back down the
meadow, noting the wink of silver as the men began to exchange coins. He
passed Piers, who had righted himself, at a trot. 'A good try, Master Piers.'
As Gaveston growled something through his visor, Edward grinned inside
his helm, returning to the starting point to take another lance from Euan.

They set off again, surging towards one another, pricking their horses to
a ferocious burst of speed. Edward saw Piers's lance swing down towards
him, saw him rise in the saddle. He leaned forward, aiming again for the
centre of that black shield, just as the Gascon aimed for his. At the last
second, Piers feinted, thrusting the lance towards Edward's face. Even
though he was protected by his helm, Edward flinched, turning his head
instinctively. His arm went wide, veering from the centre of Piers's shield
to skid along the outer edge, before pulling out of his grasp. The three-
pronged tip of Piers's lance, meanwhile, shattered on the turned side of his
helm. Edward reeled with the blow, his head whipped back and his spine
cracking against the cantle. His armour saved him from the worst of it, but
he was dazed enough to lose control of his mare, who careened wildly on.

Managing finally to bring her to a shuddering stop, he shook his head to clear the concussion, gritting his teeth as he heard the cheers, this time for Piers. Edward turned his mare and set off down the field, meaning to end the bastard. His gaze was caught by a rider emerging from the canopy of trees, through which a track led to Stirling. It was Thomas of Lancaster.

The earl rode up to the prince, who, after a brief exchange with his cousin, motioned to Piers.

Seeing the other men begin to mount up, Edward kicked his mare towards them. 'My lord, we're leaving the field?' he called, tugging off his helm, angry at the prospect of the joust ending without a chance for him to redeem himself.

But the prince had already climbed into the saddle and was riding away, Piers at his side.

39

Prince Edward's company rode into the camp, men moving quickly out of the way as the young nobles spurred their sweat-soaked horses between the rows of tents. As he approached the siege lines, the prince slowed his courser, his gaze fixing first on his father, surrounded by his barons, then moving to the walls of Stirling Castle, blackened and battered by fire and stone. Smoke and dust had turned the air a gauzy grey, diffusing the sunlight. The vapours caught in the prince's throat making him cough.

The king, on seeing him, lifted a gloved hand and beckoned. Edward steeled himself as he dismounted, holding his head high as he walked to his father. Thomas of Lancaster went with him, as did Piers, blithely ignoring the dark looks some of the older barons shot him as he swaggered through their midst, though he had the sense to bow as he came before the king.

'You summoned me, Father?'

'I want you here.' The king's pale eyes flicked from the prince to Piers. 'You've spent enough time at play.'

Edward felt his cheeks grow warm, acutely aware of the earls and lords in their midst. The barons were involved in their own conversations, but he felt sure they each had an ear open to the exchange. 'The Saracens' fire is working well,' he observed stiffly, following his father's gaze towards the castle. Beyond the walls, smoke billowed from the shattered roof of the chapel. The siege engines had paused, their crews making adjustments and rolling fresh stones from carts.

'It will not bring down the walls,' remarked the king. 'But Warwolf may. I'm having the beast brought up after nones.'

Hearing female voices lifting above the rough tones of the men, the prince turned to see the queen and her ladies filtering into the royal pavilion, which stood at the centre of the encampment. The flaps had been pulled back and several chairs were set out on the carpet inside. Pages attended the women, escorting them to their seats and handing them goblets of watered wine to quench their thirst. The crispness of dawn had dissolved with the burgeoning warmth of the morning and it promised to be a hot day. The notes of a harp rose above as one of the queen's minstrels began to play.

Prince Edward noticed his father smile as Marguerite settled into the cushioned throne. The queen, who was only two years older than himself, had been lodging with her ladies in a building in the town, but his father wanted her here for the climax of the three-month siege, as if the walls of Stirling were a stage, set for some grand performance.

'Come, Edward,' said the king briskly, suddenly full of energy. 'Ride with me. I want to inspect the damage.' As the prince made to follow, the king turned back. 'Just you.' His gaze was on Piers as he spoke.

The king's destrier, Bayard, was saddled and ready, a scarlet trapper embroidered with the royal arms covering his great rump. After speaking with his chief engineer, the king mounted, straining a little with the effort. At his gesture, Thomas of Lancaster and Humphrey de Bohun followed suit, along with a number of royal knights.

As the prince climbed into the saddle of his courser, he glanced worriedly at the castle. 'Can one of the engineers not inspect the walls?'

'I don't need another man's eyes when I can see well enough for myself. Besides, it will give us a chance to talk.'

Unease churning his stomach, Edward followed his father through the siege lines as the king urged Bayard up the craggy slope. He rode from one engine to another, pausing to speak with the crew before moving on to the next, getting gradually closer to Stirling's walls, the two earls and royal knights following at a discreet distance. The king was clearly enjoying himself, sitting at ease in the saddle of his warhorse, which he handled expertly from prancing trot to strutting walk, even occasionally flicking his spurs across the beast's muscular flanks, causing Bayard to rear up and strike the air. Edward caught his father glance at the royal pavilion and knew he was showing off for his young wife. He'd had the window of the house Marguerite had been lodging in widened in order for her to be able to view the siege. Now, here he was in full pride before his lioness, circling his prey.

The closer they came to the castle's walls, the thicker the smoke became, hanging in veils across the battlements. The prince scanned them, searching for sign of movement. Below the walls, he glimpsed limbs protruding from the debris strewn across the pathway that led to the drawbridge. Now the assault had paused a few crows had alighted on the rubble and were pecking the rotting flesh from the bones of the men who had fallen foul of the defenders' sporadic counter-assaults.

'Edward.'

The prince tore his gaze from the walls as his father called sharply to him. The king had paused a short distance from one of the trebuchets. He was sitting back against the cantle, letting Bayard crop the springy turf. Edward pricked his courser over to him. 'Yes, my lord?' He hoped his father didn't hear the tremor in his voice.

The king studied him. 'This siege will soon be over, Edward, and with it this war. I intend to return to Westminster as soon my lieutenant is in place here. I have left affairs in England alone too long. There are reports that disorder has been growing in the shires. With the barons and sheriffs at war, bands of armed felons have been terrorising towns across the country. Murder, racketeering and robbery have increased. The kingdom has been without its lord and master for too long.' The king paused. 'And there are other matters too, I have left unattended. Your marriage.'

The prince's brow knotted at the subject he had sought to avoid for months, grateful for Stirling's stubbornness and the disappearance of William Wallace, which occupied his father and kept him turned from the issue. 'I haven't even been knighted yet. Why hasten me to marriage when I am still learning the craft of war?'

'War is the very reason this marriage should be hastened,' the king responded, glancing over at Humphrey, waiting nearby with Thomas of Lancaster. 'Your sister, Bess, will have her first child by midwinter and you will have a nephew. But I want you to have a son. I am not long for this world, Edward. When the time comes for you to take my crown your line must be established. I have written to King Philippe,' he said brusquely, as his son lowered his gaze. 'To arrange terms.'

As his father continued to discuss the marriage plans, the prince remained silent, his mind wandering through dark passages of the future. He saw himself placing a ring on his veiled bride's finger. Her hands would be cold and small. He saw a marriage bed, festooned with ribbons. His jaw clenched as he saw himself climbing into it with this cold, pale stranger. He walked back from the image, repelled by it, seeking comfort. His gaze drifted to the siege lines where Piers Gaveston waited. Isabella of France, daughter of King Philippe and niece to Queen Marguerite, was only eight years old. She couldn't marry until she was at least twelve. He had four years left of freedom.

'Isabella will make a good match,' finished the king. 'Now conflict with France has ended and Gascony is returned to me, it can only help strengthen those bonds.'

Edward met the king's uncompromising gaze. 'Yes, Father.'

The king opened his mouth to say something further. Before he could, he jolted forward, slamming into his pommel. Bayard, startled by the sudden motion, bucked, almost pitching him out of the saddle. The prince saw something long and thin protruding from his father's back. It took a second for him to realise it was an arrow. He shouted in fear as more arrows stabbed down around them. Suddenly, everything was in motion. There was a flash of blue as Humphrey de Bohun swept in on his horse, lifting his shield above his head as he grabbed Bayard's reins. Kneeing his horse into action, he sped away down the hillside, the warhorse and its royal burden in tow. Thomas of Lancaster rode up alongside the prince, yelling at him to move. A rush of blood fired Edward's limbs and he kicked at his courser for all he was worth, riding back towards the siege lines, where men were shouting and running, and archers were lining up to counter the arrows thumping down from Stirling's battlements. Edward's blood pounded in his temples. Ahead of him, he saw his father sprawled over the front of the saddle, the shaft protruding from his shoulder like an exclamation. Then, the king and Bayard were swallowed by the rushing crowd.

Leaving Nes to show James Douglas a stall for the men's horses, Robert ushered William Lamberton quickly into his lodgings on Stirling's main street. Fionn greeted them with a bark and trotted over to nose the bishop. 'You found the steward,' said Robert, ordering the hound out of the way and closing the door behind them. 'Where is he?'

The bishop scanned the place, his pearl-white eye gleaming in the sunlight slanting through the shuttered windows. The house was a well-appointed timber building with two rooms leading off the central chamber. A bed stood against one wall partially hidden by a drape and a trestle and bench were placed near the shallow hearth, which had a jug of dead flowers in it. Meadowsweet covered the floor, masking the faint odour coming from a latrine, concealed behind a wattle screen. Shelves built along one wall held a collection of pewter goblets and plates, shiny with the patina of long use.

Lamberton picked up a Book of Hours that was lying on the end of a shelf, covered in a fine layer of dust. He turned it over in his hands. 'I wonder whose home this was? A burgess I presume?' He looked up at Robert. 'You've certainly won King Edward's favour, Sir Robert.'

'Your grace.'

Lamberton set the book down at the sharpness of Robert's tone. 'Sir James is in Atholl, with your brother-in-law.'

For Robert, the good tidings that the steward had been found were made all the better by the unexpected news. Having heard nothing of John of Atholl in months, he had feared the worst. 'And Thomas and Niall?'

'Your brothers are with them. Safe and well.'

Relief tempered Robert's impatience. Preoccupied by the long wait for word and the delay to his plans, he hadn't realised how concerned he had been for his brothers. 'So, James has offered to submit to the king?'

'The steward thought it prudent. He didn't want to be hunted like Sir William, with a price on his head and no safe haven. He wasn't the only one. Sir John has also offered his surrender.'

Robert nodded, taking this in. 'This way we should be able to work towards my plan without undue interest from the king. The more such threats to his peace are mitigated, the more he will turn his full attention to those that remain.' He began to pace. 'Although that does present its own difficulties. When we spoke in St Andrews you said you didn't know where Wallace had gone to ground.' Robert turned to the bishop. 'Did James have any idea how to contact him?' He continued before Lamberton could answer. 'The sooner we do so the better. Stirling cannot hold out much longer. When the castle falls, William Wallace will become the king's primary target and he will avail himself of any means by which to ensure his capture. It's a miracle he hasn't been found yet, given the number of Scotsmen already employed in hunting him down.' Robert paused, study- ing Lamberton's expression. 'You did speak to Sir James of my intentions?' His brow furrowed when the bishop didn't answer. 'You gave me your word at St Andrews, your grace.'

Robert watched as Lamberton crossed to the trestle and bench and sat himself down. Four months ago, shortly after the death of Robert's father and his return to Edward's court, the bishop had sought him out to ask why he had sent Nes to warn them of the English raid in Selkirk. Knowing he had exposed himself to the rebels by his actions, knowing too that he would need all the support he could get to set his bold plan in motion, Robert had confided in him. Admitting that although he was with the king in body he was not so in spirit, he spoke of the hope, held all this time in secret by himself and James, that if Balliol was prevented from returning to the throne of Scotland he, Robert, might one day lay claim to it. King Edward, he explained, had been a shield, protecting his interests without knowing it.

Robert had gone on to tell Lamberton his plan, inspired by the return of William Wallace: to persuade the rebel leader to build another army in secret, the like of which had been raised for Stirling. With this force, they would strike back at Edward, using Robert's knowledge of his weaknesses. If successful, he would take the throne and rally the support of the men of the realm, using Wallace's reputation to help him. He had finished by asking Lamberton to find the steward; the one man who could convince Wallace to aid him to this end.

The bishop had agreed, telling him to do nothing until he returned. Initially encouraged by the prospect, Robert had grown increasingly impatient for word. Now, by the gravity in Lamberton's bearing, he had the distinct impression his faith in the bishop had been unjustified.

'I spoke to Sir James, as I said I would,' said Lamberton, looking at him. 'I told him what you told me. Word for word.'

'He didn't agree with it?'

'He and I both agreed that there is a chance we can undermine Edward's control. Once the king has established the new government he will return to London with the majority of his men. Trouble grows for him in England, crime and poverty rising. He needs to turn his attention to his own kingdom if he is to prevent it from descending into disorder. That will be our moment for action. For a new uprising.'

Robert was nodding. 'Exactly.'

'In previous campaigns our struggle has been weakened by divisions among our leaders. Our rebellions have been wildfires, burning bright and fierce for a short time, but ultimately consuming themselves. Animosities and personal ambitions have driven a wedge between each formation of guardians. With one man in charge – backed by all factions – the steward and I believe we stand a better chance of an uprising lasting more than a season. We can win back Scotland. But to do so we need to unite it.'

'And this is what I intend to do, as king. With Wallace as my sword.'

Lamberton laced his slender hands on the table's pitted surface. 'William Wallace can no longer help you to do this, Robert. You said it yourself: he is the king's main target. Many of the nobles have been incited to hunt him down by promises from Edward that he will reduce the terms of their exile or the costs of buying back forfeited estates. Wallace cannot unite Scotland; indeed his presence would, I believe, disintegrate any attempt at unity we could make. The bastards would fight one another to be the one to drag him in irons to the king.' He fixed Robert with his gaze. 'You know I am right.'

Robert shook his head, but the denial lacked conviction. The bishop's words echoed concerns that had built in him these past months; seeing the king's desire to find William Wallace growing into the fever of obsession, listening to reports coming in, many from Scots who had sighted the outlaw in this place or another.

'In the eyes of many,' continued Lamberton, 'John Balliol still has the better right to be king. Do not forget that while he lives you are talking about overthrowing him. This is not a simple task. If you crowned yourself tomorrow, few would follow you. Even men who once supported you now see you as a traitor. In order for you to be accepted as king and for us to achieve the unification that could win us our kingdom we need the whole country to stand behind you. The only way to do that is to secure the endorsement of the one man who holds the greatest power in the realm. That man is not William Wallace. That man is John Comyn.'

Robert stared at the bishop, stunned. 'This is your plan?' He gave a hard bark of laughter. 'The steward's plan?'

'As guardian, John Comyn is invested with the right to speak for the men of the realm. But more than that, these past years he has built up a large and loyal following, supported by the army of Galloway. As Lord of Badenoch he has many vassals, augmented by his kinsmen, the Black Comyns and Comyns of Kilbride. Most importantly, he has delivered hope of victory with his triumphs at Lochmaben and Roslin.'

'Victory?' Robert shot back. 'He caused the deaths of hundreds of Scotsmen through his own greed!'

'And at whose hands did those deaths come?' Lamberton responded, rising suddenly. The accusation blazed in his eyes. 'That is what people will see if you stand before them now, Robert: your part in our defeat. I admit I find it hard not to see it myself. Alone, like Wallace, you have become a divisive force. Comyn, by contrast, has become the mortar that binds this realm together.'

'I cannot believe James went along with this.'

'He took some persuading,' admitted Lamberton. 'But in the end he saw I was right.'

Anger pulsed through Robert. Anger at the steward for agreeing to this, at Lamberton for suggesting it and at the tiny part of himself that knew the bishop spoke sense. He fought against it. 'James convinced me to submit to Edward. He put me in this position!'

'He was right to do so. At the time, he believed King John would return. We all did. Submitting to Edward was the only way to safeguard your interests. Had you fought in the rebellion you too would now be struggling to buy back your forfeited lands, perhaps spending time in exile. Instead, you are immune from persecution and find yourself in the unique position of being instrumental in setting up the new government; of being in a position of power in conquered Scotland.'

Robert stared at him. 'You've been fighting all this time for Balliol's return, your grace. You headed the delegation in Paris. Why would you help me overthrow him?'

'Because I know now that John Balliol will never sit on Scotland's throne. I know, too, that the steward and Robert Wishart pledged support for your claim a long time ago. I trust their judgement.'

'There are others with a claim,' murmured Robert. 'John Comyn included.'

'None is as strong as yours. Your grandfather would have been king, chosen by the men of the realm, had Edward not elected Balliol. Many believed the Lord of Annandale had the stronger claim. There would be a sense of justice, I believe, in making his progeny king. The world as it should have been. A slate wiped clean. It is something we could build on among the men. Something that could help your reputation.'

Robert's eyes fixed on the jug of dead flowers in the hearth. The petals were brown and brittle, curled up like dead spiders. In his mind, he saw the round hall at Peebles, himself and John Comyn in the middle of a crowd of men. He saw the hatred in Comyn's face, a hatred that had seeped through generations, fed by each, to grow to maturity in them. He saw the blade of a dagger coming up to his throat, Comyn's arm locking around his neck; saw their comrades drawing weapons, going at one another. 'You speak of the necessity of unity, your grace. You were at Peebles. You saw what happened the last time John Comyn and I were set together as guardians.' Robert shook his head. 'It cannot work.'

'It has to, Robert. None of us can fight King Edward alone. It will take the influence of John Comyn and the rightness of your claim to rally the kingdom and break his will.'

Robert turned from the bishop, his thoughts fractured. On the one hand, he was desperate to make a move – to break these shackles of loyalty to a king he loathed – to stand up and reclaim what had been taken from his family. Lamberton seemed to be offering him this. But the price?

He and Wallace hadn't always seen eye to eye, but Robert respected the man: his unerring vision for a liberated Scotland, his steadfastness and loyalty to his men, his single-minded ferocity on the battlefield. John

Comyn was another prospect entirely. The man was his blood enemy. Lamberton was asking him to forgive decades of hatred; to ignore all that the Comyns had done to his family, and his to theirs. In short, to trust him. His choice was the devil or the deep.

Robert's decision settled inside him. 'As you say, King Edward has placed me in a position of authority. Furthermore, he will need a lieutenant in Scotland when he leaves.' He turned back to Lamberton. 'I haven't lost hope yet, but if you are right and I cannot use Wallace to raise an army then I'll use whatever authority the king gives me to rebuild my influence in Scotland. I believe, in time, he may be persuaded to appoint me sole guardian. It will take longer, yes, but from that position of power I could vie for the throne.'

'Do not make the same mistake as your father, Robert,' urged Lamberton. 'He lived on the king's promises. In the end what did those scraps bring him but a lonely death in England?'

Fionn rose suddenly from his place by the bed and barked. A second later the door opened and Nes appeared. 'Sir, it's the king. He's been shot.'

40

Robert pushed his way through the crowds clustered around the royal pavilion, the flaps of which were firmly closed. There was an agitated hum of voices as knights and barons recounted the moment the arrow had shot from Stirling's battlements. A few lamented the fact they hadn't seen it coming. Others cursed the Scot who had shot the fateful bolt, swearing vengeance upon the garrison.

Robert felt a strange excitement in the tension that crackled through the throng; a sense that everything was about to change and his place in the world with it. If Edward was dead, his twenty-year-old son would be crowned king. The prince, from what his brother had told him, shared none of the king's obsession with the conquest of Scotland, his own passions lying elsewhere. What was more, young Edward would rely heavily on the experience and counsel of older men at the start of his reign. If Robert was one of those men, could he persuade him to return Scotland's liberty? Persuade him that the country needed a king if peace and prosperity were to be maintained?

As Robert neared the pavilion the flaps opened and Humphrey emerged. The earl looked drained, but he smiled and lifted his hands to the gathering, motioning for quiet. 'Our king is well.'

The ripple of relief through the crowd swelled into loud applause.

'The arrow pierced his flesh, but the wound is superficial. His physician expects him to heal quickly.'

Numbly, Robert felt men jostle him as they continued to praise God at Humphrey's words. He stared at the earl, hope seeping from him. The old bastard had survived?

'King Edward is anxious that the incident cause no further disruption to the assault on Stirling. Indeed, he intends to join us for Warwolf's inauguration.'

The applause thundered.

'*Bring the beast!*' Humphrey roared.

As engineers began to break from the crowd, moving to execute the order, Humphrey spied Robert standing there. He came over, his brow knotting. 'Robert?' He clasped his shoulder. 'You look as pale as a ghost.'

Robert roused himself. 'I just heard what happened.'

'It was a shock to us all.' Humphrey lowered his voice as men hurried past, returning to their duties, the camp now buzzing with the prospect of retribution. 'I must admit, I thought him done for. The physician said he must have lost consciousness with the pain. He came to as we were removing his armour.' The earl shook his head in wonderment. 'I swear, as the arrow was being pulled out he was sitting there telling me how he would have his revenge on the garrison by sundown. There are oxen with less—'

'Can I see him?'

Humphrey faltered. 'Now?'

'It was one of my countrymen who shot him.' Robert met the earl's gaze, the lie solidifying. 'I don't want this to jeopardise the peace we have all worked so hard to secure. I want to make sure the deeds of a few don't affect the fate of many.'

Humphrey nodded after a pause. 'Let me see if he will grant you an audience.'

Robert waited, his heart beginning to thud, as the earl ducked inside. The conversation with Lamberton, momentarily overshadowed by the possibility of the king's death, flooded his mind, charging him with a sense of urgency. He had waited months, hoping the bishop would return with the answer he sought. But all he had been offered was a poisoned chalice. He wanted to prove Lamberton wrong, prove he could get what he wanted his own way; that he didn't have to work with John Comyn to achieve it. The bishop was right – he had won the king's favour. It was time to see just what that would buy him.

Humphrey appeared and motioned to him. As Robert moved to push through the pavilion's flaps, the earl put a hand on his shoulder. 'The king may be as tough as old hide, but take care not to weary him.'

Moving past the royal guards at the entrance, Robert stepped inside the pavilion. Oil lanterns bathed the interior in a coppery glow, gleaming in the gilt work on the cushioned throne and chairs still set out in a row for the queen and her ladies. The seats were empty. A servant moved past Robert, carrying a basin of water that was tinged red. Beyond, in another section of the tent, partially obscured by richly patterned drapes, he could see the king.

Edward was sitting on a stool, his physician stooping behind him wielding a needle. The king was bare-chested, wearing only his hose and braies. His stomach was creased with loose skin, but his chest, bristling with white hairs, was still slabbed with muscle, as were his arms, which rested tensely at his sides while the physician worked. There was a knotted scar just over the king's heart; an older wound. That riddle of scar tissue showed just how close the Assassin's dagger had come to killing him, missing the target of his heart by inches. Edward had survived deadly encounters on battlefields in England, Wales, Scotland, France and the Holy Land, hunting accidents, fevers, the collapse of a tower that was struck by lightning, storms at sea. And, now, that charmed arrow. It was as if death itself was afraid to claim him.

The king wasn't alone in the tent. Queen Marguerite stood close by, wincing every time the needle swooped in for another pass through the king's shoulder. Further back, standing alone by the tent's side, was Prince Edward, his face a mask of apprehension. There were others – Bishop Bek and Thomas of Lancaster, several royal advisers and a number of pages – but Robert only had eyes for the king.

Edward fixed on him as he approached. 'Sir Robert. Humphrey tells me you have something to say.'

'I wanted to pay my respects, my lord, and to reaffirm my fealty. I am keen that the actions of Stirling's garrison do not colour your judgement of all Scotsmen.'

As the king stared at him, skeins of incense drifted between them, curling from a censer. The smoky perfume couldn't fully disguise the odours of sweat and blood. In the corner of his eye Robert saw a broken arrow lying on the chest, its shaft slick and red. He felt a twinge in his shoulder where the crossbow bolt had punctured his flesh. *We are even now*, he thought, meeting Edward's pale gaze.

'One man, not the kingdom, shot the arrow,' said the king finally. 'I was careless. It has taught me the value of caution and reminded me of the need to guard my back around my enemies. The Scots are a devious race.'

Robert didn't miss the smile that curled Bishop Bek's mouth.

Once the physician had finished stitching the wound and cut the thread, Edward flexed his shoulder carefully, then stood. 'Was there something else?'

Robert hesitated, not wanting to speak in front of Bek and the others.

The king frowned, then motioned brusquely to his family and advisers. 'Leave us.'

Bishop Bek caught Robert's eye as he passed, seeming to communicate some warning or threat. The prince looked relieved to be excused, slipping quickly out of the tent ahead of the queen, who was escorted by her ladies.

After allowing his page to help him pull on a fresh shirt, Edward took up a goblet of wine. 'Speak, Sir Robert. I am in no mood for guessing games.'

'I have been thinking, my lord, about Scotland's future and your plans for establishing a new government. This attack has exposed what has been foremost in my mind – the necessity of building a stronger union between our people in order to maintain the peace and curb the more rebellious elements who may seek to disrupt it, especially with William Wallace still at large.' Robert enjoyed the flush that mottled the king's pallid face at the mention of the outlaw.

'Go on,' ordered Edward gruffly, sipping his wine.

'More than ordinances, more than officials, you will need the consistency and cohesiveness a strong leader can provide when you leave for England. I have proven I can keep the peace in the west as Sheriff of Lanark and Ayr. I believe I could do much more as your lieutenant in Scotland. I know these men, my lord,' Robert went on, before the king could respond. 'I know their fears and their hopes. I would see the first sign of rebellion long before its fire was ever sparked again.'

The king finished his wine. 'I have already chosen my lieutenant. My nephew, John of Brittany, shall fill that role.'

The blow knocked Robert's impetus, but he fought to regain it. 'He will need an adviser. Someone who knows Scotland and its people. I would be—'

'I have also chosen my chancellor and my chamberlain, and am in the process of selecting justices and sheriffs, some of whom will indeed be Scotsmen.' Edward's tone was imperious. 'This is not the first country I have brought under my dominion, Sir Robert. I am not naïve to the delicate politics of conquest. I understand the benefits of placing natives in positions of power.' He turned to the bed where his surcoat had been laid out and picked up the garment, frowning at the bloody hole the arrow had made. 'Only, not so much that they can grow beyond their station.' He crossed to a clothes perch and took down his scarlet mantle. 'Scotland will be much as it was after I deposed John Balliol. It will enjoy its liberties, but subject to me. There will be no guardians, no regent.' He turned back to Robert. 'No king.' Edward held his gaze for a long moment, then went to shrug the mantle around his shoulders. Pain creased his face. 'Help me with this,' he commanded testily.

Robert forced himself forward and took the mantle from the king, his fingers crushing the soft material. He moved behind Edward, smelling an odour of herbs from the physician's treatment. The king was several inches taller than him, but Robert noticed he was starting to lose some of his formidable height to the stoop of old age. As he raised the garment, the three lions shifted with the movement, their open maws seeming to leer at him. He thought of the red lion of Scotland, torn from Balliol's tabard, as he laid the mantle over Edward's broad shoulders.

Time seemed to slow. Robert noticed a mole on the king's neck beneath the wisps of his thinning white hair. He saw the patches of skin on his scalp, raw from the summer sun. God, but this was just a man, bound to the same frail flesh as any other. How could this sixty-five-year-old body, weakened by human fragility, have been the cause of so much death and destruction? Robert's hands – the strong, sun-browned hands of a thirty-year-old – hovered over the king's shoulders, to either side of his neck.

Edward turned abruptly, fastening the brooch pin one-handed. 'I appreciate your offer of assistance, Sir Robert. Indeed, I welcome it. The war is ended and I want it to stay that way. I intend for a Scottish council to liaise with my lieutenant and his staff. I want John Comyn and Bishop Lamberton to be on this council, among others. But above all, I want you. You will be my eyes and ears in this new Scotland.'

'It would be an honour, my lord,' murmured Robert.

'Come,' said the king, a hard smile creasing his face. 'I want to be there when Warwolf is brought up.'

As Edward strode out of the pavilion, Robert followed. Stepping into the blinding sunlight, he barely heard the cheers of the men as they saw their king appear. Lamberton's voice echoed in his mind, drowning out all else.

Do not make the same mistake as your father. He lived on the king's promises. In the end what did those scraps bring him but a lonely death in exile?

Before Balliol was deposed, Edward had promised Robert's father the throne of Scotland in return for his loyalty. Robert remembered his father's eagerness as they made their way to Montrose that fateful summer's day. He hadn't been there when his father had gone to enquire of his reward, but he had been told later what had happened. *Do you think*, the king had demanded, *that I have nothing better to do than win kingdoms for you?* His father had never fully recovered from the loss, or the humiliation.

As the English nobles surrounded their king, offering prayers for his miraculous escape, Robert stood on the periphery, his thoughts in turmoil.

*   *   *

Warwolf rolled through the encampment, drawn by forty oxen. The animals groaned in wretched chorus as men cracked whips across their blood-streaked hides, forcing them on. In their wake the siege engine trundled, cables and ropes swinging, wheels carving up the ground, its colossal frame towering against the summer sky. Warwolf was a trebuchet; on a scale unlike anything any man had seen before. It had taken two months and more than fifty engineers to build it, frame by frame on a meadow below the town, using timber stripped from houses and the nearby woods. The men of the English army had to crane their necks to view it as it lurched slowly past, the great basket lying dormant on the wheeled platform, the other end of the beam slanting heavenward.

All was quiet on the battlements, no sign now of any defenders. Smoke floated in grey veils over the ramparts, pluming behind the walls where a large fire continued to burn out of sight. As Warwolf was brought to a halt, men unharnessed the oxen from the front of the platform, while engineers hauled and tugged the ropes and cables into position, slathering grease on to the wheel of the winch to ensure a smooth release. The crew set to work winding it, panting with the effort as the cable clanked round. Gradually, the basket of lead swung up into the air and the beam was lowered. Other crew worked close by, rolling a huge stone, far larger than those shot by the other engines, into a leather sling. Once the stone was cradled inside, the sling was attached to a hook on the beam.

The men around the base stepped back. The chief engineer looked to the king, who gave a nod. At his order, the crew released the winch. The basket hung suspended for a second as the cable hammered round, wind-ing itself free, then it dropped like an anchor. At the same time, Warwolf's arm, with the sling attached, sprang upwards in a sweeping arc. As it reached its zenith, sling and stone were sent catapulting towards Stirling's walls. It struck one of the gatehouse towers dead on, pulverising stone. The top half of the tower crumbled into the ditch with a roar of rubble. The men of the English army let out a cheer that resounded around the hillside at the sight of the jagged wound Warwolf had bitten in the castle's side.

'Again!' Edward ordered with a fierce shout. 'All the engines.'

Once more, Warwolf's crew heaved round the winch and the basket was hoisted. As another stone was loaded and sent flying into Stirling's walls, the trebuchets and mangonels joined in, the thunder of their onslaught seeming to shake the mountain. Flashes of Greek Fire thickened the smoke into a pall, blackening the sky.

After less than an hour of ferocious bombardment the men near the walls began to shout and motion to the gatehouse. Slowly, the drawbridge was lowered. The attack was halted as fifty or so figures emerged from the castle and began to pick their way through the rubble that littered the path. They were met by the king's knights, who checked them roughly for weapons, before leading them to where Edward waited.

They were a wretched band, some injured, most gaunt with lack of food and sleep. All were grey-faced and clad in the same shapeless garments. As they approached, led by the knights, Robert, standing with the king, realised that Stirling's garrison were wearing sacks over their surcoats and mail. The reason for the strange pallor of their faces became clear. Their cheeks had been smeared with ashes. Sackcloth and ashes: a show of penance and remorse. No doubt aware that some of Caerlaverock's garrison had been hanged after they surrendered, William Oliphant and his men sought the king's mercy.

Oliphant went down on bended knee. 'O great king,' he said hoarsely, holding out his fist, in which was gripped a large key on a ring. 'Stirling is yours. I humbly ask that you accept my unconditional surrender. Only, I beg you, spare the lives of my men.'

Robert glanced at the king, who remained silent, looking down on the bowed man.

'No,' said Edward, after a weighty pause. 'I do not accept.'

A few of the king's men looked at him. Humphrey was frowning in question. William Oliphant's head jerked up, his eyes filling with fear.

'It took two months to build Warwolf. I want it tested properly. I will consider your surrender when I am satisfied with the performance of my new siege engine. You will come out when I tell you to. Not a moment before.' The king gestured to his knights. 'Lead them back inside. Barricade the doors.'

William Oliphant rose, his eyes scanning the faces of the men around the king. No one came to his aid. After a moment, he turned and began to walk back up the path towards Stirling's broken gatehouse, his men following him as Warwolf's beam inched slowly skyward.

Robert stared at the king, resignation settling coldly inside him. Turning from Edward, his gaze roved across the crowd. It didn't take him long to pick out the tonsured head of William Lamberton.

41

They gathered at dawn in the courtyard of the royal manor, warming their hands around goblets of mulled wine, while grooms bridled their horses and the varlets led the dogs from the kennels. Along with the twelve running-hounds were two alaunts in leather armour and spiked collars, their powerful jaws capable of bringing down any quarry. When the huntsmen arrived with the news that the lymers had caught the scent, the company rode out, blowing their horns to entice the hounds to the chase. The sun was rising as they entered the woods, the young men's excitement spiced with apprehension, for what they hunted today wasn't stag or hare, but boar.

Spread out through the trees, the men rode through thickets of bracken and briars, spurring their coursers to leap narrow brooks and fallen branches, always with the hounds ahead, sometimes visible, other times traced only by the clamour of their barking. In their midst cantered Prince Edward, his emerald-green cloak billowing behind him. Beneath the saddle-cloth, the flanks of his horse foamed with sweat. His heart was hammering, the blood running hot in his veins. All his senses felt heightened; his eyes picking out gold flecks of sunlight in the falling leaves, ears noting the subtle shift in the cadence of the horns that now guided him eastwards on the trail of the hounds, his mouth and nose filling with the damp odours of moss and rotting acorns. The death of summer was all around him, glorious in the leaves' fading fire.

Away to the right, Thomas of Lancaster kicked his white courser up and over a tree stump. His cousin was grinning fiercely, his face flushed. Edward Bruce was just behind, raking the sides of his palfrey, determined to keep up with the earl. A spear was gripped in the Scot's right hand. His cloak was caked with mud and there was a bloody gash on his forehead, sustained in a fall, but he looked as elated as the rest of the company, alive with the joy of the hunt.

For three hours they had followed the trail, through overgrown glades and shallow rivers, the sky lightening to a glacial blue. Their quarry was cunning, evading them by doubling back on itself, but the huntsmen were skilled in their craft – reading tracks in the earth and the mud-stains the creature left as it brushed past the trunks of trees, examining piles of dung for freshness – and they were closing in. The prince had been pleased to see the acorns in the boar's droppings, which would render its meat all the sweeter. It would make a fine gift for his father, recuperating back at the manor, weakened by a complaint of the bowels during his withdrawal from Scotland. His sister Bess would no doubt enjoy it too, heavily pregnant and weary with it.

Skirting the low-hanging boughs of an oak, Edward glimpsed the sweep of a black velvet cloak disappearing between the trees up ahead. He smiled and kicked his courser on, heedless of the trailing branches he whipped past. As he gained on the rider, the velvet mantle with its embroidered knots and whorls of flowers became clearer. The rider turned in his saddle, hearing the hooves pounding up behind him. Piers grinned as he saw the prince and goaded his horse faster until the two of them were galloping madly through the woods, leaving the rest of the company far behind.

Ahead, the trees thinned out and the ground sloped down into a wide, natural ride. The two of them careened on to it, mud and leaves flying. Edward managed to manoeuvre his horse up alongside Piers, the two of them racing abreast. The trees were a blur of gold and brown, sunlight flashing in and out. A hunting horn cradled in its baldric bounced wildly against the prince's back. He fought for breath, leaning forward in the saddle. In the corner of his vision he saw Piers doing the same. The Gascon's lips were pulled back, his teeth gritted. Some distance ahead, the track narrowed, the trees closing in. Edward jabbed at his courser's sides for all he was worth, trying to get in front of Piers. But the Gascon refused to slow. The thick trunk of a beech loomed up.

At the last second, Edward lost his nerve. Pulling his horse sharply to the left to avoid the trunk, he went hurtling down a shallow bank and was almost pitched from the saddle as his horse vaulted a fallen tree and crashed through a tangle of undergrowth. Twigs scratched his face. He fought to control the animal, pulling on the reins and leaning back against the cantle until the courser came to a halt. The prince sat there, closing his eyes as his breaths slowed and the shaking in his limbs subsided.

'My lord!' called Piers, riding down to him. His horse's mouth was frothy, its nostrils flared. 'Are you hurt?'

'No thanks to you if I'm not,' snapped Edward, his blood heated by the rush of fear. 'Why didn't you slow?'

'I thought you would.' Piers smiled as he studied the prince, his dark eyes full of sly question. 'Did you not enjoy the race?'

Seeing that grin, Edward felt his own lips respond unwittingly, but fought against it. 'Just pass me the wine, damn you.'

Kicking his feet out of the stirrups, Piers jumped down and set about unfastening the skin from his saddle. He passed it to Edward, who drank deep, the wine flooding his parched throat. The faint call of horns came to them. The prince shifted round in the saddle, trying to determine the location of the rest of the hunting party.

'Look.'

Edward turned back to see that Piers had crossed to a tree, the lower bark of which was carved with scratches. The prince recognised the markings at once. They had been made by a boar sharpening its tusks. He lowered the wine skin, suddenly wary. 'Piers, you should mount up.'

The Gascon made no move to obey. 'There are more over here,' he called, heading deeper into the undergrowth.

Cursing, the prince dismounted and drew his sword. His legs felt weakened by the ride as he moved up behind Piers, blinking as he passed through a dappled patch of sunlight. He could smell wet earth and the mulch of rotting leaves. His ears were strained for any sound in the undergrowth around them. Tackling a boar on horseback was dangerous, but on foot it was foolhardy. Its tusks could split a man wide open.

Piers paused by an oak and crouched down, running a gloved finger along the gashes on the trunk. 'These seem fresh to me.'

'We should call the others,' said Edward, taking up his hunting horn.

Before he could sound it, Piers rose and grasped his wrist. 'They'll find us soon enough.'

'In pieces if that boar's skulking round here somewhere.' Edward tried to sound forceful, but the pressure of Piers's fingers around his wrist made his voice come out as a murmur. The Gascon was so close he could see the beads of sweat on his upper lip, his skin shadowed by half a day's stubble. He averted his gaze. 'Piers . . .'

'I was hoping we would have the chance to talk alone,' said the Gascon, not relinquishing his grip. 'What has the king been saying about me, Edward?'

'Saying about you? I don't know what you mean.'

'Don't play games. We've known each other too long for that.'

Edward shook his head. 'I swear, Piers, he has said nothing.'

The Gascon released his hold on Edward's wrist abruptly. 'I see the effort he makes to keep us apart. Things have changed between us these past two months. Do you not see it?'

Edward thought. After the capture of Stirling Castle, which his father had continued to bombard before eventually accepting the garrison's surrender, the king had led the army south into England. The going had been slow, his father plagued by the illness that had come upon him suddenly. It was true, he had been ordering him to take on more responsibilities in this time, but the prince had assumed this was due to his weakened state.

'No,' said Piers sharply, when Edward explained this. 'It is more than your father's health. He has been keeping me out of meetings, manoeuvring others into greater positions of power within your household. Edward Bruce – a damned *Scot* – has been given more influence than me. And your father speaks so frequently of your marriage I swear it is as if you are wed already.'

Edward scowled and sheathed his sword with a forceful stab. There was an unspoken rule between him and Piers that they never discussed his forthcoming marriage to Isabella of France. 'You're not the one facing that prospect.'

'No, my future is worse,' Piers bit back. 'Once that day comes, I will lose you for good.' He pushed past the prince and went to their horses.

Edward caught him, clutching his shoulder. 'Let's not fight.' The two of them stood facing one another, leaves drifting down around them. The calls of horns were still faint, but the pitch was higher, more urgent now. Edward knew they were looking for him. 'It doesn't matter what my father says or does. I will not let him, or anyone divide us.'

'I need to have more power and greater standing at court, Edward. That is the only way my future at your side will be secure. You must stand up to your father.'

The prince laughed harshly. 'Stand up to him?'

'He will respect you for it.'

'After he has beaten me to a pulp, maybe.' Edward's mirth vanished. 'You still don't know what he's capable of.'

Piers reached out a gloved hand and cradled his cheek. 'I know what you are capable of.' He took a step closer.

'Don't,' said Edward, trying to turn his head away.

Piers wouldn't let him. Keeping hold of the prince's face he leaned in and kissed him.

Edward felt a jolt of desire go through him like a shock. His friend's lips were warm and tasted of spiced wine and salt. He smelled of sweat and leather. He grasped the Gascon's shoulder, his fingers biting into flesh, despising and loving it at once as he opened his mouth to Piers, hungry for the taste of him. It had been weeks.

There was a flurry of motion off to their right as something large crashed through the undergrowth, quickly followed by the thud of hooves. The prince and Piers pulled apart as Edward Bruce came hurtling through the clearing in pursuit of the boar. The Scot wheeled to a stop as he saw them, his spear poised in his hand and a shocked expression frozen on his face. For a moment, the three men stared at one another. Then, the clearing filled with barking as the hounds came dashing through, followed by the huntsmen and nobles. A few halted, relieved to see their prince, but most plunged on in the boar's wake, caught up in the chase.

'My lord prince,' panted one of the men, 'are you injured?'

The prince tore his gaze from Edward Bruce. 'I'm fine,' he said roughly. Leaving Piers looking daggers at the Scot, he strode to his horse, his face feeling as though it were on fire.

On the other side of the clearing, hidden by the tangled undergrowth, Thomas of Lancaster watched his shame-faced cousin swing up into the saddle. As the prince kicked his horse after the hunting party, Edward Bruce followed, the spear lowered in his grasp. Piers Gaveston watched the Scot leave before mounting his own courser and urging it out of the clearing, his face like thunder. Thomas remained where he was for a moment longer, hands gripped tight around the reins.

Turnberry, Scotland, 1304 AD

Elizabeth stood in the window watching the gulls swoop and dive, the sea's rush and drag against the cliffs ever present. Veils of rain drifted between the dark dome of Ailsa Craig and the distant isle of Arran. It was too murky to see the faint line that, on clear days, marked the northernmost tip of

Ireland. Far below, the waves churned, making her head swim. Unlike Lough Rea, whose placid expanse she had learned to avoid as a girl, there was no escape from water on this sea-battered outcrop. Her dreams were often filled with a sense of struggle and panic, and the inability to breathe – the childhood fear stirred to the surface – and when she woke to hear those roaring waves it always took a few moments to realise she wasn't still drowning.

She glanced down at the letter she held, recently received from her father. It was a typically stilted affair, offering some cursory news about her sisters before shifting to the ongoing struggle with the Irish, who continued to press in on the borders of Connacht and Ulster. She sensed the hope, between her father's lines, that now the war in Scotland was ended, King Edward would be able to turn his attention to his other beleaguered domains.

Elizabeth moved to the stand on which she kept her personal belongings: a mirror, a comb for her hair, a phial of perfume and items of jewellery, among them her ivory cross, now kept in a silk pouch. She rarely even looked at it these days, for it offered more pain than comfort, a reminder of a time when her faith in her father, and in God, were absolute. She couldn't help but feel that both had punished her, saving her from a husband who she feared had wanted her too much, only to give her to one who didn't want her at all. She folded the letter and placed it on the stand, as a loud hammering started up in the adjacent chamber. Having completed most of the outer repairs the masons, carpenters and labourers had turned their attention to Turnberry's damaged interior.

For over a week now, Elizabeth had been unable to escape the ceaseless pounding, with autumn's storms laying siege to Carrick's coastline and turning the roads to mud. Not that there was much comfort to be found beyond the confines of the castle; just windswept dunes and lonely marshes hemmed in by tangled woodland and hills. The villagers seemed unfriendly and suspicious, and the few occasions on which Elizabeth had ventured beyond Turnberry's boundaries had done little to reassure her. Once, exercising her horse in the woods nearby, she had glimpsed an old woman with knotted white hair, staring at her from between the trees. At the woman's side was a child with a face scarred by fire. Turning her palfrey, meaning to greet the strange pair, Elizabeth had found they were nowhere to be seen. Now, whenever she thought back on them, she wondered if they had been ghosts.

Robert had brought her to Turnberry shortly after the fall of Stirling, but had stayed only long enough to inspect the repairs that had so far been made to his castle. He told her he was going to meet John Comyn on behalf of the king in order to formalise plans for a new Scottish council, but Elizabeth knew he wasn't telling her everything. Since leaving the English camp she had sensed a change in her husband, who had become even more preoccupied and secretive than usual: receiving messengers in the middle of the night, sending his squire Nes on unspecified errands, meeting with men she didn't recognise behind closed doors.

Back in Dunfermline Elizabeth thought he had begun to recognise her frustrations, for on his return from the failed raid on the Forest he had agreed to employ a governess for Marjorie. Emma, the wife of one of Sir Humphrey's squires, was a warm, matronly woman, both comforting and commanding, who had immediately taken the girl in hand. Over the past months, Marjorie, immersed in her schooling, had become a far less troublesome child. While this had been a relief, the sudden emptiness in Elizabeth's days had been filled by the growing desire for a child of her own.

Turning from the window, she went to the bed and sat. The chamber had only recently been painted, covering up the smoke damage done by the fire, and her head ached with the astringency of the whitewash. Massaging her temple with her fingertips, she thought of Bess, who would surely have her baby soon, if she hadn't already. She missed her. The loneliness inside her swelled, pushing out all else until she felt like a shell, empty of anything except the hollow boom of the sea.

'Why are you crying?'

Elizabeth looked up, wiping her eyes briskly as she saw Marjorie standing in the doorway. 'Aren't you having a lesson?'

'I learned to read a whole psalm. Mistress Emma said I could play until supper.' Marjorie lingered in the doorway for a few moments longer, then entered the bedchamber.

Elizabeth saw she had the doll her father had given her back in Writtle in her hand. The thing looked tattered and grubby. One of its black bead eyes was missing.

'I found her at the bottom of my chest,' said Marjorie, stroking one of the doll's plaits. The other had come loose, the strands of wool knotted. 'I thought I'd lost her. Do you remember?'

Remember? The girl hadn't stopped wailing for five days. Elizabeth tried not to smile. 'I do.'

Marjorie held out the doll. 'Will you help me? I can't do a plait.'

'Me?' asked Elizabeth, unable to keep the surprise from her voice. 'Will Judith not do it?'

'She fell asleep,' answered Marjorie, hoisting herself on to the bed.

As Elizabeth took the doll, combing her fingers through the woollen hair to loosen the knots, Marjorie sat closer, watching intently.

The girl reached out suddenly, touching the ring on Elizabeth's finger. 'It's so beautiful.'

Elizabeth flinched as Marjorie's hand touched hers. The feel of skin – of human contact – was a shock. She stayed still, the doll forgotten in her hand, as Marjorie turned the ring this way and that, admiring the way the light caught the ruby.

'Mistress Emma has a ring. But not as pretty.' Marjorie frowned. 'Why do ladies wear them on this finger?'

'Because there is a vein there that runs to the heart.' After a moment, Elizabeth put her arm around the girl's shoulders, closing her eyes as the cries of gulls echoed over the breaking waves.

42

Night was falling on the moors, deepening the shadows in the folds of the land. Threading his way around the upper slopes at the head of his company, Robert caught the winking glow of fires on the ridge above him. He urged his horse on up the bracken-clad hillside to where a ring of stones stood dark against the sky. As he drew nearer, the raw wind whipping his hair in his eyes, he saw a number of tents had been pitched around their circle, the canvas sides illuminated from within by lanterns.

On the camp's periphery, he was challenged by two sentries and allowed to enter. Passing through the rows of tents, not waiting for the rest of his company to catch up, Robert dismounted near the standing stones. A large fire was burning in the centre of the ring, around which many figures were seated, bowls of food cradled in their hands, their faces bruised by the flames. Some looked round, eyeing him. While Robert discerned little welcome in their faces, he did see several familiar coats of arms that gave him reassurance.

'Sir Robert.'

He turned to see a tall figure striding out of the darkness. His spirits soared. 'Sir James!' He clasped the high steward's outstretched hand. 'It is good to see you.'

James Stewart offered him a rare smile. 'And you, Robert. And you.' His smile faded quickly, but the strength of feeling remained in his brown eyes. 'It has been a long road that has led us here. In time I would hear all your tidings, but for now we . . .' He paused, looking over Robert's shoulder as the rest of the company rode into the camp. 'Welcome, your grace,' he called, seeing William Lamberton at the head.

The bishop approached, followed closely by James Douglas. Since meeting Lamberton at Perth, from where they had made their way north together, Robert had noticed the young man rarely left the bishop's side.

As the steward's gaze alighted on the youth his eyes widened. 'James? By God! I hoped you would come, but I realise now I had been waiting to meet a boy. Lamberton,' he admonished, 'you did not prepare me for the man I see before me.' When James Douglas's pale blue eyes flicked to the bishop in question, the high steward frowned. 'You have no welcome for your godfather?'

'Uncle?' The dark-haired youth took a cautious step forward.

'Have I changed that much?' Bridging the gap between them with two strides, the steward embraced his nephew. 'You have your father's strength!' he exclaimed with a laugh as James gripped him fiercely. After a moment he pulled back. 'How did you fare at Stirling? Lamberton told me he would request the release of your lands.'

'The king said he would think on it, my lord,' answered James readily. His expression darkened. 'But I know Robert Clifford is held in high esteem, so I fear the king will put some price I cannot pay upon my estates to stop me reclaiming them.'

'Do not be so hasty to assume the worst, Master James. Edward did not dismiss the matter out of hand.' Lamberton turned his attention to the steward. 'My messengers informed you of the king's acceptance of your surrender?'

'They did. Thank you, your grace.' The steward's eyes lingered on the bishop, seeming to communicate a deeper gratitude behind the words. He smiled as he looked back at his nephew. 'It is a blessing to have you back.'

Robert's attention was drawn by a group of men heading towards them. At the sight of the familiar faces joy broke like light through his soul.

There was Niall, even taller, with a new maturity in his dark eyes and a confidence in his bearing. Surprised by the change, Robert realised the last time he'd seen him had been on the banks of Lough Luioch, when he'd thrust the Staff of Malachy into Niall's hands, the hooves of Ulster's men drumming up behind them. He wondered what his youngest brother – who once adored him – must think of him now. He had his answer as Niall embraced him.

'I knew you hadn't betrayed us,' Niall murmured.

After his youngest brother let him go, Thomas Bruce stepped up, gruff and reserved as ever, but with a firm handshake for his older brother. 'Welcome back, Robert.'

'You told them?' asked Robert, turning to James.

'It was time,' came another voice, before the steward could answer.

John of Atholl stepped out of the crowd. Behind the earl was his son David, wearing his father's colours.

'I reckoned you were up to something,' John explained, gripping Robert's shoulders and smiling as he looked him up and down. 'Sir James just confirmed what I guessed.'

'By tomorrow, John Comyn will know what you are planning,' the steward interjected. 'I saw no need to keep the truth from your brothers. After all,' he said, scanning them with his gaze, 'you will need their support if you are to triumph.'

'He has it,' said Christopher Seton, moving out of the shadows.

Robert laughed to see him, feeling an immeasurable gratitude that his brothers and friends had weathered the storm and were gathered here before him, forgiving of all he had done. These past years, the thought they must hate him for his desertion had gnawed at him.

Clasping Robert's hand, Christopher went down on one knee. 'My sword is yours, Sir Robert. As ever it was.'

Robert drew the Yorkshire knight to his feet and embraced him. Over Christopher's shoulder, he saw Alexander Seton. There was no smile of greeting on the lord's face, but he inclined his head. 'How did you come to be here?' Robert asked Christopher. 'I heard you were in Wallace's band?'

'I had to know why you sent Nes to warn us in the Forest,' answered Christopher, looking past Robert to where the squire was standing with the horses. 'Wallace gave Alexander and me leave to seek out Sir John. Your brother-in-law told us everything: that you submitted to King Edward in body, but not in heart. That you still intend to claim the throne.'

'You know where Wallace is?'

'No. He went into the wild to escape his hunters.'

'We have much to catch up on,' interrupted John of Atholl. 'But let us do so with something warm in our bellies.' The earl called his pages to bring food and drink. 'Come, join me at the fire,' he told Robert and Lamberton. 'My men will show your squires a place to make camp.'

'First, I need to talk to Sir James,' answered Robert, looking at the high steward. He smiled at Niall, who lingered at his side. 'You go on ahead.'

As his youngest brother walked away with the others, Robert's smile faded. Before the night was over he would have to tell Niall and Thomas that their father was dead.

'Robert.'

Turning back at the steward's voice, he allowed James to lead him through the camp, out of earshot of the men.

Halting in the darkness near a broken cairn of stones, the steward turned to him. The pallid light of a quarter-moon highlighted the grey in his hair. 'In his last message, Bishop Lamberton told me you had doubts. I now see them for myself in your face.'

'Can you blame me?' Robert demanded. 'This isn't what we planned.'

'Our plans were built on hope not judgement. For all we knew, John Balliol was to return and you would be exiled. We could not know for certain that this day would come, that the war would be at an end and the throne still free. We couldn't think beyond that possibility, until now.'

'By doing this I expose myself to a man who is my enemy. I risk everything. Even if Comyn accepts, there is no knowing what ill may come of an alliance between us. You know the hatred in our blood.'

'You exposed yourself when you sent Nes to warn the men in Selkirk,' the steward reminded him. 'John Comyn must know you have some hidden agenda. He surrendered to Edward because he saw no other option for his survival. By this alliance you offer him the hope that he doesn't have to be a slave to English will. At the very least, I believe he will listen to what you have to say. And the prize you offer for his endorsement is no mean incentive.'

Robert's jaw tightened. 'Prize?' he said bitterly. 'It is a reward beyond any I would have ever chosen. You and Lamberton ask me for a great sacrifice.'

'Is the price not worth paying if it gains you a kingdom and our people their liberty?'

Robert turned away, unwilling to answer. Around them, the wind rippled cold through the heather. Despite his joy at the reunion, he felt the darkness of the past weeks seeping back into his mind.

'It is the only way, Robert. Comyn will not agree to our terms for anything less.'

'There may still be another way. I failed to find proof that Edward ordered the murder of King Alexander, but I know where answers might be found – at least of his prophecy.'

'I told you not to turn those stones!' the steward hissed. 'If Edward had suspected you he would—'

'He doesn't. He thinks I don't know who attacked me in Ireland. James, I swear there was fear in his eyes when he saw this.' Reaching into his surcoat, Robert pulled out the head of the crossbow on its thong. The iron fragment glinted in the moonlight. He exhaled, thinking of the Tower – all the guards and defences and locked doors between him and the prophecy box. 'I haven't been able to get to it, but there is a chance I could find the proof that will enable us to bend Edward to our will.'

'No. No more.' The steward's tone was adamant. 'For this plan to work, you need to maintain your good standing in the English court. God willing, John Comyn will agree to support us, but if he does it will still be many months before we can set things in motion. We will need to seek out allies and ready our vassals in secret, build up a force of arms and decide upon strategies for attack. Then there is your coronation to plan. In this time we cannot arouse King Edward's suspicions. You must remain loyal to him, working to establish the new Scottish council in time for next year's parliament, as he has ordered. Time is on our side; indeed, the longer it takes us to ready ourselves, the more secure the king will begin to feel. He will not be expecting the hammer blow when it falls.' James grasped his shoulder. 'Do not risk all on a whim, Robert.'

'A whim? Edward may have murdered our king!'

'And I am trying to make one,' responded James forcefully. 'Neither you nor I can bring Alexander back, whatever the cause of his passing. But if such a grave offence has been committed we can right it by setting you on the throne. Our people have lost so much, suffered so much. Freedom is worth more than justice.'

Robert looked towards the flickering campfires, hearing voices and laughter. 'I can't help but wonder, had I found you before Lamberton, whether you would have supported my initial plan?'

'When Lamberton told me of your intention to use William Wallace to raise an army against King Edward, I believed it to be a fool's errand. I stand by that. In time, I pray Sir William will be able to return to a position of standing in the realm, but not until we have the upper hand. The best thing he can do for now is stay hidden.' James's brow knotted. 'Though I fear his thirst for English blood will bring him to the surface sooner rather than later.'

Robert knew the fight was lost. In truth, it had been over the moment he had set foot on the road north. Despite his deep misgivings, he couldn't fail to see the sense in Lamberton's plan, especially since his own had so far come to nothing. But that it had come to this? He thought of his grandfather, imprisoned after the Battle of Lewes by the forces of Simon de Montfort. By the treachery of the Comyns, the Bruce family had almost been ruined by the ransom they'd been forced to pay for the lord's release. Robert tried to imagine what the old man would say if he knew what he was about to do.

He pushed the question aside. His grandfather had not lived to see such days. James was right. Any price now was worth paying if it gained him the throne.

'Does Comyn know what I'm going to ask him?'

'No. He thinks you are coming to invite him to be part of the king's new council. For once,' James added with a wry smile, 'we do not tell a lie.'

'When do we leave?'

'At first light. See,' said James, heading through the heather to the edge of the moor, which fell away into darkness. 'Lochindorb isn't far.'

Following the steward, Robert saw a great loch stretched below him in the cleft of the hills. Far out, in the moon-washed expanse of water, was a castle, its battlements jewelled by torchlight. In the glow of the fires, he caught the red of a banner. 'Tomorrow then,' he murmured. 'And may it be the last sacrifice I have to make.'

43

Lochindorb, Scotland, 1304 AD

John Comyn watched as the boat receded. He could still see Robert Bruce, marked out from the other passengers by the white of his mantle. Hearing muffled voices above him, Comyn turned. His gaze moved up the sheer face of the castle's wall to the battlements, where two of his guards, clad in his red livery, were leaning against the parapet. The tips of their bows were visible, propped beside them.

Looking back at the boat, edging towards the loch's southern shore, Comyn imagined shouting the order. He would hear the yew bows creak as the string was pulled back; would see the arrows arc towards the vessel. Bruce would tumble from the prow, his mantle clouding the surface briefly, before he went under in a swirl of blood. The act itself would be easy. The repercussions would not. Comyn knew it would be like hurling a stone into that water, as he'd often done as a boy. He'd always marvelled at how far those ripples spread.

'We have much to discuss.'

Comyn licked his dry lips as the Black Comyn spoke at his side. The Earl of Buchan's gaze remained fixed on the boat.

'We do,' murmured Comyn. He rolled his shoulders, realising just how tense he had become during the parley with Bruce and his allies. 'Let's head inside.' He led the way up the slimy boards of the jetty, past knights standing sentry, through the archway in the east wall. The two of them were met in the castle courtyard by Dungal MacDouall.

The captain inclined his head to the two lords, but his expression was one of agitated anger. 'I beg your pardon, sir,' he said in a clenched tone, 'but may I ask what I have done to deserve your mistrust?'

'Mistrust?' Comyn frowned.

'I can think of no other reason why you kept me from your meeting with Bruce and the high steward.'

'Peace, Dungal,' said Comyn irritably. 'I kept you out because I didn't think you would bear being in the same room as the man who disfigured you, without retaliating.'

Dungal flinched, his left arm pulling instinctively towards his body. The scarred bulb of his wrist jutted from the sleeve of his shirt, the skin livid and knotted.

'Come,' Comyn said, leading the way across the courtyard to the great hall. 'We must talk. The meeting did not go as planned.'

MacDouall fell into step beside him. 'Bruce did not invite you to join the king's council?'

'He did. But that was not the real reason he came.'

The doorward pushed open the double doors as the lords approached.

The great hall was dominated by a dais, behind which a red standard bearing John Comyn's arms covered the wall. Wall-hangings lined the beamed chamber, depicting various heads of the family over the ages: one standing behind a king as he sealed a document, another bowing before the throne as he accepted new grants of land, John Comyn's grandfather at the Battle of Lewes fighting alongside King Henry and a young Edward. Fires snapped and spat in the hooded hearths and the hall smelled sweetly of smoke and the straw strewn fresh across the floor for winter, the summer rushes swept out.

Servants were busy collecting up goblets and platters used during the council. Comyn dismissed them with an order, before sitting at the head of a trestle. The Black Comyn seated his broad, muscular frame on one of the benches, sending hunks of bread to the floor with a sweep of his hand. Dungal MacDouall sat opposite him, scanning the remnants of the spread darkly, as if searching for evidence of his enemy.

Comyn waited until the hall's doors thudded shut, then began to speak, apprising MacDouall of the meeting and its unexpected outcome.

The captain sat for a long moment in silence, his right hand clenched on the surface of the table. 'So Bruce intends to overthrow King John?' His voice was quiet, but it might as well have been a shout for the force in his tone.

'He has had designs on the throne for a long time,' growled the Black Comyn, 'this is no great revelation. That ambition has burned in his family for three generations. What is surprising is the confirmation that Bruce has been deceiving his English master all this time and now plans to make war upon him.'

'I would say that is no surprise,' murmured Comyn. 'The son of a bitch has twisted in the wind so many times it is impossible to know which way he faces.'

'He honestly believes you would help him do this?' MacDouall was incredulous.

'The high steward and that meddler Lamberton worked hard to convince me that such an alliance would be in my best interests. If I back Bruce in his bid for the throne he has offered me the lordship of Annandale and the earldom of Carrick.'

'Only if he becomes king,' cautioned the Black Comyn. 'Remember, John, the deal does not stand if he fails to gain the throne. He means for you to throw the full weight of your support behind him in this endeavour – your men and the vassals of your kin, all your allies.' The earl looked at MacDouall. 'The Disinherited.'

MacDouall gave a snarl of laughter and rose from his seat. 'Bruce cannot think we would do this!'

Comyn met his fierce gaze. 'I imagine they think their offer so generous I cannot refuse.' He thought back to the meeting, to the moment James Stewart had outlined the terms. After the initial surprise had passed, he had looked over at Robert Bruce. By the utter resentment in his face, Comyn had guessed the extraordinary offer of Bruce's ancestral lands and titles had not been his design. 'They have no idea I hold the desire and the will to set myself upon the throne. To overthrow the king, as you put it,' he added dryly, arching an eyebrow at the captain.

'I would rather see you sit in place of your uncle than a thousand Bruces, sir,' responded MacDouall. He sat back down, sliding one of the used goblets towards him with his good hand and pouring himself a measure of wine. His hand shook and he spilled some on the table.

The Black Comyn was studying his kinsman. 'It is still surprising to me that your father would have given his blessing for this, John. It goes against everything the Comyn family stands for, everything our forefathers worked to achieve. We are kingmakers, not kings.'

'Times have changed. We must change with them if our family is to regain its former glory,' Comyn responded, discomforted by the intensity of the man's stare. The earl, his father's cousin and fifteen years his senior, was a shrewd man, who had sat at the heart of Scottish politics for decades, appointed as Constable of Scotland under Balliol's rule. He was not a man to cross. Comyn felt relieved when the earl gave a nod and sat back.

'That's as may be,' observed the Black Comyn. 'But neither ambition nor need change the fact that Robert Bruce has a claim to the throne that is far stronger than yours. What is the likelihood of you gaining it in his place?' Before Comyn could answer, he continued. 'If Bruce was successful in his bid he would make you an earl. That is not something to be dismissed lightly, not by any means. Possession of Carrick grants you estates in Ireland and the lordship of Annandale, along with your holdings in Galloway, gives you control of the west of Scotland. He offers a great reward.'

'All subject to him,' Comyn answered, his face flushing at the thought of it. 'I will not bow before that man. Not if my life depended on it. I would rather remain under the dominion of the English.'

'Could you make a bid for the throne before he does?' asked MacDouall, nursing his wine. 'Now there is no hope for King John's return, surely the men of the realm would support you? No matter the strength of Bruce's claim, you are Balliol's kin. That would count for much in the eyes of your allies. Why not use the same opportunity they intend to? Now King Edward has returned to England, why not rally your supporters and rise up against him? As king?'

'It cannot be done.' It was the Black Comyn who answered. 'For the very same reason Bruce was forced to seek our endorsement. For his plan – or ours – to work, the whole realm must support it. Neither faction has the strength to face the English alone.' He looked at Comyn. 'Your surrender to King Edward cost you dearly. You have avoided exile by swearing to hunt down William Wallace, but you paid a high price for the return of Lochindorb and unless you deliver the outlaw you will have to pay more to gain back the rest of your estates.' He paused. 'I agree with Lamberton on this if nothing else: Scotland must be united if we are to fight our way free of the English yoke. You have many allies and an army at your command, but since Bruce inherited his father's lands his strength has increased. He too has powerful friends: the High Steward of Scotland, the Bishops of Glasgow and St Andrews, Earl John of Atholl, Earl Gartnait of Mar, the MacDonalds of Islay, numerous lords and knights. If you tried to take the throne in his stead they would stand against you.'

'Then we face a future subject to English will?' murmured Comyn. 'It is not much of a choice, is it?'

'Not necessarily.' The Black Comyn steepled his hands together. 'If the hope of Bruce becoming king was removed, his supporters would find it far harder to challenge you in your own bid. Faced with only two options for rule – you or an English king – I know which many of them would come to choose in time.'

'Removed?' Comyn's brow knotted. He wondered if the Black Comyn had had the same fantasy as him, out on the jetty. He shook his head. 'We cannot remove Bruce. Not without risk of civil war.'

'No. But King Edward could.'

Comyn sat forward. 'Share your thoughts.'

'We now know Robert Bruce is a traitor to the English. If Edward was to discover what he is planning, I'll wager you my earldom Bruce will spend the rest of his days in the Tower of London.'

Comyn shook his head. 'A fine notion. But not one that will work. King Edward trusts Bruce far more than he trusts any of us. My hatred of the man is well known. Edward is no fool. He would see it as a petty attempt on my part to discredit Bruce to further my own ambitions. I may well end up jeopardising the offer of a place on this new council. Unless I had real proof of Bruce's treachery, something beyond my own word, the king would not believe it.'

'We need not look for real proof – when proof can be manufactured to suit our needs.'

Isabel, Countess of Buchan, lay on the bed, her eyes open. On the wall beside her a tapestry depicted a man dressed in robes and crowned with a white halo, standing on the prow of a ship. In the background was an island with a cross above it, blazing in a beam of light from heaven. St Columba, she guessed, on his approach to Iona. The tapestry undulated in the draught coming through the window, making it look as though the woven sea was rippling. The fire had burned low in the grate since her husband had left and the room was as cold as a tomb. Isabel shivered, but made no move to get in under the bedcovers, or call her maids in the adjacent room to stoke the fire. Instead, she closed her eyes and rehearsed the words again, lips moving soundlessly.

Some time later, heavy footsteps approached along the passage outside. The countess pushed herself up on her hands and swung round, sliding from the edge of the mattress. For a moment she panicked, wondering where she should stand. In her husband's castles or her own manors she knew her place. Here in John Comyn's northern stronghold she was a guest, the unfamiliarity of the room making her unsure of herself. She made it to the window and sat herself on the cushioned seat, adjusting the padded net that covered her hair as the door opened.

Isabel forced a smile as her husband entered. It froze on her lips as she saw his expression: the tight set of his jaw, the creased skin of his brow. She knew that look. It did not bode well. She watched as he unfastened the pin that held his black mantle in place and swung the garment from his broad shoulders.

'Why has the fire burned low?' he growled, looking at her for the first time.

'I'll have Radulf see to it,' Isabel promised, as her husband tossed the mantle on the bed. She stood, smoothing the wrinkles in her gown. 'Did the parley go as hoped?'

The earl grunted something she didn't catch as he crossed to where his travelling cloak hung on a hook. 'Have your maids pack,' he told her, pulling the garment on over his surcoat. 'The porters will be up in an hour to collect the chests.'

'We're leaving?'

'I have urgent business to attend to.'

The words Isabel had rehearsed swelled in her mind, demanding to be spoken. She went to utter them, but faltered. 'The king's new council?' she said instead. 'Sir Robert invited you to sit upon it?'

The earl turned abruptly, the furrows in his brow deepening. He gave a bark of sardonic laughter, then crossed to her. 'Always so proper,' he murmured, cradling her face in his hand. '*Sir* Robert has played an unexpected move. The game has changed. We Comyns must now reposition our pieces. But, yes, King Edward wants me on the council.'

Isabel closed her eyes, feeling the calluses on his palm against her cheek, his skin hardened over the years from the grip of his sword. The unexpected affection emboldened her. 'That is good indeed.' She slid her hand over his, keeping it in place. 'I've been thinking, now the war is over, might we ask the king to release my nephew?' Isabel spoke the words in a rush, glad to have them out of her. They had been circling in her mind for months, since she promised her sister she would petition her husband to make the request.

The earl removed his hand from her cheek. 'I told you after St Andrews there would be no hope for your nephew's release. Edward made it plain: Earl Duncan will never set foot in Fife again. He fears to have the king-maker in Scotland.'

'Months have passed since St Andrews,' Isabel continued quickly. 'Many Scots have served their terms of exile and have returned. Why not my nephew? Perhaps King Edward will feel differently now? Duncan is just a boy.'

'Enough. I will not suffer explaining politics to a woman.'

Isabel clutched his arm as he turned away. 'But when you're sitting on his new council, the king might be persuaded to——'

'I said enough!' The Black Comyn's words rose in a shout. He shoved her away from him.

Isabel was half his size. The brute force of her husband's strength caused her to pitch back into one of the bedposts. She struck the carved wood hard, her head and spine banging against it. The net that covered her hair was only padded at the sides and offered little protection for her skull. The knock caused the world to jolt in her vision. Dazed, Isabel sank to the floor, holding the back of her head.

The earl stared down at his wife, his fists clenched, his face stained. 'Do not push me, Isabel,' he murmured, pointing a warning finger at her. 'I have no patience for it, as well you know. The matter is closed.' He straightened as the door to the adjacent chamber opened.

Agnes, one of Isabel's maids, appeared. 'My lord?' She glanced nervously from the earl to Isabel, on the floor. 'I thought I heard a — an accident?'

'My wife took a tumble, Agnes,' said the earl. 'Help her would you.' As Agnes hurried to the countess's side, the Black Comyn crossed to the door. 'I will send the porters in an hour. Make sure you are ready to leave.' He shut the door behind him.

Isabel took her hand from her head and stared at the spot of blood on her palm. She was always surprised by its redness.

'There, there, my lady,' murmured the maid, making shushing noises as she helped the countess to her feet. 'Come and sit at the mirror. I will set your hair right.'

'I am fine, Agnes,' said Isabel, but she let the maid lead her to the stool in front of a small table, which had a silver mirror on it. She sat staring at her white face in the looking-glass as Agnes removed the net and pins, and her black hair tumbled free. In the mirror it was as though it was happening to somebody else. A numbness settled over her as her body moved obediently in the glass, following the maid's instructions to tilt her head this way or that. Only her eyes showed any sign of life. So dark blue they were almost indigo, they were like two frozen pools, with glints in the depths. Deep down in Isabel, tides of anger and resentment flowed, but under an icy sheet of fear and indecision all that strength remained hidden, trapped beneath the surface.

44

Burstwick, England, 1304 AD

It was approaching twilight as Robert and his men rode into the royal manor, the clatter of hooves echoing off the walls of the buildings. Firelight gleamed in the windows and wood-smoke stung the frigid air. Servants hastened across the yard on errands, watched by sentries outside the doors of the main hall. From the stables and paddocks came the noise and stink of several hundred horses.

Dismounting, Robert saw a camp crowded with tents and wagons set up on a meadow opposite, where men moved in the gloaming. The English army had been disbanded after the fall of Stirling, infantry trickling back to farmsteads and villages, knights and lords to their estates, but the king's considerable household remained. Robert, riding hard from Badenoch to the Borders, where he had travelled into England in the footsteps of the king, had been surprised to learn that Edward hadn't moved any further south. As grooms emerged from the stables to take the horses, Fionn trotting over to greet them, he wondered what had caused the delay.

Staring around him, he sensed a strange hush hanging over the manor. No music or laughter drifted from the camp. The servants moved about their business in silence and the sentries seemed subdued. Leaving his own men to unload his belongings, Robert was going over to speak to them when a door in one of the buildings opened and his brother appeared.

Edward Bruce headed over, blowing into his hands at the chill in the air. 'I thought it was you. Welcome back, brother.'

Robert smiled, glad to see him. 'I didn't expect to see you until I reached Westminster. Why is the king still here?'

'He took ill shortly after we left Scotland. His physician advised him to rest here.'

'Is it serious?'

'No. In fact he was on the mend. We were due to leave last week, but then . . .' Edward paused. 'Your tidings first, brother.' He glanced over at the guards, but they were engrossed in their own conversation. 'How did you fare with Comyn?' He kept his voice low.

'He listened. That is all I can say with any certainty. He said he would give me his answer when he'd had time to think on it. So, for now, I wait.' Robert lifted his shoulders as if shrugging off a burden. 'I met with our brothers at Lochindorb. Niall and Thomas send their greetings. They are safe.'

A smile broke across Edward's face. 'Thank God.' He laughed in relief. 'I feared the worst when the Irish attacked Rothesay.'

'Sir, where shall we put these?'

As Nes called to him Robert saw that his men had unloaded the packs from the horses. He frowned and looked around him, wondering why no steward or official had come out to greet him. 'Can I stow my gear in your quarters for now?' he asked his brother. 'I should speak to the king if he'll see me. John Comyn and the Earl of Buchan agreed to sit on his new council. God willing,' he murmured, 'it will all serve to keep him preoccupied.'

'I would wait for now,' advised Edward. 'His daughter died five days ago.'

'Lady Joan?' Robert's thoughts went to Ralph de Monthermer.

'No, brother. It was Bess. She passed away in labour. The child too.'

Robert's mind flooded with an image of a fire-lit chamber, his wife lying limp on the bed, her ashen face greasy with sweat. Between Isobel's legs, a wad of linen was darkening with her blood. More stained the covers, the copper smell of it joined by the acrid stink of smoke from the fires that still burned around the city of Carlisle. His daughter, born in a siege, was swaddled in cloth and being cradled by the midwife. Close by the bed, a priest hovered like a crow over his dying wife. 'Where is Sir Humphrey?' he asked quickly.

'He was away on the king's business. He returned only last night.'

'Take me to him.'

'Robert, I don't think—' Edward broke off, seeing the resolve in his face. 'Very well.'

Robert followed his brother across the courtyard and into one of the timber-framed buildings. All the way down the passage, he kept seeing that chamber in his mind. He had only been married to Isobel of Mar for a year and the union had been his family's wish, a match for gain not love. Still, her death had pained him. For Humphrey and Bess their marriage had only cemented their affection. While Robert had taken comfort in his daughter, pulled alive from that bloody bed, Humphrey had lost two lives in one night.

Approaching a chamber at the end of the passage, he saw the door was open. Hoarse shouts came from within. Robert entered a scene of devastation. Covers, ripped from the bed, were strewn across the floor, along with items of armour. An overturned table, legs splintered, lay among the shards of a shattered jug and basin. Chests against the wall were open, clothes and books spilled out around them. One of the bedposts looked as though someone had taken a blade to it, gashes carving the wood. There were four men in here – Robert Clifford, Ralph de Monthermer and two of Humphrey's knights – warily watching a fifth figure in the centre. It took Robert a moment to recognise his friend.

Humphrey de Bohun was swaying on his feet, his brown hair flattened on his skull where his helm had sat, his undershirt stained with a dark stream of vomit. His face was feverish and his eyes were bloodshot slits. In one hand he clutched a wine skin, in the other his sword. The weapon's beautifully filigreed scabbard – a gift from Bess – was on the floor at his feet. He was shouting at the men watching him, ordering them to fetch his horse.

Ralph de Monthermer was talking to him, trying to calm him down, but Humphrey wasn't listening. Ralph turned in surprise as Robert pushed past him. Paying the knight's warning no heed, Robert crossed to Humphrey, stepping over the debris. Humphrey fixed on him with difficulty, swinging his sword. The strike was slow and clumsy and Robert sidestepped it easily. He grabbed Humphrey's sword-arm at the wrist, at the same time gripping the earl's shoulder. 'Humphrey,' he said, following the man's unfocused gaze with his own. 'Let go.'

Humphrey focused on him. 'Robert?' he croaked.

'Let go of the sword, Humphrey.'

The earl's grip loosened. The weapon slid from his fingers and clanged on the floor. Ralph moved in to take it. As Humphrey sagged and sank to his knees, Robert went with him, still holding him by the shoulders. The wine skin slipped from Humphrey's other hand. Claret gushed dark across the rug as he collapsed against Robert.

Crouched there in the wreckage of the chamber, Humphrey gripping his arms, Robert's mind emptied of all plans and preoccupations. The compulsion towards Scotland's throne, that goaded him like a spur in his side, faded. With it went his concerns over what John Comyn's answer to his proposal would be and the knowledge of the great fight that lay before him if his enemy agreed to support his bid. For this moment, he was just a man, holding on to a friend who might drown in the expanse of his grief.

Skipness, Scotland, 1305 AD

'My lord, you have visitors.'

John of Menteith straightened, turning from the table over which he was stooped. His steward was standing in the doorway. 'Keep working,' he ordered his accountant, tapping at the rolls that lay open on the table. 'Who is it?' he asked, crossing to the door with a frown. Looking past his steward into the hall that lay beyond his chamber, he saw a band of men standing there, a tall figure in a white surcoat at their head.

Menteith felt unease crawl in his stomach. 'Captain MacDouall,' he greeted, clearing his throat and forcing his lips into a taut smile as he entered the hall. 'This is unexpected.'

Dungal MacDouall had one gloved hand resting on the pommel of his broadsword. His other arm hung at his side, no hand visible beneath the sleeve of his gambeson. 'Why unexpected?' His tone was flat and cold. 'The Earl of Buchan told you I would come.'

'Indeed,' replied Menteith, with a thin laugh, 'but since half the barons of Scotland have been hunting Wallace without success, I imagined this business would take somewhat longer.' He stopped abruptly, realising there was a figure in the group behind the captain, being held between two men. A hood covered his head, which jerked blindly this way and that. 'Who is that?'

MacDouall didn't take his gaze off Menteith. 'You still travel to Glasgow regularly?'

Menteith flushed, knowing the captain must know full well he did by the state of his castle. He cringed as his gaze caught the whitewashed walls where brighter rectangles clearly showed where wall-hangings had once been draped. The winter straw hadn't yet been swept out and replaced with rushes, even though the new year was advancing into spring, and the top table had a broken leg bound in place with rope. Over the past year, most of the money for his hall's upkeep had trickled into the hands of the men who ran the bear-baiting pens and cock-fighting rings in the city. 'Yes,' he murmured. 'I still travel to Glasgow.'

'Good. It is from the settlements around the city where the reports of sightings have come most recently. But Wallace still has many friends among the peasantry, which is how he has managed to evade his hunters. He will need to be drawn out, as we told you.'

Menteith turned away. 'I am still not sure how you think I can do this.'

MacDouall's voice roughened. 'You'd better not be losing your nerve, Sir John. You swore to my lord you would help us when the time came.' He paused, biting back his temper. 'We know you have not fared well since the surrender; that paying King Edward the dues for your family's forfeited estates has all but ruined you. This is your chance to regain your fortune.'

'But how will I draw him out?' demanded Menteith, looking MacDouall in the eye. 'How do you know he will come?'

MacDouall nodded to the two men who held the hooded figure. One of them tugged off the hood to reveal a bald head and bruised face. Even with the torn lips, blackened cheek and swollen eye, Menteith recognised Gray – Wallace's second-in-command.

'We caught him in Lanark, gathering supplies,' said MacDouall, a note of satisfaction in his voice as he surveyed his captive. 'My men have been watching the town for months.'

Menteith went to take hold of the captain's arm, but thinking better of it settled for a jerk of his head, steering MacDouall away from Gray, who was staring at them through bloodshot eyes. 'Why in Christ's name did you let him see us?' he seethed beneath his breath. 'He knows we are both involved now!'

'That does not matter. He is just for bait. I need you to go to Glasgow and use your acquaintances there to start spreading the word that you have captured Gray and are willing to free him in return for a ransom. Do it carefully. We want Wallace to get wind of who has his man, but not the others who are hunting him, or the English. You must be the one to seize the outlaw, or our plan will be sunk.' MacDouall nodded to one of his men, who moved out of the group.

Menteith saw the man was carrying a small chest.

'This is just to help you grease any wheels,' said MacDouall. 'There will be more if you succeed.'

Menteith took the chest, feeling its weight like a promise.

45

Near Glasgow, Scotland, 1305 AD

A line of sweat dribbled down Menteith's face. As he wiped it away a cloud of flies swarmed up from the twitching flanks of his horse. It was almost midday and the sky was white with heat. The dead air rippled over the road. Insects swarmed in clouds, drawn by the sweat-stink of the men and horses who stood waiting at the crossroads as the sun arced higher.

Menteith unhooked the wine skin that hung from his saddle, his gaze passing over his men. Eighteen in number, they were grouped around a covered wagon. His knights were stooping under the weight of their mail, their visors raised to let in what little air there was. A few sat hunched in their saddles while others leaned in the sliver of shade offered by the wagon as their squires let their horses graze along the verge. To the left, the road climbed into woods. To the right it crossed a steep-banked burn by the hump of a stone bridge before meandering across a meadow where a dilapidated barn stood. Behind, it faded into the distance curving around the hills, heading for Glasgow. Shortly after they arrived, one of his men thought he'd spied figures in the woods to their left, but the scouts Menteith sent out returned without seeing sign of anyone. That was three hours ago.

Menteith lifted the skin and drank, grimacing at the taste of the wine, which had grown hot and syrupy. His eyes scanned the road, but other than the flicker of birds there was no movement. Maybe Wallace wasn't going to come after all. Or maybe he was here already, watching, waiting to wear them down in the sapping heat before he made his move? From what he knew of the rebel leader, Menteith guessed this was a tactic he would use. Since the start of the war the man had raided, ambushed and murdered his way across the Lowlands and northern England. Though he despised him, Menteith couldn't deny Wallace's aptitude for cunning and carnage.

Out here on this open crossroads, baking under the noonday sun, he felt horribly exposed. There was plenty of cover in the hills and woods around them; plenty of places for a sizeable force to keep hidden. Wallace had a number of archers from Selkirk Forest in his band. Perhaps, somewhere in those trees, a score of bows were aimed at him. Menteith returned the wine skin to his belt and took up the reins, feeling as though he couldn't get enough air in his lungs. Would Wallace take the bait? Or would he attack without warning, rescue his comrade and slaughter them to a man? His skin crawling with sweat, flies and a strengthening sense of danger, Menteith turned his palfrey with a tug. 'God curse him!'

'Sir?' questioned one of his knights, as Menteith urged his horse towards the wagon.

Ignoring him, Menteith leaned towards the closed flaps. 'I'll bake to death before the whoreson shows!'

'Patience,' came the taut reply from inside the wagon. 'Wallace will come. He will want to make certain you have no reinforcements before he shows himself to you.'

'How much longer do we wait?'

'Sir.'

Menteith didn't look round as one of his men called to him, but kept his attention on the wagon. 'How long?'

'Sir John!'

'What, damn you?'

'Riders, sir.' The knight pointed up the wooded slope to the left.

Straightening in his saddle, Menteith followed his gaze. A company of men had appeared on the fringes of the trees. It was a small group, no more than ten. They came unhurriedly, leaning back in their saddles.

'Is it him?' demanded the voice from inside the wagon.

Menteith's eyes narrowed as he scanned the approaching riders, searching for William Wallace. None of them seemed large enough of stature to be the outlaw, but the distance made it hard to tell. Most of them wore hats or hoods and it was impossible to pick out faces. If this was Wallace's band he had avoided any of the roads in, as anticipated, but Menteith was surprised by the small number. Several hundred men had gone on the run with the outlaw after the rebellion collapsed and even accounting for desertions and deaths, surely his band wouldn't have dwindled to so few? He couldn't imagine Wallace would be fool enough to come with such a modest force. Even his token eighteen men outnumbered them. Menteith licked the sweat from his upper lip, feeling a flutter of expectation.

One of the riders split away from the rest, spurring his horse down the shallow slope towards them. He came to a stop, just out of bowshot. Menteith recognised Neil Campbell. The knight from Argyll had been in Wallace's company since the early days of the insurrection.

'I have your ransom, John of Menteith!' shouted Campbell. 'Where is Gray?'

'*Is it him?*'

As the voice came again from the wagon, Menteith glanced round distractedly. 'No,' he murmured. 'It's one of his men. Campbell.' He looked back at the Argyll knight. 'What do I do?'

There was movement from inside the wagon. A tall figure emerged and jumped down. He wore an iron helm that covered his face and a plain cloak over his hauberk and gambeson. There was nothing identifiable about him – no crests or blazons – nothing except the fact his left hand was missing. Two others emerged behind MacDouall, wearing similarly plain garments and hauling Gray, hooded and bound, between them. Their captive struggled, but MacDouall drew his sword and moved in behind him. Locking his left arm under Gray's chin, pulling his head roughly back, he laid the blade across his neck.

'Tell him Wallace was supposed to deliver it. Tell him, because of their failure to comply your terms have changed.' MacDouall's voice came muffled through the helm as he spoke to Menteith. 'Say you want more money, or you'll slit Gray's throat.'

Menteith relayed this to Campbell with a hoarse shout.

Neil Campbell turned to look at the rest of his company.

'*Come on, you cur*,' murmured MacDouall, while his captive struggled and choked. After a moment, he ripped off the hood. Gray winced, turning his bruised face from the sun's white light. There was a gag over his mouth, crusted with dried blood. MacDouall kicked him hard in the back of the legs, causing him to collapse, grunting in pain as his knees struck the dusty track. His hands were tied behind his back. Fresh blood gleamed wetly in the wounds on his head and body. MacDouall stood over him, drawing back his sword as if to thrust the blade through the back of his neck.

A shout echoed from the shadows of the trees on the hillside. A rider emerged from the woods and spurred his horse down the slope towards them.

Menteith inhaled sharply. There was only one man with that giant stature. As the rider drew closer his features became clearer, evening out into a scarred, brutish face with a nose that looked like it had been broken on several occasions, framed by a thatch of brown hair. William Wallace was clad in stained hose, wrinkled boots criss-crossed with leather and a coarse blue tunic, belted at his thick waist. He would seem little more than a peasant if not for the bulk of armour visible beneath his clothes and the double-handed axe that swung from a sling attached to his saddle. Menteith's gaze was drawn from Wallace by the sight of more men emerging from the trees. A handful were mounted, but most came on foot, spears, clubs, bows and daggers in their hands. Sixty, maybe eighty strong, they came with purpose, marching down the slope in the wake of their leader.

Menteith gripped his reins. Behind him, he heard rasps of metal on leather as his men drew their swords. 'What do we do?' he questioned, turning to MacDouall.

Wallace hauled his horse to a stop as he reached Neil Campbell's side. 'Let my man go, Menteith.' His voice was rough.

At the sight of his comrade, Gray had struggled to his feet, but his two guards had moved in to grab him and were holding him tightly. He was shouting at Wallace, but his words were muffled by the gag. One of MacDouall's men cuffed him with a mailed fist, opening a new cut on his scalp and causing him to sag in their grip.

Wallace kicked his horse forward. 'Let him go and I'll let you leave here with your life.'

He stopped a short distance away, just in range, Menteith realised, of his two bowmen. Suddenly, Gray wrenched round and kneed one of his captors in the groin. As the man went down, the outlaw lunged, smashing his head into the other guard's face. The guard's nose snapped and he reeled back. MacDouall went for Gray, but he was off, running towards Wallace, bellowing through his gag. MacDouall turned with a roared command and four more men leapt from the back of the wagon. Two had horns in their hands that they began to blow, the strident notes ringing. Wallace's band, advancing down the slope, faltered at the sound. Hefting weapons, they stared around them, roused by the prospect of danger. Some were shouting at their leader, but he paid them no heed, urging his horse towards Gray.

MacDouall turned on Menteith's bowmen with a snarl. 'Bring him down!'

The archers stepped forward and drew back their bows. Wallace shouted as he saw them. Two arrows sprang forward. One punched into Gray's back between his shoulder blades, the barbed head stabbing through his shirt to bury itself in his spine. He arched, then collapsed on his stomach in the grass, hands still tied behind his back. The second arrow sailed over him and plunged into the neck of Wallace's horse. The animal reared with a scream and twisted back on its hind legs, throwing Wallace from the saddle. Rolling with the fall, he was up in an instant. Lunging for the struggling horse he grasped the shaft of his axe and pulled the weapon free. The air was rent with battle cries as his men charged down the slope, coming to his aid. Menteith drew his sword with a rush of fear. But then, from the tall grasses of the meadow and the steep banks of the burn, scores of men began to rise.

Their green cloaks soaked with sweat and dew, limbs stiff from the long wait, they emerged from their hiding places, summoned by the horns. All held bows. In the distance, along the road to Glasgow, a plume of dust stained the sky, the faint thunder of hooves unmistakable. MacDouall shouted orders at the emerging archers, who primed their bows. Raising the weapons in unison, they let loose a barrage of arrows.

Neil Campbell raised his shield to protect himself as the sky darkened, but he and Wallace weren't the targets. The missiles arced upwards, before curving down towards the mob of men. Few in Wallace's band wore adequate armour and the arrows found easy victims, piercing throats and arms, or punching through boiled leather aketons. Screams rose as men and horses went tumbling in the first wave. But more came on, leaping falling comrades, yelling furiously.

The small company with Neil Campbell was riding towards Wallace, trying to flank him protectively. MacDouall shouted through his helm to his archers, pointing at the danger. The bowmen unleashed another volley. This time, Campbell was in range. As the knight hoisted his shield, two arrows thumped into it. His horse took one in the rump and set off at a wild canter. The mounted company meanwhile rode straight into the barrage. Horses reared and crashed into one another as the barbs struck. Men were jolted from saddles to be trampled, or crushed in the panic. Others managed to spur their mounts out of the fray, kicking them out of range.

Wallace had grabbed Gray and was hauling his comrade's limp body behind his fallen horse, which was still kicking feebly. The rebel leader ducked down behind the dying animal as another hail of arrows sprang forward, plucking more men from the field. Despite their losses, the rabble kept on coming, rapidly closing the distance to Menteith's company at the crossroads. A few of Wallace's archers had now halted, priming their bows for a counter-assault.

Twisting in his saddle, Menteith fixed on the riders coming along the road from Glasgow – the rest of MacDouall's force. They wouldn't get here in time. One of his knights shouted a warning as several arrows plunged down around them, one striking the wagon, others the archers on the banks of the burn. One bowman took an arrow in the face, sending him flying back into the water. Another was struck in the shoulder and went down on his knees, gasping as he tried to pull out the shaft. Menteith urged his horse behind the wagon, panting in fear. MacDouall ducked as an arrow came darting towards him, then was up again, roaring orders at his bowmen.

Neil Campbell had managed to get control of his horse and now joined his comrades, but Wallace's band had entered the optimum range of MacDouall's archers. Those the barbs didn't wound or kill, they blinded and disorientated, men forced to duck down behind their shields. Horses panicked and veered off in all directions, knocking men down in their haste to get away. Wallace's archers kept on shooting, but they were no match for the continuous barrage coming from the roadside. Slowly, the rebel band ground to a halt, men hunkering down behind shields or fallen comrades. Less than a hundred yards of open ground lay between them and Wallace, sheltering behind his horse. Several more arrows had struck the animal, its great body twitching in death.

'Bring him in, Colban,' MacDouall commanded, turning to one of his men, who had been with him in the wagon. As Colban set off determinedly, MacDouall gestured five others to follow. 'I want him alive!' he shouted at their backs.

As the archers continued to shoot into the mob on the hillside, screams sounding whenever arrows found exposed flesh, MacDouall's men approached the fallen horse. Neil Campbell, whose own horse had been brought down, yelled a warning at Wallace over the rim of his shield. The rebel leader rose, axe in his hands, as Colban and the others came at him. Colban just managed to get his shield up as Wallace's great axe carved towards him. The blade smashed into the wood, breaking Colban's arm with the impact. Forced to his knees, he howled with pain as Wallace wrenched the axe free, roughly flinging the shield and Colban's limp arm to one side. Colban knelt there for a heartbeat, staring up at the rebel leader, before Wallace brought the axe crashing down into his skull, brain matter and blood bursting up as his head was cleaved in two. As Colban folded, Wallace heaved the blade round, swinging it two-handed into another of MacDouall's men, who came at him.

MacDouall's riders, fifty strong, were thundering towards the cross-roads, dust billowing around them. At a command from their captain, they veered off the road and charged towards Wallace's men. MacDouall's arch-ers ceased their onslaught, but the rebels, still crouched beneath their shields, were now taken by surprise by the riders. The mass of men began to break apart, some rising to counter the horsemen, hacking blades and clubs into the legs of the animals, others fleeing up the hillside trying to get to higher ground and the safety of the trees. Neil Campbell, struggling his way towards Wallace, was stopped in his tracks and forced to counter as two riders came at him.

Menteith, watching from behind the shelter of the wagon, saw Wallace bury his axe in the chest of one of MacDouall's men. The rebel leader was roaring like a cornered stag, twisting this way and that in the closing circle of men, dodging blades that flicked towards him, swinging that great two-handed axe in savage arcs towards the necks and arms of his foes. He had already killed two. Now, he hacked at a third, shattering the man's sword. They wouldn't be able to contain him, Menteith realised; not if they weren't trying to kill him. He sought out MacDouall, but the captain's attention was on his riders, rampaging through the rebels. Menteith wiped the sweat from his eyes. He couldn't let Wallace escape this field. Never mind the loss of any reward – the rebel leader would think he alone was behind this ambush. Wallace had murdered the Sheriff of Lanark in his bed. Menteith wouldn't spend the rest of his life lying awake, waiting for death in the darkness. Turning to his bowmen, he spoke quickly.

MacDouall looked round as one of Menteith's archers rose from behind the wagon and took aim. He went to shout. Too late. The arrow was loosed. Wallace had cut down a third man and taken his shield. He was turning on a fourth when the arrow punched into the back of his thigh. He staggered, dropping his guard. It was just long enough for one of MacDouall's remaining three men to grab hold of his arm, pulling it and the axe wide, while another punched him in the side of his head. Wallace was knocked off-balance by the savage strike. As he was bent forward, the third man brought a knee cracking up into his face. Blood burst from his nose and he sagged to one knee.

For a moment, it looked as though the outlaw was down. Then, in an incredible feat of strength, Wallace raised himself up with a snarl, ramming his shield into the face of one of his attackers, staving in the man's jaw. MacDouall was off and running towards him. As Wallace grappled with the last two men, the captain leapt the dead horse and came at him from behind, bringing the pommel of his sword smashing into the back of the outlaw's skull. Wallace dropped with a surprised grunt, the axe falling from his hand. MacDouall kicked him in the back, sending him crashing on to his stomach. While one of the surviving men, gasping with exertion, straddled Wallace, the other unhooked a loop of rope from his belt and roughly bound his hands behind his back.

Away across the hillside, the rest of the mob was fleeing, scattered by MacDouall's riders. They left the slopes littered with more than thirty dead.

Neil Campbell had gone, pulled out of harm's way by his comrades. The last of them were disappearing into the trees as Menteith rode over to MacDouall, who was overseeing Wallace's restraint. Several of the captain's archers had downed their bows and moved in to help. The rebel leader was still conscious. His huge body heaved occasionally trying to throw the men off him, but his wounds had worn him down and he no longer had the strength. Around him, the ground was awash with blood and gore from the bodies of Colban and the men he'd hacked apart. The stink of opened bowels was horrendous. Menteith slowed his horse and turned his head, feeling a rush of bile in his throat.

MacDouall straightened on seeing him. 'You fool,' he growled, striding towards him. 'You could have killed him!'

'Someone had to stop him,' Menteith retorted. 'He was cutting your men down like saplings!'

'Gray's still alive.'

MacDouall turned at the call from one of his men. Menteith followed as the captain crossed to where Wallace was being subdued. Gray was indeed alive, groaning through bloodied teeth, the back of his shirt slick with blood around the arrow.

MacDouall nodded to his man. 'Finish him.'

Wallace, seeing what was about to happen, bellowed in fury, but he couldn't move as Gray's head was pulled back and his throat slit by the blade of a dirk. Wallace was still bellowing as MacDouall's men tugged a hood over his head and, between three of them, dragged him towards the wagon.

With the rebel leader blinded and out of the way, MacDouall removed his helm. Several of his men, who had been tackling the outlaw's band, came riding down to him.

'A fair few escaped into the woods, Captain,' said one. 'Shall we follow?'

'No need,' answered MacDouall. 'We have what we came for.' He motioned to one of his men by the wagon.

As the man approached, Menteith saw he had a battered-looking leather bag in his hands.

He passed it to MacDouall who turned to Menteith. 'Deliver Wallace to the English garrison at Lochmaben.' He handed him the bag. 'Give them this. Tell them it was found on him. Understood?'

'What's in it?' Menteith asked, taking it. The bag felt light.

'Nothing you need concern yourself with. Remember, Menteith, you alone captured William Wallace. My men and I were not here.'

46

West Smithfield, London, 1305 AD

The late August afternoon was humid and overcast, the sky threatening rain as Robert and his men made their way west through the Outer Liberties. Ahead, London's walls dominated the view, rising over the houses, churches and workshops that clustered close along their stone line before gradually giving way to marshland and meadows interspersed by hamlets, leper hospitals and imposing religious houses through which the road curved its way down towards Westminster. Smoke from bakehouses, chimneys and open fires rose to mingle in a grey fog that hung in the muggy air, tainted by the briny stink of the marshes.

The road on which they travelled was strangely empty and the villages quiet. Robert caught sounds of cheering that seemed to swell from beyond the walls and he wondered if there was some kind of festival going on that had drawn the residents of the suburbs into the city proper. The speculation was brief, overshadowed by more internal preoccupations.

The death of the king's daughter had cast a terrible gloom over Christ Mass, lingering into the new year, at which point the court finally left Yorkshire and made its way south, down through Lincoln, towards Westminster. To Robert it had seemed as though Scotland's fate was being pulled along by the same inexorable march south, to be set, at the autumn parliament, in the stone of law. His hope, heading for Writtle in late spring, had been that the news he had been waiting for would be there to greet him. But he had found only incomplete accounts, buildings in need of repair and confused tenants who had long needed the attentions of a sober lord.

As spring gave way to summer, his impatience for an answer from John Comyn had intensified to the point where the sound of hoof-beats approaching the manor would have him at the nearest window. Still, no word had come. Now, after two months in Essex, dealing with the remnants of his father's affairs, Robert was returning to the king's court, the grim parliament upon him. After tomorrow, Scotland's new constitution would be drawn up and the council established, subordinate to their English masters.

A burst of harsh laughter drew him from his thoughts. He looked round to see four youths running fast along the verge. A fifth, younger than the others, was lagging behind, struggling to keep up. The older boys took little notice of the mounted company, but the youngest halted with a grin as Fionn bounded over to him.

'You'll miss him swing, Stephen!' shouted one of the others, glancing back.

After patting the hound, the lad sprinted after his comrades. 'We should've gone by Newgate,' he panted, his English broad and thick, as if he'd never spoken anything else.

'Dullard! The streets are packed. This way's quicker. We'll get ourselves a place on Bartholomew's wall. From there we'll see him spill his guts!'

More rough laughter rose as the youths ran on. Robert heard another cheer swell from somewhere, louder than before. He realised he could hear the low hum of a multitude of voices, punctuated occasionally by incoherent shouts. Ahead, the road turned sharply left at the same angle as the city walls, which veered south at Cripplegate. Robert's company, following its curve, soon saw the grand buildings of the Priory of St Bartholomew, less than half a mile distant. Beyond, the smooth plain of West Smithfield stretched into the dull haze of the afternoon. The sight that greeted him caused Robert to pull his horse to a halt.

The green expanse, cut by the waters of the Fleet, was covered with a seething mass of people – hundreds upon hundreds. Even as Robert watched, more joined them, funnelling out of the city from Newgate and Aldersgate like a dark oozing tide flowing to pool on Smithfield's plain. The cause of the suburbs' quiet and the empty road was suddenly clear. It was as if all of London was gathered on the fields before him. His first thought was the August Fair, which Humphrey had introduced him to years earlier. But as his gaze moved across the shifting crowds he realised there were no stalls selling wares, no horse-racing, no roasting spits.

'What is this?'

Robert glanced round as one of the Essex knights, a man called Matthew, spoke. Matthew's gaze, like that of the rest of the company, was transfixed by the sight. Looking back, Robert's eyes came to rest on the skeletal frame of the gibbet that thrust above the crowds. Often, bodies could be seen hanging there. Today, it was thronged not by the dead, but by the living, men standing on the platform beneath a row of empty nooses. The snatched conversation of the London youths came back to him with disquieting sense. 'It's an execution.'

Urging his horse into a brisk trot, Robert led his company along the road as the first drops of rain began to fall from the sullen sky. The noise of the crowds intensified the closer they drew to Smithfield and shortly the road became clogged with people flowing out from Aldersgate, forcing Robert and his men to a walk, guiding their horses through the throng. The people were a mix of commoners in coarse tunics and wooden clogs, sturdy-looking tradesmen – some still wearing aprons stained by a day's labour – and a few wealthier sorts in feathered hats and embroidered cloaks. Robert, clad in a brocaded mantle and soft hide boots, his broadsword at his hip and his escort of knights and servants, stood out like a jewel on a rough strand of pebbles. Nes, he noticed, was keeping close at his side, the squire's eyes darting suspiciously at the passing lines of Londoners.

'We should go around them, sir,' called Matthew, scowling at a couple of pimple-faced boys who tried to touch his shying horse. 'Head north to the Bar and go down through Holborn.'

'Agreed,' shouted another of the knights, turning his horse against the quickening tide. Fionn went with him, barking agitatedly.

Reaching down, Robert grabbed one of the pimpled youths by the scruff of his collar. 'Whose execution is this?' The boy tried to pull away, but Robert kept tight hold. 'Tell me!'

'William Wallace,' blurted the youth. 'The ogre of the north!'

Robert let him go, barely noticing the boy spit an insult at him before he ducked into the crowd.

'Sir!'

Robert paid Matthew no heed, turning instead to Nes. 'Take my horse,' he shouted to his squire, kicking his feet free of the stirrups and swinging down. Ignoring Nes's call of warning, he pushed his way through the press, his height and strength allowing him to force his way forward.

On the verge, he glimpsed the ragged forms of beggars, hands outstretched to the people who flowed past. Beneath the din of conversation, all of it English, he heard the tap-tap of clacker bowls proffered by lepers. There were minstrels and jugglers, quacks with their bags of cures and pardoners with their relics, drawn to the multitude as flies to honey. It was like a festival, only this wasn't a crowd eager for games, feasting and dancing. This crowd was hungry for blood. They pushed and shoved one another to get as near as they could to the gibbet, all wanting to find a space where they could best observe the proceedings.

Robert pressed on, needing to see for himself, catching Wallace's name in stray snatches of conversation. How had they caught him? When? Rain misted the air, darkening the heads and shoulders of the crowd. He stepped on someone's foot and felt a shove in his back. A woman twisted into his path, hair hanging loose around her shoulders. She smiled, looking him up and down appreciatively. With one hand, she tugged down the front of her thin dress, baring her breasts. The other she held out, uncurling a dirt-streaked palm.

'A penny for a suck on them, my lord.'

Robert felt himself caught in the surging crowd, hemmed in on all sides. He smelled the stink of stale breath as a toothless old man turned to grin lewdly at him, felt his ears assaulted as two youths pinned in beside him roared with appreciation at the glimpse of flesh. He saw the woman turn her gaze on the young men, saw a line of dark moles on her breasts as she struggled her way towards the eager men. As she was swallowed by the surging crowd, Robert was pushed along on a new current, mud and refuse squelching underfoot. He felt a tug at his side and knew his purse had gone, but couldn't move enough in the crush to look for the thief. He trod on something soft and pulpy – perhaps the corpse of some animal – that gave way with a sickening crunch beneath his boot. A pervading stench of sweat, greasy hair, smoke and excrement clogged the air, as if all the rot of the city had been boiled up in this seething cauldron of humanity.

Ahead, not far now, the gibbet loomed against the ashen sky. Some of the men who thronged its platform wore the king's scarlet livery. The others were dressed in black. A vast cheer went up from some other part of the crowd, towards the city walls, the sound rising then falling like a wave. Beneath it, Robert heard the thud of drums.

'He's on his way,' called a chubby blond boy, perched on a larger man's shoulders. His cherub-like face was sweaty with excitement. 'I can see the king's men!'

'I hear he's a giant,' said a brawny man wedged in beside them. 'Ten foot tall.'

'He'll be taller still when he's stretched,' replied a third, causing sniggers to rise around him.

Robert fought back an urge to draw his sword and hack through their red, laughing mouths. He gripped the pommel.

'No – I tell you, my cousin is a clerk of the Chancery. He heard it himself at the trial yesterday. William Wallace admitted all the crimes levelled at him, *except* treason. He said he couldn't be accused of treason since he'd never recognised Edward as his king.'

Robert turned his head to see two older men, better dressed than most around and more serious of face.

'And what did King Edward say to that?' asked the speaker's comrade, arching an eyebrow.

'Apparently the king went hunting. He wasn't there at the trial.'

The cheering rose into a shuddering roar. Now, Robert could see mounted knights dressed in scarlet surcoats riding through the crowds, which parted before them, surging like a sea. In their midst, two carthorses were being led, the beasts tossing their heads agitatedly. As a gap appeared between the shoulders of those in front, Robert saw the horses were dragging a hurdle behind them, to which was bound a naked man, face to the rain, arms outstretched like Christ on His cross.

By his stature, Robert knew it was Wallace, though he was scarcely recognisable. His body was covered with filth – night soil and offal, rotten fruit, horse dung – anything London's citizens could snatch from the streets to hurl at him as he was dragged through their city. His face was bloodied and livid red marks covered his chest and thighs, where sticks and stones had struck him. His body jerked with the motion of the horses, his bare feet jolting along the muddy ground. The mob greeted the rebel leader with roars of hate, then the gap in front of Robert closed and Wallace was gone from view.

The king's men halted by the gibbet. There was a pause, the crowds around the scaffold chanting and shouting, as Wallace was unbound from the hurdle. Moments later, held between two guards, he was forced to mount the platform, his hands now tied behind his back. The people jeered as he stood naked before them, hurling insults like they'd hurled the shit and the stones. Robert had a memory of Wallace standing in a clearing in the Forest, addressing the men of Scotland, his voice full of strength and authority, his blue eyes studying each of them in turn. He had knighted this man with his own sword. He wanted to shout – to stop what was about to happen. But he might as well try to stop the incoming tide.

A noose was pulled down from the gibbet's beam and looped around Wallace's neck. The crowd quietened as it was drawn tight by one of the black-clad executioners, the knot carefully positioned at the side so his neck wouldn't break and bring death too early in the proceedings. The punishment for treason was to be hanged, drawn and quartered. The three-fold death it was called, for victims were said to die three times over. The executioner stepped back and nodded to his fellows. Robert saw Wallace close his eyes. He seemed to take a breath. Then, three men hauled on the other end of the rope, drawing it up and over the beam. The noose tightened suddenly around Wallace's neck, twisting his head to one side. As his feet, bruised and bloodied by London's streets, left the platform, the mob erupted with a cheer. The men at the rope strained as they hoisted him higher, all seven feet of him. Wallace's ashen face reddened, his eyes widening as the breath was squeezed from him. The crowd continued to applaud noisily as the moments crawled by, Wallace's feet starting to kick and jerk. His eyes bulged obscenely, his neck stretched and his face turned purple, veins protruding on his brow. His tongue thrust out from between his lips as his body convulsed. Robert, realising he had been holding his own breath, let it out in a rush.

Slowly, the applause died away. A few women averted their eyes, unable to watch this slow, agonising expiration of life. Finally, one of the black-clad executioners, studying Wallace closely, nodded to the three men at the end of the rope, all of whom were breathing hard and sweating profusely. They let go together and Wallace collapsed on the platform with a thud. One of the men came forward and tossed a bucket of water over him to revive him. Moments later, strangled gasps of breath could clearly be heard over the almost silent crowd. A strange sense of relief seemed to rise, people beginning to laugh and talk again. Wallace was helped to his feet and led to a trestle that had been erected on the platform. There he was laid out and strapped down for the second death. The rain was falling harder now, causing people to huddle together under the downpour. On the gibbet, the curved-bladed knives and tools in the hands of the executioners gleamed.

First, they sliced off his genitals, causing a howl to tear from his lips. Then, the blood spurting dark across his thighs, the executioners began to cut through the flesh of his stomach, opening him up to get at his bowels. Robert turned his gaze to the blond boy who had been so excited by the prospect of seeing the outlaw die. Still perched on the man's shoulders, he had twisted his face away. His eyes were screwed up, his hands pressed over his ears to block out Wallace's inhuman screams, unable to bear the sight and sound of a man being opened up while still alive, his insides ripped out to be tossed into a smoking brazier, where they hissed and spat. Many more were still watching the spectacle, silent now in the main. Soon would come the last death. Merciful beheading. The rain dripping down his cheeks, Robert turned and pushed his way through the crowd.

Westminster, London, 1305 AD

Sir John Segrave stood waiting outside Westminster Hall as King Edward and his men rode into the courtyard, the legs of their horses caked with mud from the Middlesex Forest. Behind the lords, knights and squires who accompanied the king, trundled a cart laden with the corpses of half a dozen stags. One, a beast of fourteen tines, had already been unmade in the field, its carcass divided into portions. Its great head, crowned with huge, scarred antlers, was being carried on a pole by one of the huntsmen, blood dripping down the shaft. Hounds ran among the horses, barking excitedly.

Segrave made his way stiffly across the yard, his limp – a legacy from the battle with Comyn's forces near Roslin – always worse in wet weather. He had a battered leather bag gripped in his hand as he headed purposefully towards the king, past pages who took spears and helms from the knights as they dismounted, faces glistening with rain. King Edward, standing tall among them in a green hunting cloak, seemed in unusually high spirits, laughing at something his son-in-law, Ralph de Monthermer was saying. Guy de Beauchamp and Henry Percy were with them. Segrave steeled himself, praying the king wouldn't blame the messenger.

As Edward saw Segrave approaching, his smile vanished, replaced by keen question. He strode over to the lieutenant, sliding off his kid-skin gloves. 'Is it done?'

Knowing what he meant, Segrave nodded. 'Yes, my lord. William Wallace was led to Smithfield's gibbet this afternoon, where he was dealt with in accordance with your instructions.'

Edward breathed through his nostrils, nodding slowly as if savouring the news. 'And the traitor's corpse?'

'The body has been quartered. Once the crowds around Smithfield have dispersed, the limbs will be ready for transport. The head has been dipped in pitch to preserve it. It will be set on London Bridge before vespers.'

'Good.'

'My lord.' Aymer headed over. His voice was flat, his spirits markedly different to the other men of the party. 'The master huntsman asks if you will have the honour of the unmaking.'

Segrave noticed the knight didn't look the king in the eye when he spoke. He'd heard men say Valence's obsession with Robert Bruce had caused him to fall out of favour with the king. Segrave gripped the bag tighter, acutely aware of what he was about to unleash.

Edward rubbed his hands together with a rare smile. 'Indeed I will.'

'My lord,' interrupted Segrave. 'There is something else.'

Edward frowned at Segrave's tone. 'Yes?'

'This was just given to me, along with the clothes and weapons taken from Wallace at the time of his capture.' The lieutenant lifted the bag. 'According to my men John of Menteith found it on the outlaw.' Reaching into the bag, he drew out a roll of parchment. 'This was inside.'

Edward took it. While the huntsmen began dragging the bodies of the stags from the cart, the nobles talking animatedly, he unrolled the parchment and read. Segrave watched the king's face change, the hale flush of colour slowly draining from it.

'What is it, my lord?' questioned Aymer, his brow furrowing at his cousin's expression.

Edward looked up, his eyes smouldering. 'Where is Robert Bruce?'

47

Westminster Abbey towered over the precinct, a pale giant against the leaden sky, its pointed arches and buttresses gleaming in the wet. Water gushed from the yawning mouths of gargoyles and trickled down the uplifted faces of angels. The red stained glass of the rose window seemed to bleed with threads of rain. Far below, lines of men and women filed in through the colossal arched doors, heads bowed under the deluge.

Robert, riding hard along the King's Road, made straight for the abbey's white walls. Spurring his palfrey across the bridge over the Tyburn and through the grand stone archway, he drew the animal to a stamping halt by the entrance to the abbey grounds. As he dismounted, his eyes went to the great roof of Westminster Hall that thrust above the jumbled buildings of the palace behind him: the scene of Wallace's trial. Robert's sodden cloak hung heavy on his shoulders and his boots were caked in Smithfield's filth. His hair dripped water down his cheeks, while his mind was saturated with the image of Wallace on the executioner's slab. He had seen many men die bloody in battle, ripped apart by sword and axe, their insides turned outside, a feast for crows and worms. But there was something ungodly about what had been done to the rebel leader, a violation not only of flesh, but of soul. That slow degrading of the body was not a warrior's death. Not a man's death.

Hoof-beats clattered in behind him as the rest of his company caught up. Nes was the first to dismount, heading straight to him. 'Sir?' he questioned, taking the reins of Robert's palfrey, concern plain in his voice. Nes hesitated. 'My lord, there was nothing you could do for him.'

Robert turned his gaze to the ragged procession of men and women filing into the abbey. He knew that wasn't true. Had he acted on his plan, ignored James Stewart and Lamberton, he might now be heading an army raised by Wallace, the two of them fighting to free their kingdom. Instead, he had waited, futilely, for word from Comyn that hadn't come. What choices were now left to him? To Scotland? He thought of the prophecy, wondering if he had been wrong and it was genuine after all. Was that why all his plans had come to nothing? He had to know. Leaving Nes, Robert ducked through the archway in the abbey wall.

After the spectacle at West Smithfield had ended, the crowds around the gibbet had begun to disperse, some looking for more sport in the city's inns, others going back to their chores, leaving the rain washing the blood from the scaffold and the steady chop of the executioner's axe as Wallace's body was dismembered. Robert, locating his men by Fionn's barking, had continued to Westminster expecting to leave the hordes behind, only to find the King's Road teeming with people, many blighted by disfigurements and diseases of the skin, or by poverty, their flesh withered with hunger. Questioning a group of pilgrims, he'd discovered the king had declared special alms to be given to the poor at the shrine of the Confessor. What was more, the pilgrims told him, the relics of Britain were there displayed for all to see.

Robert couldn't change Wallace's fate, nor could he will an agreement to come from John Comyn. But he could open that black box. He could seek the truth. Picking up his pace, he splashed across the waterlogged ground, heading for the abbey doors.

'Robert?'

He turned abruptly at the familiar voice, to see Humphrey approaching across the yard, hood up to keep off the rain. Robert glanced back; he was almost at the doors, the candlelit gloom of the abbey's interior glowing faintly beyond. Shambling lines of the poor filed past him to where the almoners were ushering them inside. Several royal guards were there, keeping order and an eye out for thieves.

'I didn't know you had returned,' said Humphrey, coming over.

'Just now.'

Humphrey cast his eye over Robert's filthy boots and sodden clothes. 'You look as if you rode through a river to get here, my friend.'

'I was at Smithfield.'

Humphrey nodded after a pause. 'God willing, that will be the last blood shed for this war.' Despite the optimism of his words, his tone was flat and his green eyes distant. The grief wrought in him the night Bess and his unborn child had died was part of him now, etched in his face. 'You're heading inside?' He fixed on the abbey. 'I'm going to light a candle for Bess. It's been almost a year since . . .' He shook himself. 'Forgive me. It has been hard these past days. She would have celebrated her birthday last week.'

'I understand.'

'On my way here I saw the king returning from his hunt. I'm to see him this evening to discuss tomorrow's parliament.' Humphrey gestured to the abbey. 'Join me in my prayers? I would be glad of the company. Then we will go and see the king together. I know he is keen to hear any final thoughts about the new council before terms are set.'

Robert was deciding how best to answer, when Nes came running across the abbey grounds.

'Sir Robert! I have a—' The squire stopped dead as he saw Humphrey, whose hood partially hid his face. 'Message,' he finished, fixing meaningfully on Robert. 'I have a message for you.'

Robert frowned, seeing Nes's eyes dart to Humphrey. He nodded to the earl. 'I'll join you shortly.' Waiting until Humphrey had disappeared inside, he turned to Nes. 'What is it?'

'Sir Ralph de Monthermer saw me waiting for you.' Nes's voice was strained. He glanced across the abbey grounds to the wall, beyond which lay the buildings of Westminster Palace. 'He's just now come from a hunt with the king. On their return, the king was given a letter found on William Wallace when he was captured by John of Menteith. Ralph doesn't know what the letter said, but he heard the king order Aymer de Valence to arrest you.'

'Arrest me?' Robert felt something cold go through him. 'For what?'

'Ralph doesn't know.' Nes paused for breath. 'But he said he owes you this much.' The squire held out his hand and opened it. Lying on his palm, muddy from a day's ride, was a pair of spurs.

The message couldn't have been clearer.

'Run?' Robert looked up at Nes. 'Not without my brother.'

Edward Bruce pushed back the hood of his cloak as he entered the prince's chambers. Beads of rain glittered from the garment in the glow of the torches that illuminated the passageway. Except for the rushing sounds of a broom being swept across the floor somewhere above, the building was blessedly quiet, the prince and his men having gone straight to the palace kitchens on their return from Smithfield to demand food and ale. Edward had excused himself, unable to bear their abrasive talk and laughter, the death screams of William Wallace still echoing in his ears. The execution had left a bitter taste in his mouth and stripped away the illusions of camaraderie and comfort he had built around himself these past years, enabling him to play well the role of loyal vassal. A cold tide of anger, dammed by necessity, had now been unleashed in him.

He felt furious at himself, cringing from the recollection of the times he had sat and drank with these men, laughing at their jokes about the barbarous Irish, the savage Welsh and the inferior Scots. How could his father have named him after the king? Barbarous? Savage? He could think of no better words to describe what Edward had done to Wallace on that scaffold today. The king's ivory towers ran with blood.

At the parliament tomorrow, whatever liberties the king granted in the new ordinances would not disguise the bonds that would shackle Scotland to England. Robert was due to arrive from Writtle any time, but so far as Edward knew his brother had received no word from John Comyn on the proposed alliance and there seemed little hope of the move to action he had been praying for. Edward would not have taken this path. Had he been born first he wouldn't now be waiting for a Comyn to decide the fate of the Bruces and the kingdom. He would ride north tomorrow and crown himself king, using Wallace as a martyr to rally Scotland beneath his banner, and damn all who stood in his way.

Reaching the stairs that led to his quarters, Edward climbed them. So lost to his thoughts was he that he didn't notice the footsteps in the passage behind him. He halted halfway up the stairs at the sound of his name. Turning, he saw four men approaching. Their shadows came first, spreading dark along the torch-lit walls. As they drew closer, he saw Piers Gaveston at their head. The Gascon's coal-black eyes had a strange, hungry look. As Piers moved towards him, Edward realised he had his sword in his hand.

'Master Piers,' Edward greeted, his eyes on the weapon. The others with the Gascon he knew well, all men of the prince's household. They had their hands on the pommels of their blades, ready to draw them. 'The ale has stopped flowing?'

'It was flowing well enough,' answered Piers. 'Until we had a visit from one of the king's men, ordering us to find you.'

'Well, now you have, what do you want?'

'We're to arrest you.'

Edward felt the last of his gloom fade, the world around him coming into sharp clarity. His heart began to thud, but he maintained a calm expression. Ever since he'd been witness to that embrace in the woods outside Burstwick, Piers had acted differently towards him. The prince had too, but while he seemed keen to draw Edward closer, Piers had become colder, more aggressive. Perhaps he was after spilling more Scots blood today, silencing the secret that lay between the three of them? 'Arrest me?' There were seven steps between Edward and the men. He was nearer the top than the bottom. 'Is this a jest?'

Piers smiled. 'Your brother will be dealt with by the king's men. You – my prince gave me the honour of taking.'

The Gascon lunged, thrusting towards Edward, who turned and vaulted up the stairs. He had no sword, only a dirk in his belt that would be little use against four blades. At the top a passage stretched in two directions. Racing up, Edward saw a servant on hands and knees scrubbing at the tiles, a wooden bucket on the floor beside him. Grabbing it, he hurled it down the stairs. As the bucket fell with a rush of dirty water, Piers ducked. Hearing the bucket go crashing down the stairs, followed by a yelp of pain, Edward charged down the passage towards his quarters. He didn't look back as footsteps filled the corridor behind him, along with a shout of alarm from the servant. Barrelling into the chamber at the end of the passage, he turned, catching a glimpse of Piers, dripping and furious, coming straight at him, before he slammed the door shut.

Snapping the bolt across, skinning his knuckle in his haste, Edward scanned the room. He fixed on the stout armoire that stood against one wall, just as something crashed into the door. Grabbing the heavy piece of furniture, he heaved it across the boards, rucking up the rug, as the thud came again, the bolt threatening to spring off the frame with the force. The third strike was accompanied by the splintering of wood.

'There's nowhere to go, you son of a bitch!' he heard Piers snarl.

With a protesting screech, the armoire was finally wedged against the door. Edward leaned against it, fighting for breath, listening to the continuing thuds, interspersed by Piers's threats and curses.

48

After several more attempts they gave up trying to shoulder the door open. Piers's voice lifted on the other side. 'Geoffrey, Brian — you two stay here, make sure he doesn't escape. We'll fetch an axe from the wood-store.'

Edward, leaning against the armoire, had no doubt Piers meant for him to hear this. The Gascon knew he had him trapped here. The chamber had one window, filled with leaded glass, too small for him to fit through. The whitewashed walls were of thick stone. As he listened to the footsteps fading down the passage, Edward eyed the boards under the crumpled rug, wondering if he could break his way through to the floor below. Geoffrey and Brian were slamming against the door again, causing the armoire to shudder. Parts of the frame were starting to splinter. Once they had an axe they would be through in moments.

Edward's thoughts that this was a personal vendetta on Piers's part were fading, consumed by the evident gravity of his situation. Whatever they intended to arrest him and Robert for, it was clearly serious. Thoughts of William Wallace flashed in his mind. Had the outlaw, in desperation or through torture, given his executioners information that had betrayed his brother's plan to lead a new uprising against the king and take the throne? He couldn't imagine Wallace would do such a thing, but he had seen what they had done to him today. Might any man facing that kind of horror yield secrets he would have otherwise kept to his grave?

Crossing the chamber, Edward went to the chest by his bed. He opened it and pulled out his sword. Behind him, the armoire jolted at another great thud against the door. Stamping on the boards, he chose a hollow-sounding area, away from any joists.

'Open up, Edward.' Geoffrey's voice came muffled through the wood. 'Whatever you've been accused of, it'll go better for you if you come out willingly.'

Edward looked over at the door. So they didn't know what he was charged with? Geoffrey's tone sounded reasonable, but the events of the day had been anything but. He no longer trusted the men in whose company he'd spent the past two years. Jamming the tip of his sword part way between one of the gaps in the floor, he used it as a lever, trying to prise up the board. He cursed, realising it was well nailed down, the beam strong and unyielding. Rainwater and sweat trickled down his neck as he tried again, noting the pressure in the blade as the steel began to bend. Voices sounded in the passage, fainter now, as if the prince's men had moved away. He couldn't hear what they were saying.

The voices rose suddenly into shouts of alarm. Moments later, pounding footsteps were followed by the ring of blades. Pulling his sword free, Edward grasped it two-handed, his brow furrowing as he stared at the door, beyond which came sounds of fighting. A familiar voice yelled his name, sending him rushing to the armoire, heaving it away. Snapping the bolt back, Edward opened the door to see his brother grappling with Brian. Geoffrey was on the floor, his face screwed up in pain. He was clutching his shoulder, blood oozing between his fingers.

Robert was drenched, his clothes mud-splattered. He looked wild in the torchlight, eyes fierce as he battled the younger man. The passage was tight and Robert was forced half to duel, half to wrestle. Leaping Geoffrey, Edward moved in to help, managing to duck in behind Brian and lock an arm tight around his neck. The younger man began to choke. He clutched at Edward's arm in panic, leaving Robert able to step in and wrench the sword from his grip. Edward kept his stranglehold until Brian was almost unconscious, then released him. The young man sank to the floor.

'Let's go,' Robert urged, handing Brian's sword to his brother and starting down the passage.

Edward sprinted after him. 'What the hell is happening?' he demanded, as they raced down the steps, past the bucket he had thrown at Piers. 'They tried to arrest me.'

'It has something to do with a letter found on Wallace when he was captured. Ralph sent me a warning.' Robert paused as they reached the door to the outside. Catching his breath, he opened it a crack and looked out. 'We don't have time to find the answers now. Nes and my men will meet us on the other side of the Tyburn with the horses.'

'Gaveston will be back any moment.'

'Then let's be halfway to Scotland by then.' Opening the door, Robert slipped out into the dank afternoon.

The rain had eased. Great puddles stretched across the yard, mirroring the sky. The palace buildings rose around them, dwarfed by Westminster Hall. The precinct was busy as usual with clerks and lawyers, servants and courtiers. In the gaps between the buildings, Edward glimpsed the broad grey waters of the Thames. Following Robert's lead, he pulled up his hood, concealing his sword beneath the folds of his cloak as they moved alongside the exterior of the prince's chambers, which backed on to the orchards and gardens. Glancing over his shoulder, looking for sign of Piers, Edward saw a crowd of men gathered in the main yard outside Westminster Hall, some on foot, others mounted. Many had swords drawn. He recognised the colours of Henry Percy and Guy de Beauchamp among them. As Edward watched, more joined them. 'Do you think that's for our benefit?'

Robert followed his gaze. 'Only Ralph and Humphrey know I've returned. Unless they've seen any of my men the others shouldn't know I'm here yet.'

'They'll know soon enough when Piers finds Brian and Geoffrey,' said Edward grimly. 'We shouldn't have left them able to talk.'

'I'm not going to add murder to whatever charge has been levelled at me.' Robert ducked into a gap in a row of rose bushes and led the way between the fruit trees, boots splashing through the puddles. The sun shone for a moment, bright and brief, turning everything silver, before winking behind the cloud cover once more.

Ahead, beyond a low line of storehouses, Westminster Abbey rose above its surrounding wall, alongside which the road ran across the Tyburn towards London. Robert slipped between two storehouses, from which drifted a pungent smell of fermenting apples. Edward went after him, snagging his cloak on a rusty nail, stumbling free. Halfway down the narrow passage he heard the clop of hooves ahead, along with the whinny of a horse and a man's raised voice. Edward recognised the abrasive tone immediately.

Robert, intent on reaching the road, didn't seem to have noticed the danger. He had almost stepped out from between the storehouses into view before Edward caught him. Grasping him by the shoulder, he pulled his brother back against the wall. In doing so, he caught a glimpse of horsemen on the road, only yards away, all wearing the arms of Pembroke.

Humphrey headed out of the abbey grounds, the prayers he had said for Bess lingering in his mind. The words had opened up the familiar hollow in his chest, where some vital part of him had been torn away. He filled it with things most of the time: his business for the king and the running of his estates, the numbing sweetness of wine and, once, a whore's adept embrace. But nothing properly fitted the space, the edges empty, raw.

Passing through the archway in the wall, he moved through the lines of pilgrims and beggars making their way towards the abbey, all hoping for a glimpse of the four sacred relics of Britain or a boon from the almoners' box. Humphrey was drawn from his gloom by Aymer de Valence who came riding up to meet him, accompanied by several knights. Valence's blue and white striped mantle was flecked with mud, Humphrey assumed from the hunt. The king had invited him to join the party, but he had declined.

'Have you seen Robert Bruce?' Aymer demanded.

'Why?' Humphrey asked, unable to keep the dislike from his tone. He and Aymer had often crossed swords in the days when they were both Knights of the Dragon, but they had always maintained a civility despite their disagreements. Until the Forest raid.

'The king ordered me to arrest him.'

'I warn you, Aymer,' Humphrey said flatly, 'I'm in no mood for your madness.' He went to walk away, but Aymer kicked his horse into his path.

The knight leaned towards Humphrey from his saddle. His black eyes were lit with pleasure. 'Wallace had a letter on him when he was captured. It implicates Bruce in a conspiracy against our king.' The satisfaction in Aymer's eyes increased with Humphrey's frown.

'What conspiracy?'

'The letter was addressed to the High Steward of Scotland, ordering him to raise his tenants in preparation for an uprising against King Edward and the English garrisons in Scotland and to make ready for the coronation of a new king.' Aymer's lips peeled back, revealing the wire that held his front teeth together. 'Bruce's coronation.'

Humphrey shook his head, refusing to believe it. Robert had been with them for three years. He had lived among them, drank and laughed with them, feasted and prayed. He had fought with them, spilling the blood of his countrymen to aid their king. Now, he worked for peace, to end the war and create a kingdom united beneath Edward's banner.

'The letter details Bruce's plan to return to Scotland,' continued Aymer, 'to crown himself king and lead a rebellion, exploiting the weaknesses of the garrisons at Stirling, Edinburgh and Lochmaben. Wallace was no doubt on his way to deliver it to James Stewart, which was why he came out of hiding and how Menteith was able to capture him.'

'You're saying it was written by Robert himself? Bearing his seal?'

'It wasn't sealed, but the author is clear.'

'Someone planted it on Wallace,' Humphrey said, his voice rising in anger. 'Someone wanted you to find it. To discredit him.'

Aymer shook his head disgustedly. 'Why is it so easy for you to believe him when he has lied to us before? Betrayed us! No Scot would discredit Bruce if this was his plan. They would want this to happen!'

'There is some other explanation,' Humphrey insisted. He recalled Robert's comfort and his words of understanding after the death of Bess and his unborn child. It cannot have been lies. 'I will not accept—' Humphrey stopped, seeing two men riding towards them from the palace yard. He recognised them from the prince's household.

'Sir Aymer!' called one, ignoring the pilgrims who were forced to scatter out of his way as he hauled his horse to a skidding stop. 'Master Piers had Edward Bruce trapped in his quarters. Robert Bruce helped him escape, attacking our men. The king's knights are searching all the buildings.'

Aymer spat a curse, then turned on Humphrey. 'Tell me, would an innocent man run?' He spoke quickly to his knights. 'We'll place men at every exit. They won't get far.'

'Wait!' shouted Humphrey, as Aymer went to kick his horse away.

Aymer twisted in his saddle.

'I saw Robert. He was going to join me in prayer in the abbey, but his squire arrived with a message. He never came.'

'Spread out,' said Aymer to his men. 'Search the grounds. Turn the palace inside out. Find the renegade!'

As Aymer and his knights spurred away, Humphrey stood there for a moment. Lifting his face to the rain, he closed his eyes. Robert, watching him from the cover of the alley between the apple stores, saw his confusion, his suffering. Guilt tightened its knot in his chest. Leaning back against the wall, he rested his head against the stone. There it was, his betrayal finally revealed, his treachery laid bare in the face of his friend. His brother was peering around the side of the store, his brow creased with concern.

'Valence has sent two of his men down to the bridge. We'll not get out that way.' Edward looked back at him. 'Robert – what they said – the letter?' He shook his head. 'How can Wallace have had any such thing? Please tell me you didn't write it?'

'I didn't. But someone who knows the truth did.' Robert pushed himself from the wall. 'As soon as they discover we're not in the palace they'll start searching the road. Nes is waiting out there with the horses. If they get to him first we're done for.' Beyond a patch of scrubby ground and a low fence, the road bordering the wall was still busy with people filing into the abbey. Humphrey had gone, heading through the palace grounds towards Westminster Hall. Robert paused. 'Maybe I should stay? Deny it? You heard Humphrey: he thought the letter might have been placed on Wallace. Maybe I can convince them it was?'

'No,' said Edward, grasping his shoulder. 'I saw what they did to Wallace, saw the depth of the king's hatred in every act of his executioners. You are tainted by association. That letter connects you to him. The king will see Wallace when he looks at you now, will fear some ghost of the rebel. Valence may be a bastard, but he isn't wrong. You betrayed them before. It will be easier for them to believe your guilt than your innocence and I will not watch what happened to William Wallace happen to you.'

Robert, scanning his brother's face, saw a rare fear in his eyes. He nodded. 'We'll go through the abbey. We can disappear among the crowds. If we leave by the north transept we come out in the cemetery. We'll climb the precinct wall to get to the river, head along the banks.'

Close together, the brothers moved out from between the stores, hastened across the muddy ground and vaulted the low fence. Ahead, two men – peasants by their clogs and simple clothes – were making their way towards the abbey.

Robert fixed on them, an idea forming. 'You there,' he called, ducking through the archway in the wall. 'I need your cloaks.'

The men looked round, frowning at the strange request. One started to shake his head, then stopped as Robert unfastened the brooch pin that held his mantle in place.

Drawing the garment from his shoulders, Robert proffered it to the man, glancing around warily. 'We'll give you ours in return,' he said, nodding to Edward who followed suit, seeing what he was thinking.

The men stared in astonishment. The lined silk cloaks shone in the grey afternoon, the threads of silver and gold glinting. After a pause, they began shrugging off their own, the patterned wool faded by sun, patched in places and soggy with rain. Robert took one, Edward the other. Draping them around their shoulders, leaving the peasants with the spoils, the brothers jogged across the grass to join the pilgrims and poor filing into the abbey.

Robert pulled up the cloak's hood, catching the unfamiliar smell of another's man sweat. He had sheathed his broadsword, but it would only take a trained eye to detect the outline of the blade through the thin material. As they approached the doors, passing under the leering heads of gargoyles, he wedged himself in among a group of beggars, trying to conceal himself from the guards who stood talking to one another by the entrance, eyeing the shuffling procession. Keeping his head down, hunching his shoulders, he willed himself to be invisible. He needn't have worried. To be a peasant was to be invisible. The knights didn't so much look at him and his ragged fellows, as look through them. They didn't see an earl in a beggar's cloak, carrying a sword into the house of God. They saw another set of threadbare garments that concealed only poverty and hunger.

Within moments, they were through, moving in a slow tide of men and women, frankincense masking the stink of the poor. Many of the newcomers fixed on the almoners who were doling out coins. Others looked around them as they moved down the aisle towards the king's charity, pushing back rain-damp hoods to gape at the great pillars that lifted the abbey's interior heavenward, tier upon marble tier, towards God. The cavernous space was aglow with candles that gleamed in the gilt and bronze of statues, and glimmered in the murals that adorned the walls of the newer parts of the building, decorated by the king's father, Henry III. The abbey was a place of splendour, fit for Christ Himself, far removed from the dirt and drudgery of their lives.

Robert saw more guards standing sentry around two of the holy relics the abbey housed – a tooth of one of the Magi and a stone embedded with a footprint of Christ – on display for the benefit of the pilgrims. Many people were kneeling there, hands clasped. Whispered entreaties filled the nave, rising into the darkness of the vault. He kept his head lowered, eyes on the floor, which changed from worn flagstones to a pavement of gems at the crossing of the church. The people ahead of them were diverging, some heading to the almoners for food, others moving on towards the carved and painted screen at the heart of the abbey, behind which was the shrine of the Confessor. Here, Robert halted.

'Brother,' whispered Edward, nodding towards the small door in the north transept that would take them to the cemetery. 'Look. The way is clear.'

'Not yet,' murmured Robert, his gaze fixed on the screen. Beyond, lay the answers he sought. The relics had been locked in the Tower, out of reach all this time. Now, here they were, yards from him, a display of the king's might shown to his subjects on the day he set the seal on his conquest of Scotland. The shrewd old bastard had enticed them with blood, bread and blessings, so they would spread word of his authority, benevolence and magnificence. Robert had come here once today already. He would not be turned away again. The risk changed nothing. If anything, it made him more determined. This, he knew, would be his last chance.

Ignoring Edward's whispered protests, he made his way through the press of pilgrims towards the carved screen. His eyes went to the coronation chair, raised on its carpeted dais, entrapping the Stone of Destiny. He felt the pull towards it – thoughts of rescue and atonement in his mind – but he pushed the desire aside. The stone had taken three men to lift it when the Knights of the Dragon took it from Scone Abbey. Focusing on what he had come for, he made his way around the screen, his brother close at his side.

The base of the shrine was surrounded by worshippers. Some knelt in the niches, praying as close to the saint's body as possible, while those unable to get that near radiated out in a tight circle. Others paused on the periphery before moving on around the other side of the screen in a constant stream of worship. A large number, Robert realised, were afflicted by deformities, the Confessor's bones believed to be a potent cure. Above the shrine's stone base, the painted canopy hung suspended, lifted to reveal the feretory that housed the saint's remains.

Robert's gaze alighted on the altar, draped with a cloth on which were placed four objects. There was the Crown of Arthur, taken from the Welsh prince Madog ap Llywelyn after the last uprising, resting on a velvet cushion. Beside it was Curtana, the Sword of Mercy, once wielded by the Confessor himself. Between them, lying across the length of the altar, was the Staff of Malachy, its gem-encrusted sheath glimmering in the glow of several candles. Lastly, Robert fixed on the black lacquered box, in which the king kept the *Last Prophecy*. Two guards dressed in scarlet stood to either side of the altar, keeping watch over the treasures.

Robert spoke to his brother beneath his breath. 'I'm going to take the prophecy box.'

'Robert – no. It's not worth your life!'

'Please, Edward, you have to help me. Trust me on this, if nothing else.'

Edward studied him, his face registering surprise at the plea in his voice. In answer, he reached inside the folds of the tatty cloak and gripped the hilt of the sword taken from Brian.

They inched forward, forcing their way through the circle of worshippers. A few people looked up, frowning. One or two muttered at them to wait their turn. The guards glanced over, but said nothing. The brothers were almost at the altar when they heard raised voices beyond the screen. Robert went cold as he recognised the harsh tone of Aymer de Valence.

'They're in here somewhere. Those peasants saw them enter. Find them!'

Robert's heart sank as he realised their cloaks must have given them away. In desperation, he lunged for the altar, thrusting people aside. The two guards, distracted by the shouts on the other side of the screen, saw him coming at the last moment. One cried a warning and went for his sword, but Robert had already drawn his. Sweeping the blade out from under the cloak, he thrust towards the guard, who staggered back, knocking into a man kneeling behind him. He went down, cracking his skull on the base of the shrine.

The sight of the blade and the shout of the falling guard drew men and women from their prayers. People began scrabbling to their feet as the second guard drew his sword and went at Robert. The ring of blades roused the rest of the pilgrims. At once, the crowd began to move, pushing to get away from the altar and the two men battling before it. Lines of people were still making their way into the shrine and a crush formed, those trying to get in preventing others from getting out. Cries of fear rose as the elderly and infirm were caught up in the press. The first guard had pushed himself up on his knees, but had dropped his sword in the fall and was groping to find it beneath the trampling feet.

'I've got him!' shouted Edward, moving in front of Robert to tackle the second.

Needing no encouragement, Robert went for the box. A sudden surge of people caused him to lose his balance and he crashed into the altar. The Crown of Arthur slipped from its cushion as Curtana jolted into it and the Staff of Malachy was knocked into the black box, which slid across the altar cloth. Robert lunged. Too late. The box fell to the stone steps with a crack. At the same time, two of the candles toppled over, the flames gusting across the delicate silk of the altar cloth. Fire sprang to life.

Behind him, Robert could hear Aymer and his men trying to battle their way into the shrine, causing panic among the pilgrims. Screams rose as people were knocked to their knees and trampled. His brother punched the pommel of his sword into the second guard's face, breaking his nose, then kicked him in the stomach, causing him to double up. Robert bent and grabbed the prophecy box. Although the lid remained shut, a split had appeared in the side of the wood revealing the interior. A cold thrill went through him. There was nothing – nothing except the dark, shiny surface reflecting back on itself. No scraps of parchment, no dust even. The box was empty.

'Come on!' urged Edward, appearing at his side.

Robert paused, his eyes on the altar, where the cloth was smouldering. Then, thrusting the box at his brother, he took hold of the Staff of Malachy.

As Aymer and his men forced their way through the crowds now fleeing the abbey in all directions, Robert and Edward plunged into the chaos. Blades sheathed and hoods up, the treasures concealed beneath their cloaks, they were indistinguishable from the ragged multitude. Reaching the door in the north transept, through which streams of people were pressing, Robert glanced back. Canons were running to put out the fire in the Confessor's shrine, shouting in alarm as smoke plumed. He saw Aymer de Valence grabbing hold of people as they passed, ripping back hoods in a fury, then he was barrelling through the doors into the grey afternoon, the Staff of Malachy gripped in his fist. As he and Edward crossed the cemetery, leaping graves, making for the wall that ran alongside the Tyburn, a face filled Robert's thoughts – conjured by the promise of freedom. The face of the man he was certain had betrayed him.

John Comyn.

49

Dumfries, Scotland, 1306 AD

The men moved quickly through the backlands that wound behind the cramped labyrinth of wattle and daub houses. By these narrow paths they avoided the main thoroughfare where townsfolk were heading home for the day, hunched against the wind streaming up from the River Nith. It was early evening, just before vespers, and the first stars were scattered like splintered gems around the horns of a new moon. There was a breath of snow in the brittle air. Remnants of the last fall were heaped along the edges of pathways, pounded to a filthy slush by people and animals.

As the men splashed through the stinking alleys, past cesspits, water barrels and animal pens, their boots crunching over the frozen refuse of middenheaps, rats scurried ahead of them in a black tide. There was a snarl followed by a crash as something large threw itself against a fence beside them. Christopher Seton stumbled back against the timber wall of a house, grasping the hilt of his sword as the snarl rose into a volley of barking. 'Christ!'

'*Come on!*' Thomas Bruce urged, hastening on down the alley.

At an exclamation above him, Christopher looked up to catch a woman's face, white in the shadows of a window. Seeing the men passing below, she pulled the shutters closed with a bang that roused the dog to a new frenzy. Drawing the hood of his black cloak lower, Christopher moved on after his comrades.

At the end of the terrace of houses a street opened before them, the cobbles mottled with frost. On the other side rose the wall of the Greyfriars' monastery. The friary, established by John Balliol's mother over forty years ago, dominated a ridge of land at the northern end of Dumfries. Further along the cobbled street, firelight and voices spilled from dwellings, people settling in for the night, shutting out the cold and dark. Wood-smoke sharpened the air.

Robert paused in the mouth of the alley, hearing the clop of hooves approaching. Four horsemen appeared in the street, heading uphill from the bridge across the Nith. They didn't see the men who watched them from the shadows. Noting the swords protruding from their cloaks, Robert took them for another company arriving for the assembly tomorrow: one of the first gatherings of the justices chosen by King Edward for the new government. He felt a lance of fear, knowing how close he was to danger; the English garrison barracked less than two miles away at the royal castle. One slip and they would be on him. He had left the rest of his company with their horses on the outskirts of Dumfries – a necessity to keep his presence secret, but a fair distance if he had to flee.

When the horsemen had gone, Robert turned to his men and nodded. His brother Edward went first, slipping from the alley to cross the street. Niall followed, his slender silhouette lengthened by the black cloak he wore to conceal sword and mail. Four knights from Robert's estates went after them, with Thomas, Christopher and Alexander Seton. Robert let the others go, but caught Alexander's arm. 'Are you with me?'

Alexander met his questioning gaze. 'I wouldn't be here if I wasn't.'

After a pause, Robert released him, watching as he scanned the street before crossing in the wake of the others. He hadn't expected their friendship, cemented nine years earlier after he joined the insurrection, to be as it was. He understood Alexander's anger and resentment. Throwing his loyalty behind Robert all those years ago, the lord had forfeited his estates in East Lothian to the English, hoping Robert's bid for the throne would see him eventually recover those losses. That hope had been destroyed when Robert submitted to King Edward, casting the cousins adrift. Even so, he had thought to have seen some thawing in his old friend by now. It had, after all, been two months since the cousins rejoined his company.

For a moment, he hesitated, wondering if he'd made the wrong decision involving the Setons in tonight's affair. But there was no time for regrets. He was here and no one, friend nor foe, would stand in the way of the cold slice of justice he intended to serve up. He had waited five months for this.

Robert sprinted across the street, his boots scuffing the frost from the cobbles. Reaching the monastery wall he leapt up, grasping the top with his fingertips. Most of his comrades were already over, down among the cover of trees on the other side. Using rough protrusions of stone as footholds, straining with the effort – his mail coat greatly augmenting his weight – Robert pulled himself up. He was almost at the top when he heard voices. Two men were making their way up the moonlit street towards him. In his haste, he lost his footing and nearly fell, before two sets of hands grabbed his arms and hauled him up. Swinging his legs over the top, Robert jumped into darkness. For a split second he was back in Westminster vaulting from the abbey wall, the Staff of Malachy wedged in his belt, sounds of pursuit at his back. Then, he hit the ground hard, dropping to one knee, before righting himself with a nod of thanks to Thomas and Christopher who had helped him. On the other side of the wall the men's voices sharpened as they passed by, then faded.

Adjusting his scabbard, Robert made his way to the edge of the trees, beyond which the ground was carved with frozen vegetable patches, vestiges of snow glinting in the furrows. The buildings of the friary rose ahead, pale in the wash of moonlight, an imposing church looming over lower structures that surrounded a cloister. Small outbuildings clustered around the main ones: a bakehouse and brewhouse, latrines and stables. The muted radiance of candlelight shone in several windows. The ten men threaded through the gardens, their black cloaks making them part of the darkness, footsteps muffled by snow.

At a corner of the buildings, Robert pressed himself against the wall, the others lining up beside him. Before him, a small yard opened out opposite a stable. He could smell the acrid stink of soiled straw. A lantern hung from a nail, creaking in the wind and spreading a slick of light across the ground. He could hear the whickers of horses, the rustle of a broom and voices. Two men emerged from the stables and headed across the yard. As they passed beneath the lantern, Robert fixed on their red surcoats, which had a familiar coat of arms embroidered on the chests. His scouts had been right. The confirmation settled in him, hardening his resolve.

Only the rush of the broom came from the stables now the men had gone. Robert turned to Edward and Thomas. 'Find out where he is.'

His brothers came to the edge of the wall, dirks in their hands. Keeping an eye out, they stole across the yard to the stables.

'You believe he'll listen to you?'

Robert turned at Alexander's question. The lord's face was carved with darkness from the shadow of his hood. He couldn't see his expression, but the doubt was clear in his tone. 'What choice does he have?'

'He may choose to fight. If he or his men alert the English garrison we—'

'We won't give him the chance,' Robert cut across him. He looked back to see Edward peer into the gloom of the stables, then slip inside, Thomas following. There was a young voice raised in question, which became a cry that cut off abruptly. Sounds of a struggle and the whinny of startled horses were followed by silence. Finally, there was a grunt of pain, then the distinct noise of something being dragged. Edward and Thomas reappeared and made their way across to the waiting men. As they pushed their dirks into their belts beside their swords, Robert saw the blades were clean of blood. Only Thomas's fist told a tale, the knuckles red.

'He's here all right,' murmured Edward. 'He and his men have been lodged in the guest room and the abbot's house.'

'Where is he now?' Robert asked, eyeing the two buildings Edward motioned to.

'The groom said they're at supper,' answered Thomas. 'In the refectory.'

Robert cursed. He had dearly hoped to come upon his enemy unawares and alone. 'How many horses in the stables?'

Thomas shook his head. 'Hard to tell. A dozen or more?'

Edward studied Robert. 'If you're thinking of storming the refectory it could go badly for us. This wasn't planned to be a bloodbath.'

Making a decision, Robert pushed himself from the wall and headed across the yard towards the building the two men had disappeared inside. The others followed warily, looking around. There was a row of high arched windows stained by the ruddy glow of firelight. Pausing beneath them, Robert heard voices coming from within, along with muffled laughter and the clatter of dishes. Gesturing to Niall, the tallest and lightest, he crouched and laced his gloved hands together like a stirrup, nodding to Thomas to help him. As Niall stepped into their cupped hands, using the refectory wall to balance himself, Robert and Thomas hefted him up. The others gathered in a tight circle around them, eyeing the yard and the doorways leading into the buildings.

'Twenty men,' whispered Niall, when they lowered him back down. 'Three of them pages by the look of them. But he's not among them,' he finished, looking at Robert.

'We should go,' said Alexander. 'It's almost vespers. We can come back tonight when they've retired.'

'No,' murmured Robert, impatience stinging him. 'We'll split up and find him. If he's somewhere alone, this will be our best chance.' Ignoring Alexander's evident dissatisfaction, he ordered the lord to check the monastery's guest quarters. 'Go with him,' he told his three brothers and one of his knights. 'We'll take the abbot's lodgings.' Robert caught Edward's eye. 'If you find him I want to be the one to question him, understood?'

As the two parties divided, Robert led Christopher and the other three knights to the abbot's lodge, built just off the church. The windows were unpromisingly dark. As he was approaching the door, he caught the crunch of footsteps in snow. He and his men ducked into the porch as three friars went past, ghostly in their grey habits, breath misting the air. Robert peered out, following their progress with his gaze as they disappeared among the buildings around the cloister. He was turning back to the door when he caught sight of a set of footprints leading from the abbot's house. The monks had trailed dark lines through the snow on their daily processions to sing the offices, all following the same route. These prints were a single set, heading to the church across the grass where the snow was still pristine. Seeing the shimmer of light in the windows, Robert felt a flicker of antici-pation. 'We'll try the church first.'

'The monks?' cautioned Christopher.

But Robert was off, sprinting across the grass. Reaching the porch, he moved up to the door, grasped the latch and eased it down. There was a click and a creak as it opened. He put his face to the crack, scanning the nave beyond, the aisles of which faded into shadows. At the end of the nave pale gold candlelight seeped from behind the rood screen that hid the monks' choir. He caught a strong smell of incense and guessed the three friars had been readying the church for the evening office. Alexander was right. He didn't have long.

Unable to see much else from the doorway, Robert stepped inside. His four companions entered behind him, but lingered near the door at his signal, keeping watch. As Robert walked through the cold dusk of the nave, his footsteps hollow on the tiles, the glow of the candles up ahead flickered in the draught that had streamed in at his back. As he neared the choir, seeing no sign of anyone, his frustration built. At the crossing of the church, Robert halted, scowling into the peaceful gloom. He was about to turn on his heel, when he heard something.

Slipping in behind a pillar, he stared into the darkness at the end of the aisle. Moonlight slanted through the lofty windows, illuminating the floor at intervals. In the distance, shallow stone steps led into an opening – a small chapel, he guessed. A man appeared, descended the steps and turned down the aisle, heading towards Robert. As he passed through one of the swathes of moonlight his features were lit by the pallid sheen. It was John Comyn.

Robert fixed on that pinched, hungry face. It was that face that had spurred him from Westminster, fighting through the mud on the banks of the Tyburn to reach Nes and the horses; that face that had driven him into the Middlesex Forest, Aymer de Valence hot on his heels. Riding hard through the cover of the woods, stopping only when the horses were spent, he and his men had evaded capture, but the expectation of it never left him on the gruelling journey north. Taking tracks across country to skirt towns had added miles to their route and it was late September before Robert crossed the border. By the end of the month he was at Turnberry, greeting his wife and daughter, where, from his newly refortified castle, he summoned his tenants and allies. An early snowfall in late October had given him hope of a reprieve from pursuit, but Robert had known he didn't have much time. The game was up: his treachery exposed. He had to make his plans fast, before retribution came. But all through the weeks of reunions and secret gatherings that followed, the face of John Comyn had continued to darken his thoughts.

John Comyn stopped dead as the black-cloaked figure swept out of the darkness at him, sword brandished. As Robert pushed back his hood, Comyn's expression changed from startled surprise to deep shock.

At the sight of his enemy's stunned disbelief, any vestiges of doubt over the origin of the letter found on William Wallace vanished from Robert. 'What's wrong, Sir John? You look as though you've seen a spirit.' His voice shook, barely able to suppress the strength of feeling behind it. 'I suppose I am, since you intended for my life to have ended back in London, my body and plans rotting in the Tower.'

Comyn licked at his lips. 'Why are you here?'

'Did King Edward not tell you I had returned to Scotland?' Robert's tone was caustic. He enjoyed the look in Comyn's face, which told him the man knew nothing. Robert guessed the king had closed ranks after his escape. 'I imagine, when you go to his assembly for the new justices tomorrow, you will find I am the order of the day.' He stepped towards Comyn. 'But we have business of our own to finish, you and me.'

John Comyn held his ground, but his eyes flicked past Robert to the church doors, where Christopher and the other knights were barring the way. 'The friars will return at any moment. They will alert my men.'

'I have one question. It won't take long.'

'Question?'

'For months I wondered why you were delaying accepting my proposal. Now, I realise you had other plans. What I don't understand is why.' Robert's brow creased. 'Why did you do it, John? Why did you plant that letter on Wallace, betraying me to the English? Would you rather have Edward for a king?'

Anger flashed in Comyn's eyes. 'You and Edward aren't our only choices.

There were eleven other men with your grandfather and John Balliol whose claims were recognised during the trial.' He punched his chest with his fist. 'My father included.'

Robert stared at him in disbelief. 'You mean to be king?'

'Why not?' Comyn demanded. 'When you resigned as guardian I took control of the kingdom. While you were bowing to the English I was leading us to victory. Balliol is my kin and my family is still respected here, while yours is now forgotten, a relic of an age passed. You've been clinging to the last threads of power held by your grandfather. But, I tell you, it has slipped through your fingers. Scotland's crown will not be yours while I'm still standing.' Comyn's face twisted. 'You're a two-faced knave, looking to steal himself a prize beyond his honour!'

'Two-faced?' Robert's fingers whitened around the hilt of his broadsword. He thrust it towards Comyn, the tip pointed at his throat. 'Shall I tell you how Wallace died, you son of a bitch?' He flung his free hand down the aisle towards the chapel Comyn had come from. 'God damn you, I hope you were praying for forgiveness!'

Comyn laughed harshly, though his eyes were on the sword. 'Forgiveness? I need no forgiveness. Wallace was a wanted man. Edward would have strung him up sooner or later. His death is not on me.'

'No? You drew him out of hiding, using John of Menteith.' Robert caught the surprise in Comyn's eyes. 'Neil Campbell came to me at Turnberry. He told me about the ambush outside Glasgow – that Menteith had a large company of men with him, many more than are under his command, and that one was missing a hand. We both know that was MacDouall. Just as we know that you, of the few who knew what I was planning, would be the only one who would betray me.'

'You cannot prove this. Any of it.'

Robert gave a grim half-smile. 'In a small way I should thank you. Your duplicity pushed my plans forward, forcing me to take action. I'm finally free of Edward's shackles. As we speak, my allies are preparing my coronation. What is more, you're going to support me in my bid.'

John Comyn's lips peeled back in a rictus of hate. 'I would rather—'

'You'll support me or I will expose your betrayal. You gave Scotland's champion to the enemy, so he could be carved up on the executioner's slab. Wallace still commands the respect of many. Have you not heard the cries of outrage sweeping the realm since word of his death came north? What would those same people do if they knew you were behind it? You think they would follow you? They would hang you from the nearest tree!'

'Robert!'

He jerked round to see Christopher had come halfway down the aisle.

'*The monks*,' hissed the knight. 'They're coming!'

'Bar the doors,' Robert growled in response. He was only distracted for a moment, but it was all Comyn needed to shove him in the chest, sending him crashing into one of the pillars. Even as he was recovering his balance, Comyn was pushing past him. Diving behind the rood screen, he sprinted across the choir towards a side door in the opposite aisle, Robert at his heels. The candles guttered at their passing, throwing shadows across the vaulting.

Lunging, Robert grabbed hold of the back of Comyn's red surcoat, the material ripping as he brought him to a staggering stop. He ducked as Comyn swung round, aiming a fist at his face. Losing his grip, Robert snarled and thrust forward with his sword, meaning to clout him into submission. Comyn stumbled back from the blade, looking wildly around him. He leapt for the altar, grabbing a large silver candlestick. The candle slipped free, the flame extinguishing as it struck the tiled floor. Comyn brandished the stick two-handed. It was almost as long as a blade. Suddenly, he brought it carving in at Robert like an axe.

Robert twisted out of the way. 'Support me in my bid! Refuse, and when I'm crowned I'll run you and all your blood out of Scotland!'

In answer, Comyn came at him with a roar. Knocking Robert's outstretched sword to one side with a crack of the candlestick, he brought it arcing into his side. The force it struck with would have broken ribs had Robert not been wearing mail. As it was, he was sent reeling into the monks' choir stalls, one of the benches screeching across the tiles with him half sprawled on top of it. He dropped his sword. Christopher was shouting again. Faint calls rose from outside as the monks tried to get into the church and found the door barred.

Swiping his sword from the floor, Robert pushed himself up as Comyn came at him. He stooped under the strike that was aimed at his head and lashed out with his blade, his blood fired. The tip sliced Comyn's upper arm, tearing through his clothes and scoring the flesh beneath. Comyn bellowed, but didn't relinquish his grip on the candlestick. Robert's heart thumped as he circled his enemy – the rapid rhythm of the battlefield. The candlelit choir, the hammering on the doors and calls of the monks faded, along with his reasoned intentions. He had come here to threaten Comyn's reputation and standing, not his life. But that knowledge was dim now, pale in the face of the brute desire to batter the breath out of the man before him.

He pitched forward, meaning to carve another slice of flesh from him. Comyn reacted quickly, bringing the candlestick in to counter. Silver and steel met with a ringing clash that echoed through the vault. Robert felt the break before he saw it, the concussion vanishing abruptly as his broadsword snapped. The top half of the blade went flying to clatter among the choir stalls, leaving him holding the hilt and a jagged stump of metal. He stared aghast at the sword, given to him by his grandfather the day he was knighted, before Comyn stepped in through his defences and punched the candlestick into his stomach. The mail unable to absorb the savage impact, Robert doubled over.

'*Robert!*'

As Christopher's shout echoed through the nave followed by pounding footsteps, Robert grasped his dirk and freed it from his belt. He straightened and thrust at John Comyn, who was coming in again. Plunging the dagger into the man's side, he shoved it up under his ribs. Eye to eye with Comyn, Robert felt the resistance as steel grazed bone, then the release as it slid on through muscle and organs. There was a rush of something hot over his hand. Blood flowed, dark like wine in the flame light. Comyn let go of the candlestick, which clanged to the tiles. He grasped Robert's shoulder, his face changing from rage to surprise. Robert, teeth bared, twisted the knife, relishing the agony that flared in his enemy's eyes.

Comyn shoved him away then teetered back against the altar. He looked down at the hilt of the dagger embedded in his ribs, then grasped it. Closing his eyes, face clenched, he pulled it out with a ragged cry. The hammering on the church doors was louder. Comyn sagged against the altar, blood pulsing from his side. More was in his mouth, staining his gritted teeth. Robert, stooped over and breathing hard, started as Christopher appeared at his side.

The knight's face was tight with shock as he stared at Comyn. 'We've got to go,' he told Robert, tearing his gaze from the wounded man. 'Now!'

The thudding on the church door had become a rhythmic boom. The monks were trying to ram it open. Any moment, Comyn's men would arrive, if they hadn't already. Robert realised with cold shock that his brothers were still out there, searching the grounds. He looked back at Comyn, propped against the altar, blood spattering the floor around him. The prospect of capture cleared his senses. Dear God, what had he done?

Christopher propelled him towards the side door in the aisle, which the other knights had unbolted and were now pushing through. '*Go!*'

As they started towards it there was a hoarse cry. Robert jerked round to see Comyn lunging at him, eyes wild, the bloody dagger in his fist. It was

Christopher who turned and raised his sword, Christopher who plunged the length of steel into Comyn's gut. The lord convulsed on the blade, gagging blood from his mouth, before the knight wrenched the sword free. John Comyn collapsed on the church floor where he lay still, blood seeping around him in a dark slick.

The three other knights were shouting at them to come. Robert heard his brother Edward outside, voice raised. The sound snapped him to life. Shoving Christopher before him, he made for the door, the two of them plunging into the frozen darkness of the churchyard. Torchlight bobbed in the gloom as Comyn's men came running through the grounds. Edward, Niall and the others were there, gasping for breath, swords in their hands.

'They saw us,' Edward panted, seeing Robert.

'This way!' shouted Niall, making for the church wall.

The ten of them made it to the wall some distance ahead of Comyn's men. Pushing his broken sword into his belt, Robert hauled himself up. His brothers and men were beside him, jumping down the other side one by one. Christopher was struggling to find purchase on the stones, his face white in the moonlight. He slipped suddenly and fell back with a cry, sprawling in the snow. Comyn's men shouted in triumph, racing towards him, their torches throwing a red glow over the gravestones. Robert, straddling the wall, threw down a hand to the knight. Scrabbling to his feet, Christopher grabbed at it. Bracing himself, Robert hauled the knight up, gasping with the effort. Christopher reached the top, then swung himself over and dropped down. As Comyn's men ran towards the wall, the light of their torches spread across it, briefly illuminating Robert.

'Bruce!' came the shout, as he jumped. 'It's Robert Bruce!'

PART 6

1306 AD

'Make haste, therefore, to receive what God makes no delay to give you; to subdue those who are ready to receive your yoke; and to advance us all, who for your advancement will spare neither limbs nor life. And that you may accomplish this, I myself will attend you in person with ten thousand men.'

The History of the Kings of Britain, *Geoffrey of Monmouth*

50

In mid-February, when the winter snows were creeping back from the lowlands – green fields appearing, streams and rivers breaking their icy bonds and flowing free – a rumour started to spread.

It began as a murmur, carried on the lips of travellers passing through on newly cleared roads: tales of an uprising in the south. Within days, rumour had hardened into truth, settlements all along the border seething with the news that Robert Bruce had appeared in the night and roused the townsfolk of Dumfries to rebellion, storming the castle and routing King Edward's new justices who had gathered there. This was soon followed by word that Bruce and his men had captured Dalswinton Castle, a Comyn stronghold. As the furore spread, with the fall of Tibbers, Ayr, Rothesay and Dunaverty to Bruce's forces, English garrisons across Scotland began hauling up drawbridges and barring castle gates. Urgent messages were despatched south to King Edward. Robert Bruce, they said, had raised the standard of rebellion. And men were flocking to his banner.

For the first few weeks after the rising at Dumfries many Scots were still talking about it as something separate from them, something to discuss heatedly in the fields and churches of their villages where life continued much as normal in spite of the tumultuous events happening around them. Excited, troubled, agitated; all wondered if the storm would reach them, or whether it would simply blow itself out. Then, early in March, the distant rumbles of insurrection spread and grew louder, until everyone felt its coming.

To some it came in the iron-cold dawn, to others the afternoon or raw dark of evening, a burning brand carried from royal burgh to wooded hamlet, from bustling port to mountain-shadowed settlement. Passed from man to man, it was a living beacon that meant one thing to all who saw it. It was the fiery cross, Scotland's ancient call to arms. Across the realm, men took up weapons; opening chests to grasp the hilts of swords left dormant since the end of the war, hefting axes from log piles to whet the blades, hammering fresh nails into the scarred heads of clubs, fitting new flights to arrows. In the west, at Ayr and Lanark, and all around Selkirk Forest, the fiery cross passed through settlements where people were still outraged by the execution of William Wallace, word of which had come in the autumn. Here, it was as a torch set to kindling, the conflagration spreading through all who saw its flame. Some were men who had fought with Wallace in the early days of the rebellion, who had celebrated after his victory at Stirling and who had seen sons and brothers die bloody on the field at Falkirk under the steel of an English army. Men who, in the years since, had lost hope, but not heart.

All through these preparations for defence and battle, stories of the uprising and Robert Bruce's rapid victories along the west coast continued unabated. Bruce, they said, was raising the army of the realm for a new war against England and was planning to crown himself king. The revelation was met by a mixture of disbelief, anger and excitement. But it was not the only rumour. In this time, another was gaining momentum, a dark undercurrent of half-truth and hearsay, growing stronger in the Comyn heartlands of Galloway and Badenoch, Kilbride and Buchan, flowing like a riptide beneath the swelling call to arms.

Robert Bruce, they said, had murdered John Comyn.

Robert crouched down, chuckling as the boy toddled into his outstretched arms. His nephew, Donald, reached out and grasped the head of the cross-bow bolt that hung around his neck. Lifting the fragment of iron in a chubby fist, he frowned curiously at it, then tried to bite it. Robert removed the pendant from his nephew's mouth and stood, swooping the boy into the air. Donald yelled.

'He likes you,' said Christian, coming forward and smoothing a hand through her son's hair, which was fair like her own. She smiled, looking up at Robert. 'It is good for him to be around another man, with his father gone.'

Christian's smile didn't fade as she scooped her wriggling son into her arms, but Robert noticed a sheen appear in his sister's pale blue eyes at the mention of her husband. Gartnait had died a year ago, leaving Christian a widow and their son the Earl of Mar. Robert watched as she carried Donald over to the trestle erected in the centre of the tent, the canvas sides of which were being buffeted by the wind. From outside came the clamour of the encampment.

Passing the boy to his wet nurse, Christian sat to finish the meal her servants had prepared. Her sisters, Mary and Matilda, had almost finished theirs.

Mary Bruce caught Robert's eye. 'Won't you join us after all, brother?' she asked, cocking her head in question. 'In the time you've been standing there you could have broken two fasts.'

Robert met Mary's sharp gaze, struck by her similarity to Edward with her black hair and those well-defined features that lent her face a hard, almost sly mien. His sisters had arrived at Turnberry shortly before the Christ Mass, drawn from Kildrummy Castle by his summons. He was still surprised by how much the three of them had changed since he'd last seen them, Mary and Matilda especially, who, at twenty and nineteen, were the youngest of his siblings by a decade. 'I have a council to attend.'

'Elizabeth and Marjorie are joining us this evening,' said Christian, holding out her goblet as her page moved to refresh it with watered wine. Her tone carried a suggestive hint. 'It would be a rare pleasure if we all ate together.'

Matilda brightened. 'Lady Elizabeth is bringing her minstrel.' Her voice, soft and low, revealed something of her shy nature. She glanced at Mary whenever she spoke, Robert had noticed, as if looking for permission.

He gave Christian a look, irritated that his sister seemed intent on trying to soothe the troubles in his marriage. On his return to Scotland there had been a brief period of grace in which he had built some bridges with his wife. But those connections, fragile and new, had broken under the strain of the past few weeks. Elizabeth had cooled considerably towards him after the events at Dumfries, but with the march to war, he'd had neither the time nor the inclination to speak to her. 'This is a siege camp, Christian. Not a fair.' A gust of wind blew in at his back as someone entered. Robert turned, grateful for the interruption, to see Christopher Seton.

The knight nodded courteously to the three women, his eyes lingering on Christian, before turning his attention to Robert. 'You have more new arrivals, along with one you've been waiting for. Bishop Wishart has come. I've shown him to the war tent. The others are gathering there now.'

Robert gave a satisfied grunt. 'His grace's timing is impeccable.'

Christian had risen. 'Sir Christopher,' she called, as Robert headed for the opening.

The knight looked back. 'My lady?'

'I was just trying to persuade my brother to eat with us this evening. Perhaps you can convince him?' Christian smiled. 'There is room enough for both of you.'

Robert went to reproach her, then stopped as he saw his friend's expression. The knight had a fool's grin plastered all over his face.

In that moment, the years of war and hardship were stripped away and Christopher looked much as he had when Robert first met him at the siege of Carlisle – an earnest, eager young man, his life stretching before him full of possibility. Even when living hand to mouth in the Forest, even when hunger and pain had taken their toll, he had managed to retain his good-natured humour, playing his flute around the campfires to cheer the men, laughing and joking with Edward and Niall. Until four weeks ago.

Robert stared at him, wondering if his friend had known back then on Carlisle's walls – the day he'd saved his life – that ten years later he'd be jointly responsible for the murder of a man in a house of God whether Christopher would have pledged himself quite so freely to his cause. Since that night in Dumfries, he had been withdrawn, sitting in silence at mealtimes, tight-lipped and tense.

For Robert it was a relief now to see him smile, as if all could yet be right in the world, despite the events of the last month. Back in Turnberry, he'd noticed an attraction between his widowed sister and the knight. If Christian could bring back the carefree man he knew, who was he to stand in the way? 'We'll come,' he told his sister. 'Both of us.'

Leaving the women, Christopher glancing back until he'd ducked out, the two of them headed through the encampment.

It was a brisk March morning. Huge clouds scudded across the sky, sweeping shadows across the brown waters of the Clyde. The gusts coming off the wide estuary cut like glass and Robert drew his fur-trimmed mantle tighter. All around him, tents snapped and flags billowed, the multitude of colours and emblems rippling madly. New banners had joined them each day as more men answered the call to arms. Smoke blew ragged across the site, mixing with the reek from the dug-out latrines and piles of dung around makeshift stables. The camp stretched across a plain near the mighty river's banks. Just beyond a channel of mud, visible now it was low tide, reared two massive horns of rock, in the green cleft of which was built the ancient stronghold of Dumbarton Castle.

From the mud-banks a rocky path climbed to the castle's stout lower walls, beyond which rose a collection of stone and timber buildings. The dual heights ascended precipitously behind, girdled by more walls on their higher flanks. The two spurs of rock were crowned respectively by a white tower and a great hall. In a land studded with redoubtable fortresses, Dumbarton was one of the most impregnable. Inside, well guarded on his water-encircled rock, was John of Menteith. The man who captured William Wallace and gave him to the English had been generously rewarded by King Edward, who had forgiven him his debts to the crown and made him keeper of the castle.

It was the sixth stronghold Robert had laid siege to in four weeks. His campaign, beginning unexpectedly at Dumfries, had been as a boulder pushed down a hillside, gathering momentum, picking up stones and rocks in its wake, until it was an avalanche. Along with Rothesay, Dunaverty and Ayr, Dumbarton guarded the western approaches to Scotland — a vital route both for supplies and the reinforcements Robert hoped would yet come from the isles beyond. The strategic position aside, it was also the one he most desired to capture. Menteith, he was determined, would pay for the treachery against Wallace. The other castles had fallen quickly, by skill, subterfuge or threat, but Menteith had held out and without siege engines to batter the walls, Robert had been forced to content himself with cutting off his enemy's supply lines and putting the fear of God in the bastard with his ever growing force.

'Here are the new arrivals,' said Christopher, drawing Robert's attention to a small company of twenty or so men, standing around a group of dusty-looking horses.

As Robert approached he was surprised to see a woman step out of their ranks, dressed in a mulberry-coloured cloak, fastened with a silver brooch. She was in her late thirties, with a proud, weathered face and sandy hair that was greying at her temples. He was even more surprised when she came forward and embraced him. Clasping her arms, Robert removed himself from her grasp. 'My lady . . .' he began, bemused, aware of the men looking over at him. One, standing at the front, was younger than the others, in his late teens. With his sandy hair and narrow-set eyes he was too alike the woman not to be related to her. They both had an odd familiarity, but Robert couldn't place it. The young man had his arms folded across his chest and was appraising him coolly.

The woman laughed at Robert's confusion. 'Do you not remember me, little brother?'

Recognition dawned. The woman was his half-sister, Margaret, the only child of his mother's first marriage. Robert hadn't seen her since he was a boy, for she had been wed at fifteen. He'd heard word of her over the years through his mother, then, more infrequently, his father and knew Margaret's husband, a knight from Roxburghshire, had died some time ago. 'Sister!' Laughing, he pulled her back into his arms.

Smiling broadly, Margaret motioned to the sandy-haired young man. 'This is Thomas Randolph, my son. Your nephew.'

Robert smiled and extended his hand. Thomas Randolph made no move to take it, but after a meaningful glare from his mother, he came forward and clasped it briefly.

'I didn't even know you had returned to Scotland,' said Margaret, looking back at Robert, 'until the fiery cross came through our village and people said you were gathering an army.'

'I had to keep my head down while I garnered support. I knew it was only a matter of time before the English came for me.'

'I've brought you my late husband's doughtiest men.' Margaret gestured to the horsemen at her back. 'Their swords are yours, brother.'

'I gratefully accept,' Robert told her, nodding a welcome to the men. 'I'll need all I can muster in the coming days.'

'Are the rumours true, Sir Robert?' Thomas's voice cut across them, cool and clipped. 'About what happened to John Comyn?'

Margaret's eyes narrowed. 'Thomas, I swear by God, I'll—'

'No, sister,' Robert cut in, 'I'm sure you both have questions.' He levelled his half-nephew with a stare. 'But there will be time to talk later. For now, I must hold a council of war.'

Thomas Randolph, caught under that gaze, looked away.

Robert cast his eyes back to Margaret, his expression lightening. 'We have family here you should see.' He called to the squire of one of his knights, who was heading past. 'Arthur, show my sister and her men a place where they can make camp, then escort her to Lady Christian's tent.'

Leaving Margaret and her belligerent son in the squire's care, Robert headed for his pavilion, noting the vestiges of the smile had faded from Christopher's face at the mention of John Comyn.

The war tent stood at the centre of the encampment. Two banners surged outside, one white, decorated with the red chevron of Carrick, the other yellow, crossed with the banded red saltire of Annandale. There was a crowd of men and horses there that Robert recognised as Bishop Wishart's entourage. Nes was talking to them. He was wearing a new mail hauberk, the rings of which glittered beneath his cloak. Two weeks ago, Robert had knighted the young man for his part in their escape from Dumfries.

That night, Nes, hearing the hue and cry raised by Comyn's men, had led the rest of Robert's company and the horses into the town, where he'd found his master fleeing the monastery. Mounting up, Robert and the others had taken flight through the streets of Dumfries, Comyn's men following doggedly. In an effort to slow pursuit, Robert had roused the townsfolk from their homes, calling them to arms as he cantered down the thoroughfares, the voices of his men joining his until the streets resounded with their shouts. Thinking marauders were attacking, the people of Dumfries had poured from their houses, brandishing knives and flaming torches.

Their progress impeded by the swelling rabble, Comyn's men had made instead for the castle on the outskirts of the town, where the first gathering of King Edward's new Scottish council was due to take place. Robert, guessing they were going for reinforcements, had made a bold decision. Shouting to the milling, agitated crowds that he had come to liberate them from their English oppressors, he had taken command of the mob. Bolstered by more than a hundred armed townsfolk, he and his men stormed the castle, routing the garrison, who fled when he threatened to burn down the building with them inside. Robert had let them go. Their escape did not matter. With that move, his campaign had begun and there was nothing to stand in his way.

Seeing Robert approaching, Nes came to greet him. 'Everyone's here, sir,' he said, falling into step beside him.

As they reached the pavilion, Robert caught sight of Elizabeth ducking out of the tent she shared with Marjorie. Her hand came up to shield her eyes from the sun as she surveyed the camp, not seeming to see him. She looked incredibly thin, her dress hanging loose on her frame. Looking at her now, it didn't seem possible that she would ever be able to bear the life she craved. Robert had an unexpected memory of Katherine, his first wife's maid, who had been his lover for a brief time until he discovered her infidelity. When he dismissed her from his presence, Katherine had told him she was pregnant. He rarely thought about her, but a flicker of question now crossed his mind. The thought passed as Elizabeth glanced in his direction. Robert met her gaze across the distance. He had given her trinkets and fur-lined cloaks, but it hadn't been enough. He must give her a child – the child she wanted and the heir he needed. Soon now, he promised her inwardly, after his coronation, she would have this.

As Nes swept aside the tent flaps, Robert headed in, his gaze going to the large round table in the centre. It was surrounded by fourteen men. John of Atholl was there, fists planted on the table, his expression intent. Beside the earl was his son David. Edward Bruce stood next to Neil Campbell, who had a new scar on his face from the skirmish with Menteith. Thomas Bruce nodded as he saw Robert, while Niall flashed a smile. Between them was Alexander Bruce, who had joined them in the autumn after Robert ordered him to leave his position as dean at Glasgow Cathedral. He had feared for his brother's safety, the benefice having been granted by King Edward, but Alexander had seen scant reason to thank him for his consideration. Robert was relieved he would be leaving his company today. He didn't need any more priests around him at the moment. He knew well enough the gravity of his sins.

William Lamberton looked round as Robert approached the table with Christopher and Nes. James Douglas was at the bishop's side, an air of determination in his stance. Beside him was Gilbert de la Hay, Lord of Erroll, once a staunch supporter of Wallace. The lord was built like a Caledonian pine, his flop of blond hair brushing the slanting canvas roof. The last four men at the table were James Stewart, Alexander Seton and two new arrivals. The broad, stooped form of Bishop Wishart, Robert was expecting. The other, a man of his own age with a handsome, hawk-like face and sleek dark hair, was a surprise. Robert's brow furrowed as he locked eyes with Malcolm of Lennox. The last time he'd seen the earl was in the Forest after Falkirk. Several years before that, Lennox had been one of the men who had laid siege to him and his father at Carlisle.

Malcolm immediately stepped forward and held out his hand. 'Sir Robert, I hear you need men for a new war against the English.'

When Robert hesitated, John of Atholl interjected. 'Sir Malcolm has brought a hundred from Lennox.'

'Then he is most welcome,' responded Robert, grasping the earl's hand.

'Sir Robert.'

He turned at the gruff voice to see Bishop Wishart peering up at him. Dropping to one knee, Robert kissed the ring on the old man's withered hand, then rose to embrace him. They had been in contact for months via messengers, but he hadn't seen the Bishop of Glasgow for several years. He was stunned at how much the man – one of the first guardians of Scotland during the interregnum – had aged. 'Your grace, it is good to have you here.'

Wishart gripped Robert's arms. 'Sir James said you were there in London, when William . . .' The bishop inhaled, the breath wheezing in his throat. 'Did he endure great suffering?'

Robert met the bishop's watery eyes. An image of William Wallace being drawn through the stinking city, naked and bound to a hurdle, flashed in his mind. He placed a hand on Wishart's shoulder. 'He suffers no longer.'

'In the arms of God,' murmured Lamberton, 'all find peace.'

Wishart pressed his lips together. He turned away and gestured brusquely to two pages who were waiting with a chest by the side of the tent. Together, they hefted it by its handles and carried it over. Wishart opened the lid and reached inside. 'I have something for you, Robert. Something I have kept hidden, hoping the hour would come when it was needed.'

Robert watched as Wishart drew out a folded square of gold cloth. Taking its edges in his hands, the bishop shook it open. As the cloth cascaded to the ground it unfurled to reveal a red lion, rearing rampant on glimmering gold. All the men at the table fell silent, staring in astonishment at the royal standard of Scotland. Pride swelled in Robert. He felt the will of his grandfather within him, compelling him to reach out and grasp the cloth, symbol of the Bruce legacy; his inheritance. As his fingers curled around the gold, he knew that the years of waiting, all the lies and the pretence, had been worth it. In less than a fortnight, he would be crowned king.

'Dear God, your grace,' murmured James Stewart. 'Where did you get that? I thought Longshanks took all the royal regalia to Westminster after the first conquest?'

'He missed one,' replied Wishart tartly. He gently removed the banner from Robert and passed it to the pages to be folded and stowed in the chest. 'I have also brought vestments from my wardrobe at Glasgow. They will be appropriate for the ceremony.'

'So everything is set?' asked Neil Campbell, looking between the bishop and Robert.

'As much as can be,' answered William Lamberton. He glanced over at the Earl of Lennox. 'We have agreed that the enthronement will take place on the feast of the Annunciation at Scone Abbey. The abbot has been informed and will preside over the proceedings. I will perform the ceremony itself.'

Malcolm nodded calmly, seeming to take the news of this revolutionary act in his stride. Robert guessed he had heard the rumours.

'What of the Stone of Destiny?' questioned Gilbert de la Hay. 'Forgive me,' he added to Robert, 'but can a king even be made without it?'

'The ritual will be the same in every other respect and will be done on the Moot Hill.' Robert paused, aware of the secret he harboured from them all and his failure to set that wrong right. 'My grandfather always said it is the man that makes the king.'

'Indeed,' said Lamberton, nodding in agreement. 'And, with the crown and sceptre we've had wrought, the royal banner will be a welcome addition to the day. I'd say we're set.'

'Then, there is just one last thing.' Robert's eyes went to John of Atholl. 'When can you leave?'

'Whenever you order it. My men and I are ready.'

At the earl's side, David gave a staunch nod.

'Today then,' Robert told them. 'The scouts say she is still in residence at her manor, but we do not know for how long. When you have her in your custody take her directly to Scone. I'll meet you there.'

'And if she won't come willingly?'

'Do not give her the choice,' said Robert flatly.

'Who?' asked Malcolm Lennox, glancing from Atholl to Robert.

'The final piece needed for the ceremony,' Robert answered brusquely. He turned to the others. 'Is there anything new from our scouts? Any sign of movement from the English?'

Neil Campbell answered first. 'Nothing. Since our uprising began the garrisons have barricaded themselves in their castles. I imagine they will remain there until reinforcements come from England.'

'An English mouse could fart in Scotland right now and we would all hear it,' voiced Gilbert de la Hay. 'I have never known them this quiet. And given the circumstances . . .?' He scowled. 'It is troubling.'

'It is the calm before the storm,' said Lamberton. 'When the roads clear, King Edward will come. And come hard. Sir Robert's swift actions these past weeks have given us some advantage; with so many western garrisons routed the king will be forced to come by the east. But, still, we cannot underestimate him, or the strength of arms he will bring.'

'We need more men,' said Edward Bruce, his voice hard. 'We do not have enough. Not nearly.' He scanned them all, before resting on Robert. 'Have you spoken to your wife? Perhaps, if Thomas and Alexander were to delay their journey until after the enthronement, she could travel with them — speak to her father? You are about to make her queen, after all.'

'That is a path I will not risk,' Robert answered. 'Not until I've exhausted every other hope of support. The Earl of Ulster is still King Edward's man. Thomas and Alexander will be seeking more likely allies in Ireland. Lord Donough and the men of Antrim will answer my call. As will, I believe, the MacDonalds of Islay. Our sister, Margaret,' he added to Edward, 'has just arrived from Roxburghshire with twenty horse. We have the knights of Atholl and Mar, and now Lennox.'

'When I get to the Forest I can bring the last of Sir William's band to the fight,' interjected Neil Campbell. 'We aren't many, but we are more than ready for this battle.'

'And with Rothesay back in Sir James's hands we can count on strong support from his lordships,' finished Robert. For the first time since entering the pavilion he locked eyes with the steward, who had been listening in silence.

'Of course,' replied James, after a pause. 'That goes without saying. But,' he continued, as Robert went to look away, ' even with all those you have mentioned that is still only half the realm.' His gaze went to Lamberton. 'It was not the plan to go to war as a divided kingdom, your grace.'

'That plan has changed, James,' murmured Lamberton. 'There is nothing we can do about it now. We must work with the men we have and go with whatever fortune God grants us. King Edward will come for us whether we do so or not. We have no choice.'

'We could go to the Comyns, try to make reparations, offer the heads of the households some position in the new realm? Tell them, unless they stand with us in this hour of need, all will remain subject to—'

'No,' Robert said abruptly, cutting off the steward. 'We will do this without the Comyns.' He laid his hands on the table top and scanned the others. 'Now, let us go through our strategy for the coming days. Much as I hate to admit it, Dumbarton will not fall in the time we have. We must move on.'

While Robert spoke, outlining his intentions, some of the men shared troubled glances as the silence between him and the steward continued, coldly palpable.

51

When the war council was over, Robert dismissed everyone except his brothers Thomas and Alexander. While the others headed out, talking among themselves, he led them into a private area of the pavilion, stacked with chests of his personal belongings, conveyed from Turnberry. His armour hung from a stand, a sword in its scabbard propped against it. The scarred blade had been given to him by John of Atholl, a replacement for his own, broken that night at Dumfries. Fionn was sprawled on some blankets. The hound opened one eye as Robert crossed to him. Ruffling his dog's grey ears, he dragged out one of the chests. He took up a key that swung from a chain on his belt and unlocked it.

Inside the chest, under a layer of clothes, was a long thin object bound in cloth. As Robert lifted the Staff of Malachy, the black lacquered box nestled beside it was dislodged. He paused there for a moment, eyes on the split in the side of the wood, all his questions and half-formed thoughts seething inside him, then he shut the chest and locked it. There was no time for answers or action on that. Not yet.

'Here,' he said, handing the staff to Alexander. 'When you arrive in Antrim, take this to the monks at Bangor Abbey. I don't know how long they will be able to keep it safe, but for the time being I imagine King Edward will have more pressing concerns than its recovery.'

Alexander took the staff reluctantly.

'Perhaps it will appease St Malachy enough to lift the curse from our family?' offered Thomas, glancing at Alexander.

'Return via Islay,' Robert told them. 'Tell Angus Og MacDonald the Bruce family calls on the old alliance with the lords of the Isles. While you're there get word to the MacRuaries. I want to try to enlist the galloglasses for the coming fight. They would be a great asset.'

'The mercenaries?' Thomas frowned. 'Forgive me, brother, but the MacRuaries and their kin switch sides more than you do.'

'They go where the money is,' said Robert. Opening another chest, he took out a coffer that he handed to his brother. 'Tell them there will be more if they aid their new king.'

'We'll leave as soon as the horses are ready,' answered Thomas, 'hopefully make it across before the spring tides churn up the race.' He gripped Robert's shoulder briefly. 'I'm sorry we'll miss your coronation.'

'You'll make it up to me if you return with half of Ireland at your back.'

Thomas grinned and headed out, but Alexander lingered, the staff in his hands. 'Before I go, Robert, will you do as I have asked? Will you let me hear your confession?'

Robert turned away.

Alexander stepped towards him, his brow creasing. 'You may have cleaned the blood from your blade, but you cannot so easily cleanse the stain on your soul. Brother, you have committed a deadly sin. What you and Christopher did was sacrilege. You must make reparation, if not to the Comyns then certainly before God. Let me stay. Send Niall or Edward with Thomas. Use me as your confessor, rather than as a messenger of war.'

Robert twisted round. 'I need soldiers, Alex, not priests!'

Alexander started back at the fury in his voice. After a pause, he left.

Robert waited a moment, then pushed through into the main section of the pavilion. He halted as James Stewart turned to him.

'Your brother still won't be wrong, Robert. However far away you send him.'

'I don't have time for this.'

James moved in front of Robert, as he made for the tent opening. 'I meant what I said about making amends with the Comyn family. You told us it was an accident, that Sir John attacked without warning and you were defending yourself. That you had no choice but to kill him.'

'It was,' said Robert sharply, thinking he heard doubt in the steward's tone.

'The Comyns need to know that. Everything has happened so quickly. You've been running full tilt since Dumfries. You haven't paused to think about what you've done, about the harm you've caused.'

'The harm I've caused? The harm was yours — yours and Lamberton's. You forced me to agree to that foolish plan. None of this would have happened if I hadn't revealed my intentions to the Comyns. John Comyn would still be alive, King Edward would know nothing of my treason and the head of William Wallace would not now be rotting on London Bridge!'

The steward flinched at this last. 'There was no other option. That's why you agreed with the plan. Do not blame me for something you yourself knew to be true.'

Robert stalked the tent, pushing his hand through his hair. 'All the while I was in England, shackled in Edward's service – betraying my friends and fighting my countrymen, as you convinced me I must – John Comyn was here, building support for his own ambition. God damn it, James, the man wanted to be king! Of course he wouldn't endorse my bid!'

'None of us could have known he would—'

'All these years I've followed your advice, trusted you as my grandfather did. I never stopped to question why you wanted me to take the throne. Now, I think I understand. Without a king the position of high steward is fairly well redundant, isn't it? You're desperate to claw back your own power and you're using me to get it. You speak of the need for reparation?' Robert stepped up to the steward. 'John Comyn's blood is on your hands as much as mine. We'll both have to reap that whirlwind.'

This time, as he moved towards the tent opening, James didn't stand in his way.

Robert strode through the camp, ignoring the calls of greeting or question from those he passed. Finding a secluded spot on the banks of the Clyde, he sat and stared out over the estuary. Picking up a handful of stones, he tossed them viciously into the water. They peppered the surface. As he sat there, the wind whipping his hair around his face, the anger slowly drained from him, washed away by a cold tide of guilt.

You told us it was an accident.

He could lie to them all. God knows, he'd had enough practice. But he couldn't lie to himself.

Inwardly, he had attempted to defend his killing of John Comyn, telling himself it had been revenge for William Wallace and for the Comyns' crimes against his own family; an honour killing, performed in the name of his grandfather. He had even told himself what he'd told James and the others: that if he hadn't struck first the man would have slain him. But no matter the partial accuracy of these statements he couldn't deny the truth of the moment he plunged the dagger up under Comyn's ribs. The act, when it happened, had not been born out of vengeance or fear. It had been born out of pure, murderous pleasure. In that split second, he had wanted to kill Comyn, not for anyone else, but for himself; for the hot, satisfying thrill of it.

Picking up another stone, Robert ground it between his palms. In his mind's eye he saw himself at sixteen in the church of Scone Abbey surrounded by the men of the realm, all shouting furiously at one another. Word had just come of the death of the Maid of Norway and the succession was once again in question. He recalled his grandfather's harsh voice and John Comyn's father reaching for his dirk as he harangued the old man. Robert had drawn his sword to defend his grandfather. As he'd pointed it at the Lord of Badenoch's throat, all the men present had fallen into silence. His grandfather had put a hand on his shoulder, told him to lower the blade. Robert's brow furrowed as he heard his own voice, echoing down the years.

'Why would you care that I drew my sword against him, when you attacked his castles? You hate him!'

'Yes! And that hatred has the power to rip this kingdom apart!'

Rising to his feet, Robert fought off the memories. What was done was done. There was no use looking back. In two weeks' time he would be crowned king. That was, after all, what they had all wanted; these men, past and present, who now plagued him with questions and doubt. Robert glanced down at the stone in his hand, then tossed it into the river. As he turned and headed up the bank, behind him the ripples spread.

52

The young men were crushed into the abbey, in a stew of breath and sweat. Almost three hundred in number, they jostled one another, feverish with excitement as they struggled to see those in front receive the accolade, impatient for their own turn. Most had spent the night in vigil at the nearby church of the Knights Templar, numbed by the stone beneath their knees and the long dark in waiting. Around them, radiating out among the marble pillars and tombs of the dead, lords and ladies were packed into the abbey to watch the spectacle.

One by one, when called, the men moved to stand before a dais erected at the crossing of the abbey. On the platform was Prince Edward of Caernarfon, surrounded by the elite of his household. The twenty-one-year-old prince was dressed in a white surcoat trimmed with gold, drawn in at his waist by a belt studded with rubies and sapphires. His blond hair was sleek with perfumed oil, his beard clipped and neat, and golden spurs adorned his boots. He held a broadsword, the blade of which gleamed in the jewelled brilliance of the sun streaming through the abbey's rose windows. The sword had been girded on him in the palace chapel that morning, when his father made him a knight and Duke of Gascony.

The prince ordered each aspirant who came before him to kneel. With every dubbing, a hush came over the crowd as they strained to hear the oath of knighthood, before the prince raised his sword and brought the flat of the blade down on the candidate's shoulders. As each man rose, those around him roared in approval, the noise swelling back through the abbey as those who couldn't see joined in the celebration. Each newly made knight was presented with a surcoat and spurs by one of the prince's house-hold, themselves all knighted that morning. Piers Gaveston was among them, never far from the prince's side, his black hair and olive skin dark against the white of his surcoat.

King Edward, seated on his throne, watched as his son knighted another candidate. He sensed the fervour in the young men before him, many of whom would have been hungry for this moment for years. Tonight they would feast in Westminster Palace and confirm their vows over two golden swans, in a pageant to rival any witnessed in the court of Camelot. It made Edward recall his own knighthood – the transformation he'd felt during the solemn ritual; the sense of becoming. He had been fifteen at the time, several years younger than the aspirants here. The ceremony had been performed in Castile by King Alfonso. That same day he had married the king's thirteen-year-old sister, Eleanor.

The memory pricked Edward with discontent, tormenting him with the still clear image of himself as that athletic youth, full of vigour and brimming with ambition. The parchment-thin skin of his hands curled around the arms of the throne, the ache in his bones, the thinness of his hair, as white as the ermine trim of his robes: all told a tale of years passed and purpose unfulfilled. It maddened him, these young bloods with their supple limbs and fresh faces. He had the same insatiable drive he'd had in youth, but it was trapped now in the decaying body of a man in his late sixties.

Death stretched hoary hands towards him. He could feel its fingers under his skin, picking apart sinew and muscle, clawing at his bowels. The sickness that had come upon him during the withdrawal from Scotland had worsened over the winter, turning his insides to water. The rich meats and wine he had enjoyed all his life had become sources of pain rather than pleasure. His cooks now delivered small, bland morsels and even those plain meals he could barely keep inside him. The skin shrivelled on his broad frame, the muscles shrinking on to his bones. Pain was a constant companion, a gnawing ache growing in the pit of his stomach. But there was one thing that kept him going, one thing that roused him each morning and compelled him through every day. Rage.

At the end of last summer, Edward had thought his life's work done. Wales, Ireland and Gascony were under his control as was Scotland, which he had turned from a kingdom into a land, taking the symbols of its sovereignty into his custody, first the Stone of Destiny then the young Earl of Fife with his hereditary right as kingmaker. The Scottish magnates had submitted to him, John Balliol was, by all accounts, drowning in claret and self-pity in Picardy and the quartered limbs of William Wallace were rotting in the sun. In gathering Brutus's relics Edward had – in the eyes of his men – saved Britain from the ruin foretold in Merlin's prophecy, embodying a new King Arthur. But all that time he'd had a serpent in his house, just waiting for the moment to slither from the shadows and strike.

When the treachery of Robert Bruce was exposed, on the day of Wallace's execution, rage had threatened to consume Edward. Later, discovering through the interrogation of the guards at the abbey that Bruce had taken both the Staff of Malachy and the prophecy box, he thought he would go insane with it. Then, gradually, over the months that followed, that madness had subsided to a burning, white-hot desire for vengeance. Edward knew now what Aymer de Valence had warned him of all along: his obsession with bringing down Wallace had blinded him to the threat of Bruce. He had underestimated the man: had thought him to be like his father, ambitious, but ultimately pliable.

Now, reports were streaming in from garrisons across Scotland. Robert Bruce had murdered John Comyn and raised a rebellion. Castles in the west were falling to his forces and the first assembly of the king's new council had been routed. With these frantic messages came word that Bruce was planning to seize the throne. It was playing out as the letter found on Wallace had implied it would, although the murder of Comyn had been a revelation.

Often during these past weeks, Edward wondered if he could have acted sooner. Whether – the moment Valence and the company who had pursued Bruce north had returned empty-handed – he could have sent an army after the Scot. But the winter storms had been closing in and he'd needed time to summon his vassals and gather supplies for a counter-strike. Instead, Edward sent word to his garrisons along the border, ordering them to hunt down the renegade. Word had soon come back, informing him that Bruce was holed up in Turnberry, but that heavy snowfalls made it impossible for them to deploy siege engines that far west. With the castle newly strength-ened and reports of a large force of men having joined Bruce, the king's men feared an effective siege would be difficult to mount until the roads were clear. Edward had recalled them, ordering them to hold their posi-tions. He hadn't wanted to run the risk of Bruce dying in some futile skir-mish. He wanted to capture the man himself. He had to, in order to redeem himself in the eyes of his subjects, or his life's work would be for nothing, his legacy corrupted before his death. And so he had waited, all through the winter, gathering his forces and stoking that white-hot fire in his mind.

A week ago, when the spring rains were swelling the waters of the Thames, Edward made Aymer de Valence his new Lieutenant of Scotland

and sent the knight north at the head of a host of men. This advance was to
subdue Bruce's uprising and pin down the man himself until Edward could
arrive with the royal army, fortified by his son and the young bloods being
dubbed today. It did not matter that Bruce was an earl, or that he might
even be king by the time they caught up with him. Chivalry had flown in
the face of Edward's rage. He would tear the man apart in front of his own
people. His limbs, and those of any who supported him, would be strung
up to rot next to Wallace's, a banquet for the crows.

At their parting, the king had given Valence the faded banner he had
carried in war since youth. 'Raise the dragon, cousin. No mercy is to be
shown to any who have joined Bruce's uprising; kill them all. But the man
himself is mine. You understand?'

'Yes, my lord,' Valence had promised, his dark eyes burning with zeal.

To Edward, watching him ride out at the head of the host, he had seemed
like a man embarking on a crusade.

A cheer brought the king back to the present as another man was
knighted. The excitement among the young recruits in the abbey didn't
extend to the barons ranked in front of Edward's throne. These older men,
who had sacrificed much in the fight against Scotland, were watching the
spectacle in silence. Like him, they knew this was no feast day celebration,
but as much a preparation for the coming war as the supplies of grain and
meat being stockpiled in Carlisle, the taxes being levied and the soldiers
being summoned by the commissioners of array. To them this ritual was
another exercise in patience while they waited for the revenge they craved.
Bruce's betrayal had affected them all, but it had cut deepest through those
he had been closest to, none more so than Humphrey de Bohun. All now
wanted their pound of flesh; were ready to fight and die for it.

But would these silent, belligerent men who had dedicated their lives in
service to him – sworn oaths of undying loyalty around the oak of his
Round Table – be so ready and willing if they knew the truth? Edward's
hands whitened on the arms of the throne as he thought of the locked box
Robert Bruce had taken from Westminster Abbey. The box that contained
the greatest lie of his reign.

53

'We go after him now, before the bastard has the chance to take the throne.' Dungal MacDouall stalked the dais as he spoke, his voice splintered with fury. 'Give me leave to raise the men of Galloway. We can still stop this.'

The Black Comyn sat at the table, hands clasped as if in prayer, although his eyes remained open, fixed on a point in the hall before him, where his wife's servants were scattering rushes over the floor. 'No.' The earl's broad shoulders swelled as he inhaled. 'We cannot. My scouts tell me Bruce intends to be crowned at Scone on the feast of the Annunciation. That is less than a week away. I have summoned my kin from Buchan and Badenoch, but the snows still lie heavy across much of the north. My people will not get here in time. Bruce's army has grown since Dumfries. The Disinherited, however strong their lust for blood, will not be enough to counter his force.'

MacDouall strode to the front of the table. Leaning forward, he forced the earl to look at him. 'Bruce's allies are claiming he was defending himself at Greyfriars, but John's men told us the lord was unarmed when he went into that church. Bruce murdered my master – your kinsman – in cold blood! He cannot go unpunished.'

'I am not suggesting he will,' said the earl, his dark eyes fixing on MacDouall's rigid face. 'But we must have patience while we prepare our plans. Any action we take will be considered and well executed. I want our revenge to be both effective and lasting.'

MacDouall's jaw tightened, but he nodded. 'Bruce must have had some warning back in London to have escaped their clutches, mustn't he? We know the English found the letter we put on Wallace. We were supposed to be the ones planning a coronation, damn it. Bruce was meant to be rotting in the Tower!'

'I expect we'll never know what happened. We failed and John paid the price for that. All that is left to us is vengeance.' The Black Comyn rose. 'But it will be well served. When we strike, I want him to feel every inch of it.'

'It will be regicide if we kill him when he's king.'

'I do not care what crown that brigand wears upon his head,' growled the earl. 'He will never be my king.'

'What about the throne? Who will take it when we remove him?'

'Those are questions for the future. First, we rouse our supporters. The Red and the Black Comyns and the Comyns of Kilbride will be ready when the time comes, but we need others. I will head west, meet with my allies there. The MacDougalls and their kin will join us, of that I am certain. John was the Lord of Argyll's nephew. He must fulfil a blood oath against his murderer.'

'Then I have leave to go to Galloway? Raise my men for our war?'

'Yes. But when you have summoned the Disinherited you will not go after Bruce until I give the order. First, there is another alliance I want you to secure.'

Isabel watched from the window as the men gathered in the yard outside. Her husband was among them, his hulking, black-cloaked form moving purposefully through their ranks. The squares of leaded glass fragmented his progress, distorting her view as he mounted his warhorse, whipping the beast with the reins to keep it still. Around him, his knights and squires climbed into the saddles of their palfreys, the grooms leading pack-horses burdened with supplies. Her husband hadn't deigned to tell her where he was going, but her stable-master had. He was heading for Argyll to raise his allies against Robert Bruce. Captain Dungal MacDouall had left that morning, taking the road south from the manor. As she watched her husband ride out along the western road, Isabel sensed the hot breath of war in the air.

Beyond the track, fields and pastures rolled down towards the sea, seven miles away at St Andrews. Their brown contours were speckled with the first crops of oat and barley, the shades of green bright in the afternoon sun. Once, she would have felt the promise of spring, of hope in those new shoots. But now there was nothing in her heart but the wasted void of winter. As the horsemen disappeared from view, the crows settling in the fields once more, Isabel stepped back from the window. Catching sight of her reflection in the glass, she stared at the bruise that shadowed the side of her face, darkening to purple around her eye.

She received it two days ago, for asking her husband what the rebellion would mean for her nephew, still in King Edward's custody. His fist had been the answer, coming out of nowhere, shocking her to silence. Agnes had tried to put a poultice on it, but Isabel had stopped her. The bruises were a reassuring explanation for the pain. Crossing to the bed, the countess lay down, twisting the coverlet between her fingers as she watched the sky change from turquoise to indigo. Clouds were rearing in the east and the chamber was full of shadows by the time she closed her eyes.

Isabel sat up suddenly, the covers falling back. She stared around her, disorientated by the change in the room. A candle on the stand opposite her bed guttered, causing shadows to shift across the walls. Agnes must have lit it while she was sleeping. Isabel was about to settle back down, thinking her dreams must have disturbed her, when she heard a piercing cry echo outside, followed by rough shouts and the thud of hooves. She scrambled from the bed, the fog of sleep vanishing instantly.

Going quickly to the window, she saw a company of men riding in through the yard, wielding torches that threw a fierce red light up the sides of the barns and outbuildings. At first she thought her husband had returned, then she saw that these men had swords drawn. As she watched, the men the earl had left to guard the manor burst out from the door below. The horsemen spurred to meet them, the clash of weapons ringing in the night. Isabel whirled around as her door crashed open. Her maids came rushing in, along with several male servants, her cook and steward among them.

Agnes's face was drained of colour. 'My lady,' she cried, going to the countess and clutching her arms.

'Who are they, Fergus?' Isabel demanded of her steward, who was helping the cook and kitchen boys drag chests in front of the door, barricading it.

'I don't know, my lady,' panted the steward. 'The brigands slew the gatehouse guards and came at us out of the dark.'

Outside, the crash of swords continued.

As a ragged scream rose, Agnes gripped Isabel's arms until her nails bit into the countess's skin. 'God save us!'

Isabel's eyes alighted on a poker hanging by the hearth. Pulling from the maid's grasp, she crossed to it. Soot smattered the skirts of her grey silk gown as she lifted its iron length. 'Offer them whatever they want, Fergus,' she instructed her steward. 'Coins. My jewels. Anything. You understand?'

'Yes, my lady.'

There was a bang below as the front door was forced open. Agnes was cowering in a corner. The other maids, all young girls, were pressed up against the wall, sobbing. The fluttering candlelight threw mad shadows over all of them. Fergus and the cook, who was wielding a saucepan, were standing before the door, behind the stack of chests, breathing hard. Crashing sounds echoed up from downstairs, punctuated by the odd shout. Heavy footfalls thumped up the stairs. Isabel gripped the poker, her heart thrumming in her chest. She heard doors being thrown open down the passage, an exchange of voices. She started as the bolt rattled on her bedchamber door. The voices were audible now.

'This one's locked, sir.'

'Break it down.'

The door shuddered in its frame as the men outside slammed against it, the chests jolting with every impact. Agnes and the maids were crying in terror; the cook and kitchen boys had staggered back. It was Isabel and Fergus now, standing before the door. With the next bang the bolt snapped off the frame and the door shuddered open, the chests sliding a little way across the floor. Isabel flinched as a man's face appeared in the crack, torch flames lighting him from behind.

He was bearded and rough-looking, his eyes lighting up as he saw her. His mouth twisted. 'In here, sir!'

Fergus moved to Isabel's side as the men forced the door the rest of the way open, the coffers no match for their strength. One chest toppled, then the others. Isabel held her ground, though her arms were shaking. The rough man entered first, a sword in his hand. Behind him came one who was about the same age as her husband, with dark curly hair. Isabel's eyes widened in recognition. It was the Earl of Atholl.

He too had a sword in his hand, but he lowered it as he saw her. 'Lady Isabel.'

'Sir John?' Isabel shook her head in confusion. 'I thought you were a common brigand, come to rob me.' Her relief retreated as she thought of the earl's ally, Robert Bruce; her husband's enemy and murderer of his kinsman. 'Have you come to kill more Comyns?' she murmured.

Behind her, Agnes let out a whimper. Fergus stood his ground, but he was ashen in the torchlight.

'That is not my intention.'

'No?' Isabel swallowed back the terrible dryness in her mouth. 'You killed my guards.'

'Only those who resisted. The rest have been disarmed. I will let them and all your household live if you come with me.'

'The countess will go nowhere with you,' warned Fergus, though his voice trembled.

'Go where?' asked Isabel, moving in front of her steward, the poker still brandished in front of her.

John's eyes, dark and intense like her husband's, went to the makeshift weapon, then back to her. The corner of his mouth lifted, but the faint smile didn't seem cruel or mocking. 'To Scone Abbey, my lady. Sir Robert has need of your service. In five days he will take the throne of Scotland. But he cannot be made without the Earl of Fife.'

'My nephew is in England, in the custody of King Edward.'

'We know this. We need one of his blood to officiate in his absence.'

Isabel was so stunned by the revelation she almost laughed. Her arms dropped, the tip of the poker banging against the floor. 'You want me to place the crown on the new king's head?' When John of Atholl inclined his head, an icy tide flooded her. 'My husband would strip the flesh from my bones. Please, Sir John, do not ask me to do this.'

'Sir Robert will protect you, my lady. You will be well cared for in his company, of that I assure you.' The earl's eyes went to the side of her face.

Isabel had no doubt he was looking at the bruise. Ashamed, she started to turn her head so her hair would tumble in front of it, then stopped herself. 'Do I even have a choice?'

'My orders are to bring you to Scone, willing or not. I would rather it was the former.'

'You will spare my household?'

'You have my word.'

As Isabel bent and laid the poker on the floor, Agnes cried out behind her. 'My lady!'

Leaving the maids and her ashen-faced steward, Isabel walked towards the earl. Moving out into the passage, through the crowd of armed men waiting there, she felt a strange numbness settle over her. As she headed slowly down the passage towards the stairs, past open doors and broken furniture, John of Atholl fell into step beside her, after ordering his men to secure the servants in one of the rooms.

'We've been watching your manor. Your husband left earlier today. Where did he go?'

'To Argyll,' she told him, amazed at how readily the words came. 'To raise the MacDougalls against Sir Robert.' Isabel saw Sir John's face tighten in the flush of torchlight as they descended the stairs.

'And MacDouall?'

'I don't know. My husband sent him south.'

Sir John led the way out into the yard, where her husband's guards had been rounded up. They were kneeling in the mud, hands bound behind their backs. A few were injured. They stared at her as she passed. Some of them called out, their voices strained with anger and confusion. Her husband's remaining horses had been led out of the stables and were now sent galloping into the night as Atholl's men whipped at their flanks with the flats of their blades. So no one could follow, she guessed. As Sir John spoke with his knights, leaving her alone in the ring of men, Isabel glimpsed several bodies being dragged into the shadows of a barn.

'It's a raw night.'

Isabel started and turned to see a young man behind her. He looked a lot like the earl.

'Here,' he said, holding out a fur-trimmed cloak, 'put this on.'

As the young man placed it gently around her shoulders, Isabel heard him murmur.

'My father will not harm you.'

'David,' called Atholl, striding over. 'Mount up. We're leaving.'

As the men sheathed their swords and headed for their horses, Isabel felt an urge to weep, but it wasn't out of fear or sadness. John of Atholl climbed into his saddle and held out his hand to her. She took it, surprised by its strength and warmth, then dug her foot into his stirrup and pushed up, allowing him to haul her up behind him. She sat sideways, her gown cascading down the dusty rump of the horse. Isabel put her arms around Atholl's waist and held on tight as he spurred out of the yard, followed by his men. As they sped west across the dark fields, the winking lights of her manor fading behind her, the cold March wind stung her face. The tears, for so long frozen inside her, at last began to flow, the green smell of the crops and soil rising all around her.

54

Robert stood before the Moot Hill, a storm of emotion rising in him. His blood seemed hotter, faster in his veins, as if awakened by the spirit of the place that had made his ancestors kings. He felt proud to be fulfilling the ambition of his family; defiant in the face of his enemies who had tried to thwart his attempts to reach this place.

There was a great deal of activity around the low hill, which lay between the sandstone buildings of the Augustinian abbey and the royal burgh of Scone. Flags were being strung between the trees and sprigs of hawthorn spread over the freshly sawn timbers of a dais set in the centre. Two pages were hefting a chair on to the platform, under the scrutinising gaze of Bishop Lamberton. Other servants filed between the hill and the vast encampment that stretched across the abbey grounds, veiled by a gauzy shroud of smoke.

Even though it was early, the camp was bustling with life, excitement palpable in snatches of conversation and laughter. High-ranking magnates had taken up residence in the burgh, while Robert and his family had installed themselves in the abbey itself. It had been disconcerting, returning to the scene of his crime as a guest of honour. He had been relieved to find the elderly abbot he and the Knights of the Dragon encountered when they took the Stone of Destiny had been succeeded by a brisk young man, who was only too keen to put himself at the disposal of his soon-to-be king.

Following the progress of the servants, all carrying paraphernalia for the coming ceremony, Robert's gaze alighted on a couple strolling through the herb gardens a short distance away. It was his sister and Christopher Seton. They were walking close together, heads bowed in conversation. As Robert watched, Christian paused by a rosemary bush and bent to touch the leaves.

Christopher crouched beside her, his gaze on her while she talked, her smiling now and then, him nodding at her words.

The moment of simple affection, stolen in the midst of the momentous occasion, lifted Robert's heart and made him long for a time to come, untroubled by war or strife. He felt determined to offer the men and women who followed him a new Scotland rebuilt under him, a kingdom free from the yoke of England. He remembered the peace before Alexander III plunged to his death, before John Balliol took the throne and surrendered their liberties. His gaze on his sister and comrade, Robert vowed to bring back those days. With the green hill being readied for his inauguration, the lively sounds coming from the camp and the flush of warmth from the sun on his face, it all seemed possible.

Hearing the jingle of mail behind him, Robert turned to see two of his knights approaching. Both looked serious of face. He had his men guarding the periphery of the town and abbey, not willing to take any chances that this long-awaited day could yet be disrupted. Behind the knights were three others, who had halted some distance away. There was a woman with them.

'Sir, there's someone here claiming to be an old friend of yours. She requested a private audience.'

Robert stared at the woman, who was dressed in a plain gown, mostly covered by a patterned woollen cloak that swamped her thin frame. 'Did she give her name?'

'Brigid, sir. She said you would know her aunt. Affraig?'

Robert let out a surprised puff of breath at the name, focusing on the woman with new eyes. A lifetime ago, he had followed her through the bracken hills around Turnberry, trailing her to Affraig's house. He had a vague memory of her crouching before him by the fire, the day he'd fallen from his horse, a cloth bunched in her hand to wipe the blood from his face. 'Bring her here,' he murmured.

He watched as she was led to him, his knights surrounding her. Brigid's face became clearer as she approached, the skin stretched taut over the bones of her cheeks and jaw, strands of black hair drifting from beneath her hood. There was an echo of the strange, ratty-haired girl he had known in that gaunt face, but it was faint. The years had stripped any real familiarity. He motioned his men away when she came before him, but they didn't stray far. Brigid had a sack bag slung over her shoulder and her shoes were caked with mud from the road.

She inclined her head. 'Earl Robert.'

'Brigid? What are you doing here?' He frowned past her, wondering. 'Is—'

'My aunt isn't with me,' answered Brigid, before he could ask. Her Gaelic rang with the lilt of the west, reminding him of his mother. 'She wanted to be here for your coronation, but she's too frail for such a journey. She sent me in her stead.' Brigid paused, cocking her head, her blue eyes liquid in the sunlight. 'She wondered why you didn't visit her in Turnberry in the winter.'

'I wanted to,' said Robert, the lie slipping easily from him, unlike the Gaelic which he hadn't spoken for a long time. 'But I had to be wary. I thought the English would come for me.'

In truth, he hadn't wanted to see the old woman. A lot had changed since he had sat before her, asking her to weave his destiny. He had been young then and naïve, heady with the split from his father and King Edward, intoxicated by his newfound independence and his decision to be king. However solemn the ritual had seemed, events since had taught him the way of the world, had made a cynic of him. Spells and prayers did not mean what they once had. He thought of the black interior of that empty box, reflecting back on itself.

'She would have liked to see you.'

'Where is your husband?' he asked, keen to change the subject. 'You cannot have made the journey by yourself.'

'Dead. The English raid on Ayr,' she added, when his brow creased in question. 'My boy too.' Brigid held up her hand as Robert went to speak. 'These are not stories for today. I have simply come to pay my family's respects to our lord on the day of his crowning.'

'Then stay with my blessing.' Robert gestured to his knights, lingering close. 'Escort the lady to the camp,' he called. 'Tell Nes to look after her.' He hesitated as he looked back at Brigid, the prophecy box still in his mind. 'Let us speak more after my coronation. I may have need of your aunt's help in the coming weeks.'

'Another destiny?'

'No. Something else.'

As the knights led Brigid towards the encampment, Robert felt the urge to ask the question he'd avoided. 'My destiny,' he called at her back, thinking of the crown of heather and broom hanging in its web in Affraig's tree. 'Did it ever fall?'

Brigid looked round, the sunlight harsh on her face. 'Not by the time I left, Sir Robert. Perhaps now?'

He laughed dryly in response, although he noticed her expression remained serious as she turned away. Robert watched her go. He wanted to believe, but these days he thought a man might make his own destiny.

They gathered in the burgeoning warmth of the March sunshine, crowding together on the Moot Hill, where countless Scots had stood before them to watch a new king made. Earls, ladies and knights in their finery were joined by monks from the abbey, their black habits switching in the breeze. William Lamberton's strident voice carried across their ranks as he administered the oath of kingship.

In the centre of the crowd, Robert sat on the throne raised on the dais. He wore the jewelled vestments Wishart had brought from Glasgow, which smelled faintly of incense. An ermine-trimmed mantle had been placed about his shoulders by the Abbot of Scone and he had been handed a sceptre and girded with a sword, symbolising his authority and his pledge to defend his kingdom. Behind him, fluttering in the wind, was the royal standard, the red lion shifting on its golden ground. Beside him, seated on a cushioned chair set by the platform, was Elizabeth, dressed in white silk. Her hands were folded in her lap and her head was bowed. Robert couldn't see her expression.

His gaze moved from his wife to Marjorie, standing at the front of the throng, white flowers threaded through her hair. Her little face, so very serious as she listened to the bishop's words, made him want to smile. The rest of his family stood behind his daughter, his three sisters cutting dashing forms in their gowns and robes, his half-sister Margaret glowing with pride beside her unsmiling son. Robert's gaze drifted over Niall and Edward. They were no doubt both aware of the possibility of his succession passing to them in future if he had no male heirs. Beyond them, comrades, vassals and supporters stretched away – a sea of faces. His subjects. Robert caught the gaze of James Stewart fleetingly, then looked away.

When Lamberton finished reading the oath, the bishop nodded to John of Atholl. The earl stepped aside revealing a tall woman dressed in a grey gown, a winter-white mantle falling from her shoulders. All eyes were on Isabel of Buchan as she moved tentatively towards the dais at a nod of encouragement from Atholl. In the countess's hands was a gold circlet. As she approached, Robert noticed a bruise on her face, its darkness ugly against her pale beauty. He frowned, wondering if she'd had been injured during her abduction, but when they met last night Atholl had assured him she had been well cared for.

Isabel climbed on to the lower step of the dais, stretching out her arms towards his head. Her hands were shaking and she almost dropped the crown, causing a fretful murmur to rise from the crowd. Smiling, Robert leaned forward and lowered his head so she could better reach. Carefully, Isabel placed the circlet on his black hair. The crowd burst into loud applause, to the disapproval of the abbot who raised his hands for quiet. Expressing in a nod what he hoped would reveal some measure of his gratitude to Isabel, Robert sat back, feeling the crown's new weight on his head.

The last part of the ceremony – the reading of the rolls – was then observed, the names of Scotland's kings, from Kenneth MacAlpin, down through Macbeth and Malcolm Canmore to Alexander III and John Balliol, called out by a poet, whose voice rang clear across the hilltop. And with that, the ceremony was complete.

The monks began to usher people down the Moot Hill towards the church, where Lamberton was to say a High Mass, before the magnates retired to the abbey palace for a feast. As his friends and family came over to greet him, Robert smiled, but dismissed any attempts at conversation, going instead to Elizabeth. Taking her hand, he kissed it. As Elizabeth looked up at him, her face proud, but marble cold, Robert was struck by the woman she had become, overnight it seemed. He realised she was wearing the ivory cross her father had given to her. He hadn't seen it in a long while. 'Things will be different now,' he told her. 'I haven't been the husband you deserve, but I will be the king you need.'

Elizabeth shook her head. 'This is all a show, Robert. Child's play.' Her eyes went to the throne on the dais. 'This ceremony. This ritual. You cannot become king in this way.'

Robert's eyes narrowed at her words. 'It may not be as I hoped it would, but my inauguration is, I assure you, no show. I am now king by ancient right, and you are queen.'

'You aren't here by right.' Elizabeth's tone hardened, though she kept her voice low as the crowds continued to file past, people laughing and talking. 'You are here by revolution and murder. I know what you did in Dumfries. John Comyn's blood is on your hands. Do you think the rest of the realm will follow you when they know what you've done? You will be half a king, unrecognised by half your subjects.'

Robert wondered if she had been talking to her uncle – whether James had put her up to this. 'When the English come, the rest will soon acknowledge me. They will have little choice if they want to survive the war that is coming.'

'And the Comyns?'

'I am making plans to counter that threat.' Robert exhaled his irritation and placed his hands on her shoulders. 'You do not need to concern yourself, Elizabeth. I have many supporters, all ready and willing for this fight, and more being called each day. I believe we can stand against King Edward, even without the full support of the realm.'

'King Edward is not the only one who will come for you.' Some of the tension seemed to drain from her, her face filling with sorrow. 'Humphrey will come for you. All those you called brothers back in England will come for you. My father too, most likely.'

'I know this,' Robert said quietly, pricked by the mention of Humphrey. His was a name he had tried in vain to forget these past months.

Elizabeth hesitated, then put a cool hand over his where it rested on her shoulder. 'I am your wife, Robert. I have raised your daughter and kept your hearth warm these past four years. I will do my duty as your queen, that I promise, but I cannot trust in what you have done. Pride, my father told me, always comes before a fall.' She lifted his hand and kissed it, before walking away down the hill to join the crowd heading for the church.

Robert watched her go, the doom in her words lingering in his mind as he stood on the Moot Hill in the spring sunlight, the crown of Scotland a cold hard band around his scalp.

The Border, Scotland, 1306 AD

The English advance was approaching the border. Before them the green swell of hills surrounding the town of Berwick was cut by the broad ribbon of the Tweed. At the head of the two-thousand-strong host of men rode Aymer de Valence. He sat at ease in the saddle of his warhorse, the fish-scale shimmer of mail beneath his surcoat. He wore an arming cap, but no helm, feeling no threat. The king had taken Berwick a decade ago, after three days of slaughter at the start of the war. It had been an English town ever since. Here, they would gather supplies and reinforcements, before heading deeper into Scotland to hunt down and capture Robert Bruce.

Behind Aymer was raised the blue and white standard of Pembroke, the earldom to which he was heir. It was dwarfed by the scarlet sweep of the dragon banner that he had ordered hoisted that morning as they came within sight of Scotland.

'Sir!'

Aymer looked round to see one of his knights pointing to a ridge. Shielding his eyes from the sun, he followed the man's gaze. There, on the crest, was a band of mounted men. As he watched more figures appeared on the ridge behind, most on foot. Several hundred strong, he calculated quickly, catching the glint of iron from helms and spearheads. At once, Valence turned and roared at his knights. Horns were lifted, blowing a warning to the rest of the company that snaked down the road behind, their length increased by a train of supply wagons. Men, roused to the danger, rushed to arm themselves, infantry hefting falchions, archers priming bows.

The mass of men above made no move as Valence and his knights formed up, wheeling their warhorses around.

Aymer's brow creased as he drew his sword. 'Why don't they charge?' he growled.

'The churls must be scared, sir,' answered one of his knights.

Aymer, thinking he was right, was about to lead his troops up the hillside in an attack, wondering if Bruce himself might even be among them, when the small band of horsemen came riding down. The foot soldiers maintained their position, high on the ridge.

'Sir? Do we counter?'

Aymer's eyes narrowed on the company. Above the riders was raised a blue standard with a white lion emblazoned on it. As they came closer, he realised none had weapons in their hands. His curiosity mounted. 'Hold,' he ordered his knights. 'Do nothing until I say so.'

The horsemen came to a halt on the flower-speckled grass some distance from the road, where the English host was waiting, lined up along the verge, poised for battle.

'Who are you?' demanded Aymer, his shout echoing over the snorts of the horses. 'What is your business here?'

'My name is Dungal MacDouall,' came a hard voice. 'Captain of the army of Galloway, loyal servant to the late Sir John Comyn. I have been waiting for you. I seek an audience with King Edward on behalf of the mighty house of the Comyns and all their allies. We wish to affirm the vows of allegiance made at St Andrews and to pledge our swords to the fight against our shared enemy – the false king, Robert Bruce.'

AUTHOR'S NOTE

Although well documented in the main, there are gaps in our knowledge surrounding events of this period. Crafting a historical novel is rather like a dot-to-dot painting, where you have to connect what is already there with your own lines of interpretation. Furthermore, historical sources are often contradictory and while we may know who was doing what and when, we don't often know why they were doing it. The challenge for the historical novelist is to answer that question and provide motivations for our characters. Combined with the fact that history can sometimes be too convoluted or protracted to satisfy in a novel, all these things necessitate a certain amount of filling in the blanks and altering or simplifying history for the sake of pace and plot. Here, I've set out the key changes to the facts and for those wishing to learn more on the period I've included a bibliography.

The relics and the prophecy

The Staff of Malachy (also known as the Staff of Jesus) was revered by the Irish because it was believed to be connected with St Patrick. Malachy was forced to pay for possession of it when Niall Mac Edan relinquished control of Armagh's diocese, but after this point my plot diverges from the staff's actual history, as in reality it was moved to Dublin in the late twelfth century. Here it remained until the sixteenth century, when it was burned as a superstitious relic.

King Edward did remove the Stone of Destiny from Scotland during the invasion of 1296, but Robert's part in the theft is fiction, although he was in the service of the king at the time. The stone was conveyed to Westminster Abbey and set in the Coronation Chair. In 1950 it was stolen and returned to Scotland, then found and brought back, before being officially presented to Edinburgh Castle in 1996. The Crown of Arthur was taken during Edward's conquest of Wales in 1282–84 and presented at the shrine of St Edward the Confessor. In *Insurrection* I have it taken later, during the uprising of 1294. The Sword of Mercy was used in English coronations.

The History of the Kings of Britain and the *Prophecies of Merlin* were written in the twelfth century by Oxford scholar Geoffrey of Monmouth, who claimed to be translating the prophecies from an earlier source. His works include some of the first portrayals of King Arthur and Merlin, which gave birth to generations of Arthurian romances. They were hugely popular and Edward is known to have had copies. The *Last Prophecy* is my invention, but Monmouth suggested there were others that hadn't been translated. In a passage in Monmouth's *History* an angelic voice foretells that the Britons will not rule their kingdom any more until a certain time when the relics of the saints are gathered. I've connected this with Edward's confiscation of royal and sacred objects during his conquests.

Edward was clearly interested in Arthurian legend. He and Queen Eleanor reburied the bones of Arthur and Guinevere at Glastonbury. He organised Round Table tournaments and had his own Round Table made, which you can see in Winchester Castle. The Knights of the Dragon are fictitious, although the members are real. The dragon banner is authentic – Edward commanded Aymer de Valence to 'raise dragon' when he sent him north against Robert in 1306, a signal that there was to be no mercy.

The death of Alexander III and the Scottish succession

I've spoken of Alexander's demise in my author's note for *Insurrection*, but to summarise: chroniclers of the time and modern historians regard his death on the road to Kinghorn as an accident. The murder is pure fiction. That said, we can never truly know what happened that night since the king was separated from his escort and his body wasn't found until the next morning. The fact that Alexander was thought to have mooted the possibility of a union between his granddaughter and heir and Edward's son and heir in 1284, but that when he married his second wife any offspring they produced would have rendered this proposition meaningless, led me down the *what if* route. Similarly, there is no evidence that the Maid of Norway's death was anything other than a tragedy, the princess thought to have died eating rotten food on the voyage to Scotland, not through any design of the Comyns.

While Robert's grandfather had a claim to the throne of Scotland by blood, he was also said to have been named heir presumptive by Alexander II; however I've made more of this than was made at the time. Robert acquired the earldom of Carrick in 1292 shortly after John Balliol was appointed king by Edward, but it was his father who inherited the family's claim to the throne. However, Robert was accused of aiming at the crown as early as 1297 and so I chose to have the legacy passed directly from his grandfather to him.

Robert in Ireland

In *Insurrection* Robert resigns as guardian of Scotland immediately after the clash with John Comyn at the council of Peebles in 1299, before heading to Ireland in search of the staff. In reality he resigned early in 1300 and retired to Carrick. We hear nothing of him until late summer 1301, when Prince Edward attacked Turnberry Castle, but some historians believe it is possible Robert visited his estates in Ireland during this time, where he may have met the daughter of the Earl of Ulster, Elizabeth de Burgh.

All of what happens to Robert in Ireland is fiction, since we know nothing of him during this period. His foster family is fictitious, but he had possessions in Antrim that would have been in the care of a vassal and there are hints in the records that both Robert and Edward Bruce were fostered to a Gaelic magnate in youth. Lord Donough is an amalgamation of these men and Cormac is the foster-brother we later see in sources fighting alongside Robert in Scotland.

In St Bernard of Clairvaux's *Life of St Malachy of Armagh*, the monastery of Ibracense is mentioned as being founded by Malachy before he became Archbishop of Armagh, but its location is unspecified. Some archaeologists believe the ruins on Church Island, Lough Currane (old name: Lough Luioch) are those of the monastery, but this is disputed.

Robert's surrender to King Edward

John Balliol's transfer into papal custody was part of the treaty brokered between England and France through the arbitration of Pope Boniface VIII, and his subsequent release was orchestrated by Philippe IV. William Wallace spent a year at the French court trying to persuade Philippe to support the

Scottish cause and the king recommended him to the pope. We don't know if Wallace visited the papal curia, but it is possible.

In 1302, Robert surrendered to Edward, almost certainly because Balliol seemed set to return to the throne with the aid of Philippe: a disastrous prospect for Robert. He didn't travel to Westminster with Ulster as I have it, but gave himself up to the English warden of Annandale and Galloway. Edward accepted Robert into his peace and the marriage with Elizabeth de Burgh was agreed. The Earl of Ulster was an ally of the Bruce family prior to the war and Edward's chief magnate in Ireland, but the secret pact between Robert and his new father-in-law is fiction. Still, Ulster wasn't the most subservient of vassals and Edward was forced to pardon the earl's considerable debts in order to acquire his service in the 1303 campaign.

I place Robert at his father's home in Writtle after the surrender, but it's likely he would have been in Scotland for some of this time, especially after Edward made him Sheriff of Lanark and Ayr. Robert fought for Edward during the campaign of 1303; sent with Aymer de Valence to counter the rebels under John Comyn and on the mounted raid into Selkirk Forest, although this latter force was led by Robert Clifford and John Segrave, not Humphrey and Aymer. The warning to the rebels is fiction, but Wallace did manage to evade his enemies.

After the Battle of Courtrai, which heralded the end of John Balliol's hopes of returning to the throne, it seems Robert once again had his eye on the crown. An intriguing document survives from 1304, at the siege of Stirling, in which Robert and William Lamberton make some secret contract. The text is vague, but historians interpret it as evidence that Lamberton and Robert were establishing the connection that would lead to Robert's coronation.

The guardians

When Robert resigned as guardian, Lamberton and Comyn remained in the position, with Ingram de Umfraville soon joining them. In 1301 a man named John de Soules was appointed sole guardian, but the next year he was part of the Scottish delegation that went to Paris to persuade Philippe to continue to support their cause and John Comyn once again took up the role. To simplify the various permutations, I've removed Soules, who remained in Paris. James Stewart was also part of this delegation, so his appearances in Scotland at this point in the narrative are fictional, although his lands were attacked by Ulster's forces.

The capture of William Wallace

William Wallace had returned to Scotland by 1303, when he was once again active in the rebellion. Robert's plan to join forces with Wallace is fictitious. Edward is reported as being ill in 1304, after the fall of Stirling, and Robert was probably just waiting for his death before moving on the throne, well aware of the weaknesses of the king's son and heir.

Edward ordered the Scottish magnates who surrendered in 1304 to hunt down Wallace and he was eventually captured outside Glasgow by John of Menteith. According to later chroniclers, documents found on Wallace at the time of his capture implicated Robert in a conspiracy against Edward. There is, however, no contemporary evidence for this.

The plot masterminded by the Comyns to reveal Robert's treachery is fiction. Neither is there any evidence that John Comyn himself aimed at the throne, although he had a claim to it, passed down from his father whose claim was recognised by Edward at the time of the trial to find Alexander's successor. Wallace's execution is based, unfortunately, on fact.

Robert's betrayal of Edward

The historian G. W. S. Barrow says: 'Without more evidence than we possess at present, it is impossible to reconstruct the sequence of events leading to Comyn's murder and from there to Bruce's coronation' (*Robert Bruce and the Community of the Realm of Scotland*, p141). Such uncertainty inevitably makes this point difficult to reconstruct in a narrative, but I've mostly gone with the sequence put forward in John Barbour's epic poem *The Bruce*, written forty-five years after Robert's death, since it worked well with the fictional elements of the novel. The poem has some great, albeit probably fabricated touches, such as Ralph de Monthermer warning Robert, through the pair of spurs, that he was about to be arrested and should run.

Barbour and other chroniclers say that Robert Bruce and John Comyn, unhappy with Scotland's plight, entered into a pact that if Comyn helped Robert become king, Robert would give Comyn his lands. Comyn then betrays Robert's intentions to Edward, which leads to the retaliation at

Greyfriars. There are similar versions, most dismissed by historians as fiction, but there seem to be elements of truth here, for more reliable chroniclers speak of Robert's attempt to ally himself with Comyn in order to win the crown, an attempt Comyn spurned which led to the showdown at Greyfriars.

What appears in the novel is an amalgamation of these various accounts, with the chronology altered. In none of the accounts does Edward move to arrest Robert immediately after Wallace's execution, although he does seem to have grown suspicious of him around this point. Robert's escape from Westminster is fiction, as is his taking the Staff of Malachy and the fictitious prophecy box. As an interesting aside, however, the crown jewels were stolen from Westminster Abbey in 1303.

The murder of John Comyn

Accounts once again differ, according to the bias of the chronicler, when it comes to the murder of John Comyn. In reality Robert and Comyn arranged to meet at the church of the Greyfriars in Dumfries to talk, possibly about Robert's plan to take the throne, whereas in the novel Robert's appearance is a surprise to Comyn. We don't know exactly what happened next, but it seems there was an argument and Robert attacked Comyn with his dagger. There followed a skirmish, involving several of Robert's companions, including Christopher Seton, and Comyn was mortally wounded. According to some sources he was killed in two stages. After the deed was done, Robert seized Dumfries's castle and began his march to the throne. He was inaugurated six weeks later.

Chronological changes

I've moved Edward's siege of Caerlaverock from 1300 to 1301 in order to merge the campaigns of those two years, but much of what occurs, including Winchelsea's appearance with the papal order and Prince Edward's raid in Carrick, is based on fact.

The Scots attacked Lochmaben in 1301, but my account is heavily fictionalised. Likewise, Edward did make his son Prince of Wales that year, but at the Lincoln parliament rather than on campaign.

Edward's daughter, Elizabeth (Bess) died in childbirth, but much later, in 1316, and although Joan of Acre's affair with Ralph de Monthermer and their subsequent marriage is based on fact, it occurred several years earlier than portrayed.

Other chronological changes include the treaty between France and England that excluded Scotland being made in the autumn of 1303, when in reality it was made in the summer. Edward appointed Robert Sheriff of Lanark and Ayr a few months earlier than portrayed and Robert's brothers were granted their new positions the following year. The massacre at Bruges occurs slightly earlier in the novel and Robert's father died in April 1304, several months later than I have it. Although he surrendered to Edward with the other magnates in 1304, James Stewart didn't receive his lands back until late in 1305, after Wallace's death. Prince Edward was knighted by his father at Westminster in 1306 in the run-up to the reprisal against Robert, but slightly later than depicted, and Christopher Seton and Christian Bruce were already married by the time of Robert's coronation.

Robyn Young
Brighton
April 2012

CHARACTER LIST

(* Indicates fictitious characters, relationships or groups)

*ADAM: Gascon commander in a crossbow regiment of Edward I

*AFFRAIG: wise woman from Turnberry

*AGNES: maid to Isabel, Countess of Buchan

*ALAN: steward of James Stewart

ALEXANDER II: King of Scotland (1214–49)

ALEXANDER III: King of Scotland (1249–86), brother-in-law of Edward I by his first marriage, died in 1286

ALEXANDER BRUCE: brother of Robert

ALEXANDER SETON: lord from East Lothian and *cousin of Christopher Seton

*ANDREW BOYD: Constable of Turnberry Castle

*ANGUS: man from Turnberry

ANTHONY BEK: Bishop of Durham

AYMER DE VALENCE: heir to the earldom of Pembroke, cousin of Edward I and brother-in-law of John Comyn III

*BETHOC: woman from Turnberry

BLACK COMYN (THE): Earl of Buchan and head of the Black Comyns

BONIFACE VIII: pope (1294–1303)

*BRIAN: companion of Prince Edward

*BRIGID: niece of Affraig

CELLACH: Archbishop of Armagh in the twelfth century

CHRISTIAN BRUCE: sister of Robert, married to Gartnait of Mar

CHRISTOPHER SETON: son of an English knight from Yorkshire and *cousin of Alexander Seton

*COLBAN: one of Dungal MacDouall's men

*CORMAC: son of Lord Donough and foster-brother of Robert

DAVID OF ATHOLL: son of John of Atholl

DAVID GRAHAM: Scottish nobleman and rebel

DONALD OF MAR: son of Christian Bruce and Gartnait of Mar, Robert's nephew

*DONNELL: monk from Bangor Abbey

*DONOUGH: Robert's foster-father and lord of the Bruce estates in Antrim

*DUNCAN: steward of John Comyn II at Lochindorb

DUNCAN IV: Earl of Fife, nephew of Isabel, Countess of Buchan

DUNGAL MACDOUALL: (former) captain of the army of Galloway

EDMUND: son of Edward I and Marguerite of France

EDMUND COMYN: head of the Comyns of Kilbride

EDWARD I: King of England (1272–1307)

EDWARD OF CAERNARFON: son and heir of Edward I, Prince of Wales

EDWARD BALLIOL: son of John Balliol

EDWARD BRUCE: brother of Robert

*EDWIN: steward of Robert's father in Writtle

EGIDIA DE BURGH: sister of Richard de Burgh, married to James Stewart

ELEANOR BALLIOL: sister of John Balliol, married to John Comyn II

*ELENA: daughter of Brigid

ELIZABETH (BESS): daughter of Edward I and Eleanor of Castile

ELIZABETH DE BURGH: daughter of the Earl of Ulster

*EMMA: governess to Robert's daughter

*ESGAR: captain in the Earl of Ulster's household

*EUAN: squire of Edward Bruce

*FERGUS: steward of Isabel, Countess of Buchan

GARTNAIT OF MAR: Earl of Mar, married to Christian Bruce

*GEOFFREY: companion of Prince Edward

*GILBERT: steward of Lord Donough

GILBERT DE LA HAY: Lord of Erroll

GRAY: second-in-command to William Wallace

GUY DE BEAUCHAMP: Earl of Warwick

HENRY III: King of England (1216–72)

HENRY PERCY: Lord of Alnwick and grandson of John de Warenne

*HUGH: squire of Humphrey de Bohun

HUMPHREY DE BOHUN: Earl of Hereford and Essex, and Constable of England

INGRAM DE UMFRAVILLE: guardian of Scotland

ISABEL BRUCE: sister of Robert, married to Eric II and Queen of Norway

ISABEL: Countess of Buchan, married to the Black Comyn

ISABELLA OF FRANCE: daughter of King Philippe IV

JAMES DOUGLAS: son and heir of William Douglas, and nephew of James Stewart

JAMES STEWART: High Steward of Scotland, married to Egidia de Burgh

*JEAN DE REIMS: royal knight from the French court

JOAN OF ACRE: daughter of Edward I and Eleanor of Castile

JOAN DE VALENCE: sister of Aymer de Valence and cousin of Edward I, married to John Comyn III

*JOHN: a Londoner

JOHN OF ATHOLL: Earl of Atholl and Sheriff of Aberdeen, married a daughter of the Earl of Mar, making him Robert's brother-in-law

JOHN BALLIOL II: Lord of Galloway and brother-in-law of John Comyn II, King of Scotland (1292–96), deposed by Edward I in 1296

JOHN COMYN II: Lord of Badenoch and Justiciar of Galloway, brother-in-law of John Balliol and head of the Red Comyns

JOHN COMYN III: son and heir of John Comyn II and Eleanor Balliol, married to Joan de Valence

JOHN OF MENTEITH: son of the Earl of Menteith

JOHN SEGRAVE: lieutenant of Edward I in Scotland

JOHN DE WARENNE: Earl of Surrey

*JUDITH: wet nurse to Robert's daughter

*LORA: maid to Elizabeth de Burgh

LLYWELYN AP GRUFFUDD: Prince of Wales, killed during the 1282–84 conquest

MADOG AP LLYWELYN: leader of an uprising against Edward I in Wales in 1294

MALACHY (ST): Archbishop of Armagh (1132–37), canonised in 1199

MALCOLM: Earl of Lennox

MALCOLM III (CANMORE): King of Scotland (1058–93)

MARGARET: half-sister of Robert from his mother's first marriage

MARGARET (THE MAID OF NORWAY): granddaughter and heir of Alexander III, named Queen of Scotland after his death, but died on the voyage from Norway

MARGUERITE OF FRANCE: sister of Philippe IV, second wife of Edward I and Queen of England

MARJORIE BRUCE: daughter of Robert and Isobel of Mar

MARJORIE OF CARRICK: Countess of Carrick and Robert's mother, died in 1292

*MARTIN: a knight in the household of Edward I

MARY BRUCE: sister of Robert

MATILDA BRUCE: sister of Robert

MATTHEW: a knight from Robert's Essex estates

MURTOUGH: monk from Bangor Abbey

NEIL CAMPBELL: a knight from Argyll

NIALL BRUCE: brother of Robert

NIALL MAC EDAN: member of the secular family who claimed the right to the diocese of Armagh in the twelfth century

NED: servant in the Earl of Ulster's household

NES: squire to Robert

PIERRE: steward of John Balliol in Picardy

PIERS GAVESTON: companion of Prince Edward and ward of the king

PHILIPPE IV: King of France (1286–1314)

RALPH DE MONTHERMER: royal knight in the court of Edward I

RANULF: huntsman of the Earl of Ulster

RICHARD DE BURGH: Earl of Ulster and Lord of Connacht

RICHARD CROW: prison guard of Edward I

ROBERT D'ARTOIS: Count of Artois

ROBERT BRUCE V: grandfather of Robert, competed for the throne of Scotland, died in 1295

ROBERT BRUCE VI: Lord of Annandale and father of Robert

ROBERT BRUCE VII: Earl of Carrick, Lord of Annandale on his father's death and King of Scotland (1306–29)

ROBERT CLIFFORD: royal knight in the court of Edward I

ROBERT WINCHELSEA: Archbishop of Canterbury

ROBERT WISHART: Bishop of Glasgow

SIMON FRASER: Scottish nobleman and rebel

SIMON DE MONTFORT: Earl of Leicester, led a rebellion against Henry III, died in battle with Edward in 1265

*STEPHEN: a servant in the Earl of Ulster's household

STRATHEARN: Earl of Strathearn

THOMAS OF BROTHERTON: son of Edward I and Marguerite of France

THOMAS BRUCE: brother of Robert

THOMAS OF LANCASTER: Earl of Lancaster and nephew of Edward I

THOMAS RANDOLPH: son of Margaret Bruce and Robert's half-nephew

*WALTER: knight from Annandale

WILLIAM DOUGLAS: Lord of Douglas and father of James, died in the Tower in 1298

WILLIAM LAMBERTON: Bishop of St Andrews

WILLIAM OLIPHANT: commander of Stirling Castle

WILLIAM WALLACE: leader of the Scottish rebellion against Edward I in 1297

GLOSSARY

BASINET: a close-fitting helmet, sometimes worn with a visor.

BRAIES: undergarments worn by men.

CHAUSSES: mail stockings.

COAT-OF-PLATES: a cloth or leather garment with metal plates riveted to it, worn under the surcoat.

COIF: a tight-fitting cloth cap worn by men and women, it could also be made of mail and worn by soldiers under or instead of a helm.

CROWN OF ARTHUR: a coronet worn by the princes of Gwynedd, most notably Llywelyn ap Gruffudd who styled himself prince of Wales. Edward I seized the crown along with other important Welsh relics during the 1282-84 invasion and sent it to Westminster Abbey.

CURTANA: also known as the Sword of Mercy because of its symbolically broken tip, it was thought to have belonged to St Edward the Confessor and became part of the English regalia used in coronations.

DESTRIER: a warhorse.

DIRK: Scots for dagger.

FALCHION: a short sword with a curved edge.

GAMBESON: a padded coat worn by soldiers, often made of quilted cloth, stuffed with felt or straw.

GEOFFREY OF MONMOUTH: thought to have been a Welshman or Breton by birth, Monmouth resided in Oxford during the twelfth century, where he was possibly a canon of St George's College. Later, he became bishop of St Asaph. He wrote three known works during his life, the most famous being *The History of the Kings of Britain* of which the *Prophecies of Merlin* became part, followed by *The Life of Merlin*. Despite mixing established British history with romantic fiction, Monmouth presented his writings as fact and many readers of his works took them as such, accepting King Arthur and Merlin as historical figures. Monmouth's works, although criticised by some of his contemporaries, were hugely popular during the medieval period and from his *The History of the Kings of Britain* sprung the immense canon of Arthurian literature that graced Europe over the following centuries. Chrétien de Troyes, Malory, Shakespeare and Tennyson were all influenced by his work.

HAUBERK: a shirt or coat of mail with long sleeves.

HUKE: a hooded cloak.

JUSTICIAR: a chief justice official. In Scotland there were three justiciars during the period: those of Galloway, Lothian and Scotia.

MAGNATE: a high-ranking noble.

MOTTE: a castle or keep built on a mound, often surrounded by a bailey.

PALFREY: a light horse used for everyday riding.

PRIMOGENITURE: the right of the first-born to inherit.

PROPHECIES OF MERLIN: written by Geoffrey of Monmouth during the twelfth century. Originally composed as a separate volume, the *Prophecies* were later incorporated into his *The History of the Kings of Britain*. According to Monmouth he was translating the work into Latin from an older text. Monmouth has been credited as being the creator of Merlin, but it is now believed he derived this enigmatic figure from earlier Welsh sources.

QUARREL: an arrow for a crossbow.

ROUNCY: a type of riding horse.

STAFF OF MALACHY: also known as the Staff of Jesus, it was a wooden crosier covered with gold. It was believed to have belonged to St Patrick, who is said to have received it from Jesus. Highly revered by the Irish, it became connected with Malachy, Archbishop of Armagh, when he was forced to pay off the leader of the secular clan who had possession of the staff and control of St Patrick's cathedral and its diocese. According to popular law, only when Malachy had the staff could he claim to be the rightful archbishop. The staff was taken to Dublin in the late twelfth century, where it was burned as a superstitious relic in the sixteenth century.

STONE OF DESTINY: also called the Stone of Scone, it was the ancient seat used in Scottish coronations. Thought to have been brought to Scone in the ninth century by Scotland's king, Kenneth mac Alpin, its origins are unknown. It was seized by Edward I during the 1296 invasion and taken to Westminster Abbey where it was set in a specially designed throne and became part of the English coronation ceremony. It remained here until 1950 when four students stole it and returned it to Scotland. It was later sent back to England, before being officially presented to Edinburgh Castle in 1996, where it remains on display. It will be returned to Westminster for future coronations.

SURCOAT: a long sleeveless garment usually worn over armour.

VAMBRACE: armour for the lower arm.

VASSAL: a retainer subject to a feudal superior, who holds land in return for homage and services.

VENTAIL: a flap of mail that can be pulled up and secured to protect the lower half of the face during combat.

Succession to the Scottish Throne

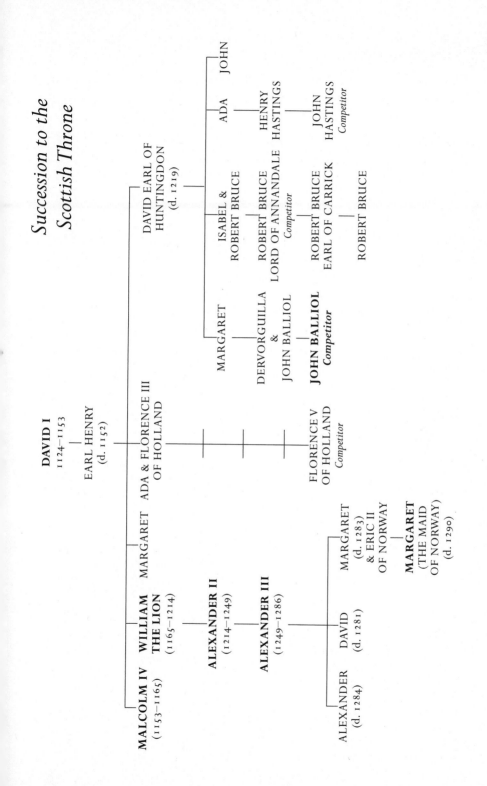

BIBLIOGRAPHY

Baker, Timothy, *Medieval London*, Cassell, 1970

Barber, Richard, *The Knight and Chivalry*, Boydell Press, 1995

Barbour, John, *The Bruce* (trans. A.A.M. Duncan), Canongate Classics, 1997

Barrell, A.D.M., *Medieval Scotland*, Cambridge University Press, 2000

Barrow, G.W.S., *Robert Bruce and the Community of the Realm of Scotland*, Edinburgh University Press, 1988

Barrow, G.W.S., *The Kingdom of the Scots*, Edinburgh University Press, 2003

Beam, Amanda, *The Balliol Dynasty 1210 – 1364*, John Donald, 2008

Chancellor, John, *The Life and Times of Edward I*, Weidenfeld & Nicolson, 1981

Clairvaux, St. Bernard of, *Life of St. Malachy of Armagh* (trans. H.J. Lawlor), Dodo Press, 1920

Cummins, John, *The Hound and the Hawk, the Art of Medieval Hunting*, Phoenix Press, 2001

Daniell, Christopher, *Death and Burial in Medieval England 1066 – 1550*, Routledge, 1997

Davis, I.M., *The Black Douglas*, Routledge & Kegan Paul, 1974

Dean, Gareth, *Medieval York*, History Press, 2008

Duffy, Seán, *Ireland in the Middle Ages*, Macmillan Press Ltd, 1997

Duffy, Seán (general ed.), *Atlas of Irish History*, Gill & Macmillan, 1997

Edge, David & Paddock, John M., *Arms and Armour of the Medieval Knight*, Bison Group, 1988

Fawcett, Richard, *Stirling Castle (Official Guide)*, Historic Scotland, 1999

Frame, Robin, *Ireland and Britain 1170 – 1450*, Hambledon Press, 1998

France, John, *Western Warfare in the Age of the Crusades 1000–1300*, UCL Press, 1999

Gravett, Christopher, *English Medieval Knight 1300 – 1400*, Osprey Publishing 2002

Gravett, Christopher, *Knights at Tournament*, Osprey Publishing, 1988

Grove, Doreen & Yeoman, Peter, *Caerlaverock Castle (Official Guide)*, Historic Scotland, 2006

Haines, Roy Martin, *King Edward II, His Life His Reign and its Aftermath 1284 – 1330*, McGill-Queen's University Press, 2003

Houston, Mary G., *Medieval Costume in England and France*, Dover Publications, 1996

Hyland, Ann, *The Horse in the Middle Ages*, Sutton Publishing, 1999

Impey, Edward & Parnell, Geoffrey, *The Tower of London (Official Illustrated History)*, Merrell, 2006

Kieckhefer, Richard, *Magic in the Middle Ages*, Cambridge University Press, 2000

Leyser, Henrietta, *Medieval Women, a Social History of Women in England 450 – 1500*, Phoenix Press, 1996

Lindsay, Maurice, *The Castles of Scotland*, Constable, 1995

Mackay, James, *William Wallace, Braveheart*, Mainstream Publishing, 1995

McNair Scott, Ronald, *Robert the Bruce, King of Scots*, Canongate, 1988

McNamee, Colm, *Robert Bruce, Our Most Valiant Prince, King and Lord*, Birlinn, 2006

Monmouth, Geoffrey of, *The History of the Kings of Britain* (trans. Lewis Thorpe), Penguin Classics, 1966

Monmouth, Geoffrey of, *The Vita Merlini* (trans. John Jay Parry), BiblioBazaar, 2008

Morris, J.E., *The Welsh Wars of Edward I*, Sutton Publishing, 1998

Morris, Marc, *A Great and Terrible King, Edward I and the Forging of Britain*, Hutchinson, 2008

Nicolle, David, *The History of Medieval Life*, Chancellor Press, 2000

Nuttgens, Patrick, *The History of York, from Earliest Times to the Year 2000*, Blackthorn Press, 2007

Oram, Richard, *The Kings and Queens of Scotland*, Tempus, 2004

Rixson, Denis, *The West Highland Galley*, Birlinn, 1998

Spufford, Peter, *Power and Profit, the Merchant in Medieval Europe*, Thames and Hudson, 2002

Tabraham, Chris, *Scotland's Castles*, Historic Scotland, B.T. Batsford, 2005

Tabraham, Chris (ed.), *Edinburgh Castle (Official Guide)*, Historic Scotland, 2003

Talbot, C.H., *Medicine in Medieval England*, Oldbourne, 1967

Watson, Fiona, *Under the Hammer, Edward I & Scotland 1286 – 1307*, Tuckwell Press, 1998

Weir, Alison, *Isabella, She-Wolf of France, Queen of England*, Pimlico, 2006

Wilkinson, James & Knighton, C.S., *Crown and Cloister, the Royal Story of Westminster Abbey*, Scala, 2010

Yeoman, Peter, *Medieval Scotland*, Historic Scotland, B.T. Batsford, 1995

Young, Alan, *Robert the Bruce's Rivals: The Comyns, 1212 – 1314*, Tuckwell Press, 1997

Zacour, Norman, *An Introduction to Medieval Institutions*, St James Press, 1977

Excerpts used as part titles taken from:

The British History of Geoffrey of Monmouth (trans. A. Thompson, revised ed. J. A. Giles), William Stevens (printer), London, 1842